P. W. CATANESE
BOOKS OF UMBER

THE END
OF TIME

ALADDIN

NEW YORK   LONDON   TORONTO   SYDNEY   NEW DELHI

This book is a work of fiction. Any references to historical events, real people, or real locales are used fictitiously. Other names, characters, places, and incidents are the product of the author's imagination, and any resemblance to actual events or locales or persons, living or dead, is entirely coincidental.

ALADDIN
An imprint of Simon & Schuster Children's Publishing Division
1230 Avenue of the Americas, New York, NY 10020
First Aladdin paperback edition February 2012
Copyright © 2011 by P. W. Catanese
All rights reserved, including the right of reproduction in whole or in part in any form.
ALADDIN is a trademark of Simon & Schuster, Inc., and related logo is a registered trademark of Simon & Schuster, Inc.
Also available in an Aladdin hardcover edition.
For information about special discounts for bulk purchases, please contact Simon & Schuster Special Sales at 1-866-506-1949 or business@simonandschuster.com.
The Simon & Schuster Speakers Bureau can bring authors to your live event. For more information or to book an event contact the Simon & Schuster Speakers Bureau at 1-866-248-3049 or visit our website at www.simonspeakers.com.
Designed by Mike Rosamilia
The text of this book was set in Bembo.
Manufactured in the United States of America 0112 OFF
2 4 6 8 10 9 7 5 3 1
The Library of Congress has cataloged the hardcover edition as follows:
Catanese, P.W.
The end of time / P.W. Catanese. —1st Aladdin hardcover ed.
p. cm. – (The books of Umber; bk. 3)
Summary: As young Hap prepares to reverse the global catastrophe on Lord Umber's world, an evil prince and a destructive sorceress threaten the kingdom of Kurahaven.
ISBN 978-1-4169-7520-5 (hc)
[1. Adventure and adventurers—Fiction. 2. Fantasy] I. Title.
PZ7.C268783En 2011
[Fic]—dc22
2010023808
ISBN 978-1-4169-5384-5 (pbk)
ISBN 978-1-4424-1955-1 (eBook)

FOR MY BROTHER RICH.
AND MY BROTHERS-
AND SISTERS-IN-LAW:
JUDY, GINA, MARC,
JOE, AND ELLEN.

THE END
OF TIME

CHAPTER
I

The book that Hap was reading slipped from his hands, and he sprang from his chair to the window. Afire with hope, and braced for disappointment, he pressed his face to the bars.

Far below was Barkin on his chestnut-colored horse, trotting up the causeway to the Aerie, the carved pillar of rock that Lord Umber called home. Hap glimpsed the corner of a box lashed to the horse, behind the saddle. "I think he got it," he said aloud, and his heart turned a cartwheel.

He flew down the stairs, out the door, and into the gatehouse as Barkin rode in. The cargo looked like a strongbox: a little wider than it was tall, and made of wrought iron. There was a keyhole embedded in its side, and hand-size padlocks secured

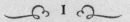

the thick chains wrapped around it, side to side and top to bottom. Barkin looked road-weary but proud, and he grinned when he saw Hap bouncing from foot to foot. "Hello, Master Happenstance. Something I can do for you?"

"Don't tease me, Barkin," Hap begged. "Not about this."

Barkin's devilish smile turned sympathetic. He dismounted and rapped the box with his knuckles. "Ah. Something important to you, inside this crate?"

Hap's nod was a blur. "Very." He didn't offer more; Umber preferred to keep these matters quiet. But that strongbox might hold all the lost secrets that Caspar, Umber's former archivist, had stolen from the Aerie. Caspar was dead, slain by an arrow intended for Umber, on a faraway island. But he'd given the box to his cousin for safekeeping, and Barkin had retrieved it.

Welkin and Dodd, Umber's other guardsmen, came forward. Welkin had a mug of ale for Barkin, and Dodd a bucket of water for the horse. "Did you have much trouble?" Dodd asked.

"Only a tad," Barkin said, with his tongue pressing the inside of one cheek. "Caspar's cousin wasn't eager to part with it. In fact, he wouldn't even admit to having it. Also, he didn't fully believe me when I told him that Caspar was dead. He thought I was trying to trick him, even when I offered him Lord Umber's bag of gold." Barkin untied the strongbox and talked over his

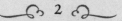

shoulder. "I could see he was tempted, but he asked me to come back the next day, after he'd thought about it."

"And what did he say the next day?" Welkin asked.

"How should I know? I was long gone by then. I came back that same night, knocked the fellow out with Umber's sleeper bottle—handy stuff that is—and searched his place until I found it."

"You *stole* it?" Hap cried.

Barkin spread his hand on his chest in a parody of indignation. "I paid for it! Left the bag of gold in its place, with a note of heartfelt apology. Oof, heavy," he said, hefting the strongbox.

Dodd patted Hap's back. "Don't forget, Master Hap. The stuff in that strongbox was stolen from Umber in the first place. He told Barkin to use any means necessary, short of violence, to bring it back."

"So it was perfectly justified," Barkin said. "Not to mention fun. I felt like such a scoundrel! Now, I wonder what's inside?"

"Old papers, I think," Hap said.

"More than that," Barkin said. "Listen." He tilted the box one way and the other. Something thumped against the side, rolled back, and thumped again. "Wonder what that is?"

"A skull, knowing Umber," Welkin said. He tired of holding the ale for Barkin and downed half of it in a gulp.

"We'll find out soon enough. Assuming Umber can get this open," said Barkin.

Welkin rolled his eyes. "You didn't bring back the *keys*?"

"Couldn't find them," Barkin said. "I'm sure Lord Umber will manage."

Hap nodded, knowing there would be no problem. Umber had a key that could open any lock in the world—one of his remarkable magical possessions. No, unlocking the strongbox was not the trouble.

Umber himself was the trouble.

"Lord Umber?"

Hap searched the gardens at the top of the Aerie. Umber was not in his usual haunt, on the bench under his favorite tree, which was bursting as always with a variety of fruits and berries. And he was not on any of the other seats or benches, or leaning on the balcony. The door to his little, round rooftop tower was shut and locked, but the window to his study high above was open, with the shutters flung wide. A curtain billowed, animated by a passing breeze. *He must be moping in there,* Hap thought. He considered leaping high to sneak a look, but decided against it.

Shortly after their return from Sarnica, where they'd recovered a cache of stolen dragon eggs, along with a living infant dragon, Umber had slipped into this hopeless melancholy. There were triumphs on that journey—a kingdom liberated, tyrants deposed, mysteries unraveled. But upon their return they were met with dreadful news: Prince Galbus, a good man who stood to inherit the throne from the ailing king, had died. It was that news, and everything it meant to Umber's hopes for the kingdom, that had sent Umber tumbling.

Umber was a man of extremes. Most often his mood was one of giddy, wild-eyed, fearless exuberance. But too often something—a reminder of the devastation he'd left behind in the world he'd escaped, or dreadful news such as the death of Galbus—would drive him into a suffocating sadness. His spirit flagged, his energy vanished, his appetite failed, and he refused all companionship.

"Lord Umber?" Hap called again. He stepped backward and finally saw the top of Umber's head as he sat slumped in the chair by his desk. "Barkin is back. He brought a strongbox that must contain your archives. We can finally learn about the Meddlers. Isn't that exciting?"

Umber's head listed to one side.

"But the strongbox is locked," Hap said. He looked around to see if anybody else had followed him onto the terrace. "I'm sure you can get it open, though . . . if you understand my meaning." He waited, but no reply came. His hope that the news might nudge Umber out of the gloom began to fade. He stomped his foot, aching to see what secrets the box contained. "Or maybe I could open it, if you don't mind," he said.

Umber stood up and moved toward the window. Hap's heart seemed to pause in its rhythm. He thought Umber might say something to signal the return of his happy nature. Or at least he might toss the key down for Hap to use.

Instead Umber reached out for the shutters and pulled them closed. Hap watched the drawn gray face vanish from sight, a face devoid of joy or cheer.

CHAPTER
2

"He didn't care at all that Barkin" was back with the lost archives?" Balfour asked.

Hap shook his head. "He ignored me."

Sophie sighed and lowered the side of her face into her palm.

"I'm *sick* of it," Balfour said, smacking his hand on the table. "Sick of this helpless waiting. Umber tumbles into these pits of gloom, and we just sit idly by, week after week, hoping he'll suddenly emerge. Or we bring him cake and coffee, as if he can eat or sip his way out!"

"It seems like we've tried everything," Sophie said. She sat on the floor with her legs folded under her dress, dropping bits of fish between the bars of the cage that held the rescued dragon. The hatchling, which had grown to the size of a small dog, snapped up the morsels and squealed for more with her neck craned and her head jabbing. She snorted, and Hap thought for a moment he saw a wisp of smoke pour from her nostrils.

"We have *not* tried everything," Balfour replied. Hap noticed a glimmer in Balfour's eye. The old man had something in mind. Even Oates, whom Hap had assumed was asleep on the sofa by the hearth, lifted his head to listen.

"Do you know what Umber needs? An *adventure*," Balfour said. Hap felt his heart deflate, and he groaned inwardly. Less than a week had passed since his ordeal with a slew of monsters, both human and otherworldly. He was sure he'd earned a rest.

Balfour punched his palm with his fist. "That's what jolted him out of it last time, wasn't it? The Creep kidnapped him, and soon he was his old self. So an adventure it must be."

The sofa creaked as Oates sat up. "That isn't going to work. Umber won't do anything but mope on the terrace. He'll just order you to leave him alone."

"We'll drag him along anyway," Balfour said.

Oates squinted. "But you can't disobey him. He's Lord Umber!"

Balfour stood, wincing at one of the countless aches in his aging limbs. He leaned forward with his knuckles on the table.

"Is he *really*? That grim ghost haunting the terrace, that's the Lord Umber you know? Because that creature is a stranger to me. Our Lord Umber is locked somewhere inside that moping imposter, a spirit shackled and trussed. We know how to set him free—shouldn't we just *do* it?" He looked from Oates to Sophie to Hap, waiting for someone to agree. But before anyone replied, footsteps were heard climbing the stairs, and Lady Truden—the tall, dour, silver-haired woman who ran the household of the Aerie—appeared. Her expression was severe as usual, but her brow was also wrinkled.

"Visitors have come, asking for Umber. They say they know him, but I have never seen them or heard their names before." She sniffed and raised her chin. "Pretenders, I imagine. I should send them away."

Balfour sighed, miffed at the interruption. "Who are they, Tru? How do they know Umber?"

"They claim to have met him in Sarnica. A woman named Fay. And a girl."

"Sable!" cried Hap, leaping up from his seat.

Sophie stared up at him. Something about her expression made Hap's collar feel like a snake constricting his neck.

Lady Tru frowned. "So you know them after all? Well. They don't appear reputable to me. And if you ask me, that Fay looks like a—"

"Let them in, Tru," Balfour snapped. "Umber was waiting for them to make it to Kurahaven."

"Lord Umber is in no condition to receive guests," Lady Tru replied.

"Lord Umber would want them treated like royalty," Balfour corrected. "Never mind. Come on, Hap, we'll let 'em in ourselves." Oates ducked into the kitchen, leaving poor Sophie alone with a fuming, red-faced Lady Tru.

They were met with a luminous smile from Fay and a squeal of delight from Sable, who didn't wait for Hap to come all the way down the stairs. She raced halfway up and nearly knocked him over with her embrace. "Hello!" Hap said, laughing. "Welcome!"

There was something different about Sable and Fay since he'd last seen them. There was a new ease in their expressions, and when Hap looked closer at Fay, the reason for the change occurred to him: The fear they'd known for so long in Sarnica was finally gone. The dangerous men who'd ruled them were nothing but memories, and they had come to a friendly shore, filled with the hope of new beginnings.

Balfour took Fay's hand and bowed. "Welcome indeed, my lady. I am Balfour, Lord Umber's friend and servant. Umber told me you were lovely, and now it seems the Lord of the Aerie is also the master of understatement."

A touch of red colored Fay's cheeks. "It is a pleasure to meet you, Balfour. We just arrived this morning. This city . . . that palace . . . this tower...I never imagined such places." She looked around the bottom floor of the Aerie, with the river gushing through its stone channel and the strange contraption that could carry passengers to the upper levels. Seeing Hap on the stairs, she smiled. "And hello to you, my young rescuer. It is wonderful to see you. We have something of yours." Beside him Sable grabbed Hap's wrist and dropped a silver locket into his palm. It was shaped like a seashell, and Hap knew what was inside: an enormous pearl.

"We did not need to use it on our journey here," Fay said. "But you were kind to offer it, and I kept it close to my heart, as I keep you." Her gaze went past Hap to the top of the stairs, searching. "And how is Lord Umber? Is he here?"

Balfour cleared his throat. "Er . . . yes, he's here. But he's not well at the moment."

Her smile vanished. "Not well? What is the matter?"

Balfour stretched his mouth wide and tickled his throat before answering. "Um . . . how to say it? Lord Umber is plagued by the occasional bout of melancholia. He comes out of it eventually, given time, but while he is, er . . . *afflicted*, he prefers to be left alone." The old fellow forced a smile and rubbed his hands together. "However! He mentioned that you two might come, and we have arranged for you to stay in a splendid inn—Kurahaven's finest, in fact."

"I would like to see Lord Umber," Fay said, summoning a tone of surprising authority. Hap felt Sable's arm slide inside his own and clamp down.

Balfour exhaled heavily. "Please, my lady. Perhaps in a few days . . . or weeks . . . he'll be in a better frame of mind."

Fay folded her arms. "Balfour, my niece and I have traveled across the sea, waiting anxiously for the day when we could thank Lord Umber for what he did for us and for all of Sarnica. Don't deny me that chance. It can't do any harm for me to see him. Even for a moment?"

Balfour looked at her again, melting under her dark-eyed gaze. Hap looked too. Her dress—the one she'd worn during the escape from Sarnica—was tattered at the hem and sleeves, and her curling brown hair had been tossed by the wind, but her beauty was undiminished. Her inner steel, which Hap had observed during their harrowing escape from the cruel tyrants of Sarnica, came shining through. "And isn't it possible that my visit might improve his spirits?" she asked.

"It would improve mine," Balfour admitted, more to himself than her. He walked to the water-powered lift and pushed the lever that engaged its machinery. Ropes squeaked and pulleys turned, and the wooden platforms began their clattering oval

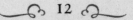

journey. "Come, my lady," Balfour said, offering his elbow. "You are right, it can't do any harm. Hap—take your friend to the grand hall, while I bring the lady to see Umber."

A curious thing happened as Hap and Sable went into the grand hall. Sophie saw Sable by Hap's side, clinging to his arm, and before Hap could introduce them, Sophie went up the stairs without saying a word, keeping her damaged arm, which ended at the wrist, tucked out of sight.

"Who was that?" asked Sable, her lips pursed.

"That's Sophie," replied Hap, frowning. "I don't know why she left."

Oates was leaning against the kitchen door. "You don't know because you're stupid about girls," he said.

Sable waved madly with the hand that wasn't holding Hap's arm hostage. "Hello, Mister Oates! How good to see you again!"

"Hello, small girl," Oates replied. Hap was relieved to see the big fellow push his way back into the kitchen. Oates was gifted with otherworldly strength, but he was also cursed, for unknown reasons, to always speak the truth. His unflinching honesty usually resulted in acute embarrassment.

"What a home you have!" Sable cried. She pulled Hap along as she turned a circle in tiny steps, gaping up and down at the wonders of the grand hall: the carved pillars, the maps and paintings, and the thousands of artifacts that cluttered the shelves and bureaus. Her bedazzled expression reminded Hap of his own arrival at the Aerie. She leaned close, and her lips almost touched his ear. "Everything about you and Lord Umber is so mysterious. Especially you, Happenstance. Will you tell me all about you?"

Hap blinked back at her, and he nearly broke into a laugh, wondering how she would react if he did what she'd asked. *All right,* he imagined himself saying. *About seven years ago I was a boy named Julian Penny. Then a stranger who we think is named Willy Nilly came and lured me to my death by drowning. He destroyed my memory and revived me as one of his own kind, something called a Meddler. That's how I got these weird green eyes. Then he brought me forward in time and left me for Lord Umber to discover in a city buried under volcanic ash. Now I can see in the dark, I never sleep, and I can leap farther and higher than any man alive. Sometimes I see these strange threads of light called filaments that allow me to steer the course of fate. Lord Umber is delighted by that, because he himself came from another world without monsters or sorcerers or any magic at all, and that world was ruined when its technology went out of control and its civilization collapsed. Of course he brought some of that technology with him: All of the amazing inventions that he's famous for have come from something called a* computer, which contains his old world's knowledge of science, music, engineering, medicine, and more. Now Lord Umber wants me to leap over to his world, back in time, and change its fate to save a billion people or more. I have no idea how to do that, and it scares the pants off me, but at least Lord Umber will come with me to help. And now you know all about me.

Sable's voice punctured his thoughts. "Are you laughing at me?"

"No," he said, wagging his head and suppressing the grin that emerged while he'd been daydreaming. "But I don't like talking about myself. I'd rather hear about how you got to Kurahaven."

"Oh, it was *such* a thrill!" she cried. While she told him, Hap tried to figure out exactly which part of the voyage she considered thrilling. She and Fay had found their way onto one of Umber's merchant ships, which stopped at several distant ports before finally arriving in Kurahaven. The roundabout trip sounded blissfully uneventful compared to one of Umber's hazardous jaunts. Sable was still recounting the nonadventure when Fay came down the stairs, looking grim and pale, with Balfour trudging close behind.

"Let us go, Sable," she said quietly.

"My lady, please understand," Balfour pleaded, raising his clasped hands. "I tried to warn you. Umber doesn't mean to be rude when he's in this state. Please don't think poorly of him for it."

"I don't know what to think," Fay said. Her eyes glistened. "That is not the man I knew."

"But he will be again," Balfour said. "I promise you. And I'll send for you as soon as he is. In the meantime, come downstairs and I'll have the carriage take you to your inn. Later on I'll escort you to the market and get anything you need. Those were Umber's wishes."

They were in the gatehouse, waiting for Dodd to ready the carriage, when another, larger carriage with green doors and gilded wheels came up the causeway, pulled by a team of white horses. Balfour scowled as the carriage rolled to a stop.

Hap recognized the sinewy, cold-blooded fellow who opened the door and stepped out. It was Larcombe, the head of Prince Loden's personal guard. He licked his lips in a reptilian fashion, as was his constant habit, and smirked directly at Hap.

"What can we do for you, Larcombe?" Balfour asked in a monotone.

Larcombe grinned without saying a word and moved aside as Prince Loden stepped out of the carriage.

Hap felt a jolt go through his body, and he swallowed past a lump in his throat. He hadn't seen Loden in person since they'd returned. Once he had known Loden as the youngest of three princes. Now Loden was the only prince still living. Umber was convinced that Loden had murdered his eldest brother, Argent, by pushing him from the top of a mist-shrouded waterfall during a hunt. And Galbus, the middle prince, had died while Umber and Hap were away. It was said that Galbus tumbled down a flight of stairs in a drunken stupor—though he'd told Umber that his days of intoxication were behind him. As Umber was slipping into his dark mood, he'd mumbled that Loden was surely behind the death of Galbus as well.

Hap and Umber had been fond of the middle prince, and now, with Loden before him, Hap battled to keep his temper in check. He wanted to scream; he wanted to pound that smug, handsome face with his fists.

Prince Loden tugged at the hem of his embroidered tunic and jutted his chin. "I wish to speak to Umber."

"Lord Umber is not well," Balfour said. "Your Highness," he added dryly. His face, Hap saw, was flushed a dark shade of red.

"What, moping again?" the prince asked with a sigh. "And after I've taken the trouble to come all the way up to this dreary rock." He waited for a reply, but Balfour only stared back. Loden's eyes narrowed. He seemed poised to rebuke Balfour when he noticed Fay standing nearby. In an instant his features rearranged themselves into an expert simulation of warmth and charm. "And who is *this*?"

"My name is Fay. And this is my niece Sable."

"Fay," Loden said, taking her hand and kissing it. "How can it be that you and I have never met before?"

"We only just arrived, after escaping from Sarnica during the revolt," Fay said. A blush flooded her cheeks.

"Yes, I have just been informed of this uprising," Loden replied. "A monarch overthrown, I hear." Loden's glance darted toward Hap, and Hap felt the fine hairs on the back of his neck quiver like grain in the wind.

"A cruel tyrant, sir," Fay replied. "And his son. The world will miss neither of those monsters."

"Aunt Fay was the princess of Sarnica," Sable chirped. "But she didn't want to be. Lord Umber and Happenstance saved us!"

Loden bent with his hands on his thighs and smiled broadly at Sable. "Did they really! Still, we mustn't make a habit of casting down monarchs, don't you think?" He straightened and chuckled at his own joke, and Larcombe laughed with him. "Of course, I would say that—I am the prince of Kurahaven, and heir to the throne of this magnificent kingdom."

Bile rose in Hap's throat when he saw Fay's head tilt in admiration and heard the gasp of delight from Sable. Fay bowed her head. "Forgive me, Your Highness. I did not know whose presence I was in. I feel so ashamed, dressed in these ragged clothes . . ."

This time Loden took both her hands. "My lady, no apology is necessary. You have my gratitude, in fact. I have spent many days mourning the death of my dear brothers. So my sadness has been as deep as Umber's, but perhaps easier to understand. Now I find my spirit soaring again, just to look upon your face."

Fay bit her bottom lip. "I am sorry for your loss, Your Highness."

Hap glanced at Balfour, who looked ready to vomit.

"You are as kind as you are lovely. But where are you staying while you visit my fair city?" Loden asked her.

It's not your city yet, Hap thought bitterly.

"Balfour has arranged for us to stay at an inn," Fay replied.

"An inn! I won't allow it," Loden said. "I'd sooner plant a rosebush in a pigsty. You will come to the palace and stay in the rooms we reserve for visiting royalty." Sable gasped again, and Loden turned to her. "Would you like that, little princess? The view will take your breath away, as your aunt has taken mine. Do you see my wonderful palace over there, the color of sand, rising above everything else? Do you see the balcony under the great clock tower? That is the porch outside your room!"

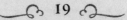

19

Sable's mouth hung open as she stared at the soaring tower.

"Please tell me you'll stay. I can always command you . . . I am the prince, you know!" Loden grinned and winked at Sable.

"You are kind, Your Highness," Fay said, looking downward. "But Balfour has—"

"I'm sure my subject Balfour would want you treated like the royalty you are," Loden said. He took her hand and gently pulled, leading her to his carriage. "Besides, I must hear about this revolt. A prince has to keep informed about such things. Really, I insist you come along, you and your lovely niece."

Fay shot back a look of regret, and called out as she stepped into the carriage. "Good-bye, Happenstance. Balfour, you will send word as soon as Lord Umber recovers?"

"You can be sure of that," Balfour said flatly.

"That could be many weeks, unfortunately, if I know Umber," Loden said, shaking his head. "These bouts of sadness are all too frequent." He closed the door behind Fay and ambled back to where Balfour and Hap stood. "Tell me, you green-eyed whelp," he whispered, leaning down. "Does Umber fancy this one?" He smirked as Hap's eyes watered and his jaw trembled. "I think that answers my question!"

Loden and Larcombe climbed into the carriage, the driver atop cracked his whip, and the white horses pulled the carriage in a tight circle and back down the causeway. Balfour watched it roll away with a hand clamped over his jaw, tapping his cheek with one finger.

"Just think: That wretched sack of goblin droppings will be king one day."

...structive and creative impulses have ...

...coexisted. Blood was surely the first pa...

...primitive soul who raised a club to bludgeo...

...his prey may also have used it to drum out

the first rhythm. I remember myself as a boy,

staring at the glittering beauty of a cascade

...f icicles, only to reach for a ... momen...

...ter and...

CHAPTER
3

Umber was brooding on the bench under the tree of many fruits. He lifted his chin an inch and stared at the trio before him. Hap's heart ached to see the sunken cheeks and the dark crescents under his eyes.

"What?" Umber muttered.

"We're going on a journey," Balfour told him.

"Leave me alone."

"Please, Lord Umber," Hap said. "Come with us."

Umber turned his face aside and tucked his hands under his armpits.

"Go ahead, Oates," Balfour said. "Gently, now."

Oates seized Umber by the arm, hauled him off the bench, and tossed him across his shoulder. Umber thumped the broad back weakly with his fists. "Put me down, you miserable oaf."

"Blame Balfour," Oates said, and he led the way down the stairs, where they stepped onto the lift that would take them to the waiting carriage.

Curious stares followed them as they walked up the plank and onto the deck of the *Bounder*. Captain Sandar watched with a bemused smile as Oates carried Umber through the hatch to the lower deck. Oates came out a moment later, shaking his head. "He said mean things to me."

"Don't take it personally," Balfour began to say, but Oates was suddenly staring at the crowded docks like a fox that had spotted a rabbit. Without a word of explanation, the big fellow raced down the plank, which bounced merrily under every heavy step. Hap saw a figure in the crowd spin and run. A terrible limp slowed his escape, and as Oates closed in, the stranger ducked behind a stack of cargo.

Sophie peered down from the railing with her hand shading her brow. "Who is Oates chasing?"

Oates looked left and right, and then leaned over to peer behind a row of crates. He reached down and pulled a flailing figure up by the collar, and then tossed whomever it was over his shoulder just as he'd carried Umber, but not as gently. When this fellow kicked and punched him, Oates squeezed his midsection, and the struggle ended. Soon Oates was back on the *Bounder*, where he dumped the man rudely onto the deck.

The stranger landed on his stomach, and then turned over, coughing and wheezing. The face was covered with half-healed bruises, and the nose, which once was straight, had been bent to one side, but Hap still recognized the man. He spit the name out like a bug he'd nearly swallowed. "Hameron!"

"Saw him skulking around on the dock, watching us," Oates said.

Hameron got to his knees, rubbing an elbow, and glared at Oates. "I would have come on board if you'd asked, you beast."

Balfour grinned down at Umber's rival. "Hello, Hameron. Umber wondered if you'd made it through the rebellion alive."

"Barely," Hameron said, standing up and wincing. "But this leg will never heal right. And look at my nose, my face!" He poked his bent, broken nose. Hap noticed that a third of his teeth were missing.

"Looks like you took a beating," Balfour said, trying to temper his smile.

"Yes. Because somebody released a bunch of angry prisoners who decided to take their wrath out on me," Hameron replied, glaring at Hap.

"You're lucky they didn't kill you," Hap replied. It wasn't his way to talk back to adults, but he couldn't help himself with Hameron.

"Hmph," Hameron said. "Well, I lost everything, thanks to you people."

"And you're following us for what reason?" Balfour asked. "Revenge?"

"Hardly," Hameron said. "I'm not the vengeful type. But I am destitute, and it's all Umber's fault. It's compensation I want."

"Compensation?" Balfour looked at Oates, and they both roared with laughter.

Hameron puffed out his chest and crossed his arms. "Restitution for my losses. And my suffering! It's only fair. Those were *my* dragon eggs that Umber stole. And I had to escape from Sarnica with nothing but the clothes on my back and the coins in my pocket."

Balfour bent with laughter, and finally wiped the tears from his eyes and collected himself. "Oh, you are an amusing fellow, Hameron. Compensation, ha-ha!"

Hameron's mouth cinched tight and his face turned purple. "I demand to speak to Umber. And speaking of which . . . why did this great buffoon carry Umber onto the ship?"

Balfour shook his head and chuckled again. "Oh, you'll

speak to Umber eventually. Not yet, though. But I think we may have something in the way of compensation for you, Hameron."

Hameron raised an eyebrow and waited.

"See, you're going on a journey with us," Balfour told him, thumbing toward the sea. "And if you help us do something, Umber might see fit to reward you. How much of a reward will be up to him, but you know he's a generous soul."

"Help you do *what*?" Hameron's eye narrowed to a squint.

"Ah—this is why your appearance is so timely," Balfour replied. "You're just the man to help us take the dragon eggs back where they belong. Since you're the one who stole them in the first place."

Hameron's jaw dropped like a trapdoor. "Take them *back*? Tell me you're not that crazy!"

"We truly are," Oates said, shaking his head.

"That is more dangerous than you can imagine," Hameron said, backing away. "Sorry, Balfour. You can leave me out." He turned to limp down the plank. But after a nod from Balfour, Oates's meaty hand clamped down on his shoulder. Hameron shrieked.

"Lock him up till we're at sea, Oates," Balfour said. He tapped his fingertips together. "You know something, Hap? I think I'm getting the hang of this adventuring stuff."

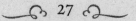

The sea billowed with long, rolling waves, so that the *Bounder* was rarely level. She rose up one watery slope, burst through its foaming crest, and plunged down the other side.

Sophie nudged Hap with her elbow and pointed to the starboard railing, where Hameron leaned over, sending a jet of half-digested food into the green sea. He turned toward them, sweaty and pale-faced, and wiped the corner of his mouth with his sleeve. "I *despise* ocean travel," he said. A deep, wet hiccup followed, and he leaned over the rail once more.

Sophie turned away to hide her smile. "Come on, Hap. Let's go see Jewel," she said. They fetched a pair of fish from the galley and went down to the hold, at the bottom of the ship. The steps ended at the carpenter's walk: the aisle that ran the length of the ship and was used to find and repair any leaks that sprang up during a journey.

The vessel was alive with conducted noise and vibration. There were groaning beams and planks, dim steps and voices of sailors above, and the muffled rush of water washing past the hull. It occurred to Hap that they were standing below the waterline, inside a bubble of wood. *Don't think about that,* he ordered himself.

The carpenter's walk divided the hold, where barrels of food, fresh water, rum, and beer were stacked high. Plenty of

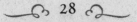

storage space remained, since this was a merchant ship, but this journey was not for commerce. Their primary cargo was a small chest filled with crystalline dragon eggs, and a cage with an infant dragon that was small but growing fast.

"Hello, Jewel," Hap said, as he and Sophie sat beside the cage, next to where the thick main mast was rooted at the bottom of the ship.

The dragon had been sleeping with her head resting on her scaled legs. She lifted her face and opened her sapphire eyes. The long mouth cracked wide, and she squeaked out a yawn. The copper-colored scales shimmered as she stretched her limbs. Her tiny wings fanned out, experimented with a single tentative flap, and folded tight against her back once more.

"Jewel is such a perfect name," Sophie said. "Did you or Umber give it to her?"

"It was Sable's idea," Hap said. Sophie's head dropped, and she seemed to shrink beside him. Hap frowned, wondering what the problem was this time. All he'd done was answer the question. "Here, Sophie, give Jewel the fish," he said. "I think she likes you better, anyway."

That night Hap was summoned to the main deck, where he found a small group waiting: Balfour, Oates, Sophie, Captain Sandar, and Hameron. Hameron was partially recovered from his seasickness, but he still clung to a stay with a handkerchief pressed to his mouth.

Balfour nodded at them. "Follow me, please. Umber should hear this discussion." He led them to a cabin at the front of the ship, knocked twice, and opened the door.

They crowded into the room, with Oates pushing Hameron ahead of him. Umber was slumped on a chair with his chin on his chest. His eyes rolled up to look at his visitors, and then down again as if the effort was too great to sustain. "Told you I wanted to be left alone," he mumbled.

"My apologies, Umber," Balfour said. "But we need to figure out exactly how we're going to return these eggs."

Umber just shrugged. Hameron gave him a sour look. "What's the matter with him?"

"Put off by your presence, perhaps," Balfour said.

Hameron sneered and turned to Oates. "What's the matter with Umber, Oates?"

"He falls into these moods, and we never know when he'll come out," Oates replied.

Hameron dabbed at a corner of his mouth with the handkerchief. "Always knew there was something nutty about him."

Balfour cleared his throat loudly. "You all know why we're on this journey."

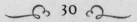

"To suffer a brutal, fiery death," Hameron muttered.

"That's enough of that," Sandar snapped. He stepped so close to Hameron that their noses nearly touched. "You will respect my passengers, and you will say nothing more against Lord Umber, Hameron. It's a long swim home if you don't."

Balfour twiddled his thumbs and looked sideways at Hameron. "Our mission is to return the eggs and the infant dragon to the land where they belong. Hameron, you were the one who found them. If you're so concerned for our safety, maybe you could advise us on how to pull this off."

Hameron crossed his arms and rolled his eyes. "You ruined my life, all of you. And kidnapped me for this journey, against my will. Why should I help you?"

"This ship is going to the dragon's lair, Hameron, with you on it. So you'll be saving your own skin, too, mind you," Balfour told him. "And I think you can expect some reward for your help. It was compensation you were after, wasn't it?"

Hameron's jaw worked from side to side. "How *much* compensation?"

"That will be up to Umber. Enough to put you back on your feet, though, I imagine."

"My weight in gold," Hameron said.

"I beg your pardon?" Balfour replied.

"That's what I demand. I'll tell you how to safely return the dragon eggs. But I want my weight in gold in return."

"Preposterous," Balfour began, but he was interrupted by a weak, emotionless voice.

"He can have it," Umber muttered.

"Umber, really," Balfour whined.

"I don't care," Umber said. His eyes were shut, and he rubbed at one lid with his fingertips. "Anything to get this over with. Just do what he says. And get out of my cabin, all of you." He stepped out of the chair, never straightening, and flopped onto his bed, facedown.

Hameron smirked at Balfour. "You heard him, old man. Do what I say. This is my expedition now." He turned to Sandar. "You have a map of Chastor, I presume? Fetch it for me like a good captain. We should leave dear Umber to marinate in his despair, and gather at the dining table. Suddenly I'm feeling quite hungry."

Hap lingered for a moment after the others filed out. "I hope you feel better soon, Lord Umber."

Umber never looked up.

The others were at the table, gathered around the map that Sandar unrolled. Hameron's lip curled as he looked at it. "This is the best map you've got?"

Sandar glared. "The land is full of dragons. Mapmakers tend to avoid it, like everyone else."

"Ugh," Hameron said. "My chart was better. But I guess this will do." His fingernail rasped across the parchment and stopped. "Here. See that notch in the coast? It's like a bite taken from the land. That little crescent is where the dragons have their nests. It's easy enough to spot if the mists aren't too thick. There's a sharp point of rock that juts out of the sea a few hundred yards from the shore. I call it Hameron's Needle." Hap looked at Balfour, who watched with his nostrils flared wide.

Hameron's finger slid south on the map. "We'll put ashore here, a few miles away, in a sandy cove that I discovered. Hameron's Cove. The cliffs along the coast are riddled with crevices and caves, and we can use those to approach unseen. I know the path. But the wind has to be right—it must not carry our scent to the dragons." He lifted his head and looked at the others. "We can take the eggs ashore and leave them for the dragons to find. But we can't take the infant."

"What?" said Balfour. "Why not?"

"Are you losing your wits in your old age, Balfour? It's too risky. The dragon may cry out or reveal our presence some other way. And that will mean death for us."

"But we can't keep her," Hap cried. "She's getting big—she'll be too dangerous!"

"True," Hameron said. "You'll have to dispose of her."

"*Dispose* of her?" cried Sophie.

Hameron sighed. "If we can't return her safely, and you can't keep her, you have no choice, my dear. It will be done humanely, of course. Not like those barbaric Dragon Games. And the creature will make a lovely museum piece once it's stuffed."

Sophie made a sound Hap had never heard from her before: half grunt, half shout, from a closed mouth. She stomped away, down to the hold, where Jewel was caged.

"Balfour," Hap pleaded.

Balfour raised a hand. "Nobody's killing the dragon, Hameron. Umber has bottles of sleeping potions; we'll use some on her, and she won't make a sound."

Hameron rocked his head back and puffed air at the ceiling. "You think you have all the answers, don't you, Balfour?"

"Hardly," Balfour replied. "I never said I was unfallible."

"The word is *in*fallible."

Balfour shrugged. "See?"

CHAPTER
4

Captain Sandar steered the Bounder
near the eastern coast of Celador, keeping the rugged shore just visible to starboard. They passed through the channel that separated the mainland from Norr. The sailors kept close watch on that island, in case one of its hostile ships bolted out in pursuit, but Sandar was unconcerned. The *Bounder* could outsail any rival craft, except for others in Umber's merchant fleet. They were the sleekest ships the world had known, and it was rumored that Umber had better, faster vessels on the way, even as envious shipbuilders copied his current designs.

The sky turned gloomy, and clouds obscured the setting sun. As the ship sailed blindly through the night, Hap wondered how Sandar could know which way to steer. He'd seen navigators use instruments of Umber's invention to plot their courses based on the position of the sun and the stars. But those tools were useless under a canopy of cloud. Sandar, who had taken a liking to Hap from the beginning, was happy to explain.

"I have charts to tell me the distance between lands. And I have a compass to show me our heading. All I need, then, is to know our speed. Now, Hap, have you seen my crew let that knotted rope slip into the water every so often? That's how we judge our speed, depending on how many knots pay out in one turn of the glass. Then I mark our progress on the chart. We can be more accurate than you'd imagine this way. I once got through the Straits of Maur in a driving rainstorm with that sort of reckoning."

Hameron had said that the coast of Chastor was often enveloped by mist, and his words proved to be true. The next day the *Bounder* sailed into a thickening vapor. Hap felt moisture collecting on the fine hairs of his arms. It was high noon, according to the ship's glass, but the light was dim and diffused, and there were no shadows. The ship nudged forward under a single sail, in a gentle breeze that carried them toward the land of the dragons.

Hameron stood near the prow, leaning over the rail. "You'd

better know what you're doing, Captain Sandar," he called back. His neck craned forward. "How far from the coast are we?"

"About a mile," Sandar replied.

"*About*, he tells me," Hameron muttered. He waved a hand in front of his face, as if he could push the fog away, and cupped his hands beside his eyes, peering forward. A sailor named Hannigan was in the crow's nest at the top of the foremast, and his urgent cry came down: "Land ahead—a spike of land!"

"No!" cried Hameron. "That's my needle! Hameron's Needle! Sandar, you incompetent fool, you've got us too close! Quiet, everyone," he screamed, though he was the only one making a sound. He rushed back toward the helm with his eyes bulging. Hap saw a narrow, jagged rock, taller than the ship's masts, resolving in the mist before them.

"That way!" Hameron hissed, jabbing at the air. "Take us that way!"

"Starboard, hard," Sandar said, and the helmsman spun the ship's wheel. The fog overhead dimmed for a moment—a flash of darkness that passed swiftly from east to west. Hameron's head snapped upward, and his mouth sagged open.

"Did anyone else see that?" said Oates. "Hap, could you see?"

Hap shook his head. His vision was sharp, even in the dark, but it couldn't penetrate this fog.

It happened again: a shadow moving swiftly inside the vapor. Hap thought he heard a sound this time, a great *fwoop* of air being pushed, like a sheet snapping on a clothesline. Part of the mist billowed into whorls, disturbed from above. Hameron made a dash for the hatch, but Oates grabbed him by the collar. "Where are you going?" Oates asked, as Hameron flailed.

An orange plume flared within the mist. The thing passed by again, but closer this time, and its form could be seen: long-necked and long-tailed, with diamond wings on either side. It was half the length of the ship.

"Oh no, no, no, oh no," whined Hameron, clutching his skull. He turned to Sandar with every tooth showing in a ghastly grimace. "You've doomed us all!"

Sandar's face had gone pale, and his throat bobbed. He looked at Balfour with watery eyes. "The map," he said hoarsely. "I know how to sail; the map must be wrong!"

A terrible sound came from directly above: a loud screech that fell in pitch to a booming roar. All eyes turned up to see a golden serpent drop out of the cloud with its wings spread wide. Hap was sure it would crash onto the deck of the ship, but the sprawling wings flapped once, arresting the descent. The gust of air nearly knocked Hap off his feet. The dragon seized the top of the forward mast with all four of its legs. In the crow's nest, Hannigan was eye to eye with the creature. He yelped and dropped out of sight in the half-barrel platform.

The dragon's claws bit deep into the mast. The wings spread wide and flapped again and again, forcing the ship into a dangerous tilt. Sandar and Balfour wrapped their arms around the helm, and the sailors seized the stays and rails to keep from sliding across the deck. Hap heard things rolling and crashing in the hold below, and he saw Oates with one arm curled around the foremast and the other hand holding a sprawling, squirming Hameron by the collar, saving him from a painful tumble. The dragon turned its jaws toward the sky and unleashed a plume of fire. The wings kept flapping, and the ship was nearly sideways. The sailors wailed and screamed.

When the *Bounder* seemed inches from capsizing, the dragon made a chuffing sound and folded its wings. The ship rolled back to horizontal and beyond, and a few men lost their grip and tumbled across the deck into the port-side rail.

Why did it stop? Hap wondered. The dragon extended its long neck and stared down with smoke drifting from its jaws. As its muscles moved, the metallic scales shimmered. Hap followed the serpent's gaze and saw Sophie lying on the deck just outside the hatch, with her hand pushing Jewel's cage in front of her. Jewel raced back and forth within the bars, taking two strides and whipping her slender body around to face the other way.

The golden dragon climbed halfway down the mast and angled its head, inspecting the cage. It called out again: not the earsplitting roar they'd already heard, but a long, warbling cry.

Some of the crew stood cautiously as the ship stopped rocking, while the rest stayed low, cowering. Hap saw Hameron tug at the cuff of Oates's pants. "You're the fighter, you big oaf—do something!"

Oates laughed bitterly. "Do what? Get my head bitten off?"

The dragon stared down, turning its gaze on anyone who moved. All motion stopped, except for the blinking of eyes and heaving of chests.

Hap looked at Sophie, who had gotten to her knees next to the cage, clutching it with a shaking hand. "Should I open it?" she whispered.

Hap nodded. "Do it!"

"I'm scared," she said.

Hap craned his neck to watch the dragon and took a slow, sliding step toward Sophie. When the dragon didn't notice him, he took another, and a third. And then the serpent's long snout swiveled toward him, and its sapphire eyes narrowed and focused. Terror fused Hap's feet to the deck, and hot beads of sweat sprang up along his hairline. He looked sideways at Sophie and saw someone appear in the threshold over her

shoulder, coming slowly up the stairs from the deck below.

Umber looked like a man roused from a drunken stupor as he wobbled up the last step, gripping the rail to steady himself. His eyes were slits, and he blinked at the daylight as he stepped onto the top deck. His mouth opened and twisted sideways in a long, loud yawn, which froze wide when he spotted the dragon on the mast. His tongue wagged, and he might have said something if a second dragon had not burst out of the mist.

It was larger than the first and more coppery in hue. With wings flexed wide it glided to the front of the ship and landed on the prow, gouging the planks and snapping off the bowsprit. The copper beast sang a warbling reply to the golden dragon, and then growled at the cowering people on the *Bounder*.

Then the copper dragon did something astonishing. It bent its neck and lowered its head to the deck. Hap saw a man perched on the dragon's shoulders, in a leather saddle. The man swung his legs to one side, kicking off the loops that secured his feet. The dragon raised its foreleg, offering a place to stand, and lowered the man to the deck. He stepped down and took two strides forward. The dragon's head hovered over the man's shoulder, teeth bared.

The man was dressed head to toe in spotted goat hide:

boots, leggings, tunic, and gloves. His forehead and ears were covered by a leather hood with long flaps down the sides. On the parts of his face that Hap could see, and across his bare arms, metallic scales had been painted or tattooed.

Hap remembered reading in one of Umber's books about a legendary being. The name sprang to mind: the Dragon Lord.

The man looked at the cage with Jewel inside. His lips pulled back in a snarl, and he called out in a fierce, strangely accented voice, "Who commands you?"

All eyes went to Umber, who stood unsteadily, looking bewildered as he gaped at the dragons. He didn't seem to hear the question.

"This is my ship," Sandar said in a quavering voice, from the helm.

Balfour cleared his throat and stepped forward. "But this is my mission. We are here to return something that belongs to you. Are you . . . are you the Dragon Lord?"

Hap saw Umber mouth the words: *Dragon Lord*. His fingers twitched against his lips.

The Dragon Lord ignored the question. He pointed at Jewel's cage with a gloved hand. "How did you come to possess that?"

Balfour glanced at Umber, perhaps hoping that Umber was ready to join the conversation. "It was stolen from you,"

Balfour said. "And we took it back so we could return it. But that's not all. We have also brought back your stolen eggs."

The Dragon Lord reached up to cradle the copper dragon's great jaw in his arm, and he sang softly into its ear. The creature rumbled and snorted, and a puff of smoke shot from each nostril. Hap gulped. He saw Hameron try to edge away, but Oates held him by the sleeve. Hameron's bottom lip trembled, and his head moved in tiny sideways shakes.

Balfour's voice cracked as he called out the side of his mouth. "Perhaps someone could fetch the eggs?"

"I'll go," Hap said. As he ran by, he tugged Sophie's arm. "Help me," he said, and he breathed a little easier when she followed him into the lower deck, out of reach of the dragon's toothy jaws.

"Stay below," he told her when they'd made it down the first flight of stairs.

"I will not," she replied, and ran ahead of him, down into the hold. But he darted past her, picked up the chest before she arrived, and bounded back up the stairs as fast as his powerful legs would take him. When he arrived on the top deck again, it didn't seem as if any more words had been exchanged. The Dragon Lord stood like a sculpture with his fists on his hips. Jewel was out of her cage and clung to his shoulder with her tail wrapped tight around his arm. The golden dragon had slithered farther down the mast, spiraling around the beam as it descended, until its snout was just over Oates's head. Hameron ducked behind the bigger man.

Hap felt Sophie's hand on his shoulder. "Let's go," she whispered, "before we lose our nerve."

They passed Umber, who stood with his mouth agape, blinking up at the dragon on the mast. "Are you all right?" Hap asked, but Umber didn't respond.

With Sophie gripping the back of his shirt, Hap edged slowly forward until he was two strides from the Dragon Lord. "The eggs are in here, sir," Hap said, and he lowered the chest to the deck.

The Dragon Lord's pale eyes narrowed in the shadow of the hood. "Open it."

Balfour cleared his throat. "I have the key." He came forward with tiny, hesitant steps and opened the lock with a shaky hand. The lid yawned. Inside, the crystalline eggs gleamed. The Dragon Lord stepped up to the box, and the copper dragon slid up beside him with fluid grace. Hap felt its breath on his head, like the heat of a furnace.

The Dragon Lord kneeled and counted the eggs. He stood with one in each hand. "Ten and six were stolen from us. Here are ten and *one*."

Balfour opened his mouth again, but no words came out.

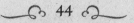

Hap gulped, and his voice squeaked as he answered. "The infant dragon hatched from one. Four were . . . killed in a barbaric game in a distant land. But the men who killed the dragons died themselves, as we rescued the eggs."

Hap heard the Dragon Lord's breath hiss from his nostrils. The copper dragon's wings ruffled, and it flexed its claws, splintering the wood below. "And the person who stole the eggs," the Dragon Lord roared, for every person on the ship to hear. "What became of *him*?"

Hap looked behind him and saw exactly what he feared. Oates was biting his lip. He looked like he was struggling to keep a violent sneeze from escaping. Over Oates's shoulder, Hap saw the growing alarm in Hameron's expression. Hameron knew what was about to happen. Oates was compelled to speak the truth, and when a question was asked, nothing but a muzzle could keep him from answering. He crammed his fist into his mouth, but it popped back out like a cork. "It was this man right here," his voice boomed out, as tears drizzled from his pained, squinting eyes.

Hameron gasped. He darted away from Oates and raced for the hatch. The Dragon Lord sang out, and the golden dragon on the mast dropped onto the deck. Hap and Sophie leaped aside to avoid the lash of its tail. Umber never moved, and found himself within arm's reach of the dragon's rear haunch.

He put a hand up and touched its scales, and his gaping mouth curved into an infant smile.

Hameron darted into the hatch, but the dragon's head and the entire length of its neck followed. When the head came back out, Hameron's short cape was clamped between its teeth. The dragon reared up on two legs, and Hameron dangled under its chin, shrieking and pinwheeling his arms.

Hap was dizzy with terror. He leaped toward the Dragon Lord, a gesture so rash that the copper dragon arched its neck and snarled, showing a row of pearly daggers. Hap dropped to his knees with his hands clasped before him. "Show mercy! He helped us bring the eggs back!"

"Where was mercy for my lost children? Can your thief return the fallen ones, as well?" the Dragon Lord snapped, slamming the lid on the chest of eggs. He called out again in that strange song. The golden dragon tossed its head, flipping Hameron into the air. It caught him neatly, almost gently, with its jaws around his waist. "Umber!" Hameron cried, spotting his rival on the deck. "Umber, do something!" The words seemed to register dimly, as Umber looked stupidly about him, trying to find the source of the voice.

The golden dragon's wings snapped open, blotting out the misty sky. They flapped once, so hard that Hap and Sophie

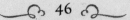

were driven to their knees. A second flap bore the dragon aloft, with every head turning to watch its ascent.

"Ummmmberrrrrr!" came Hameron's faint, desperate cry. The dragon's chest expanded, its neck straightened, and its breath came out as a river of flame. Beside him Hap heard a choking sob from Sophie. He put his hand over his throat. The dragon opened its jaws, and a tiny, charred form dropped into the sea.

Hap stared, numb with horror. Balfour had covered his face with his hands, and Oates kneeled with his forehead on the planks and his fist pounding the deck.

"The same fate could be yours," the Dragon Lord said. "But I spare you because you have returned these eggs." He lifted the chest and tucked it under one arm. "Now leave this shore. Come back again if you wish to die." The copper dragon offered its foreleg as a step, and the Dragon Lord climbed into the saddle. Jewel clung fast to his shoulder, but she turned her head toward Sophie and squeaked once. Soon the dragon was airborne, but before they flew from sight the serpents wheeled and soared past the sides of the *Bounder*, slashing the waves with their tails and scorching the port and starboard rails with their fire.

Time passed. Hap couldn't have said if it was a minute or

an hour. Oates sat up and sniffed. "Curse this curse," he said. "I didn't like Hameron, but I never wished that on him."

"We know," Balfour said thickly.

Umber had a hand on each cheek. He was watching the place where the dragons had melted into the fog. He patted his face and blew air out of puffed cheeks, and then looked around him, blinking at Balfour, Hap, and Sophie. His eyebrows flickered as a thought seemed to occur.

"Er . . . I don't suppose we have any coffee?"

CHAPTER
5

As the Bounder sailed from Chastor, there was mug after mug of coffee, and then Umber gorged himself on fruit, bread, fish, and cheese and washed it down with a mug of ale. Color dawned in the face that had long been a dreadful ashen shade. Hap sighed with relief as signs of Umber's good nature reappeared: a twinkle in his eye, a waggle of his eyebrow, the fidgeting of hands and feet. Umber said little, but he finally looked up and offered a weak smile. The tightness in Hap's chest, which had plagued him since Umber plunged into his dark mood, began to loosen.

Umber picked up a napkin and dabbed the corners of his mouth. "Well," he said, with his voice weak from disuse, "that was a terrible fate for Hameron." Hap and the others nodded. "He was a louse, there's no denying it," Umber continued, gaining strength. "But nobody deserves that. Here's to his memory." He raised his goblet, and Balfour raised his, while Hap and Sophie sipped the cider that Balfour had brought them.

Umber leaned back, quietly burped, and patted his swollen stomach. "Where's Oates?"

"Moping in the cabin," Balfour told him. "He feels bad about . . . you know."

"Hum," said Umber. "It wasn't his fault Hameron stole the eggs. And imagine if the Dragon Lord hadn't learned the truth; those dragons might have burned the whole ship if they hadn't taken their revenge on Hameron alone. Come to think of it, Hameron probably saved every one of us." Umber slapped the table. "But, Sophie, did you see those gorgeous creatures? Did you get a good look, so you can sketch 'em? Those *wings*, those *tails*—incredible! Though I think it best that we investigate no further, wouldn't you agree? Fancy me, saying that! Ha!" He drummed the table with his palms. Hap shook his head, amazed at how quickly Umber had emerged from his near-fatal melancholy.

Umber froze abruptly with his hands hovering over the table. His head swiveled toward Balfour. "Er . . . Balfour. My latest episode . . . it was a bad one, wasn't it?"

"You could say that."

"Weeks, I believe?"

"That's right."

Umber pinched the end of his nose. "I don't remember much, as usual . . . but I have an odd feeling. . . . Did I see Fay? Balfour, did Fay come to the Aerie . . . while I was . . . you know?"

Balfour puckered his mouth and scratched at a knot in the tabletop. "Who? Fay? Oh. Well. She did, in fact."

Umber put his palm to his forehead. "And she saw me? Face-to-face, I mean? You let her up to *see* me?"

Balfour's head shrank between his shoulders. "I . . . I thought it would help. You know. Jolt you out of your state."

Umber tilted his chair back and chuckled ruefully at the ceiling. "Well, now. I don't imagine I made a wonderful second impression."

Balfour and Hap glanced at each other, widening their eyes, and Umber noticed. "What?" he said. "Something else? What happened? Fay is still in Kurahaven, isn't she?"

Balfour seemed to be shrinking. "She is."

"Well, where'd you put her? Someplace nice? Your old inn, right, Balfour?"

Balfour stared down at the table without answering.

"Sophie? Hap?" Umber said, turning from one to the other. "Care to tell me?"

Oates chose that moment to lumber into the cabin, dour

and puffy-eyed. Umber shot a frustrated glare at Balfour and called to the big man. "Oates, there you are!"

"Yes, I am," Oates rumbled. "And you're better, I see. About time."

"I cherish your kind words," Umber snapped. "But what I need right now is an honest answer: What happened after Fay came to the Aerie to see me?"

Oates frowned at the others, unhappy that it fell on him to deliver the news. "Loden showed up, right when Fay and that little girl were leaving. He became very charming and convinced Fay to go back to the palace. She's still there, as far as we know."

Umber's mouth hung slack. Oates shrugged, dropped his bulk into a chair, and piled food on a plate.

Hap watched with alarm as the color started to drain from Umber's face. He leaned across the table and clutched Umber's forearm. "The archives that Caspar took, Lord Umber. With your stolen documents about the Meddlers. Caspar kept them in a strongbox, and it's on the ship right now!"

Umber's head sprang back up. "Here? In a strongbox? What was in it?"

Hap grinned. "It hasn't been opened yet. I was waiting until you felt better."

Umber pushed himself to his feet and rubbed his hands

together. "Then your wait is over. Let's crack it open now!"

Hap stood, and Balfour got up to go with them. Umber put a hand on Balfour's shoulder. "My dear friend," Umber said. "I think Hap and I ought to do this alone. Do you mind terribly?"

Balfour's shoulders sagged. "Not at all, Umber. Go right ahead. The strongbox was in your cabin all this while."

Umber and Hap sat cross-legged on the floor with Caspar's strongbox between them.

Umber rolled his shoulders and cracked his neck, still coming back to life. He narrowed his eyes, peering at the top of Hap's head. "Hap—you've got more of those hairs now. Twice as many as before."

"I know," Hap said, almost moaning the words. He'd plucked one of those strands once to examine it. It looked white at first glance, but on closer examination it gleamed with color, like diamonds spun into string. In fact, it looked a bit like the filaments that he would sometimes envision. The change in his hair, he supposed, was part of the process of turning into a Meddler. It made him squirm to think about it, so he turned Umber's attention back to the strongbox by tapping it. "There's something else in there. You can hear it rolling around."

Umber raised an eyebrow. He gave the box a shove, and

there was a muffled thump from inside. "Now I'm extra curious." He pulled the loop of a chain over his neck, with his remarkable key dangling. Even as it swung back and forth like a pendulum, its shape changed to match the nearest lock. Umber opened the padlocks first, and the chains slithered to the floor. Then he slipped the key into the embedded lock and turned it. The lid rose with the faintest squeak from its well-oiled hinges.

Hap dug his fingertips into his knees. Inside the strongbox were the stolen secrets of the Meddlers: the answers he'd been seeking since he'd woken, devoid of memory, in an entombed city months before.

Umber peered into the interior. His eyebrows rose and his mouth formed a tiny, puckered smile. With both hands, he reached down and lifted out a large object wrapped in heavy canvas. He turned it from side to side, showing Hap its fat oval shape. "Hmm. Any guesses, Hap?"

Hap's nose wrinkled. The guess that someone had already made seemed all too likely. "A skull?"

"Good answer! Let's find out," Umber said. He turned the object in his hand to unwind its wrapping. Hap braced himself, fully expecting to see gaping sockets and a frozen grin.

"Ouch!" Umber sucked on the pad of his thumb. Then he put the thing on the floor and carefully removed the last flaps of canvas, revealing a large tan object that tapered to a blunt point at one end. It was covered with inch-long thorns.

Hap put his nose near the thing. "What is it?"

"A nut!" Umber pronounced. He squinted at it. "I think, anyway. Here we have a big, prickly nut."

Hap frowned. "That doesn't have anything to do with Meddlers, does it?"

"Probably not. I suppose Caspar found it in some lost corner of the Aerie and decided to steal it, too." Umber interlaced his fingers and cracked them. "But let's put that aside for the moment. The answers we've been waiting for are right before us!" He reached into the chest and picked up a leather-bound notebook.

"That looks like one of *your* notebooks," Hap said.

"Caspar used the same kind," Umber said. His expression softened as he skimmed the first pages. "And that's Caspar's writing. Oh, this'll be mighty helpful." He noticed Hap leaning in, and turned the page so he could see. "In this notebook he's summarized everything he's learned from the documents."

Umber put the notebook on his lap and scooped a pile of old parchments out of the chest. "So here we have the source materials, and, in the notebook, Caspar's conclusions. This is excellent! I'll tell you what—you have a go at the old stuff, since you can understand all those languages, and I'll peruse the notebook."

Hap was halfway through an old document in a forgotten language from a faraway land, which told of a seldom seen, mischievous green-eyed people, when Umber lowered the notebook from his face to reveal a solemn gaze. "Happenstance," he said.

Hap was always mildly alarmed when Umber used his entire name. "What is it?"

"Do you want to know how Meddlers are made?"

All the moisture left Hap's mouth in an instant, and his pulse seemed to triple. "H-how?"

"There is an essence—a liquid. It is poured into the eyes of someone who is recently . . . you know." Umber took a deep breath. "Departed."

Hap's limbs started to shake. This was hardly a shock; they were almost certain that Julian Penny, his former self, had drowned, and that the death had been connived by the Meddler they'd come to know as Willy Nilly. But still, the confirmation struck him like a spear in the belly.

"An . . . *essence* made me?" Hap asked, touching the corners of his eyes.

Umber nodded. "It gave you your abilities—your grasp of

all languages, your nocturnal vision, your springy legs, and, of course, the power to see the filaments. It also wiped away your old memories." He glanced at the notebook. "And there is only one source for the essence."

Hap waited.

"You won't like this," Umber said. He closed the notebook, with his finger marking the page he'd been reading.

Hap gulped. "I haven't liked any of it, ever."

Umber's bottom teeth sawed his upper lip. "The essence is taken from the eyes of another Meddler. That's the only way to get it."

"So that means . . ." Hap's mind swirled, desperately evading the obvious conclusion.

"It means that another Meddler died so you could be made," Umber said. "Or was blinded."

Hap pressed his palms over his eyes. He rocked back and forth and groaned. The list of horrors was still compiling. He thought about poor Julian Penny—the boy who was *him* and yet also a stranger. He thought about Julian's parents, and the fateful chain of circumstances that had delivered them into the hands of a monster. And now someone else had lost his eyes and likely met his doom so that Hap might become a Meddler. "Do you think Willy Nilly did it? Killed another Meddler?"

"It's possible," Umber said. He touched Hap's shoulder. "Don't blame yourself. You didn't ask for any of this. It just happened to you. And you have to remember—you may have been born from tragedy, but you have to think of what's ahead. We're going to save a world, you and I. A billion lives, or more."

Hap nodded and smeared a tear across his cheek. "What else did Caspar know?"

Umber opened the notebook again. "Do you want to hear it as I learn it, or all at once when I'm done?"

"As you learn it."

Hap finished reading the parchment and turned to another. It listed all the names that had been used for Meddlers across the world: Hoppers, Tinkers, Fate Lords, Leapers, *Interferi*, Wanderers, Greeneyes . . .

He looked up to see Umber staring blank-faced, holding the notebook limply in his hands. Umber stood and put his forehead against the wall. "How could I not have realized it?" he muttered. The notebook slid from his hands and thumped on the floor.

Hap got to his feet, feeling twinges in his stomach. "Lord Umber?"

Umber slapped his palm on the wall. "Happenstance. I told you . . . I promised you . . ." He rolled his eyes upward and

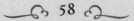

closed them. "I said when your powers develop, and you can leap back to the world that I came from . . . I promised I'd go with you."

Hap nodded, even as a spidery panic twitched through his arms and legs. "And you will, won't you? You'll help me?"

Umber stared at the notebook at his feet. "We know that a Meddler can transport another person. Willy Nilly carried you—he took you hundreds of miles, and seven years into the future, to where I would find you. And I'm sure a Meddler must have carried me, the same way, from my world to this world. Maybe that was Willy too, because he brought us together. That makes sense, right?"

"Yes," Hap said.

"So that is not the problem; carrying someone with you."

Hap clutched his hands together to still them. "But there *is* a problem?"

"*Time* is the problem." Umber grimaced and pinched an eyebrow. "If what Caspar learned is correct . . . nobody can pass through the same time twice. No human and no Meddler."

"But . . ." Hap tried to speak, but couldn't form a question, and finally his jaw went slack.

"Hap, to fix my world, you have to go into its past. And *you* can, because you've never been there—it's not your past. But it's *my* past. I can't return, except after the moment I left. And

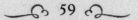

then it would be too late, of course. All the catastrophes would have already happened."

Hap's mind struggled with the full weight of the implications. "You mean . . . I have to do this on my own? You won't be there to help me?"

Umber shook his head. "You know I would if it were possible. But I don't think it is." He picked up the notebook. "Hap, maybe Caspar was wrong about this. His source could be wrong. We'll keep reading, all right?"

"All right," Hap said, but while Umber went back to inspecting the notebook, Hap wrapped his arms around his knees and stared at nothing.

"You know," Umber said after a while, "I think we could both use a break, and some fresh air." He picked up the canvas and wound it around the thorny nut. "I wish I knew what this was," he said, and then his eyes widened and his neck stretched. "You know what? I know someone who might. Come with me, Hap!"

Umber and Hap stepped into the ship's central cabin. Balfour was at the dining table, slumped with his chin on his hand. "Balfour!" cried Umber. "Have you seen Sandar? Is he on the top deck?"

Balfour looked up. There was an odd pause, and then he

jabbed his thumb in the direction of the captain's cabin.

"Excellent," Umber said. "Old friend, that coffee did me a world of good. Might there be another pot in my near future?"

Balfour exhaled heavily. "Whatever you say, *old friend.*" He shoved his chair under the table with a clatter and vanished into the galley without another word.

Umber watched him go with his mouth scrunched sideways. "Odd. Someone else is in a funk for a change," he said, and he shrugged. He walked to the rear of the deck and knocked on the door to the captain's cabin. "Enter," Sandar called from within. Umber opened the door, waving Hap in before him.

The captain's cabin on the *Bounder*, as on any sailing vessel, was the ship's largest and finest room. The wide, curving wall opposite the door was the stern, and it was lined with panes of glass, overlooking the sea. Sandar stood there watching the *Bounder*'s frothy wake, with his arm propped on the wall and his forehead resting on his elbow. They had sailed clear of the mists of Chastor, and the waves were molten gold in the late afternoon sun.

"Captain," Umber said, "I'd like to change our heading. Nothing drastic, just a place I need to visit on the way home."

Sandar kept his back to them. "Are you sure you trust me to find it, whatever it is?"

Umber's head inclined. "Of course I do. Why would you even ask?"

Sandar turned stiffly. "Because I owe you an apology. I brought the *Bounder* too close to the coast. Hameron died because of me. And we could have lost the whole ship, and every man on it."

Umber pursed his lips and scratched his temple. "Listen, Sandar, this was a risky endeavor. Foolhardy, even! But we accomplished what we set out to do, and righted a terrible wrong. Was Hameron's life worth more than those dragons'? It's not for us to say. So don't flog yourself over one mistake, Captain."

Sandar took a deep breath and nodded. "Thank you, Lord Umber. Please understand . . . it is my pride and pleasure to serve as your captain. And I worry that your trust in me has been shaken."

"Not at all. Which is fortunate, because I have an important favor to ask regarding our voyage home."

Sandar stood straight and thrust out his jaw. "Name it, Lord Umber."

"I need to be in Kurahaven soon. But there must be a detour first. Take us to the Verdant Isle. And I'll say it again: Speed is paramount. How quickly can you get us there, my captain?"

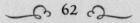

The heel of Sandar's boot struck the wooden planks, and a fiery look came to his eyes. "We'll put up every scrap of sail we've got. And I'll string up my laundry, too, if that'll push us faster. The *Bounder* will have you there before sunset tomorrow, or you can toss me overboard."

Sandar burst past them and raced out of his cabin. They heard him bellow as he charged onto the top deck: "Look lively, set sails! Have we fixed the bowsprit yet? Scamper up those ratlines, boys, and let's see what she can do!"

Umber grinned and poked Hap with his elbow. "We're not really in such a hurry, but our good captain feels the need to redeem himself."

Hap barely heard the comment. He'd experienced enough of Umber's destinations to have developed a healthy fear of them, and his mind raced uneasily forward. The crack in his voice betrayed his concern. "What is the Verdant Isle, Lord Umber?"

Umber's smile widened, and he ruffled Hap's hair. "Nothing to worry about! I have a friend there who might identify our thorny nut. And it's been far too long since I've seen him. You haven't met an actual wizard yet, have you, Hap? Soon you will—and a peculiar breed of wizard at that!"

everal who specialize in botanical
wizardry. They collect and cultivat
world's magical plants, and use the
own craft to develop new exotic

CHAPTER
6

Hap and Umber went belowdecks, where
Balfour sat by himself in a corner. Sophie was busy at the large
dining table, sketching with charcoal on broad sheets of paper.
Already she had produced three large drawings of the dragons
and the Dragon Lord. "How do you remember so much, so
well?" Hap asked, admiring the detail that she'd included,
down to the collar of feathers that ringed the dragons' necks.
Sophie just smiled and shrugged.

"Wonderful," Umber told her. His eyes sparkled as he
spotted the familiar silver pot on its tray, with steam drifting
from its spout. "And do you know what else is wonderful?"
He turned, looking for Balfour, but his expression fell when
he saw just the heels of Balfour's boots as he climbed the stairs,

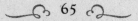

departing without a word. Umber watched the vacant steps with his bottom lip jutting out, and then shrugged and turned to Hap. "Let me enjoy a mug or two, Hap, and then we'll dive into those documents again."

"What have you got now, Hap?"

Hap held the scroll up for Umber to see. "It's in the Dwergh language. This is some old history about someone they called Emerald Eyes, who must have been a Meddler. There was a war for power going on between two Dwergh kings. On each side they'd be terrified any time they saw a green-eyed man, because something would go wrong soon after."

"That story has many variations, all over the world," Umber said. He poked at a page in Caspar's notebook. "Here's another strange fact. As we suspected, Meddlers can vanish at will and reappear in another place. But apparently they can't disappear if they are being watched—only when no eyes are upon them!"

"So if we see Willy Nilly again . . ."

"Right. We don't let him out of our sight. Now, Hap, allow me to sum up the rest of what Caspar learned. You know those filaments you've seen? Humans have them. And Meddlers, too. But most other creatures do not."

"Occo had them," Hap said, thinking of the horrible eye-stealing creature that had once pursued him.

"Yes. Occo, the Creep. I wonder why? Maybe because his kind is partly human. Or because they steal human eyes. Well, at least we don't have to worry about him anymore. Now, where was I? Many of the Meddlers—most of them, probably—are just pranksters. Small-time stuff. Others have brought down whole kingdoms with their schemes and machinations. It's impossible to say how many Meddlers there are at a given moment, because they move through time at will. A Meddler who is with us today might decide to leap forward ten years, or a century. And once they go forward, they cannot go back.

"Meddlers seem to come in pairs—but not friendly pairs. They are rivals, nemeses, and they each manipulate events with a different goal in mind. For example, while one Meddler tries to bring two lovers together, the nemesis keeps them apart. Or they take opposing sides in a conflict of nations." Umber closed the book and balanced it on his knee. "And that's just about all we know. Unless you've learned something more."

Hap shook his head. "Nothing important. But I wonder who Willy Nilly's nemesis was. Do you think . . . ?" His hands rose, subconsciously, and touched the corners of his eyes.

Umber winced. "I had the same thought. Perhaps they

were both in my world, working their mischief. And then, for some reason, Willy decided to make a new Meddler. And he might have used the eyes of his nemesis to do it."

"Do you think one of them caused all that trouble in your world?" Hap asked.

Umber dwelled on that question, tapping the space between his nose and mouth with one finger. "Maybe. It would have been easy enough for a Meddler to wreak havoc there. But now Willy wants to set things right. Remember the note he'd left when I first found you? You're supposed to undo the damage. Head off the global catastrophe. Who knows, maybe the nemesis caused it. Or Willy himself, and he came to regret it. We won't know unless Willy shows up and tells us, will we?"

Hap followed Umber to the main deck and nearly walked into his back when Umber abruptly stopped and looked up. He had the sort of mouth that could flash every tooth when he smiled wide, and suddenly they were all on display. "Hap, look!"

White sails were spread wide everywhere on the *Bounder*, giving her a top-heavy appearance. There were vast, bulging sprawls of canvas on the foremast and mainmast, smaller spreads on the topmasts, three triangular sails stretched toward the repaired bowsprit, and more sails improvised in places Hap had never seen them before.

Sandar shouted endless instructions to sailors who'd clambered high among the ship's roping. He noticed Umber and Hap on deck and flung his arms wide. "Lord Umber, have you ever seen so much sail? And look how she flies—two knots faster than ever. We'll reach the Verdant Isle in no time!"

Every sailor on the deck and up in the rigging watched Umber, struggling to suppress their grins. Hap puzzled over it briefly, and then saw the reason: A pair of ropes had been strung across the ship's deck, and laundry pinned there from top to bottom. Shirts, pants, and undergarments billowed in the breeze like the sails above. Umber's eyebrows rose when he finally noticed them, and he bent and guffawed. That was the moment the crew was waiting for, and they howled along with him. Some of the sailors above laughed so strenuously that Hap was afraid they might lose their grip and tumble to the deck. "Told you I'd string up my laundry to push us along!" Sandar shouted to Umber above the din.

Hap's own laughter faded when he saw Balfour trudging back downstairs. He waited for Umber to wipe a happy tear from his eye, and then spoke to him quietly. "Something's wrong with Balfour."

"I know," Umber said, growing serious. Oates wandered past at that moment, and Umber pinched his sleeve. "Oates, do you have any idea what's eating Balfour?"

"Yes," answered Oates.

Umber made a whirling motion with his fingers until his patience expired. "For pity's sake, Oates, would you mind telling me what it is?"

"I don't mind at all. You mean you don't know?"

"I do not."

Oates angled his head. "So I know something that you don't?"

"Right you are, but we can do something about that, can't we?"

Oates folded his burly arms. "*You're* bothering him, Umber."

"Me?" Umber cried. "But . . ."

"You're keeping secrets from him."

"I *always* keep secrets," Umber protested.

"You always kept secrets from everyone, but not anymore," Oates replied. "Balfour is your oldest friend. The first man you met in Kurahaven, isn't he? After you came from wherever you were before. He's been loyal all these years. But now you've made Hap your favorite. You share things with the boy that you keep from Balfour. Balfour figures he's earned your trust. And he has, you know. This has been eating at him, and he can't pretend to take it any longer. Listen, it doesn't bother me when you don't tell me things. That would be daft—I can't keep my mouth shut! But Balfour can hold a secret. And look

at all he's done for you. You'd be in the Aerie moping around right now if it wasn't for him. It was his idea to take the dragon eggs back!"

Umber's mouth shrank to a pinhole, and his forehead wrinkled. "Curse me for a fool. You're absolutely right." He walked to the rail and stared at the foam in the *Bounder*'s wake. Then he thumped his fist and hurried down the stairs.

Oates snorted. "For a smart man he can be quite stupid at times."

Hap saw Umber and Balfour later, in the central cabin, sitting on chairs pulled close. He went back on deck, not wanting to interfere. Hours later, when he ventured downstairs again, the two were still talking, and it was obvious from the look on Balfour's face—a shining, moist-eyed, grateful, and mildly astounded expression—that his humor had been restored.

Again Hap kept his distance, ducking into Umber's cabin to take another look at Caspar's notebook. Umber came in a while later.

"Oates was right," he said, yawning. "Balfour is too loyal a friend not to trust. He knows everything now."

"Everything?" asked Hap. He was thinking about the strange machine that Umber kept hidden in his tower in the Aerie, the source of all of the miraculous innovations that Umber had brought to this world. Hap had accidentally discovered the "computer"—a slender, metallic, folding thing with the word REBOOT engraved on its silvery face—and had always figured that Umber would otherwise have never told him about it.

"The whole crazy tale," Umber said.

Hap remembered how dizzy he'd felt when Umber told him his story. "What did Balfour say?"

"He said he'd believe any fool thing, where you and I were concerned. But he posed a question that has me thinking. He asked if I was the same lunatic back where I'd come from. Referring, of course, to my mood swings and my wanton disregard for personal safety." Umber chuckled at his own expense and dropped heavily into a chair. He picked at the stubble on his chin. "And you know, I think he's onto something. Sure, my emotions always ran deep, and I was plagued by the occasional melancholy. I even took some medicines for it. But . . . coming to this world transformed me in some fundamental way. I mean, I was always curious and lively. But not the way I am now. I do get reckless at times, don't I?"

Hap coughed and nodded, thinking about all the moments he'd spent on the brink of death, owing to Umber's mania.

"Something to ponder, at any rate," Umber said, ending the sentence with a powerful yawn. "Time for bed, I think. Does it bother you, Hap, that you never sleep?"

Hap shrugged. "I don't see the advantage of it, I suppose. It's like dying for a little while."

Umber's head rocked back. "*There's* a lovely thought to comfort my dreams. You want advantages? Well, if you have a rotten day, it's a chance to turn the page. You fall asleep and tell yourself the next one will be better. And it helps you mark time. Does it all blur together for you?"

Hap considered that and nodded. "It's all been a blur. From the start." He said good night and left the room, bringing Caspar's journal to read during the lonely night.

"I see it now," Umber said.

The Verdant Isle was on the horizon. Hours of sunlight still remained; Sandar had gotten the *Bounder* there even faster than promised. The island was modest in size and hilly, with vegetation thicker and wilder than any Hap had seen before.

"Looks like a jungle, doesn't it?" Umber said.

"I suppose," Hap said. He'd never seen a jungle. "Lord Umber, who is this man we're going to see?"

"A friend of mine with a particular expertise: botanical wizardry. His name is Fendofel. You've seen those remarkable plants on my terrace, like the tree of many fruits? Most of them came from Fendofel. If anyone can identify that thorny nut, it's him."

"How long have you known him?" Hap asked.

"A while—we met soon after I got here. He's a dear old man, and I owed him a visit long before this. Things have been hectic since we met you, though." He turned and called to Sandar with one hand cupped beside his mouth. "Not too close, Sandar, or that living weed will foul her rudder!"

"I remember," Sandar said, frowning at a memory. The *Bounder* reduced sail until it nudged forward with the island looming ahead. "That'll do—drop anchor, boys!"

Hap stared at the island. It had no beach—the thick and tangled vegetation reached to the sea and formed a formidable barrier along the island's perimeter. But on the shore just ahead he saw a stone ramp that emerged from the growth and sloped into the water. *I guess that's where we land,* he thought.

The *Bounder*'s jolly boat was lowered, with Umber, Hap, Oates, Balfour, and Sophie on board. Oates rowed them closer to the island. Hap's fear of water was not as intense as it used to be, but he still wasn't fond of the sea, especially in a small vessel that bobbed so vigorously in the waves. He looked over the side, hoping to see the bottom close below. Instead a forest of seaweed swayed and rippled a few feet below. He gasped as the weeds sprang to life and broke the surface, surrounding the boat. The passengers lurched as their progress was abruptly stopped.

"This again?" groused Oates. The weeds were wrapped

around both his oars. When he tried to raise them from the water, the weeds tugged them back down. The boat shook from side to side, a sudden motion that felt like a warning.

"Be calm, Oates," Umber said. "This isn't your first time here, for heaven's sake. You know how it goes." He leaned forward and gazed at the edge of the jungle.

"I wish someone would tell *me* how it goes," Hap said quietly to Sophie.

"I thought you knew," she said. "Don't worry. Dendra will be here soon."

"Dendra? Who is Dendra?"

Sophie smiled. "I don't want to ruin the surprise."

Hap pouted back at her. "You've been hanging around Umber too long."

The edge of the heavy undergrowth shifted, and an enormous vine that was spiraled tightly at the end pierced through. It hovered for a moment, and then, as Hap watched with his jaw sagging, it uncoiled and reach toward them, extending across the waves. "*That* is Dendra," Sophie whispered.

Umber leaned over the prow with a shining grin, waiting. The vine had diamond-shaped leaves the size of hands sprouting from it, and along its length more curling tendrils sprouted, all light green with jagged red stripes. When the vine finished uncurling, barely a foot from Umber's face, Hap saw a long, red flower shaped like a trumpet, and he was amazed to hear a *voice* coming from the flower—the thin, quavering voice of an old man. "What is it? Who's out there?"

Umber smiled over his shoulder. "It's like a speaking tube, Hap. The wizard talks into a blossom at the other end, and the vine conducts the sound." He put his mouth near the flower. "It's me, Fendofel! Your friend Umber."

"Umber?" said the voice from the vine. "Umber . . . Umber . . . Umber . . ." it repeated, puzzling over the word. Umber looked back at his friends again with a raised brow.

"Of course, Umber!" cried the voice, rising with happy recognition. "My dear boy. You're back! Come ashore, come ashore."

"I have friends with me—some you've met, and one you haven't," Umber told the flower.

"Friends! How nice! Come, all of you! Welcome to my home!"

The seaweed sank into the depths again, and the strands released the oars. The boat bobbed freely, and Oates, shaking his head with his mouth stretched wide, rowed them to the stone ramp. As they drew closer, the vine withdrew ahead of them. The ramp was covered with smaller vines that looked much like Dendra. Oates picked up a line, meaning to tie the boat off, but the smaller vines sprang to life and twirled around the cleats, holding the boat fast.

"This is the oddest place," Oates muttered, dropping the line and lifting the pack with the strange nut inside.

They disembarked and walked up the ramp to where the riotous growth barred further progress. Hap felt Sophie's elbow nudge his side. "Watch this," she said.

From inside the jungle, Hap heard rustling sounds, as if a stiff breeze was coming or a flock of birds had taken flight. The tangle of leaves and limbs that blocked their way pulled back, swinging inward like a pair of doors. The rustling extended deeper into the growth, and soon a shadowy tunnel had been created before them.

"You look stupid with your mouth hanging open like that," Oates said to Hap. Hap's jaw popped as he snapped it shut.

"Really, Oates," Umber chided. "Hap's never been here before. I envy him—it's such fun to be astonished!"

"Not for me," Oates muttered.

Umber nearly broke into a skip as he headed down the living tunnel. The vine called Dendra led them, slithering back along the path like the tail of a snake. The tunnel floor was paved with stones worn smooth. Fragments of sunlight pierced the thick canopy, spattering them with shifting flecks of light.

Hap heard a rustling sound again, this time at his back. The path they'd taken closed in behind them, sealing their exit as if the tunnel had never existed.

CHAPTER
7

After a few dozen paces the tunnel ended and they stepped into a clearing. Within the giant hedge that encircled the island, butterflies flittered about, and the hum of bees filled the air. They followed the stone path into the heart of the island, crossing narrow bands of sharply differing landscapes. There was a fragrant meadow with bright blossoms of a hundred different shades, where deer grazed, watching them pass with dull, unconcerned expressions. Next was a stand of pine trees amid a soft carpet of fallen needles.

"I'll remind you not to pick the flowers, everyone," Umber said. "And don't take any fruit unless a vine offers it to you."

They passed next through a sandy spot where cacti grew

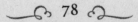

and tortoises sauntered and craned their necks. Still, the vine pulled away ahead of them, arching like an inchworm as it retracted.

"How long is that thing?" Hap asked Sophie.

"Very."

They arrived at the heart of the island, a strange and watery garden filled with exotic plants, bushes, and trees. The path they'd followed branched into smaller trails that meandered through the clearing. "Step on the stones, not the plants," Umber said, though Hap had already decided that would be wise. "There are a few mats of moss that don't mind if you rest on them, though."

They went by a shrub with brilliant orange blossoms, which snapped shut as they passed. "Shy around strangers," Umber explained. A stand of pale blue mushrooms stood nearby, so tall that Oates could have walked under their caps. Towering ferns waved in the gentle breeze.

As they moved into the clearing, a bird with a long blue tail burst out of tall grass. When Hap followed its flight with his gaze, he saw an ancient building ahead.

It was a dome built of rough white stone, with arches in its curving walls that let air and light pass. On either side of the dome stood more modern structures: long, rectangular

wings made of wrought iron and milky glass. Hap saw a riot of strange plants inside, growing in steamy air and pressing against the misty panes.

The vine they'd followed curled itself like a snake, with the coils stacking high overhead. More of the pale green and blood red arms emerged from every arch of the dome and slithered into the garden like the tentacles of a sea creature. Some grew up and over the dome, dividing into slender fingers that might have been holding the stones in place.

Hap tugged on Umber's sleeve. "Those vines. Are they all from one plant?"

Umber nodded. "One vine, one mind. It's all Dendra."

An old man in a long, brown robe hobbled through one of the archways, leaning on a twisted cane. Another small vine hovered by his elbow, a living banister. He was not a tall man, and his height was reduced by the curve of his spine, which forced his head down so that he had to crane his neck to squint at his visitors. His hair was thin and silky, dangling past his ears, and he might have been bald on top except for what appeared to be stringy gray moss growing there. Tiny white flowers emerged from his thick beard. "Who is it? Who's there?"

Hap looked sideways at Sophie. "Didn't Lord Umber just tell him it was us?" She shushed him quietly, her forehead creased with worry.

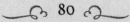

"It's me, Fendofel," Umber called out, quite loudly. "Umber. Remember?"

Fendofel's mouth broke into a nearly toothless smile, and he rapped the side of his head with his knuckles. "Foolish me! Ha-ha, of course, you just told me you were coming a minute ago!"

The dome was surrounded by a narrow moat, and Fendofel limped across one of the short bridges that spanned the water. The vine slithered behind him with its tip elbow-high, darting left and right, depending on which way the old man teetered.

Umber trotted ahead to close the distance, and took the old wizard by the elbow. "How wonderful to see you again."

Fendofel was a head shorter than Umber, and his rheumy eyes glistened as he looked up. "And you, and you! But look at you, Umber—so thin! You're skin and bones, my boy."

"I'm fine, Fendofel," Umber told him.

The wizard looked at him from head to toe, squinting. "Well, you don't *look* fine. But tell me, how is my tree of many fruits? Healthier than you, I hope?"

"Strong-limbed and thriving, just like me," Umber said, chuckling. "And, Fendofel, you remember these good people." Umber swept his arm toward Balfour, Sophie, and Oates.

"I . . . oh, of course I do," Fendofel said. He put his hand beside his mouth and tried to whisper to Umber but was plainly heard by all. "Be a good fellow and remind me of their names, will you, Umber?"

Hap saw the concern in Umber's smile. "Of course," Umber said, putting his hand on Fendofel's shoulder. "We have here my dear friend Balfour; the always delightful Oates; and the kingdom's finest archer and artist, young Sophie. But this young man you have not met," Umber said, with an open hand aimed at Hap. "This is my ward, Happenstance. Or Hap for short."

Fendofel leaned toward Hap, squinting and grinning. There was a silver chain around his neck with a locket that held an enormous green crystal. The old wizard reached toward Hap, and a thin, bony arm slid from the loose sleeve. His hands were spotted by age, with soil caked in the wrinkles and under the nails, and Hap was sure he saw a patch of lichen growing on the wrist. "Happenstance. What an excellent name . . . and my, what eyes you have!"

Hap was usually bothered by the attention his eyes drew, but he felt nothing but warmth for this fragile, charming man. "Thank you," he replied, with a smile that came easily.

"Your eyes are *green*," the old man said. He winked at Hap. "The finest of colors! Come in, all of you, come in!"

They crossed the bridge that spanned the moat. Aquatic plants teemed in the water, with blossoms on the surface. One specimen propelled itself through the water by wriggling its roots behind it. There was a splash, and another plant rose from the water with a squirming frog inside spiked, leafy jaws. "Ew," Hap said, gaping.

When they stepped inside the building, Hap's lips formed a silent whistle. The arms of Dendra had grown steadily thicker the closer they came to the roots. Inside the arches the red-lashed vines were as thick as pillars.

Under the center of the dome, Dendra had sprouted long ago, erupting like a volcano through the thick foundation. The arms all sprang from a massive round growth, easily a dozen feet across, with the bumpy skin of a gourd. Dendra was never still for long; every so often one of the arms would give a little shrug, or the tip of a vine would slither back inside the dome.

Benches of stone were all around, with mats of moss on the seats. Fendofel eased himself down with a happy sigh. "Oh yes, Umber, you must tell me: How is the tree of many fruits? Is it well?"

Umber froze for a moment, and his eyes softened. "It thrives, my friend," he said. He looked carefully at the old wizard. Hap's glance met Balfour's, and Balfour raised his eyebrows.

"I'm very glad to hear it," Fendofel said with a contented smile. One of Dendra's fat arms slid across the stone floor and rubbed gently against Fendofel's leg. It looked to Hap like something an affectionate cat might do. "But what brings you here, my dear boy?"

"It's been too long since my last visit," Umber said, squeezing the old wizard's arm. "But really, I came for your advice."

"My advice, eh?" said Fendofel, straightening up and lifting his chin. "And I'm happy to give it. But I want the truth first: How have you been? Honestly, now."

"Me?" Umber's gaze dropped. "Oh, I've been fine."

"What do you mean, fine?" roared Oates. "You were moping for weeks. We thought you'd waste away and die."

Umber slung a lethal glare at Oates. "I think I'll take a walk," Oates muttered.

"Oates, there's a plant just outside, covered with razor-sharp needles," Umber said.

Oates stared back from the archway. "So?"

"I'd like you to sit on it," Umber said. Oates rolled his eyes and left the dome.

Fendofel tapped his fingers together and gave Umber a reproachful frown. "At least he's honest. There's no reason to hide anything from me, Umber, you scamp."

"I don't want you to worry," Umber said quietly.

"Ridiculous. I can *help* you, silly boy," Fendofel said, smiling. "I've been working on something for you, and it's finally ready." He reached down and touched the vine by his knee. "Dendra, fetch the elatia, will you?"

Another arm of the great vine responded. It slid into one of the glass-and-iron wings. A moment later it returned, its tip wrapped around a dark ceramic pot with a bushy plant inside. The vine passed the plant into Fendofel's waiting hands, and he held it out to Umber.

"Looks like mint," Umber said, taking the pot.

"It is *elatia*," Fendofel said, pronouncing the name with care. "This might cure your episodes of sadness, my friend."

Hap looked at the others. Sophie had a delighted, openmouthed smile, and Balfour's eyebrows had gone halfway up his forehead. "How wonderful that would be," Balfour whispered. Sophie nodded.

Umber's gaze was fixed on the plant. He brushed the leaves with the tips of his fingers. "Will it really?"

Fendofel nodded and chuckled. "It took all my craft to create it. Listen carefully, now, Umber: If you feel one of your bouts coming on, pluck seventeen leaves and make a tea of them. Boil it until the leaves turn black."

"Until the leaves turn black. Seventeen," Umber said. He looked at Balfour and raised his brow. "Seventeen," Balfour repeated.

Umber placed the elatia on the bench beside him. "What

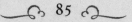

a gift, Fendofel! And all I can offer you in return is a mystery."

Fendofel laughed, and the laugh turned into a cough that went on until the old man was out of breath. Umber put a hand on his back, and one of Dendra's vines twirled tenderly around the old wizard's calf. "I'm fine, I'm fine," Fendofel said, waving a hand and wheezing. "What is your mystery, Umber?"

Umber fetched the pack that Oates had left on the floor. He dug out the skull-size object, still wrapped in canvas, and sat again with the thing in his lap. "I want to know if you've ever seen anything like this," Umber said. He threw off the canvas flaps, revealing the enormous nut. "Careful of the thorns."

Fendofel leaned close, narrowing one eye and widening the other. "What have you found?" he whispered. Umber raised the nut, nested on the thick cloth, and Fendofel slid his hands under the thing, hefted it with care, and set it down again on the bench. He stuck his fingers between the thorns and prodded; he put his nose as close as he dared, inhaling deeply; he scratched his chin and tugged his ear. "I . . . I feel like I've seen this before. Knew what it was . . . long ago." He looked mournfully at Umber. "But I can't recall."

"Is it magical, you think?" Umber asked.

Fendofel concentrated, and Hap could see the frustration growing on his face. His nose wrinkled, and his mouth twisted. He tapped himself on the head—softly first, and then much harder—"Curse me. Umber, my memory isn't what it used to be." He looked up at Hap. "You must think I'm an old fool, Master . . ." He grunted as he struggled to remember.

"Happenstance," Hap told him gently.

"Ah," Fendofel said. His shoulders slumped. "Yes. Happenstance. I'd have gotten it if you hadn't said it."

"Don't worry about it, Fendofel," Umber said. "Tell me, though. What do you think I should do with this thing?"

Fendofel looked at the nut again, prodding the tip of a thorn with his thumb. "Where did it come from?"

"It was with some stuff my former archivist stole from me. I guess he thought it was valuable. Unfortunately he's dead now, so I can't ask him where he found it. Who knows? Maybe it was somewhere in the Aerie."

"Looks awfully old," Fendofel said. "Might not even grow if you planted it."

"Is it worth a try?"

Fendofel narrowed his eyes at the thing. "Not sure. Something about it . . . worries me. Wish I could remember. Perhaps in the morning I shall. You will stay the night, won't you all?"

Umber bit his bottom lip. "I'm sorry, Fendofel. We can't stay for long. But I'll come back soon."

"I understand," Fendofel said, lowering his eyes.

"Fendofel," Umber said, with his fingertips on the old wizard's shoulder, "you're not a young man anymore. You need people to look after you. It might be time to leave this place."

"*Leave?*" Fendofel looked up with watery eyes. "This is my home, Umber. Everything I know is here. And I have Dendra to watch after me." One of the vines was beside the old man as usual, and Fendofel laid his hand upon it. Hap felt a tingle of fear on his spine, because the vine had risen up and arched itself like a viper when Umber suggested that Fendofel leave the island.

"I know," Umber said. "But . . ." He looked at Balfour. "Balfour, would you take Hap and Sophie outside? I'll catch up with you."

Hap paused for a moment, waiting to catch Umber's eye. When Umber looked back at him, Hap jabbed his chin toward the vine. Umber just smiled warmly and waved him away.

Before Hap could follow Balfour and Sophie out of the dome, an animal sound erupted outside: the terrified bleating of a beast in distress. Nearby, the thickest of the vines was in motion, flexing like an enormous muscle that filled one entire arch. The sound grew louder.

Balfour and Sophie backed into the dome and stepped aside, looking wild-eyed. When they moved, Hap saw a full-grown deer coming at him, hovering off the ground with its four legs stabbing at the air. One of the striped vines was coiled around its midsection, propelling it forward. The hooves of the deer clattered against the stone arch. Its brown eyes bulged and spittle flew from its mouth. Dendra was too strong; the vine shoved the terrified animal through the arch, and Hap leaped aside to avoid the flailing legs.

"Dendra!" cried Fendofel. He swatted the vine with his palm. "This is most impolite!"

Beside the old wizard, Umber sprang upright, spilling the thorny nut and canvas onto the floor. His avid gaze darted right and left, absorbing the scene.

Hap backed away from the vine and bumped into Sophie. She wrapped her good arm around him and pulled him against her. He felt her warm gasp in his ear as the body of Dendra— the enormous, gourdlike thing at the heart of the vines— cracked open in four sections that peeled down like the petals of a flower. The inner surface was yellow and studded with glistening white knobs, and when the vine shoved the terrified animal inside, the poor deer stuck to the knobs like glue. The vine uncoiled and withdrew, leaving the thrashing, squealing animal inside. The four sections rose again and closed tight.

For a while Hap heard thumping inside Dendra's body. Sophie's hand was on his chest, and he wondered if she felt his heart leaping under her palm.

The sounds of struggle faded. Hap heard a thump, and hoped it was the last. But there were two more after that, much weaker. Then Dendra shivered, and another sound started from within, a grinding and sloshing that made his stomach go sour.

Fendofel dabbed at his eyes with the end of one sleeve. "My friends, I am so sorry," he said with a sniff. "I . . . I don't know what got into her. . . . She's not supposed to feed with guests here . . . and not like that. There are gentler ways."

Umber put a hand on his shoulder. "Don't trouble yourself over it, Fendofel." He looked at the others and gestured toward the exit. "Go on," he told them.

"By all means," Balfour said thickly. His face was a few shades paler than usual. Sophie was suddenly conscious of her hand around Hap's chest, and she pulled it away. Hap followed her and Balfour out, and the three of them shuffled as if they'd forgotten how to walk properly.

When he stepped outside the dome, Hap saw Oates lying on a stone bench under a tree with long, drooping branches that burst with pink blossoms. Petals were scattered across the big fellow's chest. He snored like thunder, and his mouth hung open with a trickle of drool running down one cheek. "The man can sleep through anything," Balfour said, shaking his head.

The three of them sat on one of the moss-covered benches

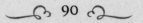

and waited quietly. Sophie lowered her head, and Balfour patted her shoulder. A thought occurred to Hap, and he looked over his shoulder to make sure none of Dendra's vines was near. He leaned forward to catch Balfour's eye, and spoke as quietly as he could. "It . . . I mean, she . . . has never done that before, when you were here? Eating something alive like that?"

Sophie looked up. A tear had trickled and paused at the corner of her mouth, and Hap fought a powerful urge to reach out and brush it away. She shook her head.

"I didn't even know she was carnivorous," Balfour said. He shivered.

"Do you think Dendra wanted to scare us?" Hap asked. "Because Umber talked about taking Fendofel away from here?"

Balfour looked toward the dome and thrust out his bottom lip. Then he nodded. "Absolutely. That was a warning."

"But Lord Umber is right. Fendofel needs help," Sophie whispered. "He's gotten so forgetful."

"Why doesn't somebody stay here with him?" Hap asked.

"Umber has tried that," Balfour said. "He's sent people to assist Fendofel and keep him from getting lonely. But after a while that vine starts to unnerve the assistants. Dendra becomes jealous and threatening. So Fendofel remains alone."

There was more silence, until Balfour thumped the bench

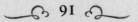

with his fist. "Scares the life out of me how an old man's mind can start to slip like that. My aching bones are bad enough. I don't need my wits falling to pieces along with my joints." He dropped his head, cupping his jaw with one palm.

Hap was going to say more, but he saw the tall grass near them moving, and caught a glimpse of one of Dendra's arms. It stopped there, mostly hidden. The others noticed, and the conversation died. Under the tree Oates went on snoring, oblivious to all.

As night fell, Hap saw dim lights appear throughout the garden. Flowers were glowing in the dark. Something moved at the corner of his eye, and he turned to see a small shrub boost itself out of the soil and creep toward the moat on roots that looked like spider legs. When it neared the pond, the foremost root reached out and slurped water.

"It is an amazing place, isn't it?" Sophie mused.

Voices caught Hap's attention and broke the spell. Umber and Fendofel ambled into the garden, with a pair of Dendra's arms slithering beside them on either side.

Fendofel squinted toward Oates. "Oh dear. I should have warned him about that tree. Those flowers have put him to sleep."

"Oates doesn't need any help with his naps. He excels at dozing," Umber said.

"This is different," Fendofel said, wagging his beard. "He won't wake for hours no matter what you do."

Balfour stood up and stretched. "Well, that's a problem. That man's as heavy as an ox. How can we drag him back to the boat?"

Dendra's long arms glided over the ground. They wormed their way under Oates's neck and the small of his back, and curled around his knees and ankles. With no effort they lifted Oates, who never stopped snoring.

Hap realized that the vine was wrapped around Oates just the way it had been wrapped around the deer, and his chest clamped down on his heart.

"Fendofel?" Umber said, his voice cracking a little.

"Eh? Oh, don't fear—Dendra will just carry him to your boat," said the wizard.

"I think Dendra wants us to leave," Sophie whispered sideways.

"I'm not going to argue," Hap said, barely moving his lips.

Umber put his hands on Fendofel's shoulders. "My friend. What are we going to do with you? You can't stay here forever." The great vine by his feet twitched, and the leaves trembled for a moment.

"But this is my home, Umber," Fendofel said. "Go on, now. Get back to . . ." His face grew pinched. "Back to . . ."

"Kurahaven," Umber said.

"Yes, Kurahaven. I would have remembered if you hadn't said it." Fendofel looked at the others, and his face twisted with concentration as he looked at Hap. "And . . . good-bye to you, young man. And you, and you," he said to Balfour and Sophie.

Umber and Balfour took the oars, with Oates still unconscious and drooling at the bottom of the jolly boat. The lantern lights of the *Bounder* bobbed in the night, drawing closer with every stroke.

"Will Fendofel be all right, Lord Umber?" Sophie asked. She had the elatia cradled in her lap.

Umber's shoulders rose and fell. He wore a defeated expression. "I don't know what to do. His memory is fading and his body is failing. But he won't leave. And nobody can stay with him, because of Dendra. It's his home, but it's turned into a trap." He shook his head. "We'll just have to check on him as often as we can."

Hap looked at the bulging pack. "You didn't learn anything about the thorny nut, Lord Umber."

"No. And back where I come from, we'd call that a 'bummer.' But I think Fendofel knew something that his mind couldn't retrieve. Maybe it'll come to him eventually."

CHAPTER
8

Unfriendly winds made the voyage home longer than expected, but the *Bounder* finally sailed into Kurahaven Bay. Hap was glad to see the familiar soaring palace, the colorful marketplace, the busy docks, and most of all the Aerie, with his own room high in one corner, within the great carved face with windows for eyes.

When they disembarked, Umber kept Hap from stepping into the carriage with the others. "Come with me, Hap. I have an errand in the market, and then I want to stop by the shipping offices."

"I'll get my hat," Hap said. He fished it out of his pack and pulled it low over the unusual green eyes that drew so many curious stares.

The tents of the marketplace were drenched with sun and awash with the salty breeze. There were rows upon rows of goods from all over the known world, and the chatter of people filled the air like birdsong. Umber led Hap through the maze of byways, and paused where a young woman stood by a cart packed with flowers. "These are lovely," he told her, burying his nose in a lavish blossom.

She bowed her head. "Thank you, my lord. My family grows them."

"What I would like," Umber said, digging into a vest pocket and pulling out silver coins, "is for you to assemble the biggest bouquet you can fit in a vase, and deliver it to the palace for me. I'll give you a note to include with the flowers. Can you manage that?"

"Of course, my lord!" The woman's mouth hung open at the sight of the coins tumbling into her palm. "But this is more than I would ask."

"That's all right. It's what I wish to pay. Could it be sent right away?"

"My brother will take it, quick as lightning," she replied. "He's just run over to get some pie."

Umber pulled notepaper and a pencil from his pocket, scratched out a message, folded it in half, wrote something else on the outside, and handed it to the woman. "Put this on

the bouquet. The flowers should go to the person named on that note."

"Within the hour, my lord," she said, dropping into a curtsy.

Umber smiled and bowed. "Onward," he said to Hap, and broke into a brisk stride.

Hap trotted beside him. "Were those for Fay?"

Umber smirked and ignored the question. He patted his stomach with one hand. "She had to go and say 'pie.' Now I can't stop thinking about it! I've been ravenous ever since I emerged from my funk. How about a slice of . . ." Umber came to an abrupt stop and drew up straight. His eyebrows strained high, and his mouth formed a gaping circle.

"What is it?" Hap asked.

Umber didn't answer. He turned in one direction, and then another—not looking, but listening with hands cupped behind his ears. Hap tried to guess which of the many sounds in the crowd had caught his attention. "What do you—"

Umber cut him off with a violent wave. He shut his eyes and sang along to a tune that was being whistled not far from where they stood.

"*Buy me some peanuts and Cracker Jack, I don't care if I never . . .*" Umber's eyes sprang open, and his hand shot out and seized the front of Hap's shirt. "Hap—quick! Help me find that whistler!"

At first it wasn't easy to tell where the sound was coming from, with all the noises that surrounded them. Hap pointed. "The other side of those tents, I think." Umber sprinted down the narrow space between a pair of merchants stalls. Hap followed, wondering what had gotten into his guardian. Whatever the tune was, it wasn't familiar to him.

They burst into the open space on the other side of the byway. It was the farmers area of the market, cluttered with barrels and boxes of fruits and vegetables. Hundreds of people milled about the lane. Chickens clucked and ducks quacked in their pens. A cart went by with screeching wheels. Still, Hap heard the song cut vaguely through the din, somewhere to their right.

"Who's whistling?" Umber shouted. Heads turned his way, and recognition dawned on many faces when they saw the kingdom's most renowned citizen.

From the corner of his eye, Hap saw someone duck inside a tent. Near that spot, people's heads turned to look at where the man had been, as if they might have heard someone whistling there a moment before.

"This way!" Hap said. He sprang ahead of Umber as a voice cried out inside the tent. "What? What are you doing in here? Stop that! What are you up to?"

Hap rushed in, under a hanging board with the words BART THE BEEKEEPER and a painting of a dripping honeycomb.

Pots of honey sealed with cork lined the shelves inside the modest space. A short, round, curly-haired man in a yellow apron stood with his back to Hap. His fists were on his hips as he glared at the other side of the tent. Hap was about to say something when Umber burst into the tent and plowed into him. They tumbled to the ground, side by side.

"Have all the lunatics come to the market today?" shouted the man, who must have been the beekeeper himself. He seized a cane and raised it over one shoulder, ready to strike. But his complexion paled when he saw Umber's face. "Lord Umber!" Bart squeaked. He tried to hide the cane behind his back.

"Hap," Umber said, panting. "What did you see?"

"A man ran into this tent," Hap said, scrambling to his feet and picking up his fallen hat. "Didn't he?" he asked Bart.

"Yes, a moment before you. Thought he was going to rob me! He wiggled out under the tent, over there."

Umber ran to the spot, dropped to his belly, and wormed his way under the flap. Hap looked at the beekeeper, who seemed a little dazed.

"You have the strangest green eyes," Bart said.

"Excuse me," Hap said. He tugged his hat down and dove under the flap. Behind him he heard the beekeeper's voice falling away: "Young man, tell Lord Umber I'd be honored to sell him some honey. At a discount, of course!"

Umber was in the middle of the next lane, whirling about. "Did anybody see a man climb out from under this tent?" The people nearby shook their heads. Umber stomped his foot. "Hap, what was he wearing? Did you notice?"

"I only saw him for a moment," Hap said. "I'm sorry."

Umber blew air from the corner of his mouth as he looked at the many narrow lanes between stalls and tents. "It's a labyrinth. No chance of catching him now."

"The beekeeper got a better look at him," Hap offered.

Umber brightened. "Yes he did!"

Bart the beekeeper had barely seen the man's face, and what he could recall—light tunic, dark trousers, a thin man who was neither tall nor short—wouldn't have distinguished the whistler from a thousand other men in Kurahaven. Umber and Hap left the tent with little useful information and a small pot of honey crooked in Hap's elbow. Hap wiped his palm on his leg, because he'd shaken Bart's hand before they left, and it was the stickiest handshake he'd ever shared.

"Lord Umber, why did you want to catch the man who whistled?"

Umber looked left and right as they walked through the market, and dropped his voice to answer. "That song he was whistling—it was from my world, Happenstance.

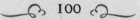

The one I left behind. Do you know what that means?"

Hap considered the question. "You think someone else from your world is here?"

Umber's mouth was bent in a tight, tense frown. "It's the only explanation."

"Maybe *you* whistled it once, and someone learned it from you?"

"Good theory. But I haven't given that tune a moment's thought in ten years."

"Maybe someone here wrote a song that sounds just like it?"

"But then why would the whistler run like a thief when he realized I was after him?"

Hap furrowed his brow. "This is strange, Lord Umber. If someone else from your world is here . . . well, they might realize that *you* were one of them. Because of everything you've done."

"Right you are. The inventions I've introduced, the works of Mozart and Beethoven . . . I've been sending signals out for years, for anyone to notice. So why run away? Why not make yourself known to me? If I learned of someone else from my world, I'd seek him out immediately!" Umber plowed his hand into his scalp, and his hair stuck up between his fingers. "I can't believe it, Happenstance. I always assumed I was unique. And now . . . it seems I have company."

Hap noticed the pie-man's tent. "Did you still want pie?"

"Lost my appetite," Umber said. "Let's go to my shipping company."

Hoyle, the squat, domineering woman who oversaw Umber's business interests, pounced the moment they walked up the marble steps and through the tall doors of the Umber Shipping Company. "So you're better, eh?" she said to Umber. She tried to scowl, but Hap could see the relief in her eyes.

"I am."

"Then I suppose I'll forgive Balfour for borrowing one of our ships, and getting the mast clawed by a dragon so that it will have to be replaced, at no small expense." She took a longer look at Umber, and pursed her lips in dismay. "But look at you—gaunt as a scarecrow. You need to eat."

"And I will, like a pig," Umber said. "I just stopped in to make sure all is well with our ventures. I know I haven't been attentive these past weeks."

"You say that as if you are ever attentive at all. Of *course* things are fine. Do you think I'd ignore business matters? That's more your style, I'd say."

Umber rolled his eyes. "Anything important I should know about?"

"Hmph." Hoyle folded her arms. "Well, Nima is due back

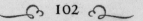

soon with a cargo of silk and spice. There's a shipment of your beloved coffee beans just arrived—yes, I knew you'd be happy to hear that, you can wipe that ridiculous grin off your face. The new fleet is coming along in the shipyards; not as fast as I'd like of course. And . . . well, I've decided to put off any ventures within a day's sail of the Far Continent."

Umber's head tilted. "Why? Trouble with those ruffians?"

"More than the usual trouble," Hoyle said. She looked around her, and then dropped her voice. "We always try to steer clear of those savages. But a few weeks ago Captain Sylvan's ship, the *Gull*, was blown off course by a fierce wind and ended up within sight of that coast. She came upon what was left of a ship from Vernia. It had been shattered into pieces. All the crew was lost except for two, floating amid the burnt wreckage. They spoke of something that came after them—a monster in the sea. It hurled smoke and fire from a great distance, destroying their ship instantly." Hoyle shivered and stretched her mouth wide. "Terrible. Umber, what do you suppose that was?"

Umber gnawed at the back of his thumb. "I . . . I haven't the faintest idea."

"Dragons?"

"No. Not so far from Chastor. Perhaps I could guess, if I spoke to those survivors."

Hoyle shook her head. "You can't. One died from his wounds, and the other disembarked at a port along the way."

"A shame," Umber said. "Well . . . whenever one of our ships comes back, ask the captains if they've heard anything else about this monster, or whatever it was. They'll be the first to know."

"I already thought of that," Hoyle said.

"How clever of you," Umber said out of the side of his mouth. "Since my wisdom is apparently superfluous here, Hap and I will return to the Aerie. Contact me if you need anything."

"Frankly, things run more smoothly when you're not around," Hoyle said. "I'll get the carriage for you."

"You know, I think we'll stroll," Umber said.

Umber walked with his hands clasped behind his back and his brow furrowed. Hap wondered which mystery preoccupied him more: the whistler in the marketplace, or the ship that had been destroyed.

"Lord Umber, what is the Far Continent? I've seen it on your maps, but I don't know much about it."

Umber looked up, emerging from deep thought. "Eh? Oh . . . it's an enormous landmass several hundred miles to the west. Well beyond Sarnica. Soon after it was discovered, it became a haven for pirates, outlaws, and warlords. The king has worried about those folk forever, but our ships can sail circles around theirs, so they haven't been much of a threat." He lowered his head and went back to brooding.

When they were halfway up the causeway, where the River Kura surged under the road and splashed into the bay, Umber stopped to stare at the churning collision of water below. Mist rose up, and Hap felt cool drops on his face. Umber took a deep breath of moist air and exhaled slowly. "I hope Fay likes the flowers," he said.

"Are you . . . you know. Fond of her?" Hap asked.

Umber gave Hap a crooked smile. He had to speak a little louder to be heard over the roar of water. "And what if I am? Romance is problematical for me, Hap, for many reasons. One is that computer up in my tower. Nobody can learn about the true source of my inventions, and so I can't let people get too close to me. And those dark moods of mine . . . it's hard to expect anyone to put up with that." He leaned down, picked up a small stone, and flung it into the bay. "Listen to me, spilling all this to a boy. But you've pegged it: I do like her. If nothing else, I have to pry her away from Loden. The poor woman just escaped one foul prince; we can't let her fall into the clutches of another, can we?" Umber started up the causeway again, at a brisker pace.

Hap felt a wave of hot, prickly anger as he thought about Prince Loden. "Lord Umber, do you really think Loden murdered both his brothers?"

"We'll never know that for sure, unless a witness comes forward," Umber said. "But I think he did, to clear his path to the throne."

"What are you going to do?" Hap asked.

"There's not much I *can* do. Let's just hope King Tyrian's health improves, and he stays on the throne for years to come."

"But he's sick, isn't he."

"Very. Odds are we'll be bowing to King Loden before long. And won't that be a dark day for all of us." Umber sighed heavily, and slowed.

The Aerie loomed. Hap saw Welkin and Barkin on a pair of stools outside the gatehouse, playing a game of cards. Barkin waved.

"What do you think Loden would do, if he were king?" Hap asked.

Umber didn't answer. He'd fallen behind. Hap looked back and saw a face drained of color with eyes half-closed. "Lord Umber?"

"Huh?" Umber said. His voice dropped until he was almost mumbling. "Oh. Loden. He'll move against me, I'm sure . . . but let's talk about this some other time."

Hap felt a pang in his chest. He had seen that look and heard that tone of voice before. *Not again,* he thought. *Not so soon after the last time.* "Lord Umber, are you feeling all right?"

Umber spread his hands across his face and rubbed the bridge of his nose with his little fingers. "No . . . not really."

At the gatehouse, Welkin and Barkin sensed the trouble. They bolted from their seats and came swiftly down the causeway. Hap grabbed Umber's arm and tugged. "Come on. Let's get back to the Aerie. Quickly!"

onathan, my old friend, I wish you were
still alive and could see what your creation
has made possible. You conceived Reboot as
a way to preserve and rebuild the best of our
civilization, never dreaming that it would
one day be used for the good of another world
altogether. With that device I have saved
and uplifted lives and even planted

CHAPTER
9

Hap threw the lever, and the water-
driven lift lurched into motion. Umber shuffled along like a
sleepwalker, with Welkin on one side and Barkin on the other.
Dodd, the third guardsman, had dashed up the stairs to fetch
Balfour.

Hap stepped onto a moving platform, and the guardsmen
guided Umber on beside him. The space was crowded, and
the four stood shoulder to shoulder. "Steady, Lord Umber,"
Barkin said.

"Just bring me to the terrace and leave me alone," Umber
said dimly.

The lift would have brought them all the way to the third
level, just under the terrace, but as soon as they rose into the

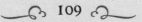

grand hall they saw Balfour and Oates waiting for them. "It's happening again," Hap cried out.

"Bring him here," Balfour said. "I sent Sophie up to get the elatia."

"Really, I'm fine," Umber muttered. He tried to shake free of the guardsmen's grip, but they led him to the large dining table and lowered him into a seat.

"Thanks, boys. You can go back to the gatehouse," Balfour told Welkin and Barkin. They took another mournful look at Umber and went back to ride the lift down.

Umber tried to stand, but Balfour gestured to Oates, and the big fellow pressed down on Umber's shoulders, keeping him seated.

"Curse you, Oates," Umber said.

"Someone already has," Oates reminded him.

Balfour put a hand on Umber's forearm. "Stay here, my friend, and drink the tea we give you. Then we'll see if Fendofel knows what he's doing."

There was a shriek from the stairwell as Lady Truden raced in. "What's happening?" she cried. Nobody answered immediately, but when she saw Umber slumping at the table, she covered her mouth to muffle a gasp. "No—not again, so close to the last one . . . this will kill him!"

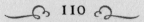

"Just the encouragement we need right now," Balfour said under his breath.

Sophie appeared behind Lady Truden on the stairs, with her arms wrapped around the elatia's large clay pot. "Excuse me, Lady Tru," she said, brushing by.

Lady Truden's mouth was stretched wide, and her teeth were bared. "Sophie! Is that the plant from the wizard?"

"Yes, my lady," Sophie called over her shoulder. She passed the plant to Balfour, who headed for the kitchen.

Lady Tru stepped in front of Balfour. Her chest was heaving, and her eyes looked ready to spill tears. "Wait! What are you supposed to do with it?"

"Make a tea from seventeen of its leaves," Balfour told her.

"And this will make Lord Umber better?"

"We hope so."

"Give it to me!" she pleaded, and when Balfour did not respond she wrestled the plant from the old man's arms. "I'll do it! I'll make the tea! Were there any other instructions?"

Balfour huffed and threw his hands in the air. "Boil the leaves until they turn black."

"Yes, yes!" she cried, running for the kitchen. "I'll do it, and Lord Umber will recover!" Hap watched Lady Truden go, thinking back to the night when he'd accidentally spied on her. He remembered her gazing at the small portrait of Lord Umber that she'd secretly asked Sophie to paint, and how she had clutched it to her heart. He wondered if Lord Umber had any idea just how much she adored him.

A pot clattered in the kitchen, and Lady Tru cursed the water for not boiling fast enough. That brought a chuckle from Balfour. As they waited, Oates lumbered to a sofa and stretched out with his hands clasped behind his head. Sophie retreated to a chair in the corner and gnawed at the fingernails of her only hand. Hap sat on one side of Umber, and Balfour was on the other, reminding Umber of funny things they'd seen together. Umber tried to smile, but his mouth seemed too weak to maintain it.

The door to the kitchen squealed open, and Lady Truden burst out with a mug trailing steam. She moved as fast as she could without spilling it, and put it on the table in front of Umber. "I made it for you myself, my lord," she said, squeezing his shoulder and whispering into his ear. She kissed the ear, and then straightened up suddenly, looking from side to side with thinly disguised alarm.

Yes, we all saw that, Hap thought.

"Where are the leaves?" Balfour said, looking into the mug.

"I strained them out, of course," Lady Tru snapped, her combative nature surfacing again. "Did you want him to choke on them?"

Balfour scowled at her and slid the mug closer to Umber. "Come on, my friend. Drink it up, and let's make this the last of your days of sadness."

Umber stared down at the tea, and then turned his face away.

Balfour took Umber's wrist and slid the mug into his palm. "Umber, I swear, I'll have Oates pry your mouth open and we'll pour it down your throat. For your own good, of course."

Hap leaned close and whispered. "Lord Umber, we have important things to do, you and I. Drink the tea."

Umber raised his chin and looked at Hap. He nodded, took a deep breath, and raised the mug to his lips. Lady Truden closed her eyes and clasped her hands. When Umber lowered the mug again, half the tea was gone. He wrinkled his nose, tilted the mug again, and drank the rest. "Yuck," he said, sticking out his tongue. He shoved the mug an arm's length away and leaned back in his chair.

Hap stared at Umber, searching for the slightest shift in expression. Balfour squinted to sharpen his vision. The sofa squeaked as Oates sat up to watch.

Umber's face was impassive. Then one eyebrow flicked up, and he blinked his eyes wide open. His mouth puckered, and the expression that formed was one of surprise. He looked at Balfour, and Hap, and over his shoulder at Lady Tru.

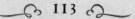

"What do you know," he said.

"What? What?" Tru said, as if she couldn't breathe.

"I think I feel . . . better," Umber said.

Balfour slapped the table with his palm and cried out. "Just like that? Wonderful!"

"Better. Yes, better," Umber said, wiping the corner of his mouth with his cuff. "Although it's also left me a little . . . a little . . ."

"Tired?" Balfour guessed.

Umber's mouth bent into a crooked, frozen grin. His eyes rolled up, and his body went limp, and he would have bashed his forehead on the table if Hap hadn't clutched the back of his collar. Lady Truden choked on her own breath and clapped a hand across her mouth.

"Is he all right?" Hap said, easing Umber's head down.

Balfour bent close and snapped his fingers by Umber's ear. "Maybe this is how it works. Oates, can you carry him upstairs to one of the spare bedrooms?"

Oates lumbered up the stairs with Umber across his shoulder like a sack of grain, with Balfour leading the way. When they were gone Lady Tru pressed her shaking fists against her forehead.

Hap wondered if it was wise to speak. "I think he's going to be better," he finally ventured.

Lady Tru's eyes blinked open again. "Yes," she said quietly. "I believe he will." She straightened her posture and cleared her throat, then folded her hands at her waist in her usual style. Hap watched the emotion drain from her features. "I almost forgot what I was in the middle of," she said, and her voice had resumed its commanding tone. "Young man, I need your help."

"Me?" squeaked Hap.

"Yes, you. I wanted Umber to come as well, but we should do this right away." She turned to Sophie. "Run up and get your bow and a quiver of arrows, and meet us down here as soon as you can."

The passageway took them past the archives and storage rooms and plunged into the foot of the stony mountain behind the Aerie. Not far ahead was the side corridor that led to the chamber where the sorceress Turiana was kept prisoner.

"Wait," Hap said. Lady Truden, who held a jar of glimmer-worms to light her way, peered over her shoulder at him. "We're not going to see the sorceress, are we?" he asked. That was perhaps the last thing on earth he wanted to do. Turiana had terrified him the only time he'd met her, when Umber brought him to her chamber seeking answers to Hap's origins. It wasn't just her ghastly appearance that bothered Hap. It was the way she taunted him, hinting that he was dead, which turned out to be at least partly true. And it was the scary knack she had for picking thoughts out of the minds of her visitors.

Lady Tru pursed her lips and frowned. "No. I don't want to visit that chamber any more than I have to. It's my job to care for that abomination, you know. There's no point to it, if you ask me. She stays in a trance all the while, and never eats the food I bring." She moved on, still talking. "I want to show you something in the caverns. You can still see in the dark, I presume?"

"Um. Yes," Hap said.

"Good," Lady Tru said. "Strange boy," she added under her breath.

They walked through the caverns, winding among undulating pillars of rock. Countless more glimmer-worms crawled over the walls and ceiling, filling the space with a rainbow of dim light. The air was damp with the mineral scent of the underworld. They walked by the subterranean pond, where drops from the toothy stone above plunked musically into the water and transparent fish glided near the surface.

The massive portcullis was ahead: a fanged iron gate with thick, tightly spaced bars that blocked the passage leading deeper under the earth. It held back the terrible creatures that lurked on the other side. They had served the sorceress when she held the city in the grip of terror, before Umber stripped her of her dark powers and locked her away in the Aerie.

Before Lady Truden reached the portcullis, she ducked behind one of the largest stone pillars and beckoned for Hap and Sophie to join her. Sophie's jaw tensed. On her damaged arm, where her hand should have been, she had strapped the pronged device that held the bow Umber had designed for her. The bow was already locked in place, and she reached over her shoulder and plucked an arrow from the quiver. Hap watched her, amazed at how her timid nature vanished at moments like these, when she transformed into a fierce defender. "What is it, Lady Truden?" Sophie asked.

Lady Truden put a finger to her lips. "Wait," she said. She peered around the edge of the pillar. "Do you smell that?" she said.

"Ugh," Sophie replied. Hap smelled it as well—something rotten and foul. His throat knotted.

"I *hear* something too," Sophie whispered. "Hap, do you?"

Hap turned his head. He heard drops of water spattering stones all around. And something else: a sound from the darkness beyond the gate. It was slow, labored breathing, rasping in and gurgling out, at a deep pitch that suggested enormous lungs. *Something big,* he thought.

"I brought you here because of your eyes," Lady Truden hissed at him. "Why don't you use them?"

Hap swallowed—not an easy thing to do with his mouth so dry. He eased his head out from behind the pillar to look.

It was dark beyond the portcullis. The glimmer-worms that roamed everywhere on the Aerie's side of the gate did not venture past the iron bars, as if they sensed something wicked and dangerous there. His eyes penetrated the darkness and saw the natural tunnel that plunged deep into the rock and twisted to hide its depths from sight. With the cones of rock stabbing up from the floor and down from the ceiling—stalactites and stalagmites, Umber called them—the tunnel looked eerily like a throat, and those pointed stones like teeth.

More thick columns, where the tapering stones had touched and merged over the eons, stood before the dark throat. Hap thought the sound came from behind one of them. And then he saw something move at the edge of one column. It was thick and round, and part of something much larger. "I see it," he whispered.

"What is it?" Lady Truden hissed back.

Hap looked at her and shrugged. He stepped sideways, into the open, to find a better angle. *There are strong bars between us,* he reminded himself, but that didn't stop his knees from twitching. When he glanced back at Sophie, he saw that she was with him, edging sideways with her bow raised halfway up.

The part of the thing that he could see was level with his eyes. It moved, subtly and slowly, in time to the breathing. As Hap eased to his left, more of it came into view. It looked like a shoulder. "I think—," he whispered, but then he cut himself off with a gasp as the creature leaned out, and an enormous head turned to peer back at him.

Hap saw a small, silvery eye and a wide, brutal mouth with lips pulled back to bare jagged, broken teeth. The cry escaped Hap's mouth before he could snuff it with his hand. "Oh!"

The thing grunted and ducked out of sight. Hap grabbed Sophie's arm and tugged her back into hiding next to Lady Truden. His heart pounded like a fist on a door.

"Did you see? What was it?" Lady Truden asked with her back pressed tight against the rock.

"It was a . . . I think it was a . . ." Hap panted. Then their heads all turned at a new sound: scraping, and the thump of heavy feet. Hap peered out again just in time to watch a hulking gray mass rush down the tunnel and disappear.

"I think it was a troll," he said, not whispering anymore.

"As soon as Lord Umber recovers, *I* will tell him," Lady Truden said. Her jaw tensed. "There are horrid things deep in those caverns, but none has approached the gate for years. Why now?"

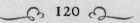

Umber was still sleeping hours later—peacefully, Balfour reported after checking on him—and eventually the others found their own ways to occupy their time. Sophie worked on her paintings in her studio upstairs, and Oates went to the gatehouse for a game of cards with the guardsmen. Balfour popped into the kitchen to bake something, while Hap wandered down to the archives. He expected a harsh, unpleasant reply when he knocked on the door, and Umber's archivist did not disappoint him.

"Go away! Or at least say why you're bothering me."

Hap peeked through the small window in the door. He saw Smudge, wild-haired and dirty-faced as always, sitting at a large oak table with scrolls spread out before him. "It's me, Smudge. Happenstance. I was wondering if you wanted any help with translations."

Smudge's fierce expression softened a bit. Once he'd learned about Hap's uncanny understanding of all languages—another gift of the Meddlers—he'd come to value Hap's ability to decode ancient documents. "Fine," he grumbled. "Come in." He didn't look up from his scroll as Hap approached the table, but he pointed at a dusty leather-bound book. "That's a Dwergh book that somebody just sent us."

Hap picked it up. "Do you mind if I take it to the grand hall to read it?"

Smudge looked up with his shaggy eyebrows gathered in a scowl. "Don't spill anything on it."

"Also," Hap ventured, "if you have anything about trolls, or the caverns under the Aerie, I'd like to read those, too."

Smudge shook his head and said something distasteful under his breath, but he plunged into the rows of shelves and returned with an armful of volumes. Hap scooped them up and headed to the door, eager to leave, but Smudge cleared his throat and said something to him from behind. "Boy . . . tell me again how Brother Caspar died."

With a gulp, Hap turned back. He saw Smudge with his head tilted down and his eyes peering up, tugging at the mess of his beard with both hands. Hap bit his lip. "Didn't Balfour explain?"

Smudge nodded. His voice was quiet and ragged. "But Balfour wasn't there. You were. I want to hear it from you."

Hap hugged the ancient books to his chest. "We . . . we went back to the island of Desolas, where your brother was trapped by the curse of the bidmis. A man who was chasing us fired an arrow at Umber, but it struck Caspar instead."

Smudge twisted his beard. "Did he suffer greatly?"

Hap felt a lump form in his throat. They had all agreed that Smudge should never learn what happened next: that they had brought Caspar's body to be devoured by the soul crabs, so those awful creatures could speak in his voice and reveal the location of the archives that he'd stolen from Lord Umber. They did it because the fate of another world might depend on the retrieval of those secrets. But now they had to live with the terrible notion that they might have committed Caspar's soul to an even darker fate.

"No," Hap said, when he was able to respond. "That was the end of his suffering. I think he was relieved, in a way. To finally escape the bidmis."

Smudge smoothed his beard, coughed, and raised himself out of his perpetual hunch. "I see." Something else was on Smudge's mind, Hap could see, and so he waited.

"I suppose I am Umber's archivist now. For good, I mean. Since Brother Caspar will not come back."

Hap inclined his head. "Yes, I suppose you are."

Smudge squeezed his eyes nearly shut and scratched inside his ear. "Is it wrong to be glad about that, while I also mourn the loss of my brother?"

"I suppose not," Hap said, uncertain of his own reply. "I'll see you later, all right?"

CHAPTER
10

Hap was nibbling on muffins that Balfour had baked, with Smudge's volumes pushed safely aside, when Sophie rushed down the stairs. A patch of fresh paint glistened on her smock. "Lord Umber is awake, but I think something's wrong with him!"

Lady Truden shot up from her chair. "What? What's the matter?"

Sophie gulped and averted her eyes. "You should come up and see."

Tru dashed for the stairs, running with the sides of her gown bunched in her fists. Hap and Sophie followed, not daring to pass her. Hap heard Balfour and Oates rushing to join them.

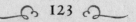

When they reached the terrace, they were startled to hear Umber hooting and laughing. He was shirtless, standing behind one of the largest planters on the terrace with a shovel in his hand. Dirt was flung all around him, and the small tree that previously occupied the planter had been uprooted and cast aside. Umber climbed onto the waist-high planter to stomp down the fresh pile of dirt. Oates snorted out a laugh. It was clear then that Umber was pantsless as well as shirtless, and in fact was entirely naked except for the striped socks that reached to his knees. He began to sing loudly, drawing out the notes and laughing: *"Oh give me a home, where the buffalo rooooooaaaaam!"*

Sophie turned away, blushing. Lady Truden cried out and covered her face with her hands, though Hap was pretty sure he saw her peering out from between parted fingers.

"What's the matter with him?" Tru shouted.

"At least he's not depressed," Balfour said, chuckling.

"This isn't funny, you old fool," Tru shot back. "What sort of plant did that idiot wizard give you?"

"You're the one who made the tea," Oates reminded her.

Umber raised his face to the sky and howled more of the song. *"And the deer and the antelope plaaaaaaay, ha-ha!"*

Tru jabbed Balfour's chest with a finger. "Don't blame this on me. I did exactly what you told me! I made tea from seventy leaves!"

"What is an anti-lope?" Oates wondered.

"Seventy?" cried Balfour. "There's the trouble. I told you seventeen."

Umber held the shovel horizontally in two hands, and kicked one way, and then the other. *"Where seldom is heeeard . . ."*

"You told me seventy!" Tru shouted, snarling. "There's nothing wrong with my ears."

"I heard him say seventeen," Oates said flatly. *That settles that,* thought Hap.

". . . a discouraging wooooooord!"

With an anguished cry, Tru fell to her knees. She dropped her face into her hands, and her body convulsed with sobs. "Oh, my dear Umber, what have I done to you?"

"Give him time, Tru," Balfour said, patting her shoulder. "I bet he'll calm down. And it's better than moping for weeks, isn't it? Oates, why don't you help Umber down from there and put his clothes back on him."

"I'd rather not touch him," Oates replied, looking at Umber from head to toe.

"And the skiiiies are not cloudy all daaaaay! Ha-ha!" Umber tossed the shovel over his shoulder and scooped up soil with both hands and flung it in the air. He smiled upward with his eyes and mouth closed as it rained back down on his face.

Balfour sighed heavily. "Come on, Hap. You too, Oates.

We'll all do it. Sophie, help Tru downstairs, will you?"

Hap gathered the clothes that were scattered around the terrace. Oates gripped Umber below the armpits and held him up. Balfour tugged Umber's pants back on with his face turned away, and he couldn't help but laugh while he did it. Hap chuckled as well, despite his own concern for Umber's sanity. Umber found their struggle hilarious. "Looky, boys, I went and did it!" he cried, barely able to squeeze the words out between his guffaws.

Balfour pulled the shirt over Umber's head. "Did what, Umber?"

"Helloooo!" cried Umber as his head popped up from the collar. "I planted it, of course!"

"I think he means that thorny nut," Hap said.

"Exactly!" Umber said, and he started to sing again. "*In a canyon, in a cavern, excavaaaaaating for a mine . . .*" But then his eyelids fluttered, his head lolled, and his voice slurred. "You guys are my pals. I think I'll take another nap."

"That's a fine idea," Balfour said. Umber drifted off a moment later, and Balfour turned to Hap and Oates. "But this time, let's keep an eye on him."

Once Umber was tucked away again, they gathered in the great hall. Sophie's cheeks were still as red as a rose, while Lady

Tru's face was hidden behind her hands as she slumped at the table. "The only misstep," Balfour said, "was quadrupling the dosage." That observation prompted an inarticulate groan from Lady Tru.

Dodd strode into the room. "Visitors coming," he said. "On horseback, not in a carriage. I believe it's Umber's female acquaintance." He winked at Hap. "And her little friend, too."

Hap straightened up and stretched his neck. Sophie was across the table from him, and he saw vertical lines appear between her eyebrows.

Lady Tru took her hands off her face. "That woman again? She's a regular nuisance, if you ask me."

Balfour puffed air out of the side of his mouth. "Everything's happening at once today, isn't it? Dodd, this is not the best time for that young lady to visit, especially after what happened last time. Let's just tell them Umber's not in, shall we?"

"I'll handle these visitors," Lady Tru said, and she pushed away from the table.

"I bet you will," Balfour muttered.

Dodd stepped back, allowing Tru plenty of room to pass. When she was out of earshot, he put his hand next to his mouth and, always the impromptu poet, quietly recited:

"Of all the beasties, there are few,

Who frighten me like Lady Tru."

Hap was suddenly aware that he was fidgeting madly in his seat, with his knees bouncing and his hands rubbing together. "Come on, Hap," Balfour said, with a sly look on his grizzled face. "Why don't we go down and say hello? They're your friends too."

"All right," Hap said. He stood, with a flush of anticipation that faded when he saw Sophie twist away to hide her face. Hap wondered why she did that; she could be difficult to understand at times. But his own feelings were just as hard to decipher, he realized; at that moment he was torn between going downstairs to see Fay and Sable, and remaining where he was at the table with Sophie. Balfour was already on his way, so he followed the old man.

"You could take the lift and save your knees," Hap said, catching up to him.

"I'm feeling spry at the moment," Balfour said cheerfully. He stopped at the top landing and raised an arm to hold Hap back. Balfour cocked his head to listen, and Hap was surprised to hear Fay's voice inside the Aerie.

"She let them inside?" Balfour muttered with a frown. "Why would she do that?"

"I'm sorry, but Lord Umber is in no frame of mind to receive visitors," Lady Tru said.

Balfour's expression darkened and Hap felt his own blood

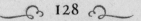

begin to boil. "But, Balfour, you said we should tell them—"

"I know!" Balfour tried to mask his anger as he made his way down the stairs. Hap followed and saw Fay and Sable below.

"You have to understand, Lord Umber is not well," Lady Truden said to Fay. Her hands were clasped at her waist, and the smug set of her mouth made Hap want to scream.

Balfour coughed, loudly, and Sable looked up. She gasped when she spotted Hap, and hopped up and down with her hand waving madly. Fay looked up next, and seemed relieved to see Balfour and Hap, if only to have someone else to speak to besides the contemptuous silver-haired woman who towered over her.

"Balfour," Fay said. "How good to see you again. And you, Master Happenstance."

"Hullo, Hap!" cried Sable.

"A pleasure, my lady," Balfour said, wincing as an ache flared in his leg. He started to limp, and Hap stepped down next to him so that Balfour could put a hand on his shoulder. They were halfway down the stairs. "I don't know what Lady Truden has just told you, but I'm sure Lord Umber will—"

Lady Truden interrupted to finish Balfour's sentence. "Be quite happy if you leave him alone to recover in peace." Hap felt Balfour's grip tighten on his shoulder.

"That terrible sadness ... Lord Umber still is not recovered?" Fay said.

"I'm afraid not," Lady Truden said.

"Tru!" snapped Balfour.

Fay looked up at Balfour and back at Lady Tru. "But he sent flowers to the palace. I assumed he was well again, and came to thank him."

"He *is* well," Balfour said with a vigorous nod. "Recovering just fine, in fact. But he's resting now. I know he's eager to see you, however, and . . ." Balfour's voice creaked to a stop, because a faint sound echoed from the upper floor of the Aerie, through the gaps in the floors that allowed the lift to pass. They heard it faintly over the rush of water that flowed through the channel in the ground floor of the Aerie. It was a wild, almost maniacal laughter, followed by another song: the one that Umber had heard whistled in the market.

"Take me out to the ball game . . . take me out with the crowd!"

Fay peered up past the ropes and platforms of the lift. "Is that Lord Umber?"

"Um. I believe it is," Balfour said. His eyes stretched wide, and his fingers clutched Hap's shoulder.

"Buy me some peanuts and Cracker Jack, I don't care if I never get back!"

"He doesn't sound sad at all," Sable said, squinting up.

No, he sounds like a lunatic, Hap thought. He and Balfour had frozen side by side, and he didn't think either one of them was breathing.

Something terrible happened. The gears of the lift were suddenly engaged, and the platforms began to move. On one of the first platforms to drop down from the floor above, Hap saw a pair of empty trousers dangling. They slipped off and fluttered to the floor below, not far from where Fay and Sable stood. "Oh, crackers," Balfour muttered. He spoke quickly into Hap's ear. "Bad news. Umber started the lift from upstairs. Go throw the switch at the bottom and stop it, as fast as you can. I think he's naked again."

Hap thundered down the steps. He tried to present a calm, friendly smile to Fay and Sable as their heads turned to watch him, but the best he could manage was a maniacal clenching of his teeth. At the foot of the lift, where the rushing water powered the machinery, he shoved the lever back. The lift rattled to a stop with the ropes quivering. Hap looked up with his breath poised inside his chest. High overhead, just below the hole in the ceiling, he saw a pair of skinny bare legs up to the knees. *That was close,* Hap thought.

"What's this?" Umber cried merrily. The bare legs hopped up and down on the platform. "Something's amiss with the lift! Is anybody down there? Start me up again! Helloooo!"

Oates's head appeared at the top of the stairs. "Umber is awake again," he said.

Balfour squinted and rubbed the side of his face. "That's helpful, Oates. Can you put him back in that room for the time being? Sit on him if you have to."

Oates stuck out his tongue and vanished back into the grand hall. A moment later Umber's bare legs levitated up and out of sight. "What's this?" Umber cried with a laugh. "Oh, it's you, Oates! Are we going somewhere? I just remembered a song—I'll sing it for you!" The voice faded away.

Hap puffed out a deep breath and looked back at their visitors. Fay and Sable were gaping, openmouthed. Hap saw the corner of Lady Truden's mouth turn up, and his hand crunched into a fist.

"I don't understand," Fay said, looking at Balfour with her hand pressed to her heart. "Before, it was sadness. Now he sounds giddy, almost mad. This . . . this is not the man I met before, who saved us in Sarnica."

"He is a troubled man," Lady Truden said, shaking her head sadly. "Perhaps you both should leave us now. I believe you were staying with Prince Loden at the palace? The rumor is you and he are quite inseparable."

"Tru!" Balfour snapped. He'd finally hobbled to the bottom of the stairs. His face was an angry shade of purple as he stepped inches away from Lady Truden. He spoke quietly, his voice filled with fury. "I know what you're doing, and why. Now get upstairs. All the way upstairs, and out of sight. When Umber recovers, I'm telling him how you treated our guests. Now *go*!"

Lady Tru's lips pressed so tightly together that they turned white. She whirled and stomped upstairs, with Balfour's glare practically igniting the hair on the back of her head.

"Golly," whispered Sable when Lady Tru was gone. Hap could see the whites all around her eyes.

Fay took Sable's hand and stepped back. "Perhaps we should go."

"Please don't," Hap said.

"That's right," Balfour said. He took Fay's free hand and clasped it inside both of his. "Umber will never forgive me if I don't explain what you've seen these last two visits. The Umber you first met is the true Umber, I promise you. And you will see that man again, before long. Please, my lady. Stay for a while, and let us talk."

Sable tugged at Fay's other hand. "Please, Aunt Fay. Just for a little while." Her dark eyes stared at Hap in a way that made his stomach flutter.

Fay heaved out a deep breath, and she nodded. "Not for too long. We'll be missed at the palace." She blushed and grinned at Balfour. "We snuck away, to be honest. We were only supposed to ride around the palace grounds."

Balfour smiled back and extended his elbow. "Ride the lift with me to the grand hall, my lady, and we'll share a glass of wine while I explain the inexplicable. Hap, perhaps you'd like to show your pretty friend the view of Petraportus?"

"Oh, please," said Sable. She slipped her arm inside Hap's, and it clamped on his elbow like a vise.

Hap and Sable sat at the edge of the path overlooking the ancient crumbling castle in Kurahaven Bay, with their legs dangling over the edge. Below them the enormous spout of fresh water, fed by a subterranean stream, jetted out from the base of the Aerie and splashed into the salt water below.

"You're still at the palace?" Hap asked.

Sable nodded and pushed her dark curls behind one ear. "Everything is so beautiful there."

"And Prince Loden is treating you well?" Hap watched her face carefully.

"He's very nice to Aunt Fay. And to me," she replied. She rocked from side to side, inching closer to Hap.

Hap's teeth gnawed on his upper lip. He wasn't sure if it was safe to tell what they suspected about Loden and his

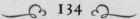

murderous desire for the crown. "But nothing . . . bothers you about him?" he ventured.

Sable peered at him with her head at a curious angle. "What do you mean? No, the prince is very nice. Although . . ." She kicked her legs, hitting the rock below with her heels.

"What?" Hap said, urging her.

"He doesn't want us going off on our own. We had to sneak away just to visit you! Whenever Fay wants to see the other parts of the city, he insists on coming along. Or he sends another man with us . . . and I don't like that fellow very much."

Hap knew who she meant. "Larcombe, right?"

She looked up, startled. "Yes, that's him!"

"He reminds me of a lizard," Hap said.

"Me too!" she cried. She leaned as she laughed, and their shoulders met. The touch sent bolts of lightning down Hap's legs and into his toes. He took a deep breath and tried to reassemble the thoughts that had just been scrambled inside his brain. He wanted to tell her that Loden was a wicked and ruthless man, and that she and her aunt should leave the palace as soon as they could. His mouth opened, but he hesitated, and at that moment another voice called out from the gatehouse.

"Sable! Are you there?"

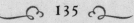

Sable groaned. "Yes, Aunt Fay!"

"Come along. We have to go," Fay called. Hap thought there was an urgent edge to her voice.

"Oh, so soon?" Sable whined, only for Hap's ears. Hap stood, and she raised her hand. "Help me up?" He clasped her hand, and she sprang up beside him. "It's scary on this narrow path," she said, tightening her grip. Hap gulped and raised an eyebrow. The path wasn't especially narrow at that point, and she hadn't seemed afraid on the way out. But he walked with her, hand in hand, back to the gatehouse.

"There was a girl here last time," Sable said, with calculated innocence. "With only one hand."

"Yes, that's Sophie."

"Who is she?"

Hap looked back at her and saw a sunny smile replace her frown. "She lives here," he said. "She creates art for Umber's books. And she is a great archer."

"She's your friend?"

"Oh yes," he said. He felt her hand twitch against his palm. The path rounded the gatehouse, and they found Fay inside, already mounted on her horse with Dodd holding the bridle.

Fay's eyes looked watery, and her expression was dazed. Her voice shook when she called out. "Come now, Sable. We've stayed too long. The prince may think we've stolen his horses."

Sable ran to the second horse, and Barkin lifted her onto the saddle. Fay turned and looked at Balfour, with a troubled shake of her head. "Mister Balfour, I don't know what to make of what you've said. I can't reconcile those words with the prince I've come to know. He's been nothing but kind to me and my niece."

Balfour clasped his hands, pleading. "Forgive me, good lady, I hope I didn't offend you. Promise me you'll come again? I assure you, Lord Umber will recover soon from this temporary affliction."

Fay gazed up at the top of the Aerie. "I will . . . if we can. Please tell Lord Umber we were here," she said, and she kicked her heels against the sides of the horse. She and Sable trotted down the causeway. Sable looked over her shoulder and waved at Hap, with her lip quivering and her eyes shining.

Barkin gave a low whistle. "What a filly. And I don't mean the horse. Did you say something you shouldn't have, Balfour?"

Balfour clutched his head and squeezed his eyes shut. "Please don't salt my wounds. I tried to warn her about Loden. But that scoundrel has her fooled, and now I think I've offended her. Two visits, two catastrophes, both my doing. How will I explain this to Umber?"

Hap's heart ached for Balfour, and for another reason he could not understand. He noticed Dodd tugging at his small rectangular beard with his eyes rolled upward, and he knew what was coming. Sure enough, Dodd raised a finger and recited:

"For peasants, soldiers, lords, and kings,

Love's a mighty messy thing."

"Stuff your poetry, Dodd," Balfour grumbled, and he limped back into the Aerie, shaking his head.

...e known varieties. There are
...untain or stone trolls, like those that
...well in the rocky Barren Gray in the
northern reaches of Vernia, with flesh that
resembles various minerals; marine trolls,
...the semi-aquatic creatures whose nostrils
...e located at the top of their heads,
...re trolls, distinguished by

CHAPTER
II

Hap was at the table in the grand
hall, absorbed in his translation, when he heard the thump
of descending feet, heavier than usual. Umber's voice echoed
down the stairwell. "Oates. Put me down. This is humiliating."

Hap popped out of his chair, feeling a wave of relief. There
was no singing, no mad laughter. Umber didn't sound delirious
or despondent, just cranky and weak.

"You said you were dizzy and might fall," Oates said.

"But that didn't mean you should scoop me up like an
infant and—oh, never mind, we're almost there." Umber's
head appeared, and then the rest of him, cradled in Oates's
arms. When Oates took the last step down into the grand hall,
Umber swatted the big fellow's arms. Oates set him down on

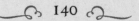

his feet, and Umber wobbled for a moment, and then yawned and stretched with his arms thrown wide. "Ah, Hap," he said, raising his hand.

Balfour eased the galley door open and peered out, before venturing into the room. "You look better," he said.

"I *am* better." Umber plopped down at the table and took a pear from the bowl of fruit. "Apparently the elatia works."

Balfour grimaced. "There was a small problem with the dosage."

"Yes, Oates told me." Umber chuckled, but then he winced and pressed his palm to his forehead. "It left me with a little headache. But can you believe it, Balfour? After all these years, I may have put those dark episodes behind me." He rubbed the pear against his shirt. "You know, I have only the haziest memories of what I did during my, er, euphoria. It seems I planted the thorny nut, though. But I hope I didn't embarrass myself in any way." When a grim silence followed, he looked from Hap to Balfour. "What? Did I?"

Balfour stared at the floor, and Hap bit the inside of his cheek. Umber's alarm grew. "Oates?" he said, looking over his shoulder. Oates had made a hasty escape, and Hap saw just the heel of his boot as he fled upstairs.

"Umber," Balfour said hoarsely. He raised his hands, and they were trembling.

"Good heavens, man, did I kill somebody?" Umber cried.

Balfour shut his eyes and blurted out his reply in a high, tight voice. "You were laughing and singing like a madman, and you stripped off all your clothes."

Umber goggled, and then shook his head and chuckled. "Did I? I must have scandalized poor Sophie and Tru. Well, it's just a body. Every person has one." He raised the pear for a bite.

"Fay was here," Balfour said.

There was the crunch of the pear, and then a splat as the bite flew out of Umber's mouth and landed on the table. "She came back?"

Balfour nodded.

Umber breathed sharply in and slowly out. "And you let her inside, while I was . . . in that state?"

"Well . . . Tru let her in. But we thought you were sleeping."

Umber stood up. The pear was still in his hand, and he raised it to his shoulder as if to dash it against the wall. Then he lowered his hand and let it roll onto the table, and hung his head. Hap glanced at Balfour, and the old man's bleary-eyed, despondent expression made his heart dissolve.

Finally Umber raised his face again. His mouth was small and tight, and his gaze drifted, unfocused. "To sum things up: She came to visit once, and I was hopelessly depressed. She came back a second time, and I was a naked singing lunatic.

Well. I believe we have thrust a dagger deep into the heart of that possibility." He rapped his knuckles on the table. His shoulders twitched, as if he was trying to shrug off the unhappy development. "It's probably for the best. I'm an ill-suited suitor when it comes down to it. Hap, come upstairs with me, will you? We have some catching up to do."

"Umber?" Balfour called from behind.

Umber turned. "Yes, Balfour?"

Balfour's bottom lip quivered. "May I . . . put up a pot of coffee for you?"

Umber lifted his chin, and Hap was glad to see a tiny smile on his weary face. "That sounds splendid," Umber said. "Bring it up to the terrace when it's ready, will you, my best of friends?"

"I had the strangest dreams while I slept just now," Umber said, as they stepped into the open air and the last rays of the setting sun.

"About what?"

"My former life. Do you mind hearing about them? I feel the need to talk."

"I don't mind at all," Hap replied.

"Ugh," Umber said. He scratched the back of his head and looked at the mess on the terrace. Dirt was flung everywhere.

He lifted up the uprooted tree and inspected it. The only sounds were distant and serene: the dash of waves, the cries of the gulls, the shushing of the wind. Then, amid those, Hap gradually detected an alien noise, much closer. Umber turned his ear—he'd heard it too. They glanced at each other, and their heads swiveled toward the source.

The sound was coming from inside the enormous stone planter where the tree had once grown. Umber set the tree back on the ground and squatted low to put his ear against the planter's side. "Something's moving in there," he whispered. The familiar twinkle returned to his eye.

Hap heard something new: a faint squishing. He pointed at the inside of the planter. The rich black soil, a foot below the rim, was bubbling and falling, like oatmeal coming to a slow boil. "The . . . the nut?" Hap asked.

Umber grinned. "What else?" He spread his arms wide, gripped the sides of the planter, and leaned in with his nose an inch from the soil.

"There," Hap squeaked. He pointed near Umber's right hand, where something poked out of the dirt. It was pale, almost white, glistening and caked with dirt, and it moved with the slow, oozing patience of a slug. "What is it?" Hap said.

"A root, I think," Umber told him, eyeing it from inches away.

They watched for a minute as it crept up the side, exposing more and more of its length. It reached the edge of the planter, curved over the lip, and started down again. "Amazing," Umber whispered. "I wonder what it's going to be." Hap wasn't sure he wanted to know.

"Tell you what," Umber said. He sat on the terrace floor with his elbows on his knees. "Let's stay right here and keep an eye on this new wonder while I tell you about my dreams."

Hap sat likewise beside Umber, but put a little more distance between him and the eerie root.

"They weren't dreams so much as memories," Umber said. "I saw moments of my life replayed in my mind, as if I were there all over again. I haven't remembered those days so clearly since I first arrived in this world. An effect of the elatia, I suppose. But then again, I wonder if hearing that mysterious whistler triggered the memories." Umber leaned forward to where the root was nudging down the side of the planter, and gave it an experimental poke. His fingertip came away with a coating of slime, which Umber wiped off on his pant leg. The root paused for a moment, as a worm might when prodded, and then resumed its cautious journey.

Umber's inward journey resumed as well. "I dreamed about people I used to know. The friends I left behind. Saw their faces, heard their voices."

Hap looked at Umber, searching for any omens of the terrible sadness that might afflict him. But he saw none, and breathed easier. "Did you have a mother and father?"

"I did once, of course. But they passed away when I was still a very young man."

"What friends did you see?"

"One, most of all. And it's funny you ask about my parents, because this man was like a father to me. His name was Jonathan Doane. Do you remember me telling you about him?"

Hap looked skyward, searching the vault of his memory. "Yes. He was the man who asked you to help him with his idea."

"Right. Project Reboot . . . preserving all of humanity's learning and achievements, and storing it all on the Reboot computer, so that people could rebuild civilization one day if they had to. That was Jonathan's brainchild. And he chose me, out of all the people who could have led that mission. Hap, sometimes two people come together, and the bond is instantaneous. That's how it was with Jonathan and me. What a genius he was. He spent his life studying the history of technology, especially military technology. He finally decided that it was all rushing forward too quickly. The ability to destroy, combined with the worst impulses of human nature, would some day result in global chaos and destruction." Umber fell quiet and gazed at the evening's first stars. "I guess he knew what he was talking about." He tapped his knuckles against his chin, immersed in memory.

"What happened to Jonathan?" Hap asked.

Umber sighed and shrugged. "I told you before how I barely made it out alive from the place where we'd been working on Project Reboot. Doane was there too when the mob attacked and the fire started. I hate to imagine what became of him."

Balfour appeared at the top of the stairs with a pot of coffee, a pitcher of cream, and three mugs on a silver tray. "Coffee for you, cocoa for the boy, and—*what on earth!*" The tray came unbalanced in his hands. As the pitcher and mugs wobbled to a stop, he gawked, openmouthed, at the planter. Five more roots had wriggled down the sides, like enormous fingers gripping it from above.

"Not wasting any time, is it?" Umber mused. Hap stood alongside him and looked into the planter. In the middle the soil rose like a small hill. A crack appeared, and something pale and gray pushed through the dirt from below. It rose, sluggish and arching, and Hap saw that it was the stem of a plant, as thick as his wrist. Its tip broke loose from the soil, and there was a dense cluster of infant branches at the top, all bristling with tiny thorns.

Balfour shook his head and sighed. "It's always something around here."

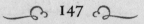

When Balfour returned to the kitchen, Hap followed Umber into his study, a room once forbidden to anyone but Umber. But there were no more secrets between them, as far as he knew. "Sit," Umber said. Hap lowered himself into the padded chair on the other side of Umber's desk.

Umber went to the wall beside his desk and pushed a tapestry aside, revealing the round door of the safe where he kept the miraculous machine that belonged, like Umber himself, to another world. With his remarkable key that could magically alter its shape to open any lock at all, he opened the safe. The door gave a tiny kitten squeak as it swung wide.

"You should know something," Umber said. He lifted out the smooth, flat silver case with that word engraved on its surface: REBOOT. "My computer isn't the only thing of value in this safe. There's other stuff that could be even more dangerous in the wrong hands."

Hap coughed and squirmed in his seat.

Umber laid the computer on his desk. He opened its lid and pressed a button, and it hummed to life. "Remember Turiana, the 'guest' we have locked away downstairs? What am I saying—of course you remember, she tried to scare the life out of you!"

Hap nodded. He'd been through many frightening

moments in his brief conscious life, but one of the worst was his encounter with the sorceress.

Umber reached into the safe and pulled out a box made of a material that bore an unsettling resemblance to bleached bone. He took off the lid and showed Hap its contents: rings, pendants, bracelets, and enormous crystals and gemstones. Hap looked up at Umber with his head at a curious angle. "Jewels?"

"Talismans," Umber replied. He closed the box, shoved it deep into the hole in the wall, and closed the safe. Next he went to the hearth in the opposite wall and made a stack of twigs and wood.

Hap's thoughts turned inward, to something Balfour had once told him. "Those talismans—they used to belong to Turiana."

"That's right," Umber said. "Now, a warlock or sorceress has a certain amount of natural magical ability. Turiana can pull thoughts out of people's heads, remember?"

A shiver coursed through Hap's shoulders. "I remember."

"But talismans are used to amplify those abilities. That's true of Fendofel, too—he has a talisman for his botanical wizardry."

"The crystal around his neck," Hap said.

"Exactly. Turiana collected the objects in that box over many years, usually by seizing them from other warlocks and sorceresses. With every talisman she won, she grew more

powerful. She could cast spells and call out the foul creatures that live deep underground and force them to serve her."

Umber took a burning candle from his desk and used it to light the finest twigs at the bottom of his pile of wood.

"Why don't you use the talismans yourself?" Hap asked.

Umber flashed his black-stone ring at Hap. "I use this one, to open the black door downstairs. But the rest? Too dangerous. Remember what happened to Turiana when she amassed too much dark power: It drove her mad and turned her thoughts to evil. But really, Hap, I'm telling you this because those talismans must be destroyed if anything happens to me," Umber said.

"Nothing will happen to you," Hap blurted. He wanted it to be true, and he also believed it. Umber had survived so many harebrained, reckless adventures already that it was hard to conceive of him actually coming to harm.

"You never know," Umber said, smiling. "Now, I've already told Balfour what to do in the event of a tragedy involving myself. But I want you to know as well. You're to get this key from me, which I wear around my neck or keep in my pocket at all times. The Reboot computer should be tossed into the sea. The talismans must be melted down or smashed to pieces. Is that clear?"

"Nothing will happen," Hap echoed softly.

"Nevertheless," Umber said. And then he did another curious thing—he seemed to have an endless supply of unexpected things to do. He reached behind his desk and lifted a small statue. It was as tall as Hap's knee, made of rough stone, and blackened by soot. The form was vaguely human, but also amphibian, with a froglike mouth opened wide and glittering white gems for eyes. One arm was broken off, and one leg was replaced with an iron peg. Umber laid it faceup on the burning wood.

"What are you . . . ?" Hap began to ask.

"Watch," Umber said.

The stone figure settled into the burning sticks. Flames lapped over it, and sparks crackled and flew. Hap leaned over with his hands on his knees, staring.

The fingers on the statue's only arm twitched. Then they curled into a half-formed fist. The elbow bent and straightened, and the statue flexed its knee and ankle.

"You don't look all that surprised, Hap," Umber said. "Don't tell me I've lost the ability to astonish you!"

"There have been so many surprises," Hap said. The statue used its one arm to turn itself over, exposing its face and belly to the flames. "What is this thing?"

"It was a gift from the Dwergh. I returned some treasures of theirs that Turiana had hoarded, and this was their thanks.

It's called a Molton—an enchanted statue that's animated by fire. It'll perform whatever task you give it. They're extremely rare. This one had been damaged, but it's perfectly useful for the tasks I give it."

The Molton sat up with a burning stick in its hand. It opened its frog mouth and shoved the stick down its blackened throat. "What tasks are those?" Hap asked.

Umber smiled. "Haven't you wondered how I get it all done—the plans for ships and buildings, the music, the books of instruction, and all that other stuff? I have this Molton to transcribe them." He pulled a stack of parchment from a drawer and set it beside the computer in two piles. One pile, Hap could see, was densely covered with musical notations. The second pile was blank. Umber swiveled the computer until the screen faced him and spoke a command. "Reboot: Show the score for Beethoven's Third Symphony, beginning with the second movement." The thing that Umber had summoned appeared on the computer screen: countless symbols, numbers, and slashes arranged across horizontal lines.

The Molton rose up inside the hearth, unsteady at first on its one leg and the iron peg. It hobbled stiffly out of the fire and helped itself to a few lumps of coal in a bin that Umber kept nearby, tossing them into its gaping mouth.

"Hello, Shale," Umber said to the Molton. The creature turned its stone face up, expressionless except for the glitter of its gemstone eyes. Umber set a feathered pen and an inkwell on the desktop and pulled a stool out of the corner of the room. Hap hadn't noticed that stool before, with rungs between its legs that made it easy for the Molton to clamber up. "You can pick up where you left off, transcribing this symphony. And keep feeding yourself coal so you don't cool down, all right? That's a good lad." The Molton nodded, apparently understanding every word.

"His name is Shale?" Hap asked.

"I thought about changing it to Rocky, but kept the Dwergh name after all," Umber said. He watched happily as the stone creature picked up the pen, dipped it into the ink, and went to work.

Hap was in Sophie's studio, watching her prepare an engraving. It was an illustration of the sea-giants: the enormous creatures they'd encountered on the rocky coast of Celador. She had depicted them just as Hap remembered, slumbering on the ledge of the sea-cave, with ocean-refracted light shimmering on their grotesque forms. The memory quickened Hap's pulse. Umber could be reckless, but never more so than when he'd nearly woken those titanic beasts. After all, those were the

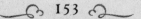

same giants that had smashed Kurahaven into rubble more than a century before.

"It really is remarkable," Hap told her. "How do you remember what you see so well?" She smiled and shrugged. Sophie had a habit of looking away as soon as Hap's eyes met hers. But this time she held his glance for so long that he felt his face turn warm.

"You seem different lately," she said.

"I do?"

She nodded, and her gaze grew more intense. "When we found you, you were like a little boy. So lost. But you've changed."

Without thinking about it, Hap put his hand to his temple and felt his hair under his palm.

"I don't mean what's happening to your hair," Sophie said. "It's you. You're . . . older somehow."

Hap felt tiny dots of perspiration at the top of his forehead. "I am?"

The door to the studio squeaked open, and Umber's head angled into the threshold. Hap let out a deep breath. Somehow the interruption was both welcome and unwelcome.

Umber's eyes were avid and wide, and he spoke quickly, louder than necessary. "Happenstance! There you are. Get to your room and put on your best clothes."

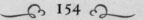

"Are . . . are we going somewhere?" Hap asked.

"We've been summoned to the palace," Umber replied.

"We've *both* been summoned?"

Umber grinned. "Well, just me, obviously, but you know how it is—I need you to come with me. So put on your finery and meet me downstairs, right away." Umber's head vanished, and his footsteps tapered.

Hap turned to Sophie, but she'd put her back to him and was cleaning her brush, swishing it inside a glass jar with unnecessary vigor. "Have fun at the palace, Happenstance. I suppose you'll see your little friend."

The carriage trundled down the causeway. Hap noticed how carefully Umber had primped himself for this visit. He wore his best boots, freshly blackened and with shining gold buckles. Instead of the many-pocketed and well-worn vest that he favored, he had donned a black surcoat embroidered with gold, over a snowy silk shirt. His chaotic hair was combed and tied back with a black ribbon. Umber was normally an energetic sort, but he was particularly effervescent at the moment, humming loudly with his feet tapping. He stuck his arm out the window, cupping his hand to catch the wind.

Hap, meanwhile, slumped on his bench, so low that his knees were almost at eye level. Umber eventually took note.

"Now, Happenstance, I know you don't like being dragged to these things. But you know the reason."

Hap nodded. "The note from Willy Nilly told you to take me on all your adventures. But this isn't really an adventure, is it?"

"One never knows when adventure will strike," Umber said, spreading his arms.

Hap put his hands on the bench and pushed himself straight. "Who wants you at the palace, Lord Umber? Is it Fay?"

Umber shook his head. "I wish it was. But no, it was the king himself."

"The king?" For months it was rumored that King Tyrian was near death. He had even been too ill to attend the funerals of the two sons he'd recently lost, only weeks apart.

"Yes," Umber said. "Apparently he's felt a little better these last few days. Thanks to some friends of mine, I might add."

"Friends of yours?"

Umber nodded. "Improving the quality of medicine in this world has been one of my priorities. I've established a school of medicine to train a new generation of physicians. But some people are stubborn about the old ways. King Tyrian was among them. He insisted on using his royal physician—who is the practitioner of some of the most outdated quackery that you can imagine. Tyrian finally relented and allowed a pair of my best physicians to treat him."

That's good, Hap thought. The conniving Prince Loden had seemed on the verge of taking the throne. But perhaps that day would not come so soon after all.

They were met inside the palace by a servant of the king, a well-fed man in a green robe. When he saw Umber, his expression softened like butter in the sun. "Lord Umber—how nice to welcome you to the palace again!"

"Hello, Tattersall," Umber said, clasping the royal servant's hands. "I hope it's all right that I brought my ward, Happenstance."

Tattersall stared, captivated like so many before him by Hap's eyes. But this time Hap stared back, because there was something on Tattersall's face that he'd never seen before: a round piece of glass over each eye, connected by a thin frame that bridged his nose and metal bands that hooked behind his ears.

"Oh, you've noticed my spectacles," Tattersall said. He took the thing off his face and held it out for Hap to see. "I have your Lord Umber to thank for these!"

"How are they working?" Umber asked.

"Perfectly. What a delight to see clearly again!" Tattersall replied. He'd been squinting since removing the spectacles, and he put them back over his eyes and grinned.

"Another one of my ventures," Umber told Hap. "Just getting started, really. I hope to make them widely available."

"As for this young fellow," Tattersall said, putting a hand on Hap's shoulder, "I haven't had the pleasure of meeting you, but I have seen you. When you were here for Prince Galbus's birthday party."

"Poor Galbus," Umber said. He looked over Tattersall's shoulder, and back over his own. When he spoke again, his voice was almost a whisper. "Tattersall . . . it's being said that Galbus died after a drunken fall. I was surprised to hear that. It seemed to me that he'd forsaken wine."

Tattersall's body went rigid. His jaw lifted and his throat convulsed as he swallowed hard, and he seemed on the verge of speaking when a sound came from the second-floor balcony—a foot scraping, or a back sliding against a wall. "It . . . it was a terrible tragedy," Tattersall stammered. He suddenly adopted a stiff and formal manner, but his eyes were locked on Umber's, wide and filled with alarm, with his eyebrows lofted high on his forehead. Hap saw him give Umber the tiniest shake of his head, something that could not have been seen if they hadn't been standing so close.

"Tattersall," Umber began, but Tattersall raised a hand to silence him.

"Please, Lord Umber," Tattersall said, dropping his voice

to a whisper, and barely moving his lips. "You must understand . . . I can't be heard discussing such things." He gulped, and his throat bobbed. Then he composed himself and raised his voice. "Let me take you to the king." His heels clicked on the marble floor as he walked away.

They followed Tattersall through an enormous room where a throne sat empty before a long table lined with tall chairs, and up a wide, curving stair that climbed past the lofty first floor of the palace. At a landing they turned down a corridor, while the steps continued higher into the palace. There, a voice floated down from above.

"Lord Umber!"

Umber jolted to a stop. Hap looked up and saw Fay at the top of the stairs.

"Why, Fay," Umber said, putting a hand to his heart. He stared up, blinking. "You look as lovely as a metaphor."

Fay glanced down at her exquisite dress, and her hand wandered up to cover the glittering necklace at her throat. "Thank you. And you, Lord Umber. You seem . . . restored?"

Umber patted the side of his face and chuckled. "Ah. Yes. Certainly an improvement over the last two times you saw me. I'm happy to tell you, the moods that afflicted me are probably gone for good."

Fay's foot was poised at the top of the first step. She peered sideways before speaking again, with a tremor in her voice. "I hardly know what to expect when I see you. But now you're the man I remember . . . the one who saved us."

Umber mounted two steps, caressing the banister as he rose. "Could I speak with you again, Fay? I have an audience with the king. But after that?"

Fay's lips paled as she pressed them together. "I . . . I don't think we can."

Hap looked to Fay's left and right, wondering if Sable was nearby. He heard Tattersall clear his throat and saw him pull a handkerchief from his sleeve to dab his forehead.

Umber nodded at Fay. "Not here? Then come to the Aerie, as soon as you can. Or name a place, and I will meet you there."

Fay's hands were shaking. "The . . . the prince worries for my safety, and wishes me to stay at the palace."

"Your *safety*?" Umber said, narrowing his eyes. He mounted another step.

Fay leaned forward, and seemed ready to rush down the stairs, when a sound came from her right. She glanced sideways and clamped her teeth on her bottom lip. With her eyes glistening, she mouthed a silent word toward Umber. It might have been *help*. Then she rushed away, as Umber watched with his hand raised toward her.

Behind her, where the noise was heard, Hap saw a profile

appear. Eyes stared down, and then the face withdrew from sight. But it was there long enough for him to recognize Larcombe, the dangerous man who served Prince Loden.

Umber stared at the place where Fay had disappeared, until Tattersall pulled at his elbow. "Please, my lord. We mustn't keep the king waiting."

CHAPTER
12

A pair of tall doors angled together at the top, ten feet high. A guard stood before each, leaning on the shaft of an inverted battle-ax, but they stepped aside when they saw Tattersall approach.

Tattersall pushed one door open. "Your ward will stay here?" he said to Umber. It sounded more like an order than a question.

Umber had quietly seethed since the encounter with Fay, but he composed his expression and put a hand on Hap's shoulder. "Actually, he will join me for this audience."

Tattersall's head jolted back, hard enough to shake his jowls. "I hardly think the king—"

"Oh, never mind, Tattersall, send them in and get on with

it," came a voice from beyond the doors, weak and raspy but still bristling with authority. Tattersall's neck seemed to shrink. He extended an arm, guiding Umber and Hap into the room. When they were inside, Hap heard Tattersall's heels clicking down the hall at an urgent pace.

The walls of the room dazzled Hap's eyes. They were golden, reflecting the light of the candles that stood on gilded tables. The row of windows in the opposite had the purest glass Hap had seen, offering an undistorted view of the coastal city of Kurahaven, the market, and the glittering blue harbor. The room was filled with kingly trappings: soaring tapestries on the walls, woven carpets on the polished wooden floors, claw-foot chairs, and a silver-faced clock as tall as a man. When Hap saw the canopied bed at the far right, he realized that they had entered the king's bedchamber. *I don't belong here,* he thought, as a rush of doubt dizzied him. Umber leaned sideways, trying to peer through the gauzy purple curtains that surrounded the bed.

"Over here, you fools," came that creaky voice. Hap and Umber turned together to see King Tyrian sitting at a lavish desk made of dark red wood. Parchments were piled high, and a feathered pen stood at the ready. The stuffed head of an enormous hart loomed over him, staring with brown marble eyes.

"Your Majesty," Umber said. With his arms spread wide, he bowed low, putting a leg forward with his heel on the ground and toes up. He used one of those arms to prod Hap, who copied the bow as best he could. Hap looked up sheepishly, and was glad to see the king ignoring them to scratch the parchments with the pen. The feather was so long that it could have tickled his ear as it shook in his trembling hand.

Umber remained deep in his bow. "So good to see you, Your Highness . . ."

"Good to see me out of that accursed bed for once, you mean?" growled the king. "I should hope so." He rolled his hand in the air, which seemed to mean that they could stop bowing. When Hap straightened up, the king peered at him. Hap lowered his gaze to the floor, but he'd gathered his first impression of the monarch's face: red-rimmed eyes with dark satchels suspended below, hollowed cheeks, and wrinkled skin spattered with the discoloration of great age. The hair was yellowed gray and thin at the top, with a beard cropped straight across the bottom.

"Heard about this boy," Tyrian muttered. "And those green eyes."

"Your Majesty," Umber said. "Let me first offer my sincerest condolences for the tragedies that have—"

"Enough of that," Tyrian snapped. He slapped the desktop

with an open palm. "I've mourned for weeks. You weren't brought here to wring more pain from my heart."

Umber lowered his head. "My apologies, sire. Please tell me how I can serve you today."

The king smacked his lips wetly, and winced as he shifted in his seat. "What are we to do with you, Umber? You've done so much for the kingdom. And yet I wonder, have you done enough?"

"I don't understand, Your Highness."

Tyrian snorted like a bull. "Don't you. Hmph." He rolled his shoulders and arched his back, seeking some comfort that eluded him. "Tell me about that vile prisoner of yours. Does she still live?"

"Turiana," Umber replied. "Yes, Your Majesty. She is alive, but spends her days in a trance, unmoving."

"We should have executed her. It was a mistake to let her live."

"She is no danger to us now, my king," Umber said.

"We'll see. Remember our agreement—it's your neck on the chopping block if the sorceress escapes."

Umber massaged his throat. "I remember perfectly, Your Majesty. I've grown attached to my head—I'd hate for it to become unattached to me."

Tyrian's expression soured at the joke, but then he looked

past them to where Tattersall had just entered with a young man beside him. The man was barely out of his teens, if out of them at all, and he held a striped cat in his arms that stared around the room with sleepy eyes. Tyrian waved them closer, and Tattersall tapped the young man on the shoulder and pointed. The man walked past Umber and Hap and stood before the king.

"This fellow was on a ship of our navy that approached the Far Continent," Tyrian said. "His name is Burrell."

"Pleased to meet you, Mister Burrell," Umber said, extending a hand. Burrell did not respond, and kept his eyes downcast before the king.

"He can't hear you," Tyrian said. He picked up the parchment he'd written on and thrust it under Burrell's nose. Hap's sharp eyes read the words written in the unsteady hand: *Tell them what happened.*

Burrell shifted the cat to cradle it in one arm, and he took the note with his free hand and studied it carefully, laboring to comprehend. He finally nodded, and looked at Umber and Hap—taking a second, longer glance at Hap's eyes, of course. When he spoke, his voice swung between too loud and too soft, as if he wasn't sure how to temper his volume.

"I was on the *Gabrielle*," Burrell began. Hap saw the king sigh and turn toward a portrait on the wall over his desk. The subject was a woman with dark hair braided at the temples and embraced by a slender crown on top. She stood on a balcony overlooking the sea, with the folds of her blue-green dress rolling like waves, and the white fur on the hem draped at her feet like foam on sand. The face reminded Hap of poor Prince Galbus. He was lost in sad memory for a moment, and when he emerged he found that Burrell had plunged into his story.

". . . orders were to approach as close as we dared, and perhaps send a small boat in under cover of night, with a party of spies who might see what was happening. I was the carpenter's mate, understand, and so heard most of this from others in the crew." His voice had dropped low, and when he saw Umber leaning close to hear better, he raised his voice so loud that Umber winced and reared back.

"But we never got that far. We were miles from the coast when it happened. I was plugging a leak in the hold with the carpenter, so I didn't see anything. All of the sudden we heard shouts up top, and feet pounding, and the ship made a hard turn. We ran up the stairs to see what was about. When we got to the middle deck I heard my mates shouting, and the captain calling for more sail, and from high above—the crow's nest, I think—I heard someone shout, 'What is that thing?'"

Burrell pulled the cat close to his chest. The cat stretched, rubbed its cheek against the sailor's chin, and started to purr, unconcerned with the drama of the tale. "Then came a . . . a roar," Burrell said, growing louder still. "In the distance. Like thunder, or a great wave crashing, or some sea-beast I'd never heard before. But that was nothing next to what happened next. There was a sound I can't explain that consumed the ship . . . the world ending. It was the last thing I ever heard, except for the great bells still tolling in my skull.

"And the ship . . . it broke apart. A gap appeared right in front of me, all ragged and splintered. The carpenter . . . his name was Jake, and a fine carpenter he was too, and a better friend, and the sea flooded right into the middle of the boat, and I tried to grab Jake's hand but no force on earth could have held him . . . the sea just smashed him down like a fist. I wrapped my arm around a beam, and the ship turned upside down, and then the water came and tossed me, and a barrel rose from the deep and saved my life. I wrapped my arms around the barrel and it floated up . . . and a hand or two tried to grab me, but I was still deep underwater and afraid to die, and I kicked those hands away like a coward, and right before my lungs were ready to open up and drink the sea, I came up, and everything was smoke and fire.

"Pieces of the ship were all over, hissing and burning. The smoke stung my eyes and I couldn't see much. My mates were bobbing all around me, not alive, not any of them, except for one, and that was Pressley . . . he was floating near me, sprawled on the ship's wheel, or half of it anyway, and he was bleeding all over, the water gone pink all around him . . . I asked him, 'What happened? What was it?' And he answered me, but I didn't hear anything, and that's when I knew my ears were ruined . . . but he said it again, and I watched his lips, and I think he said *fire* and *monster*, or maybe it was all one thing: *fire monster*.

"Well, a big piece of the ship was right behind Pressley, and it rolled over on top of him, and it sank and took Pressley with it. Then the wind took the smoke away, and I looked back to see if the monster was still there . . . but I didn't see anything, except maybe for something big and dark, far away, heading back to the Far Continent, but I couldn't be sure. Then I looked around and called for my mates, but the only living thing was the ship's cat. I found her clinging to a broken spar, and I grabbed her."

And haven't let go since, Hap thought, watching Burrell pull the cat into a hug and close his eyes.

"I collected some of the pieces of the wreck and lashed them together," Burrell said.

"That will do," said Tyrian.

"The cat and I drifted for days, getting weaker by the hour," Burrell said.

Tyrian waved his hand in the air. "You there! We've heard enough!"

"A storm arose, and I thought I was done for."

Tattersall stepped forward and put his hand on Burrell's shoulder. Burrell's mouth snapped shut when he saw Tattersall with a finger to his lips. The king waved his hand toward the door, and Tattersall ushered the carpenter's mate out.

Umber watched him go with a sympathetic twist to his mouth. "A carpenter without ears is still a good carpenter. He can work for my shipbuilders if you—"

Tyrian interrupted, which seemed to be his habit. "You're not the only one who can treat people kindly, Umber. Our navy has a place for him." Umber bowed his head.

"So you have the story now," the king said. "He floated for days, but then a foreign trader picked him up, and he made his way back here. Umber, we have heard strange tales about the Far Continent—a new secrecy, foreign ships utterly destroyed near their waters, vast columns of black smoke over a hidden harbor. Loden proposed that we send a ship there, to land some spies. And now you've heard what happened to the *Gabrielle*—a ship of your design, I might add, and one of the fastest afloat. Tell me, Umber. There seems to be some terrible magic at work here. Do you know what this might be—this *fire monster?*"

Umber paused with his hand sliding down the side of his face. Hap was sure that the room had suddenly grown cooler. He shivered and felt the hair on his arms stand at attention.

Umber shook his head. "I'm afraid I don't, Your Highness."

The king grunted as he raised his hand to point at Umber. "We have asked you many times, Umber, to use your talents to improve the defense of our kingdom. Give us weapons to keep us safe. And over and over you refused. Now this strange threat has appeared . . ."

Tyrian went on, his voice rising as his temper flared, but Hap's attention was distracted. His eyes suddenly felt warm, and the chill left his body. Filaments appeared, flowing from the chest of every person in the room: the king, Umber, and himself. They were sharper and better defined than he'd seen before, as if he'd seen all the others through cloudy glass. And they glowed steadily, without the flickering of his earlier visions. Umber's thread swirled in tight circles before passing through the tall doors, and his did the same. Those threads were bright and filled with color, while the king's was thin and weak. And it was riddled with spots where its pale light dimmed into a black nothing. Hap had never seen anything like it. *The opposite of sparkling,* his mind suggested.

The thread reached from the desk to the bed, passing just an arm's length from where Hap stood. It was easy enough to slide over and raise his hand so that the thread passed through his palm.

As soon as he touched it, he heard the song of the filament. He had learned that each one had its own sound, ethereal and indefinable. There was a meaning locked inside, which he knew he must learn to interpret. *What are you telling me?* he wondered. A vague feeling was all he could gather, and he struggled to match words to the feeling: *Loss. Anguish. Regret. Despair. Acceptance.*

He focused his mind, concentrating, but a voice pierced through, and his head jolted up.

"I said, what are you doing there, boy? What's the matter with you!" Tyrian glared at him with his eyebrows fiercely angled. Umber covered his mouth with his hand, but the wrinkled corners of his eyes gave away his amused expression.

Hap's hand was still suspended chest-high. He let it flop to his side. "I am terribly sorry, Your Majesty. I felt a draft."

Tyrian stared, narrow-eyed. "Lord Umber, you keep the oddest company."

Umber smiled back, but his smile faded as he saw the king slump low in his chair, with his beard crumpled against his chest. His breath came out in a wheeze.

"That's enough," the king said, waving them off. "Leave me now."

"Are you feeling all right?" Umber asked. "Is there anything I can do?"

The king shook his head. "Tattersall should be waiting outside. Send him back in."

Umber bowed, and Hap bowed alongside him, and they walked to the door.

"One thing more, Umber," the king called after them.

Umber turned with his arms clasped behind him. "Yes, Your Majesty?"

Tyrian had the feathered pen in his hand, and he drew the feather between two fingers. "Is there a problem between you and my only living son?"

Umber hesitated, and his lips twitched. Hap's breath was trapped inside his lungs. He wondered if Umber was on the verge of blurting out his suspicions: that Loden was a murderer, consumed with a lust for power, and unworthy of the crown.

"None at all, Your Highness," Umber replied at last. "Or is there something I should know?"

The king's energy was fading, and his head wobbled. He jabbed the pen's tip in Umber's direction. "Loden will wear my crown, sooner than later. That must be obvious. It is to me, at any rate."

Umber raised his chin a fraction of an inch, and bowed

again. "May you stay strong and healthy, King Tyrian, and rule Celador wisely for years to come."

The king wheezed and waved Umber away once more.

"You saw the filaments again, didn't you?" Umber asked as they stepped outside the palace.

"Until a moment ago," Hap said.

Dodd was waiting beside Umber's carriage, across the circular courtyard. He saw them coming and climbed onto the driver's perch.

"Was it different this time?" Umber asked.

"Clearer than before," Hap replied. He looked back at the palace. "I saw King Tyrian's thread."

Umber arched an eyebrow. "And did it tell you anything?"

Hap stared at his palm. "Sort of. I still can't understand them . . . but I can sense things now."

Umber bent to look Hap in the eye. "What did you sense?"

Hap chewed on the corner of his thumbnail. He blinked and felt warmth pooling in his eyes. "I think the king will die very soon."

...tted out a particularly good rhyme today. I really ought to collect his verse in writing. It went: "In the caves beneath the Aerie/If you go there best be wary/for there dwell things...and

CHAPTER
13

Umber held his black ring high and uttered the foreign command: *Hurkhor.*

The inky stone door parted in the center and swung silently open, and they stepped into the Aerie, welcomed as usual by the rush of water that flowed through the bottom floor. This time they were greeted as well by the urgent voice of Lady Truden, standing at the top of the stairs engraved into the rock. "I thought you'd never get back!"

Umber raised his face. "Something the matter, Tru?"

Lady Truden's hands were clasped at her waist, but Hap noticed her thumbs tapping together at a frantic rate. "*She* is awake."

"She?"

"The guest!"

Hap's shoulders jolted. Umber's mouth formed a circle.

"What is she doing?" Umber asked her.

"Chanting."

"Chanting what, Tru?"

"Some horrid tongue that I don't understand! I just went down to check on her, as my duty requires, and she was out of her chair, standing in the middle of her cell. It nearly scared the life out of me."

Umber blew air from his cheeks and turned to Hap. "Er . . . Happenstance . . ."

Hap whipped his head from side to side. "Don't make me. Please don't make me."

"You have to come with me. For the usual reason, of course. But also . . . if you can understand that language . . ."

Hap hung his head, deflated. The last time he saw the sorceress, she tried to trick him into setting her free, and taunted him by informing him that he was dead. "Right. I guess you need me, don't you."

They paused in the stone corridor deep under the Aerie. The door before them was black iron, a little taller than it was wide, with burly hinges to hold its weight. Beyond that was Umber's prisoner, in a comfortable chamber behind sturdy bars.

"I can feel the cold out here," Hap whispered.

Umber nodded, staring at the door. "Me too." He exhaled into his palms and rubbed his hands together. The tunnels and caves were always cool, but there was a harsher, unnatural chill inside the sorceress's chamber that now penetrated the door and infected the corridor. Hap's muscles already ached from the cold.

Five cloaks lined with wool hung from pegs on the wall. Umber took two, passed the smaller one to Hap, and exhaled deeply when both had put them on. "Ready for this?"

"No."

Umber somehow managed a smile. "Me neither." He used his key to unlock the door, and heaved it open.

The cold struck Hap like a slap across the face. He squeezed his eyes nearly shut and drew his hands inside the sleeves. He pulled the hood up and pinched it under his chin, while Umber did the same. "Remember, the cold isn't real," Umber reminded him.

Umber stepped into the room, leaning as if into a stiff breeze, and Hap followed. The air seemed to push back, and the chill passed through the fabric as if he wore nothing at all. His fingers went numb, and then his toes.

She's gotten stronger, Hap thought. And there she was, a skeletal figure standing in the middle of her cell, amid the

splendid furniture that Umber had provided. She faced away from them—*Thankfully,* Hap thought—toward a corner of the room, with her head tilted back. Her arms were extended, her hands shoulder-high. Her bony wrists emerged from the draping sleeves of her gown, and the thin, knobby-knuckled fingers twitched, each to its own jerky rhythm. The fingers ended in overgrown nails that looked like ragged, twisted talons.

Little black spiders lived in the folds of her garments. When Hap saw her for the first time, the spiders had woven a veil that covered her face. Now her head and shoulders were shrouded in a silky membrane. Flies had been trapped and mummified in the silk, lined in rows like beading. Hap remembered that terrible face, with streams of dark blood coursing under translucent skin, and he was glad it was out of sight.

She was chanting, as Lady Truden said, in that silky, beautiful voice that was so ill-matched with the horror that produced it. *Vocturas timias, vocturas timias, ildrum tal runia . . .* Hap couldn't have named the language, but with his Meddler's ability to understand any tongue, he effortlessly translated: *Almost time, almost time, hear me, children, and know what must be done. . . .*

The chanting ceased, abruptly. Turiana's fingers fell still and the angle of her head changed, swiveling a fraction toward them. Umber looked at Hap with an eyebrow lifted high. "Turiana. You're awake," he said, quite loud.

A blast of cold washed over them, frigid to the point of pain. Hap's teeth chattered, and he blinked his eyes, afraid that they might freeze solid.

Turiana turned. Slowly. Her gown reached the floor, hiding her legs, but Hap had the terrible impression that she spun in place without moving her feet at all.

"This chill is not polite," Umber said. "Can you do something about that?"

The sorceress did not reply, but Hap felt the cold diminish, just a fraction.

Umber shifted from foot to foot. "A little better. Tell me, Turi. What's that you're saying? What are you up to?"

She lowered her arms and glided toward them until she was near the bars. Hap felt a powerful urge to bolt, like a rabbit from a wolf, but he pressed his trembling teeth together and willed himself to stay.

Through the partly transparent shroud, Hap saw her tiny shriveled eyes, deep in the twin craters of her skull. "Something approaches," the sorceress said. The silk across her jaw stretched and relaxed as she spoke.

Umber's fidgeting stopped. "Don't tease us, Turi. What do you mean? What approaches?"

"A menace. Something unknown to me. I cannot define it." She lifted her chin, and Hap heard the whispery sound of air drawn into the gaping holes where her nose once was. "But its eyes are here already. And the thing itself draws near."

Umber stared at her, and Hap could see his mistrust. "A menace to you, or to us?" Umber asked.

"A threat to all we know."

Umber's jaw tensed. "What are you up to, Turi? What is this chanting?"

Turiana wrapped her spindly fingers around a bar. Hap felt his stomach convulse as he looked at the translucent skin that barely concealed the bones and tendons of the fingers. It was unthinkable that this creature had once been, with the help of her talismans, a legendary beauty.

"You think I deceive you," she whispered. Her shrouded face drifted toward Hap. "Ask the little one, Umber. A Meddler knows what lies ahead."

"I . . . d-don't," Hap said, stammering from cold and terror together.

"Pity," she replied. She reached out, extending her arms between the bars. Hap knew that he and Umber were out of reach, but his blood ran colder still. "Release me, Umber. I have spent time enough in this dungeon."

"You know I cannot," Umber said.

Turiana opened her hand, palm out, with fingers spread wide. Umber stared at the hand, and then at her face. His eyes widened, and he stepped back. "Get out of my head, Turiana. I can feel you prodding around in there!"

The silk at Turiana's cheeks bulged, and Hap pictured the toothy skeletal grin underneath. Umber's hand clamped on his shoulder, and he almost shrieked. "We have to go," Umber said, and he pushed Hap ahead of him, out the door.

Umber slammed the door and slumped against the wall. "I don't know how, but her powers have grown. . . . Maybe she's been resting up. Or whatever she's sensed out there has given her this urgency." He thumped his temple with the heel of his hand. "She was searching my mind, looking for something. Feels like ants wandering across your brain." He wriggled out of the cloak and hung it from the peg. Hap did the same, and they hurried down the subterranean passage until the sensation of cold was gone.

"The chanting . . . did you understand any of that?" Umber asked.

Hap told Umber what he'd heard. Umber plucked at an eyebrow and stared back toward the iron door. "Is she plotting against us? Trying to warn us? I don't know—but it worries me, her digging into my mind like that."

Hap jumped from foot to foot to drive away the chill. "She can't get out, can she?" He was thinking about the king's warning, that Umber's life depended on her remaining a prisoner.

"The bars are strong. It would take a battering ram to knock that door in. And I have the key. So no, I don't think she'll be getting out."

Hap nodded, eager to believe it. But her words haunted his brain: *Almost time, almost time.* "That menace she was talking about . . . I wonder if she meant the troll we saw in the caverns."

Umber's head rocked back. "Troll? What troll?"

CHAPTER
14

Hap led Umber through the blackness.
It was Umber's idea to approach this way, to take advantage
of Hap's ability to see in the dark. Umber carried a jar of
glimmer-worms, but he'd thrown a cloth over it to hide their
light.

As they approached the portcullis, Hap caught a whiff of
decay and pinched his nose. "Smell that?" Umber whispered,
squeezing Hap's shoulder.

"Yes," Hap said nasally. He led Umber behind one of the
pillars of rock that stood before the gate. "We're here," he
whispered.

Umber stared blindly. "Can you see anything? Is it there?"

Hap leaned sideways to peer at the portcullis and had to

stifle a gasp. The troll was sitting in the open, with its broad back against the iron bars. "It's there."

"What does it look like?"

Hap took a longer look. The troll wore a shredded hide around its waist. It held a broken piece of tapered stone in one hand, and it lifted it and let it drop, stabbing lazily at the cavern floor. It didn't seem to hear their whispers.

"It's sitting against the bars, so I can only see its back," he told Umber in a hush. "It's huge—maybe nine feet tall and six wide. The skin's gray and lumpy, with scars all over."

"Old or fresh?"

Hap took another peek. "Fresh, I think."

A low growl issued from the troll's throat, and it sounded like *charrrrr*. Umber smiled and sucked in air. He bounced on his heels as his excitement mounted. "Fresh scars! Do you suppose it fought another troll and was cast out from its pack?" He reached for the cloth that covered the jar of glimmer-worms. "I have to see it!"

As soon as the soft light of the glimmer-worms appeared, Hap heard the troll's great bulk scrape against the stout bars of the portcullis. He leaned out and saw that it had whirled around and was grasping a bar with one enormous, clawed hand and wielding the stone dagger with the other. Its legs were short and bowed, its arms thick and long with knotty muscles. The face was brutal, with a twisted nose and a wide mouth with ragged teeth slanting in all directions. The eyes were tiny pools of quicksilver with black dots in the centers, and those specks moved to follow Umber as he stepped into the open.

The troll edged back. It looked ready to turn and run, but Umber spoke in a soothing, encouraging voice. "Wait—don't go away. Nobody will harm you."

The troll lowered its head, and its lip arched high on one side of its mouth. It spoke again, a rumble that turned to a growling purr: *Charrrrrr.*

"Maybe we should call you Charrly," Umber said in a hush. He advanced in dreamy, gentle steps, holding the jar high. "What a specimen you are! What brings you here, Charrly? Are you lost? Are you hungry?"

The troll angled its head to one side and then the other. It sank into a crouch as Umber approached. Umber was entranced by the enormous creature, eyeing it from head to toe as he cooed. When Umber was barely two strides away, Hap saw the muscles in the troll's legs go taut. Before he could shout a warning, the troll sprang up and thrust its long arm between the bars.

CHAPTER
15

The troll's claws raked the air in front of Umber's face. Umber barely moved. He had sized up the troll's arms, and seemed sure that he was out of reach. The troll snorted and grunted as it struggled in vain to grasp him.

"Come on out, Hap, and meet Charrly," Umber said. Hap took a deep, fortifying breath and stepped out from his hiding place. He nearly dove back when the troll's face swiveled his way and it hissed. The appearance of a second person seemed to worry the beast. It looked around for more intruders, and then it pulled its arm back from between the bars and loped into the caverns beyond the portcullis, with a single fierce glance over its shoulder before it vanished. From the depths of the passage, its voice rumbled out again:

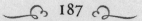

Charrrr.

"Well. What do you think of that, Hap?"

"I think these bars better be strong."

"No worries there," Umber said. "They can't be broken down. And they can't be raised, except by that winch in the alcove. The winch can't be turned unless it's unlocked. And I have the only key." Umber tapped the magical key he wore around his neck.

"There are other creatures in those caverns, aren't there?" Hap asked, staring into the dark passage.

Umber nodded. "Yes. Foul flesh-eating things. When Turiana ruled here, she summoned them from the depths to be her servants."

"But you sent them away, didn't you? When you stole Turiana's talismans."

"That's right. I sent them back to the depths. And let's hope that's where they've stayed."

Hap was in the kitchen with his hands wrapped around a mug of hot tea that Balfour had brewed. He closed his eyes and took a long, deep breath.

"Feeling all right?" Balfour asked.

"I was thinking about the sorceress," Hap said. "It scares me just knowing she's down there."

Balfour snorted. "She'd give a snake the creeps."

Hap heard a familiar pounding of feet come downstairs and approach the grand hall, and he braced himself. "This can't be good," he muttered.

The kitchen door burst open and Umber charged inside. It was hard to tell if he was panicked or delighted. "Where's Oates?"

"Asleep in his room, if I had to guess," Balfour replied.

Umber capered in place. "Hap, get Oates, wherever he is, and meet me on the terrace. Tell him to bring an ax!" And then Umber was gone, and his feet assaulted the stairs once more.

Hap and Balfour looked at each other with both their mouths curving sharply down at the corners. "Trouble at the palace, trouble below, trouble above," Balfour said. "My dear boy, we are surrounded."

Hap's fist thumped on Oates's door. "Mister Oates! Umber needs you on the terrace! Bring an ax!" He heard a mumbled reply, followed by a clatter of iron: Oates reaching into the stack of weapons he kept standing in the corner of his room and knocking them all over. The big man opened the door with such violence that the hinges nearly tore loose. In his hand was an ax that no ordinary man could lift.

Balfour stood back so that Oates wouldn't trample him, but Hap sprinted ahead of them both and took the stairs seven steps at a time with his powerful legs. At the top of the landing he saw a sky filled with inky gray clouds that looked ready to weep. With a final stride he soared onto the terrace.

Umber stood there with one hand plowed into his unruly hair, staring at the tree that had sprouted from the thorny nut. The tree was already twice his height. It looked as if it were twisting as it grew—its pale green bark was grooved like a towel being wrung dry. Inch-long thorns jutted from the trunk and the leafless branches that spread wide and loomed overhead.

"How?" Hap said. "How could it grow so fast?"

Umber shook his head and laughed. "Quite a specimen, isn't it? But those roots have me worried." Already two of Umber's finest plants had been strangled in their planters by the roots of the thorny tree. Now another root was closing in on Umber's beloved tree of many fruits—it had slithered up the side of the planter, and its tip was at the edge like a crooked finger.

"I tried moving it myself, but it's strong," Umber said.

They heard Oates's heavy steps, and a clang of metal as his ax struck the stone wall. He reached the top with the ax poised in two hands, ready for assault. "What?" he cried, still

blinking away his sleepiness. "What is it? Oh!" He spotted the thorny tree, and as he stared at the spreading branches and wandering roots, the head of his ax drooped until it rang against the terrace floor.

"Put the ax down for now, Oates," Umber said. "Can you can pull that root away from my fruit tree? I can't bear to lose that one."

Oates grimaced and laid the ax on the ground with obvious reluctance. "I think I ought to toss the whole infernal tree off the roof." He spat on his hands and rubbed them together.

Hap heard wheezing behind him. Balfour had just made it to the terrace, and he stood with his chest heaving. He reached for Hap's shoulder to steady himself.

Oates wrapped his meaty hands around the root and pulled. Hap had rarely seen Oates struggle with a feat of strength, but the big fellow's face turned purple as he strained. He braced his foot against the planter and heaved. Spittle flew from his gritted teeth. Slowly he was able to bend the root backward. He took three deep breaths, freshened his grip, and tugged again. Suddenly his face turned into a mask of pain, and he cried out, pulling his hands off the root.

"It stung me!" Oates shouted. He held his hands up for Umber to see. Hap saw dots of blood on his palms. Umber's mouth puckered and he stepped closer to examine the root.

"Thorns," he said, pointing at the place where Oates had gripped the root. "But only here."

"They weren't there a minute ago," Oates said.

"No, they weren't," Umber said. His eyes gleamed with avid curiosity. "It defended itself! You're all right, though, aren't you?"

Oates pressed his lips to the wounds. His reply was muffled. "It stings."

At the solemn pace of a slug, the root bent back toward the planter where the tree of many fruits stood. The tip began to burrow into the dirt.

"The ax, then," Umber said, with a touch of apprehension.

"My pleasure," Oates replied. He seized the ax and held it just above the length of the root that was flat on the terrace floor. Umber watched intently with his fingers interlaced and his thumbs tapping together. Hap felt Balfour's hand tugging on his shoulder, and he gladly retreated a step. He wasn't sure what to expect, but his stomach had knotted nevertheless.

Oates brought the ax down in a blur. It bit deep, nearly severing the root. When Oates yanked the blade free, liquid boiled from the wound—thick, glistening, yellow and pink, like something infected and poisonous. A sharp odor stung Hap's nose a moment later. Oates smelled it too, and he cried out in disgust: "Eeww!"

Umber pulled the collar of his shirt up to cover his nose and kept observing. The wounded root rose slowly off the ground, with its nearly severed end dangling, and hovered waist-high. Umber's eyes traced the root back to the trunk, and his mouth fell open.

The whole tree shuddered and wriggled. The trunk untwisted a fraction, and twisted back again. The bark squealed and the branches quaked.

A stiff wind washed over the terrace. Hap heard a rushing sound, and realized that it was rain sweeping across Kurahaven Bay, far below. The storm arrived moments later, a few fat drops that turned to a downpour. The deluge had a soothing effect on the thorn tree. The writhing of the trunk and the quivering of the limbs ended, and the wounded root slumped to the ground and fell still.

The rain soaked their clothes, but nobody moved. Hap felt it dripping from the end of his nose. Umber turned and grinned widely, with his thumb pointing back over his shoulder. "Now *that* was interesting. Looks like the show's over for the moment, though."

Hap shook his head and raised a finger, pointing at the nearest horizontal branch. Near the end, a bulge had appeared, growing out of the smooth bark until it was the size of a fist. It split open, and a blossom unfolded within a minute. Its petals were the color of bruised skin, with edges like torn paper, and they surrounded what looked like a mass of dead worms.

"That," said Oates, "is the ugliest flower I've ever seen."

Umber went up on the tips of his toes and put his nose close to the blossom. "Doesn't smell any prettier," he reported. Hap's stomach soured, as the stench reached his nose. Remarkably, Umber went back for a second whiff. "Smells like rot, actually."

More flowers began to emerge on other branches. The rain fell harder, splattering the stone, and the wind whistled through the stony corners of the terrace. Dimly, amid all that noise, Hap heard another sound that made him turn an ear to the city. "Listen," he said, raising his voice.

A bell was tolling; the great bell in the palace tower; the largest bell with the deepest, gravest voice. It clanged slowly, with seconds passing before it boomed again and faded to a gloomy drone. Umber forgot the thorn tree and its foul blossoms. He drifted like a ghost across the terrace, his face unmoving except to blink away the rain, and stood at the balcony, staring at the palace. In the buildings that surrounded the city, flickering points of candlelight appeared.

Hap didn't have to ask what the ringing meant. He'd heard it before, and not so long ago. That bell meant death—the death foretold by the filament he'd seen. And the news was doubly grim, because Prince Loden was going to be King Loden.

As he thought about that, the deep, solemn knell began to sound like a word.

Wrongggg . . .

Wrongggg . . .

Wrongggg . . .

CHAPTER
16

The rain ended but the gloom lasted the
day and through the night and into the morning that followed,
as criers and couriers on horseback clattered out of the palace
gates and into the streets with the news. It was still dark a day
later, when all of Kurahaven lined the harbor road for the
funeral procession.

Hap stood with Umber and the others on the steps of the
Umber Shipping Company, at the foot of the great columns
that lined the building. He saw the procession approach with
the king's guard leading the way. The king's favorite horse, a
towering black beast with an empty saddle, was led by a grim
young page on foot. A team of white horses came next, pulling
a funeral carriage that had seen far too much use recently. Hap

felt something roil deep in his gut when he saw Tyrian's corpse, his body wreathed by flowers, and his gray face turned to the gray sky. He was dressed as a warrior, in mail and light armor, with sword and helmet by his side. Across his chest lay his shield with the four-part coat of arms: crown, sun, mountains, and seashell. As he passed, the people kneeled and lowered their heads, and men held their hats to their hearts. Mournful cries filled the streets, echoed by the gulls that wheeled above.

"Look at Loden—the perfect mourning son," Balfour muttered. Umber peered sideways at Balfour with a finger tapping his lips.

Hap saw Loden walking behind the funeral carriage, leading his own horse. If the prince was not truly grief-struck, then he was playing his part to perfection. He trudged along, holding his trembling chin up bravely. There was a handkerchief bunched in one hand, and he used it to dab an eye.

As he walked, a ragged gap appeared in the clouds above. The rays of the sun beamed through the misty air and cast Loden and the procession in golden light. A murmur passed through the crowd. Loden turned his face to the sun and closed his eyes, accepting the warm rays with a sad smile.

"That's no omen, you murderous swine," Balfour whispered, his face twisted with contempt. Umber coughed and gave him a gentle elbow to the ribs.

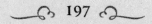

Loden opened his eyes. He must have realized where the procession was, because he turned toward the shipping company and searched the steps until he spotted Umber. When their gazes met, one of Loden's eyebrows lifted, and a smirk teased the corner of his mouth. Hap heard Umber take a deep breath and hold it. Finally Loden moved on, nodding solemnly at the people in the crowd who wept and called his name.

"So is Loden king now?" Hap asked, as Umber took a seat in the carriage.

"Not until the coronation," Umber said.

"When is that abomination?" asked Balfour. He grabbed a handle to steady himself, because the carriage rocked as Oates climbed in.

"Tonight. And I wasn't invited, by the way." Umber rapped the side of the carriage. "All set, Dodd." The carriage rolled, and soon Hap felt the familiar tilt of the causeway under their wheels, pressing him against the back of his seat.

Long before they reached the Aerie, Dodd called to the horses, and the carriage slowed. Hap leaned out to see why they'd stopped and saw a couple of boys, years younger than him, sitting in the middle of the causeway. They were beside a small cart filled with straw. It was harnessed to a donkey, but the beast had apparently suffered an unexpected death and

was sprawled on its side, blocking the way. This circumstance had driven both of the boys to tears. They kneeled side by side, mashing their palms into their eyes, mouths open and bawling. Perhaps because the river was nearby, passing under the causeway and splashing thunderously into the bay, they hadn't heard the carriage approach.

Dodd called down through the carriage window. "Mister Oates, I think we're going to need you."

Oates grumbled and stepped out.

A sharp exhalation whistled out of Umber's nose. "I'm in no mood for delays after that procession." He followed Oates out of the carriage.

Hap leaned out to watch. The boys finally noticed that someone had arrived, and the older boy punched the younger one's shoulder to alert him. They wiped their tears and scrambled to their feet with chests heaving, and the younger one kicked the older one in the shins to repay him for the punch.

"Boys, what's happened here?" Umber said. The boys looked up at him and gawked at the towering bulk of Oates.

"Our stupid donkey died," the older boy said, pointing at the beast. "She just dropped right there."

"I mourn with you," Umber said. "But why are you on this road?"

199

The boys looked at each other. They grimaced and gulped and fidgeted from foot to foot. The younger one spoke next, and his words tumbled out, blurring together. "We were bringing something to that place up there, where a man lives, and he's supposed to pay us for what we're bringing."

The older boy reached over and pinched the younger one's arm. "You always say too much," he said out of the side of his mouth. His eyes, big and bulging like a toad's, were locked on the intimidating figure of Oates.

Umber scratched the tip of his nose. He spoke kindly to the boys, but Hap sensed a hint of impatience. "Who is this man you're looking for?"

"His name is Hum-ber," said the older boy, keeping an inch of his brother's flesh between his thumb and finger. The younger boy lashed out with an elbow that jabbed his brother under the armpit.

"Well, that is me. I am Lord Umber, of the Aerie." A duet of gasps was the instant reply. Umber looked at the hay sticking out of the cart. "But what are you bringing me? I don't have a crying need for hay."

The younger boy pulled his arm from his brother's pinch and fired out a hailstorm of words. "The man told us you'd pay us, and so we took the cart without asking our dad, and came all these miles from our farm, and now you have to pay us, and plenty, too, because we need a new donkey, because our dad's going to be so mad that we took it, and it dropped dead all of a sudden in the middle of the road!"

Umber groaned and rubbed his hand up the length of his face. "Right. And what a charming pair you are. Just answer this, will you: What is it you've brought me, and what man told you to bring it?"

The older boy covered his brother's mouth with his palm. "Well . . . you see . . . Lord Hum–ber . . . the *man* is the thing."

Umber's mouth silently echoed the last five words. His brow contorted and snapped up. He looked back at the cart.

The younger boy pried his brother's hand off his mouth. "But we think he might've dropped dead too!"

Umber stepped to the cart and raked the straw with his fingers. Hap couldn't see what was revealed beneath. Umber's hand floated up and landed on the top of his head. "Happenstance," he called. "Would you come over here, please?"

CHAPTER
17

Hap stepped out of the carriage with his heart thumping against his chest. He glanced up at Dodd in the driver's perch. Dodd lifted his chin, a nod of encouragement, and returned his anxious gaze to the cart. *He can see what's inside from up there,* Hap thought, and he gulped. Dreading every step, he approached the cart. When the younger boy got a closer look at Hap, he elbowed his brother in the ribs and whispered, "Lookit his eyes!"

"Is this who I think it is?" Umber said. He had pushed the straw aside to reveal the man who lay senseless in the cart. When Hap looked, his knees buckled, and Umber gripped his shoulder to steady him.

The man had a narrow strip of cloth tied across his eyes.

The fabric was stained and crusted with blood. More blood had flowed from under the cloth and caked around his ears and nose. The long hair was a strange color—so white that it was almost clear. But a closer look showed flecks of brilliant color inside the hair. Hap had seen such hair only twice: in his own rapidly multiplying strands, and on the head of the one who'd created him.

"It's him. It's Willy Nilly," Hap said, barely moving his lips.

"Are you sure?" Umber asked.

Hap looked again at the prominent but delicate nose and the cleft in the long chin. "I'm sure. Even the clothes are the same." He leaned heavily on the side of the cart.

Umber turned to the boys, just as the younger one seized the older one's earlobe and pulled it like taffy. "Stop that fighting at once, you imps, or this large, angry man will throw you into the sea," Umber snapped. Their horror-struck faces turned toward Oates, who cracked his knuckles and flashed a menacing grin. The boys straightened and froze.

"Why does that man have a bloody cloth over his eyes?" Umber asked.

"He hasn't got eyes," said the younger.

"Somebody took 'em!" cried the elder.

Hap's breath hitched, and his stomach convulsed. Umber reached for the cloth with his nose wrinkled and his lip twisted on one side. Hap turned away before Umber peeled the cloth away from one eye, but he heard Umber suck in air and let out an *ugh*.

Umber wiped both sides of his hand on his pants. "Where did you find him?" he asked the boys.

"Near the great forest," the older boy said. "That's where our farm is. We heard him crying out, and he was walking around blind, you know, like this." The boy closed his eyes and staggered in place with his hands groping the air before him.

Umber frowned at the boy. "The great forest—it must have taken you two days to get here." The brothers nodded. "And you didn't tell your father you were going? Well, of course he'll be angry. Now, this man in the cart—he told you to bring him to me?"

"That's right!" blurted the younger brother. "He said you'd give us a bag of gold if we did, 'cause you're a wealthy man, he said just that!"

Hap stared down at Willy Nilly's face, wreathed by straw. "Lord Umber . . . is he . . . ?"

Umber bit his bottom lip. He reached into the cart and put two fingers to Willy's neck, close to his ear. With his eyes staring at nothing, he waited, concentrating.

"He's weak, but . . ." Umber would have said more, but

Willy stirred just then, turning his head. His jaw slackened, and a shallow breath rattled out. Umber turned back to the boys. "And why is he packed in straw?"

The younger one aimed a finger at his brother. "It was his idea."

The older one tucked his head between his shoulders. "Um. I didn't want nobody to ask why we had a sick man with no eyes."

Umber squeezed the back of his neck and nodded. "That logic has merit." The boy smiled tentatively, clearly not understanding the words. "Oates," Umber said, "will you move that beast aside for the moment, and can I trouble you to haul the cart up to the gatehouse? We'd better take Willy up to the Aerie and stuff him with medicine."

The boys' mouths turned into gaping round holes as Oates took the harness off the donkey and hoisted it as easily as most people would lift a cat, setting it gently aside. He stood between the shafts of the cart, grabbed one in each hand, and pulled it up the causeway without a hint of exertion.

"You two," Umber called to the boys. He pointed at the carriage, then seemed to think better of his idea and flapped his hand toward the Aerie. "Just walk up there, will you? I'll deal with you later."

The boys skipped up the causeway until they caught up

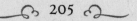

to Oates, and then irritated him immensely by walking just behind him and gawking the rest of the way.

Dodd chuckled and shook his head. "I am so pleased that I have no offspring."

Umber ruffled Hap's hair. "They're not all so bad. Now, Dodd, take the carriage to the medical university and bring the sisters back to the Aerie, as quick as you can."

Balfour stepped out of the room and closed the door softly behind him. He held a bucket of bloody rags in water. "Cleaned him up the best I could," he said, looking grim. "He never stirred."

"The sisters are here," Lady Truden announced. She stood at the top of the stairs at the end of the corridor with her chin raised high, and stepped sideways to clear a path. The physicians entered: the women whom Umber had called the sisters.

The sisters were short and round-faced, with upturned noses and bright blue eyes. They dressed identically in billowing wheat-colored dresses with wide red sashes around the waist. Their blond hair was tucked under plain white headdresses. Each had a large wicker basket hanging from a bent arm. They smiled cheerily up at Lady Truden, who stared impassively down, more than a head taller than either.

"Lord Umber," said one, and they both bent a knee.

"My friends," Umber replied. "Happenstance, these are the best of the healers from my school of medicine: Laurel and Lily."

"Laurel is me," said the plumper of the two, smiling at Hap. "And this is Lily." The other sister lifted a hand and waved. Their smiles were open and honest, and their cheeks filled with color.

"Hello," Hap said.

"You look starved but well, Lord Umber," Laurel said, looking closely at Umber's face.

"I'm fine," Umber told her. "But there is another patient here for you, and you must do everything you can for him."

Laurel dipped her head. "And of course we will. Where will we find him?"

Umber turned the knob and swung the door open. "Right here."

The sisters smiled and bustled inside. Umber did the thing Hap was dreading: He motioned with a twirl of his hand for Hap to follow him into the room.

The sisters set their baskets on the floor and stepped up to a basin that Balfour had readied. They poured warm water from a kettle into the basin, lathered their hands with soap, scrubbed furiously, rinsed, and dried their hands on clean towels. Only then did they approach the bed where Willy Nilly lay covered

by a white blanket. There was a fresh cloth over his eyes, with orange-brown stains already seeping through. Laurel peeled the cloth back. Hap looked away, but not before he'd glimpsed the raw cavities where bright green eyes should have nestled.

"Such cruelty," Laurel said. Beside her, Lily shook her head and closed her eyes, squeezing out a teardrop that tumbled down her cheek.

Hap wondered if she'd feel such pity if she knew what Willy Nilly had done. *The boy I was drowned because of him,* he thought. *And he probably murdered another Meddler to resurrect me.* Hap had spent many of his solitary nights stoking his anger for this strange man.

"Is he a friend?" Laurel asked, as her sister gently held her wrist to Willy's forehead.

"An acquaintance," Umber replied.

Acquaintance, Hap thought bitterly. He'd made that acquaintance only twice. Once deep in the subterranean city where Hap had been left for Umber to discover. And next on the islet when Hap had been lost at sea. On both occasions, Willy was mysterious, mocking, and strangely lighthearted, with a maddening songlike quality to his voice.

But despite all that, to Hap's surprise, his heart softened at the sight of Willy's maimed face.

Lily looked at Laurel, and with both hands made intricate

gestures in the air, finally putting her hand to her own forehead and then yanking it away as if it were painful to touch.

Laurel nodded. "Yes. And what shall we give him for his fever?"

Lily can't speak, Hap realized. He watched her open her basket, revealing dozens of colorful ceramic jars within. She ran her fingers across the cork lids of the jars, and then extracted one and held it up for Laurel to see. Laurel smiled and nodded. "And the willow extract as well, I think. But first let us clean his wounds."

"When I first heard of the sisters, Hap," Umber said, "they were midwives and herbalists, living in the hills above Kurahaven."

"Some called us witches," Laurel said. "Can you imagine!"

Umber laughed. "Those insults came from the quacks and blood-letters that thought of themselves as physicians. But things are improving, Hap. When I established our university of medicine, I found that, for the most part, the country healers were quicker to embrace modern medical ideas."

"Modern, indeed," Laurel said. She lifted another jar from the basket and held it up for Hap to see. This jar was made of clear glass and filled with brown powder. A serious look transformed her cheerful face. "Young man, you have witnessed many of Lord Umber's innovations, I'm sure. His ships. His buildings. His printing press. His symphonies. But I would sacrifice them all for the medicine in this jar. With this I can heal folk whose blood is fouled and whose infections would lead to suffering and death. Already I have seen it save hundreds of lives. This is the wonder of all wonders, but there is nothing magical about it. And do you know where this medicine comes from?"

Hap shook his head, impressed into silence.

Laurel smiled again. "The mold that spoils your bread and fruit!" She moved abruptly to help her sister, who had turned Willy's head to the side to pour a clear liquid into the ragged wounds. The liquid turned to a bubbling froth, faintly hissing. Willy moaned softly, and Laurel took his hand between hers. For a moment Hap thought the Meddler might wake, but his body went limp once more, even as Lily dabbed at the grisly sockets with her cloth.

"Antibiotics," Umber said to Hap. "That's what those medicines are called. It's not a simple matter—impurities are still a concern. But we're getting better." He stepped closer to the bed and looked down at Willy. "Will he live?"

Lily looked at Laurel and gave the slightest shrug of her shoulders. Laurel turned to Umber. "We aren't sure. He is very ill."

"Anything you can do . . . please do," Umber said. "I am most eager to speak to this man."

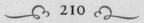

through the use of talismans that enh...

their innate magical abilities. One of th...

...ost notorious of these objects was a stone...

...nown by many names, including the Se...

...Stone and the Eye of the Warlock, wh...

...wed its wearer t...

CHAPTER
18

Umber and Hap walked down to the grand hall to find Oates holding the brothers by the fronts of their shirts, one in each hand. Their legs dangled, kicking wildly at air. Balfour watched from his seat at the table with his head wagging from side to side.

"They were fighting again," Oates said when he spotted Umber.

Umber glared at the boys with his fists on his hips. "All right, you twitchy little monsters. What are your names?" They started to answer, but Umber waved his hands to cut them off. "On second thought, I don't even want to know that much. Listen: I wasn't the one who promised a reward, but I'll give you one anyway."

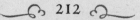

"Hooray!" cried the older boy, flapping his arms like a bird.

"And you'll get a ride home, too, because your parents must be sick with worry, and because I don't think you can make it that far without killing each other. Balfour, would you make the arrangements?"

"The idea fills me with joy," Balfour said.

"Excellent. Now, Hap, why don't we find out what that overgrown weed on the terrace is up to?"

"I wish Fendofel could see this," said Umber.

The thorn tree's branches had sprouted thousands of narrow, pointed leaves. The reeking flowers had withered, their petals dropped to reveal small, flesh-colored fruits. Umber reached up and gently pinched one. "Wonder if these are edible?"

"I wouldn't eat it," Hap said. Everything about the tree unnerved him, even those egg-shaped fruits.

Umber stared at the roots that sprawled across the terrace floor like frozen serpents. "At least it stopped trying to kill my other plants." He took a second glance at one of the fruits, and leaned closer, almost touching it with his nose. "I might be wrong . . . but I think this fruit is growing, even as we speak. We'd better keep an eye on this. Hap, would you take a look tonight, while the rest of us are sleeping?"

Hap looked out the twin windows of his tiny room, into the night. Below lay what was left of the ancient castle Petraportus. There was a new tomb inside those ruins. Umber had it made for the fisherman and his wife, the reclusive pair that had turned out to be Hap's brokenhearted parents. It was Willy Nilly's fault they were dead. Willy had never laid a hand on them, but the events that he set in motion years before had led to their deaths. And wasn't that how Meddlers worked: indirectly?

Now Willy was a few doors away, close to death himself. Hap felt the urge to burst in and shake him into consciousness. *Why me?* he wanted to scream. *How dare you make me one of you! And now you and Umber want me to leave this world and save another. But I never asked for these powers. I don't want this burden!*

The hour was late, and he figured that everyone else was asleep. He eased the door to his room open and stepped quietly into the hall. Every other door was closed, except for one threshold that still cast a rectangle of golden light. When he reached it, he saw Willy Nilly's still and senseless form. The Meddler's face was pale, his jaw slack, his breathing raspy and labored.

Laurel was sleeping on a second bed in the room with her face to the wall. Lily, the silent one, was dozing in a chair beside Willy. Something alerted her to Hap's presence, and her eyes fluttered open. She smiled and put a hand over her mouth to cover a yawn.

Hap waved but couldn't smile. He pointed to Willy. "Has he woken up at all?"

Lily shook her head.

Hap gnawed on the knuckle of his thumb for a moment. "Do you think . . . he's going to live?"

Lily stared at the Meddler with her lips in a pout. Then she touched her hand to her temple and shrugged.

Hap could think of nothing else to say. Finally he waved. "Good night." She smiled back, and he left the room and took the stairs to the terrace.

In the darkness his gifted eyes saw the thorn tree. The roots and branches hadn't grown, but the fruits had swollen to the size of skulls, and the branches drooped with their weight. Hap's finger jabbed at the air as he counted them. *Eleven.*

He walked among the other plants of the terrace, and past Umber's little tower, a cylinder on top of the soaring slab of the Aerie. At the corner of the terrace he leaned over with his forearms flat on the stone railing and stared out at the bay. His eyes widened, and he sprang straight up and laughed with delight.

The great leviathan Boroon was floating a hundred yards away, gently swirling his enormous fins to hold him in place.

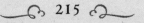

The barge was strapped to his back as usual. Hap leaned over, trying to spot Nima, the amphibious captain of the craft. He was even more surprised to see her swimming through the water, into the space between the Aerie and Petraportus. She reached the crude bridge of stone that connected the two and climbed onto the rocks.

Hap hopped from one foot to the other, grinning madly. He cupped his hands around his mouth, trying to project his voice in a narrow beam that would not wake the others. "Nima!"

The night was so still that she heard him. She looked up, unable to see in the dark as Hap could, and waved in his direction. "Let me in," she called up.

"Of course!" Hap called down. He soared to Umber's tower in a single, joyful leap, and pounded on the locked door. "Lord Umber! Wake up!"

A squeal of shutters came from above, and Umber stuck his head out, grinding the back of his hand against the narrow slits of his eyes. "Hap? What—something happen?"

"Nima is here! She's coming up to the Aerie!"

Umber blinked and managed to open one eye entirely. "Coming up to the . . . she's on *land*?"

Hap cocked his head to one side. "Well . . . yes. Hurry, we have to let her in!"

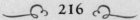

Umber ducked back inside. Hap heard the thump of his feet on the inner stairs, and then his door flew open and he stumbled out, pulling a pair of trousers up under his nightshirt. "This must be important. Nima hates the land—more than you hate the sea!"

Nima followed them into the grand hall, looking ill at ease with every step. She took a seat at the table, but perched on the edge, never sitting back in comfort.

Umber squeezed her wrist. "What is it, Nima?"

She put her hands on the table with her fingers spread wide, as if she felt unsteady in a world that did not move or roll beneath her feet. Hap couldn't help but look at the webbing that connected her fingers as high as the knuckles. "There is something strange in the sea," she said. "To the west."

Umber glanced at Hap and nodded. "Near the Far Continent?"

"No," she said. "Much closer than that. I . . . wish I could tell you more, but I have not seen it. Boroon *heard* it as we were returning to Kurahaven with cargo from Ornast. The thing was many miles away, but Boroon still heard a sound like nothing he has ever known, a constant roar of thunder in the water, thumping like a heart. I have never seen Boroon so afraid. He refused to go any closer. And it was beyond the horizon, so I could not see what it was." She folded her arms tight against her body and fixed her dark-eyed gaze on Umber. "Do you know what it was, Lord Umber? This terrible thing roaming the sea?"

Umber sat with his chin in his hand and a finger sawing his bottom lip. "I don't, I'm afraid." He turned to Hap. "The same thing as that sailor's fire monster, do you suppose?"

Hap squirmed in his seat. The thought had crossed his mind. "Nima, could you tell which way it was going?"

She shook her head. "What is this fire monster?"

"We don't know much about it," Umber said, "except that it has destroyed more than one ship, with unbelievable violence. And it seemed to come from the Far Continent—which means that it is crossing the sea. It would be nice to know where it's heading."

"Can't you send your friend and his flying craft to find it?" Nima asked.

"Pilot?" Umber smiled crookedly and rolled his eyes. "He only comes to me when he needs money, and I paid him a fortune on our last adventure. We won't be seeing him or his spidery crew anytime soon."

Nima stood abruptly. Hap could see tension in the flare of her nostrils and the muscles of her jaw. "I must get back to Boroon," she said. What she really meant, Hap knew, was that she needed to return to the supple embrace of the sea.

Umber popped out of his seat. "What will you do next? Where will you be?"

"I have a rendezvous with one of your ships offshore, to unload my cargo," she replied. Her shoulders trembled, and she rubbed one arm with the other hand. "After that I await another assignment from Hoyle."

"Be careful," Hap told her. "I mean, stay away from that thing. Whatever it is."

She smiled despite her nerves. "Boroon will keep me many miles from this monster, Happenstance. I promise you."

They watched Nima dive off the rocks, into the inky water. She surfaced again minutes later, close to Boroon. "She's waving," Hap told Umber, who couldn't have seen the gesture in the murk of night. He watched her climb onto the back of the leviathan. With a gentle thrust of his wide tail, Boroon began to cruise toward the open sea. Hap wished the filaments would appear just then, so he could see what fate might have in store for Nima.

When they walked into the Aerie again, they met Laurel, rushing down with a candle held high. "There you are," she cried. "Hurry—the patient has woken!"

"What an interesting evening this is," Umber observed. Hap followed Umber and Laurel to the third floor. With every step closer to Willy Nilly's room, his stomach tightened and soured. He paused for a moment outside the door, lingering after Umber stepped inside. He covered his face with his hands, exhaled between his fingers, and followed.

Willy had his head propped up by a pillow. Lily poured something into his open mouth—a remedy, or perhaps just water. He swallowed weakly, and some of the liquid spilled down his chin.

"I have brought them," Laurel told him.

Willy licked his lips with a swollen tongue. His skin was blotchy red and dotted with perspiration. Lily wiped his forehead with a cloth.

"Umber . . . you are here?" said the Meddler. His words trickled out as a thin wheeze, a dim echo of the mocking, musical voice that Hap had known twice before.

"I am. And Happenstance as well," Umber replied, lowering his own voice in empathy.

"Ahh . . . Happenstance," Willy said. He tried to sit up, but winced with pain and fell limp against the pillow.

Hap's hands shrank into stony fists, and his lips mashed together. He bit back the words he wanted to say, about all the pain this Meddler had caused.

"I led him on a merry chase, Happenstance," Willy said. "To keep him away from you . . . give you time, for your skills to ripen." Already, his skin was shining with new perspiration.

Umber saw Hap struggling to contain his emotions, and spoke first. "You led *who* on a merry chase, Willy?"

Willy managed a pitiful, openmouthed smile. "Good for you. You've guessed my name! But is Happenstance truly here? I have not heard his voice."

"I'm right here," Hap said. He could not keep the venom out of his tone.

"So angry," Willy said. He laughed, but it was a silent, ghastly laugh. "It was the Executioner, of course. I warned you about him. Tried to keep him occupied. I shook him off once or twice, in the Neither. It's cold in the Neither, and if you stay long enough, move fast enough, it confuses the signs, makes the filaments hard to read . . ."

"The Neither?" asked Hap. "I don't know what you're talking about."

"The Neither is where we traverse, my boy—from place to place, time to time. A cold, dark nothing, not of this world. *Neither* here nor there . . . you see?" Willy's strength ebbed, and his body sagged. "But I grew tired, let my guard down, and he caught up with me . . . obviously." His hands rose, quaking, and his fingers brushed against the cloth that concealed his wounds. Lily leaned away with a sickened expression.

"Who is this Executioner, Willy?" Umber asked quietly.

Willy tried to answer, but something bubbled in his throat. His chest convulsed as he coughed it out. "You've seen his kind already," he finally wheezed.

The words struck Hap like a bolt of lightning. "His kind—you mean, like Occo?"

Willy nodded.

A flood of terrible memories jarred Hap's brain. He saw, as vividly as the night he first encountered it, the awful face of Occo the Creep—a vile being who plucked the eyes from others, human and animal, and planted them in the sockets that dotted his own face. Occo had hungered for the green eyes of a Meddler, and almost taken Hap's.

"Occo was a child. This one—this Executioner . . . older. Larger. More formidable," gasped Willy. "Already has a Meddler's eyes . . . more than one pair, in fact. And that gives him a Meddler's powers—something Occo did not have. The Executioner sees the filaments. Can follow you anywhere, even into the Neither . . . appear out of nowhere . . ."

Hap gaped at Umber—but Umber was looking at the confused faces of the sisters. "Laurel, Lily," he said gently. "Don't mind his ravings. But if you don't mind, Hap and I should talk to Willy alone."

Laurel nodded, but the quizzical look remained. "He is weak, Lord Umber. Don't keep him too long with your questions." Lily stood and followed her out, and they eased the door shut behind them.

"Willy," Umber said, "if this Executioner has Meddler eyes, why isn't he just a Meddler—a mischief-maker—like you?"

"He is no Meddler. His nature is too strong . . . a murderous thing, always thirsting for new eyes. . . . So the boy must escape to your world, Umber. Are you ready, Happenstance?"

"I'm *not* ready," Hap said, slouching in his chair.

"Very bad news," Willy said. "You don't have . . . much time."

"How much time *do* we have?" Umber asked.

Willy's head doddered from side to side. "Can't be sure. . . . He will take time . . . to absorb my eyes . . . let their powers sink in. . . . Days? A week? I do not know."

Hap seized his own hair. He stared at the floor and stifled a moan. Occo was terrible enough. But a larger version, with the ability to read the filaments? He could not imagine surviving an encounter with such a creature.

"Can you see them now, Happenstance?" Willy asked. "Are the filaments here? You tell me: How long do I have?"

"I don't see them," Hap muttered, his voice thick with dread. "I don't know how to make them appear."

"You need more . . . experience . . . adventure . . ."

Hap bolted out of the chair with such violence that his heels left the floor, and the chair crashed onto its back. "*More* adventure? Do you *know* what I've been through?"

"Not enough, whatever it was," Willy said. "Don't know how much it will take. . . . There has never been a child Meddler before . . ."

Hap rushed at the bed. He wanted to grab Willy by the collar and shake him, but the Meddler looked so fragile that he just slashed at the air with his hands, a frantic display that Willy couldn't see. "No? Never a child Meddler before? *Then why did you do it this time! Why me?*"

It was the question he needed to ask more than any, and he'd finally gotten it out, expelling it like a poison. His chest heaved with great, gasping breaths, and he waited for the answer.

Willy turned his face toward Hap. That weak smirk returned. "Why you? Because the signs told me . . . you were the only one who might be able . . . to do it."

Hap felt the hard rock wall against his shoulder blades. He had backed away from Willy, barely conscious of his motion, until he was on the other side of the small room. "To do *what*?"

Willy's grin was ghastly. "The task, of course. The thing Umber has asked of you."

Hap looked at Umber and saw dread in his expression. *He's afraid,* Hap thought. Umber was terrified that Hap would be unable to do—or would refuse to do—what Umber desperately wanted him to attempt.

"I don't believe you," Hap told Willy. "Why would I be the only one?"

The Meddler's head sank back into the pillow. "I don't know why. But I searched everywhere for you. I read countless filaments. The Meddler who would cross to that other world had to be powerful. Gifted beyond the ordinary. And . . . what is the word I am looking for?" Willy paused and licked his parched lips. Umber sat on the stool by his bedside and poured a sip of water into his mouth.

"Benevolent," Willy finally said. "And so you are. But you cannot blame me for choosing Julian Penny, Happenstance. Blame Julian's filament. *Your* filament. It told me you were the one."

Hap thumped the wall with his fists. Umber looked back and patted the air, asking Hap to calm himself.

"Willy," Umber said, "did your meddling have anything to do with what happened in my world? The way everything went wrong?"

Willy laughed again, and it turned into another violent cough. "Think it's my fault, do you? That world of yours needed little help to come crashing down. But you can blame the nemesis, more than me . . ."

"The nemesis?" Umber narrowed his eyes. "Yes, that's how you Meddlers operate, isn't it? Always two of you,

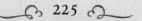

locked in battle, working toward opposing purposes."

Willy clucked his tongue and shook his head. "We are not supposed to share our secrets with ordinary folk."

"You've broken enough rules already, it seems to me. And besides, what else can they do to you now? I should point out: You're not even a Meddler anymore."

Willy's mouth twisted. He sniffed wetly and groaned. "Salt in my wounds. Hurts to cry," he said, waving his fingers above the cloth. "But how right you are, Umber. Nothing left to lose. Yes, we opposed each other. That is the game we love to play. One tries to start a war, the other stop it. Make one people flourish, make another fall. Bring a man love and fortune . . . bring him heartache and destitution."

Hap crossed his arms. "And who was your nemesis, Willy?"

Willy perked up at the sound of Hap's voice. "His name, you mean? Why, it was Pell Mell, of course."

"Of course," Umber said. He smiled at Hap, but Hap's bitter expression remained.

"Happenstance, Willy Nilly, Pell Mell," Hap said. "It's all a joke to them. They toy with words. They toy with fate." He pushed himself away from the wall with his elbows and stepped closer to the bed. "But Pell Mell is dead, isn't he?" He pointed an accusing finger that Willy could not see. "Or blinded, like you. Because you used his eyes to make me!"

Willy seemed to melt into the bed. His voice was weaker still, a puff of air barely forming words. "Was . . . the only way . . ."

Hap's anger flared, white-hot. "You're a monster. You murdered him to make me," he shouted. "How many have died because of you?"

"Hap," Umber said gently.

"Lord Umber, it wasn't just Julian and his parents who died. What about all the people in your world? What about them, Willy? *How many are dead because of you?*"

"Hap, he can't hear you. He's unconscious. He needs to rest."

Hap sucked his bottom lip into his mouth. Willy Nilly's head had rolled to one side, and his mouth hung open. "I bet he's faking. I hate him so much."

"Let him rest. We'll talk later. There's more we need to know."

There was a knock at the door. Hap opened it and saw Laurel's stern face. "There was shouting," she said. "The patient must not be agitated."

"You can have him," Hap said, earning a disapproving glance from the physician as he brushed past her, out of the room.

CHAPTER
19

Hap couldn't stand to be near Willy Nilly, not even on the same floor. With the stench of illness haunting his nose he went up to the terrace, eager for the cleansing air of the sea. The tip of the sun had just cleared the horizon. He glanced toward the thorn tree, and the exclamation flew from his lips: "Oh!"

The tree was dying. That didn't bother Hap at all. The ugly thing had filled him with unease since it sprouted, and he was relieved to see its leaves brown and shriveled on the terrace floor and its roots cracked and dry.

He walked toward it with small, cautious steps, eyeing the eleven fruits hanging from the drooping limbs. They had tripled in size since he'd seen them last, as if all the life in the

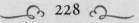

tree had been channeled into those hideous swollen things. The mottled skin of the fruits was stretched tight. As Hap watched, with disgust percolating at the bottom of his throat, he saw the nearest fruit twitch and convulse. Something inside was stirring to life, pressing against the skin.

Umber's voice piped up from behind him. "Holy smokes!"

"This one's moving," Hap cried, pointing.

"They're all starting to move," Umber replied, rushing to Hap's side. "I wonder if we should get the others."

Before Hap could agree, the nearest fruit split open at the bottom. A cloudy fluid oozed out like honey, and then the tear opened wide and something large and solid spilled onto the terrace floor with a moist, heavy plop.

"What do you suppose . . ." Umber sank into a squat, staring down at the green, dripping thing on the stone. It was contorted into an oval shape, but parts of it began to pry loose. A thin appendage quivered and straightened, and revealed itself as an arm with a knobby elbow.

Umber goggled at the thing with his fingers digging into his cheeks.

"It's . . . a little man," Hap said. The legs that were bent tight against the chest trembled and unfolded. They looked thin and weak, while the body was grotesquely swollen. The head was tucked down, out of sight, as the creature lay curled on its side.

"Look!" Umber cried. He pointed at the fat body, which had begun to twitch and convulse. "It's pumping liquid into the limbs—making them stronger! Like a new butterfly does to its wings." Hap could see the belly shrinking, even as the arms and legs expanded and the muscles took shape. There were thorns sprouting as well, rising to a needle-sharp point on every inch of its body. As the thing transformed, Hap could hear watery sounds from within, squishing and squelching.

A second fruit split open, spilling another balled-up creature onto the terrace. Then a third, and then the rest fell as one.

"Lord Umber—what are these things?" Hap asked.

"Thornies."

"You've heard of them?"

"No, but we have to call them something, don't we?"

The first creature straightened its neck and lifted its face. It had milky white globes for eyes, set close together. The mouth was a nightmarish thing: a round, pulsing membrane surrounded by a circle of thorns. It had no ears or nose, and a cluster of tendrils grew where a man might have a beard.

Umber straightened from his crouch as the thornie pushed itself to its feet with its long arms. The quivering of its limbs had stopped. The swollen belly was now lean, and the limbs sculpted and strong. The thing looked up at Umber from half his height, and turned to peer back at its fellow creatures, revealing the taller thorns that ran down its spine. Hap heard high-pitched sounds, like cricket calls. The membranes that covered their mouths vibrated as they chirped back and forth.

"Hap. Maybe you ought to get the others. Especially Oates," Umber said. There was a mild edge to his voice.

"Um . . . why don't we both go and get him?"

Umber waved him away. "I'll be fine. Just get the others. And hurry."

Hap backed off three steps and then bolted down the stairs. "Oates! Sophie! Balfour! Anybody!" He burst into Oates's room and found the big fellow just rousing himself from sleep.

"Come on, Oates, we need you on the terrace! Get up!"

Oates smacked his lips and raised his head an inch off his pillow. "What now?"

"The fruit on the thorn tree opened up and little monsters came out!"

"Of course they did," Oates said, wiping sleep from his eyes with his knuckles.

A faint scream from above drifted down the hall. It was Umber, calling their names and crying for help.

Oates whipped his blankets aside and rushed for the door, grabbing his favorite ax again. Hap raced after him and saw Sophie in the hall with her bow under one arm and a quiver of arrows slung over one shoulder.

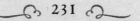

Hap bounded ahead of them all. When he leaped up the last flight of stairs he saw Umber on the ground, pale-faced and wide-eyed, with one arm clutched tight to his stomach and the other hand pressed on his neck. Two thornies stood over him, swatting with their prickly three-fingered hands and driving him backward. Their high-pitched squeals made Hap want to plug his ears with his fingers.

Umber saw Hap and shouted. "They took my key—and they're in my tower! Where is Oates?"

"Here," Oates answered as he mounted the last step. He glowered at the waist-high creatures and they stared back, bristling with thorns.

"Careful—they're dangerous!" Umber held his hand up, and Hap could see blood trickling from a dozen scratches.

"Can I kill 'em?" Oates asked, spinning the great ax in his hand.

Umber hesitated and bit his lip. A noise came from the window of his tower room—objects overturning and crashing. Normally, when faced with some exotic creature, even a deadly one, he was seized by a breathless joy. But this time fear was etched on his face. "They're after something—we've got to stop them! Do what you have to do!"

"Finally," Oates said with a grim smile. He stepped toward the thornies and swung the ax at the level of his knees. With shocking speed, they sprang up and over the whooshing blade and clawed at his face. Oates threw his elbow up to block them, and his sleeve tore open as the thorns raked across it. One of the thornies landed behind him and wrapped its limbs tight around his legs. The other leaped once more, clawing for his eyes. The creatures were too close for Oates to swing the ax again, and so he used one arm to backhand the jumping thornie. The thing tumbled through the air and over the balcony, heading for the rocks far below. The second thornie clung tight to his leg until Oates reached down with a bleeding hand to grab its throat. The thornie hopped off and scrambled away on all fours. Oates swung the ax again, producing sparks as it struck the terrace stone, but the thornie leaped back. Its head rocked from side to side, and it waved its hands in a taunting gesture. Its screech sounded like a laugh.

An arrow whistled through the air and pierced the creature's side, so deep that the arrowhead emerged under its other arm. The thornie staggered sideways and stared down at the thick white fluid that drizzled from the wound. Its head snapped up, and it searched for the one who had harmed it. Hap saw its gaze land on Sophie, who was already stringing another arrow.

The thornie rushed at Sophie. Oates swung his ax again, so quickly that its blade was a silver blur. The thornie's head tumbled off and rolled to a stop with its eyes still moving and its tendril beard wriggling. The headless body ran on and nearly reached Sophie before it wobbled and sprawled on the ground with its limbs still thrashing.

"What do they want?" Hap cried.

Umber looked back with an expression filled with dread. He'd found a long-handled shovel near one of the terrace plantings, and he wielded it like a spear.

They can't be after Umber's computer, Hap thought. *How could they know about it—and what would they want with it?*

"Oates, the rest are in my tower—come on!" Umber cried.

"You'll let me in there?" Oates said, disbelieving. But as Umber raced to the tower door, Oates followed.

Umber vanished through the threshold, but scrambled back with a pair of thornies at his feet, swatting at his legs and inflicting them with tiny punctures. The rest of the thornies spilled out from the tower as one. The last had something tucked under its arm. It wasn't the computer that they'd been after, Hap saw. It was a familiar pale box made from a material that looked like bone.

"The talismans!" Hap cried.

Umber swung the shovel at the thornie with the box, but it dodged the blow and tossed the box to another creature. Oates swung his ax again, but the agile things eluded him.

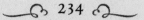 234

Another one of Sophie's arrows flew by and pierced one of the creatures in the shoulder, but it barely slowed.

The thornies bounded toward the stairs. "No!" cried Umber, and he and Oates pursued them, but the nimble creatures were too fast.

Hap gathered himself and leaped high, soaring over Umber and Oates. He'd aimed himself well, and was about to land with his feet on the thornie that carried the box, but the creature sensed him coming and tossed the box to its right. Hap came down with both feet on the back of his first target. The thornie crumpled under his weight but grabbed Hap's boot as it fell. Hap tumbled to the ground, thumping his shoulder and elbow as he rolled.

The threshold was ahead, and nobody was there to stop the thornies from escaping, until Balfour and Lady Truden appeared, with a kitchen knife and cleaver for their weapons. "Stop them!" Umber screamed. Lady Tru swung the cleaver at the first thornie, and it struck the box, breaking it open. Amulets, rings, and charms spilled down the stairs. Every thornie that remained screeched and leaped on Lady Tru. She lurched back, crying out as the thorns pierced her skin. Her heel missed the step behind her and she lost her balance slowly, awkwardly, with arms wheeling. Balfour reached to save her, but his fingers only brushed the end of her long sleeve before she fell.

CHAPTER
20

The thornies sprang off of Lady Truden
and scooped up the fallen talismans. Balfour stabbed at them,
driving them down the steps. One of the creatures slapped
at his arm, sinking its thorns into his flesh, and Balfour cried
out and dropped the knife. The creatures swarmed toward
Balfour, but then Oates was there, swinging his ax, and the
thornies fled with whatever they'd picked up, leaving half of
the magical things behind.

Umber rushed down the steps and knelt beside Lady
Truden, who was sprawled over the bottom steps. "Tru!" he
cried, touching her cheek. "Tru!" He looked up at the others,
and the fear in his eyes had been joined by pain. "Balfour,
stay with Tru! Sophie, get the sisters from Willy's room and

tell them Tru's fallen and struck her head. Hap and Oates, with me!"

They followed Umber to the grand hall, and into the corridor that led to the archives and beyond to the caverns behind the Aerie. When they reached the door to the archives, Smudge was there in the corridor, staring down its dark length.

"Smudge!" Umber shouted. "Did some nasty creatures come this way?"

Smudge nodded, and then glared at Oates. "And here comes another."

"Not now, Smudge," Umber snapped. He darted into the archives and came out again with a glass jar filled with glimmer-worms to light his way. He shouted at Smudge over his shoulder as he ran on. "And come with us if you want to be useful for once!"

Smudge's reply was to snort and shove the door closed.

"Where are we going?" huffed Oates.

"I think they're trying to free Turiana!" answered Umber.

"The sorceress? But she's all locked up," Oates said.

"They got the *key*, Oates. And some of her talismans!"

Hap remembered the wounds on Umber's throat. *They tore the chain right off his neck,* he realized, as the full danger dawned on him. *And that key can open anything!*

They turned down the side corridor that led to Turiana's

cell. Hap saw from a distance what the others could not, in the gloom. "The door's already open!"

Umber skidded to a halt. "And Turiana's cell?"

"Empty," Hap said, squinting at the dark place. The cell door was open, and the ghastly sorceress nowhere in sight.

"Need to be sure," Umber said. He jogged to the door and stuck his head through the threshold. "She's gone," he panted. "And we didn't run into them on their way out . . ." His eyes expanded with alarm.

Hap guessed what Umber was thinking. "The gate to the caverns!"

They dashed again, threading their way through the underground passages and past the subterranean pond. Glimmer-worms clung to the cave walls and pointed stones, casting light too dim to form shadows. Umber wheezed and puffed with the effort, while Oates ran with a scowl on his face, ready to strike at anything that confronted them.

"Do you hear that?" Hap cried. From ahead came a tortured, rusty screech, and the deep ring and clatter of thick chains in motion.

"They're raising the portcullis," Umber shouted.

The passage made its final turn. Ahead was the portcullis, and beyond that the cavern that plunged deep under the mountains. Hap saw the surviving thornies in the shadowy alcove, struggling to turn the winch and raise the portcullis. The lock that kept it from turning had been opened and cast aside.

The iron bars crept upward, groaning and shivering as the portcullis moved for the first time in years. The sorceress was there, facing the deep cavern. The spiderweb cowl that she wore fluttered back, waving in the cold breeze that flowed from the depths. She sensed their arrival and turned slowly.

The silk that always covered her head was torn down the middle to reveal her face. Umber, Hap, and Oates stopped as one with their feet scraping on the stone. Hap heard Umber gasp aloud. "She's beautiful," Oates said.

And beautiful she was, a skeletal horror no more. Turiana was lovelier than any flower, any jewel, any sky filled with stars. When she used a hand to slide the waves of dark hair behind one ear, Hap saw the rings restored to her fingers, and the amulets that hung around her long, graceful neck. *The talismans,* he thought. He felt a twist inside his heart as her crimson lips curved into a smile.

The beauty was an illusion, he knew, and still he was frozen, entranced, even as he watched the portcullis rumble slowly up behind her, already as high as her knees. Umber and Oates were just as stunned and motionless beside him; Oates's ax had drifted down until its head touched the stone at his feet.

 239

When Hap finally saw the single thornie creeping up behind them with Balfour's knife, it was reaching up to stab Oates in the back. There was no time to move, no time to shout. But in the next instant the thornie squealed and dropped to the floor, writhing and trying to pluck out the arrow that had sunk deep into the soft flesh of its head.

Sophie was behind them, reaching over her shoulder for another arrow while her eyes scanned right and left for the next target. Oates shot her a thankful look, and then stomped twice on the thrashing thornie at his feet, putting an end to its throes.

"Oates, stop the winch!" cried Umber, shaken from his trance. Oates grunted and charged at the thornies in the alcove with his ax poised to swing.

The portcullis was already waist-high. As Turiana bent low to pass under the bars, the next arrow struck her between the shoulders. The sorceress straightened, whirled about, and stabbed her fingers in Sophie's direction. Sophie's face twisted with pain, and she cried out and dropped her bow.

"You think you can hurt me?" the sorceress cooed in her silken voice. She raised her arms, and the arrow fell down behind her, bloodless, extracted by some mysterious means.

"Turiana, you must not leave," Umber said, stepping toward her. "You told me you were no longer the evil creature you once were. Prove it now by returning to your cell."

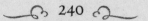

Her eyes narrowed and her glance darted left as the thornies in the alcove cried out under Oates's blade. The portcullis had still been rising, but it shuddered and stopped. Three thornies—the only still alive—scuttled across the floor and hunched at the sorceress's feet.

"Oates—drop the gate!" Umber shouted. Oates threw a switch, and the chains rattled again, spinning fast and free. The portcullis fell, but something enormous rushed out from the depths of the cavern. It was the wounded troll that Umber had named Charrly. The troll seized the bars and howled as he staggered under the weight, and spittle flew from his quivering purple tongue. Charrly could hold the massive weight of the portcullis for only a moment. But that was enough for the sorceress to flow with liquid grace under the bars, with the thornies right behind her.

"You heard me well," Turiana told the beast. Hap realized that when she was chanting in her cell, the sorceress had been calling out to this troll as well as to the thornies.

Charrly bellowed as he released the portcullis. The pointed iron bars slammed into the ground like a clap of thunder that echoed into silence. The sorceress stared back at Umber, and the thornies hopped and twirled and slapped the ground.

"Don't do this, Turiana," Umber said, clasping his hands.

"Do not dare to follow," replied Turiana. She glided into

the passage that led to the bowels of the mountains, and the troll and thornies followed. Umber watched them vanish, chewing on his bottom lip.

Hap heard a moan from behind them. Sophie sat on the ground, holding her stomach. He shot to her side in one great leap and fell to his knees, taking her hand between his. "Are you all right?"

"Yes," she said. "When she pointed—I felt claws inside me. But it wasn't real, I think—I hardly feel anything now. But . . . Lord Umber?"

Umber was standing over them now. "Yes, my dear brave girl?"

"The king's law," she whispered, afraid to speak it loudly.

Umber nodded. "The law that says I will be executed if the sorceress ever escapes?"

"Oh no," Hap whispered.

"I won't tell if you don't," Umber said, rubbing the back of his neck. His gaze went to the crushed thornie at their feet, and his eyes narrowed. He dropped to one knee and tugged something out of the creature's curled fingers. It was his precious transforming key.

They trudged back through the caverns, moving slowly until Umber stretched his neck and said, "I hope Tru wasn't hurt too badly." He broke into an urgent run and led them back to the Aerie.

Tru was still at the bottom of the stairs, lying peacefully on her back with her hands folded at her waist. Balfour sat on the bottom step with one hand across the lower half of his face. Laurel and Lily were treating his other arm, dabbing the wounds with ointment. They looked up as Umber approached, with their mouths drawn tight, and deep lines at the corners of their eyes.

"Shouldn't somebody be helping Tru? She's just . . . ," Umber said, but his words faded. He took a few more steps to her side, each less steady than the one before, and sagged to his knees.

"The blow to her head when she fell . . . ," Laurel said quietly. Umber laid one hand across Tru's and clutched the front of his shirt with the other.

"She loved you, Umber," Balfour said in a half-choked voice.

"I know she did," Umber replied. He reached out and brushed a strand of silver hair away from Tru's closed eyes. Then he bent low and pressed his forehead to hers.

Hap felt a hand touch his. He reached without looking and pulled Sophie to him, and buried his face in her hair and felt her tears on his neck.

CHAPTER
21

Correspondence arrived at the Aerie the next morning. Dodd set the letters and packets on the table in front of Umber, who was slumped in his chair with his hair hanging over his eyes. His hands were wrapped around a mug. Inside the vessel was not his usual dose of bitter coffee but the last drops of tea brewed with elatia. He stared at the boiled leaves at the bottom, perhaps trying to divine any meaning.

One of the envelopes captured his attention, and he set the mug aside and tugged it out of the pile. With his bread knife he sliced through the splatter of wax that sealed it. "It's from Fendofel," he murmured, pulling out a leaf-shaped note. "I've asked some of our captains to stop at the Verdant Isle regularly to see how he's doing."

Umber's lips moved faintly as he perused the letter from the botanical wizard. He lowered it to the table, looked up at the ceiling, and uttered a vulgar phrase that Hap had never heard him speak before.

"What does it say?" Hap asked.

Umber dug his fingers into his eyelids and groaned. "First, some notes about how to care for and propagate the elatia plant. Advice that slipped his mind. And that's splendid. But then, this." He raised the note and read aloud: "'My memory finally stirred concerning that thorny nut you showed me. It might be the seed of a thorn imp tree, one of the most sinister plants of legend. In fact that nut may well belong to the sorceress you have locked away, and any thorn imps that are born from the tree's fruit would be quite dangerous. Those wicked but short-lived creatures would know her thoughts and do her bidding. I am terribly sorry that it took so long to remember, but hopefully you heeded my advice and did not plant it,' blah, blah, blah." Umber let the letter fall to the table, and he rested his forehead on the heels of his hands.

"You couldn't have known that," Hap said to the back of Umber's head.

"He said it worried him. But I still planted it," Umber muttered. "Now the sorceress is free, and Tru is dead."

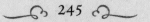

"But you weren't yourself when you planted it. Lady Truden gave you too much elatia and—"

"Don't!" Umber snapped. *"Don't* blame her. It was my dark mood that started it all. And if I wasn't so insatiably curious about that sort of thing, I wouldn't have planted the nut. So don't blame anyone but me." He rapped his temples with his knuckles. "Oh, Hap, I didn't mean to scold you. But the circumstances—so ill-fated. All our ships these last few days have been slowed by bad winds. *Bad winds*, Hap! If the letter came a day sooner, none of this would have happened. How can death be so capricious? Why should someone die because the wind blew north instead of south?"

Hap didn't have an answer. He curled up in his chair with his arms wrapped around his knees. When a minute passed, he spoke softly. "That's what you want me to be someday. Like the wind. Steering fate this way or that."

Umber stared, and shrugged, and nodded. "But always for good, Hap. Always for good. There are a billion lives to save in my world—maybe twice or three times as many. And yes, you will be the capricious fate that rescues them. But you could never be an ill wind. Your heart is too . . . benevolent." Umber raised his cup of tea and let the last drops fall into his mouth.

"What do you think Turiana will do, now that she's escaped?" Hap asked.

Umber tapped the table with his cup. "No idea. I'm not even sure which powers she's regained. The thorn imps only got half of her talismans, and I don't know exactly what each of them was for. If I'm lucky, she'll go into hiding or find a new lair far from here. If I'm unlucky, she'll make her presence known around Kurahaven, and everyone will find out that she's escaped."

"That would be bad, wouldn't it?"

"Only if you're not in favor of my execution," Umber said with a sad grin. "In which case, I might ask you to use your Meddler powers to whisk me away."

"What powers?" Hap mumbled. "I haven't seen the filaments in so long. How will I ever do the thing you need me to do?"

Umber tugged at his nose, thinking. "I am getting worried, honestly. It feels like we're running out of time. Both of us." He tipped back in his chair, balancing it on two legs. "Maybe if Willy wakes up again he'll have some answers."

Hap tried to eat but found his appetite lacking. He wanted to talk to Balfour, but his aged friend had wandered outside to stare at the sea, and asked to be alone when Hap came near.

So Hap went upstairs, meaning to return to his room. His chest tightened as he approached Lady Truden's room, and he

was startled when Sophie stepped out in front of him. She gasped and jolted, and her posture went rigid. There was something in her hand, a small rectangle, and she tucked it swiftly out of sight behind her. "Oh—Happenstance," she said.

"Hello, Sophie."

"I . . . I wanted to take this before anybody found it," she said. She brought the thing out of hiding. It was the small but perfectly rendered portrait of Lord Umber. Hap had seen it before, accidentally, when he saw Lady Truden gazing at the painting in her candlelit room. "Remember this? She asked me to paint it for her," Sophie said softly.

"I remember." Hap felt the wound in his heart open a little wider.

Sophie tucked the picture into the pocket of her paint-stained apron. "She would have been so embarrassed if Lord Umber found it. So I took it back."

Hap nodded. "That was nice of you to think of that. Even though . . ."

She shook her head and sniffed. "Yes. Even though she's gone. She wasn't always kind, and I know she was mean to you at first. But she always thought she was doing what was best for Lord Umber. Do you know what makes me saddest, Hap? That she felt the way she did about him, and she never got the chance to tell him. Now she never will." Sophie leaned against the wall and bent her head sideways until it touched the stone.

"That is sad," Hap said.

Sophie straightened up. "It shouldn't be like that. People should tell people how they feel, before it's too late."

Hap looked at her, and she was leaning toward him, gazing into his eyes without blinking. His feet felt like they were melting into the floor.

"I care about *you*, Happenstance. I care about you greatly. When we found you I thought you were just a little boy. But you're so much more than that." Her hand brushed his cheek, and her fingers pushed into his hair, over his ear. "I'm afraid, Hap. People are dying. A wicked man is king. The sorceress has escaped. And Lord Umber might be in trouble. I don't know what's going to happen to any of us. But I think you might not be around for much longer. I've never spied on you, but I've overheard things. There's something Lord Umber wants you to do, far away from here. I'm right, aren't I?"

Hap's mouth opened, but only a silent stutter emerged.

"You don't have to say it," Sophie said. "I know it's true. And that's why I want to show you how I feel." She leaned close and put her lips against his. Hap's eyes flew open wide, and then they closed, until she pulled herself away an eternal moment later, leaving a cool, soft feeling that lingered on Hap's mouth.

Hap's brain spun like a top inside his head. His knees buckled underneath him. "I . . . I feel the same way about you."

Sophie tried to smile, but the curve of her mouth faltered and fell flat. "It doesn't matter. Because you're going to leave. But at least we said it." She touched the corner of her eye with her fingers, and walked into her room, closing the door behind her.

It took Hap a moment to remember how to breathe again. His heart felt like it was swelling and shrinking, healing and breaking all at once, and he suddenly felt weary. Behind him he heard a throat being cleared.

Umber stood awkwardly at the landing, as if he could not decide whether to advance or retreat. Something in his expression made Hap think he'd been there for a while. "Uh. I was on my way to see if Willy was awake," Umber said, pointing at the door where the stricken Meddler lay.

"Oh," replied Hap, with his eyes downcast.

Umber stepped to the door and gripped the handle. "Come with me?"

Hap felt dizzy and befuddled, with no will of his own. "All right."

The sisters had left Willy by himself for the moment. The Meddler looked ghastly, lying with his head sunken into his pillow and his mouth hanging open. But at least the white

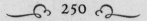

cloth that covered his eyes no longer had twin stains of blood.

"Willy?" Umber asked softly, putting two fingers on the Meddler's shoulder. There was no response. Umber sank into the chair by the bed, and Hap took the second seat, still preoccupied by his moment with Sophie. The sensation of her lips on his haunted him like a ghost. He touched his mouth experimentally, then looked sideways to see Umber smiling at him.

"First kiss, obviously," Umber said.

Hap felt his face redden. He squirmed in his seat.

"You really care about her," Umber said.

"Well . . . yes."

"You have a fine heart, Hap. Your feelings run deep."

"I . . . I guess," Hap said. At the moment his feelings were running amok.

"No," came a rasping voice from the bed.

Umber's head snapped toward Willy, and he popped out of his chair. "Willy, it's Umber. And Happenstance. We're both here."

Willy wriggled his shoulders and lifted his head, and Umber tucked another pillow behind his neck. He raised a glass to Willy's mouth and tipped in a sip of water.

"Why did you say no, Willy?" Umber asked.

"Now I understand. The boy *feels*. He *cares*. This is why he . . . fails," Willy said faintly.

"Because I *care*? What is that supposed to mean?" Hap cried. His anger had always been quick to rise in the presence of his murderer and creator. Now the emotions that Sophie had sent spinning suddenly oriented themselves, pointing straight to fury.

"Meddlers are not meant to care," Willy said. The words leaked out with little breath to shape them. "We pass . . . blithely . . . through the years . . . indifferent to whatever suffering or . . . joy our machinations bring . . . entertaining ourselves and giving those we torment or reward no more thought than . . . a chess master gives his pawns . . ."

"Why would I want to be like that?" Hap said. His words dripped with venom. "You sicken me." He felt Umber's hand on his shoulder and shrugged it off. Umber patted the air with his hand, urging Hap to calm down.

"Willy," Umber said. "Are you saying that the reason Hap is not seeing the filaments the way he should is because of his feelings? His attachments to the rest of us?"

Willy nodded. "He remains too human. I don't . . . understand. Signs told me he would be strong . . . more powerful than me, and perhaps any Meddler who ever was . . . skilled enough to fix that world. . . . I must have misread the filaments . . . never should have chosen a child, that was the flaw . . . emotions too raw, too unrefined . . ."

"You don't even make sense," Hap said. He shoved himself off his chair and paced to the middle of the room. "If you're so indifferent to the fate of humanity, then why do you care about Umber's world? You created me to save all those people. Why bother if you don't even care?"

Umber stared at Hap, looking both impressed and worried. He turned toward Willy, just as curious to hear the answer.

"Ah," Willy said. "The child is clever, at least. You are right, Happenstance. I found something to care about. And that has been my downfall. See what it has cost me." He touched a fingertip to the cloth on his eyes. "But . . . I didn't make you to save all those people. I made you . . . to save *one*." His trembling hand went to his chest and touched his shirt. A look of horror contorted his mouth. "This . . . not what I was wearing!"

"Calm yourself," Umber said, patting his arm. "We bathed you and gave you a clean set of clothes, for the good of your health. But the tunic and leggings you wore are here."

Willy breathed out a deep sigh. "And did you . . . go through my pockets, Umber?"

"Of course not," Umber said, but he shrugged and nodded toward Hap, looking genuinely embarrassed.

"There is a lining in the tunic," Willy whispered. "Something hidden within . . . you can reach inside through a slit, here." His hand quivered as he tapped a spot near his heart.

Umber took the tunic from a peg on the wall, near the door. It was a strange, silvery material, something like silk, marred by dirt and caked with dried blood across the chest. The inner lining was black. Umber's finger fumbled and probed until he finally slipped his hand into the space between. Hap watched Umber's face—there was a frown of concentration as he searched within, and then his eyebrows rose and his mouth formed a circle at the moment of discovery. The hand came out clutching a flat rectangle of some otherworldly, transparent material. It looked like liquid glass, and surrounded a torn square of paper.

Umber held it up, regarding it with wonder. "Well. Haven't seen one of these for years," he said. He smiled at Hap and held the object up for him to see. "It's a bag made from what we called *plastic*. Seals tight to protect whatever you keep inside. In this case . . ." Umber turned the clear bag around, showing Hap the other side of the ragged-edged paper. "A photograph."

Photograph, Hap thought. He had seen photographs before, on Umber's remarkable computer. It was an image of perfect fidelity—not a painting by an artist, but the object itself, captured and reproduced by a technology that did not exist in this world. This photograph showed a woman's face and shoulders. He stared with his nose just inches from the picture. The woman was beautiful, but underneath the beauty Hap could sense an aching sadness.

"Yes . . . photograph," Willy said. "Of her. The only one I cared for."

Umber's eyebrows contorted, and he turned the picture to look at it again. "*This* woman? You knew *this* woman?"

Willy shook his head weakly. "Never knew her. Learned of her. Later, when it was too late to save her. That is the joy of your world, Umber . . . memories live forever, preserved in your photographs and films, newspapers and magazines . . . and your computers. I did not know her, but I learned to love her, just the same. Umber . . . do you know who she was?"

Umber looked sideways at Hap with an expression that shouted *this is crazy.* "Of course I knew of her. She was famous. Everyone did. And a lot of them felt the same as you. They loved her from afar. And pitied her."

"Her life . . . her death . . . such tragedy."

"Yes, it was. But what does this have to do with us, Willy?"

Willy reached up, groping at air. Umber offered his hand, and Willy grasped it. "This is what I ask," Willy said. "All I ask. If the boy saves your world . . . save her as well. Give her . . . a better life." Willy raised his other hand toward Hap. Hap stared at it with his lip curled on one side.

Willy reached farther, groping toward Hap. "Happenstance, how can you refuse? I offer the chance to save billions. To head off unspeakable death and destruction, starvation, murder, and

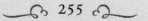

255

madness. This . . . the only thing I ask in return. One small thing. Take my hand, Happenstance. Vow that you will save that woman when you save the rest. Umber will tell you who she is, how to find her. *Make your vow.*"

Umber drew in a great breath and held it. He raised his free hand to Hap, offering to complete the circle. Hap stared at the hand, and kept his own by his sides. "Fine. I vow to save her. But what's the point? I can't even do what you're asking." He turned and left the room, without bothering to slam the door.

I have tried to ferret out any
evidence that Loden murdered both
of the elder princes. I know people
within the palace, but none of them
dares speak. Larcombe, Loden's
henchman, is a menacing presence
and I am sure they all fear his
arisal of the

CHAPTER
22

A familiar sound cut through Hap's dark contemplation: carriage wheels rolling over the stone causeway, and the hollow applause of hooves. Every set of wheels had its own voice, and Hap had heard this one before. When he looked out his window he was not surprised to see the royal coach approaching the Aerie.

He wondered who was inside. *Could it be Loden?* The thought filled him with sharp, sour anger. *Or could it be Fay . . . and Sable?* That notion conjured up strangely mixed feelings, particularly where Sable was concerned. He was shocked to feel a surge of unease over wanting to see her again, and found himself touching the place on his lips where Sophie's kiss had landed.

The carriage entered the gatehouse without offering a glimpse of its passengers. Curiosity propelled Hap down the stairs. He made it to the grand hall just as Dodd stepped in to announce the visitor—something Lady Truden would have done if she were still alive.

"Loden's pet lizard, here to see you," Dodd whispered to Umber.

Hap's spirits curdled, and he retreated out of sight, a few steps up the curving staircase. *Larcombe,* he said to himself, picturing that sinewy, angular man with a perpetual look of disdain on his pale face. Larcombe was cold and ruthless, and he had certainly murdered at least once to help his master seize the throne. His arrival could hardly mean glad tidings.

Hap heard the clack of boot heels. Larcombe was not alone; there must have been two or three of the new king's guard with him. It was easy to picture them, with the royal crests on their surcoats, short green capes hanging over their shoulders, and swords at their sides.

"Larcombe," Umber said.

"Umber," Larcombe replied, rudely omitting Umber's title. "I bring news from His Majesty King Loden."

Umber's reply was cool. "I am eager to receive it."

There was a rustle of parchment. "The king wanted me to read it aloud to you. And so I shall: 'Whereas we have taken into consideration the best interests of the glorious nation of Celador and its loving subjects, we hereby declare it to fit our Royal Will and Pleasure: First, the Umber Shipping Company and all of its associated enterprises, and the full value of its treasuries, assets, profits, and holdings, are as of this day the property of His Majesty King Loden.'" The paper rustled, and Larcombe paused.

"The king is taking my ventures away from me," Umber said. He sounded almost in awe.

"There is more," Larcombe said, with thinly veiled pleasure. Hap had not heard him speak much before, and now the sound of his thin, grating voice made Hap want to plug his ears with candle wax. "'Secondly, all of Lord Umber's remaining movable-type printing presses shall be surrendered for immediate destruction, and any printed materials created by said presses shall likewise be delivered to the palace, where they shall be reviewed and, if the king so wishes, destroyed, so that the minds of the common folk and the young and unwary may not be contaminated by exposure to corrupting influences.'"

"Do you even perceive the irony, Larcombe?" Umber said while Larcombe paused. "That proclamation is printed on one of those presses, which was my gift to the previous king."

Hap stepped back into the grand hall, barely aware that he

was moving, but magnetically compelled to stand by Umber's side. At the same time, he saw Balfour come out of the kitchen, moving likewise toward Umber with his jaw thrust forward, defiant. Sophie was already next to Umber, with her arm inside his elbow.

There were three guardsmen with Larcombe, all gawking at the soaring roof, mighty pillars, and endless curiosities on the shelves and walls of the grand hall. Larcombe was focused solely on his prey, Lord Umber. He slid his tongue across his lips and read on, smiling. "'At Lord Umber's urging, construction has begun on halls of education in the hinterlands of our nation, solely for the misguided aim of spreading unfortunate ideas among the common folk; these projects are hereby canceled, and those schools at an advanced stage of construction shall be converted to garrisons for the king's expanded armed forces. The whole of Lord Umber's other initiatives are likewise suspended, pending the review and approval of the royal court.'"

"Pathetic," Umber said.

"Ah, but I'm not finished," Larcombe said. "'The court does not by these actions wish Lord Umber to think his talents are unappreciated. Rather, his ingenuity needs only to be properly channeled, and thus he will henceforth serve His Royal Highness under the direct supervision of the king's appointed representative.'"

"And that is who?" Umber said.

"That is me," Larcombe replied. "The new Lord of the Aerie. Your lordship is to be revoked, but that is a matter for another proclamation. Yes, Umber, I'll be taking possession of your beloved hollow rock very soon. In fact, I think I should like that rooftop tower of yours for myself; it's quite charming. You will remain on these premises, where I can keep an eye on you. But as for the rest of this riffraff . . ." He grinned at Sophie, Balfour, and Happenstance, showing a row of small, widely spaced teeth. "They'll have to go, of course. To make room for my retinue and my guard."

Sophie gasped and tightened her grip on Umber's arm. Hap looked up at his guardian, who gazed back at Larcombe with a pleasant expression, except for the flare of his nostrils.

"Unacceptable," Umber said.

The guardsmen behind Larcombe stopped eyeing their impressive surroundings and stared, narrow-eyed, at Umber. Larcombe laughed. "Did you think you could get away with it, Umber? With your open disdain for King Loden? With your wild accusations, blaming him for the deaths of his brothers? Yes, we know you've been asking questions about the king."

"Don't be so modest. I blame you, too," Umber said.

The mirth vanished from Larcombe's face. "You are a

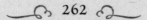

man who doesn't know when to close his mouth."

"It's time for you to leave," Umber said. Hap wanted to hide behind Umber's back, but he willed his trembling legs to stay where they were.

Larcombe's men stepped forward. Swords whispered as they were drawn from their scabbards, and metal glinted in the light. "The fact that you believe you can order me to do anything is almost comical," Larcombe said, giving his lips another reptilian lick.

Heavy steps on the stairs behind them drew the attention of Larcombe and his men. Hap looked over his shoulder and saw Oates lumber into the grand hall. Oates had strapped his muzzle across his mouth—probably, Hap figured, so he wouldn't blurt out the news of Turiana's escape. Oates had his enormous battle-ax in one hand. In the other was a mace, a club with a spiked head that looked as big as the full moon. Any other man would have struggled to lift either weapon, but Oates wielded both with the ease of a quill pen.

The men gave one another uneasy glances, and their swords wavered in the air. Larcombe looked at them with his nose curling, as if he smelled something foul. He turned to Umber and his grin returned. "A shame you had to be so rude, Umber. After all, I had an invitation for you." He paused, waiting for Umber to ask the obvious question, but Umber refused the bait. "To King Loden's wedding, of course," Larcombe said. "Just three days from now. A king must have a queen. I think you know who the fortunate woman is. Despite your differences, the king would have loved for you to attend."

Hap's fists trembled with barely contained rage, and his head shook from side to side.

"How absurd," Umber said. "He must know she doesn't love him."

"But you should have seen how she wept when he proposed," Larcombe said. "Tears of joy, I'm certain."

Umber's face went crimson. "Get out," he said. Oates clashed his weapons together, producing a gong that echoed through the grand hall. The guardsmen hopped back and widened their stances.

Larcombe held his ground and clucked his tongue. "Really, Umber. Is this how you choose to handle your fall from grace? With one brave moment that will cost you so dearly for years to come? Or are you only this foolhardy when that trained bear of yours is near to keep you safe? I would be more respectful if I were in your position."

"Your position is about to be horizontal and airborne," Umber said through his teeth.

Larcombe's lips mashed together. "This will end on my

terms, very soon." He turned to the guardsmen behind them and gestured toward the door that led down the stairs to the gatehouse. The guardsmen exhaled, all at once, and tried to mask their relief with stoic expressions.

"Make sure they find the door, Oates," Umber said. But Larcombe and his men hurried down the stairs before Oates could take a single step.

Around the long table in the grand hall, they gathered: Umber, Hap, Balfour, Oates, Sophie, and Dodd, who'd come up from the guardhouse to see why Larcombe had departed in such an agitated state. They exchanged uneasy glances until Umber broke the silence.

"We seem to be in dire straits."

"We are almost always in dire straits," Oates muttered.

"Aren't we, though?" Umber said, plucking at the tabletop. "But never like this. We'll have to leave, I suppose. Slip away in the dark. They may have seized my shipping company, but I'll find a craft to transport us. You can all come with me, of course. Unless anyone would rather stay. Dodd, if you and the boys don't want to join us, I'll have a generous parting fee for all of you."

Dodd shrugged. "I'll talk it over with Welkin and Barkin."

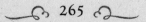

"Where will we go?" asked Sophie.

"I'll figure something out," Umber told her. "We'll track Nima down and impose on her for a while. Bear in mind, my friends, I am still a man of considerable resources, with friends far and wide. There will be a place for us."

An acid voice rose from the floor. "What a sorry gaggle of cowards. And you're the worst, Umber."

All eyes turned down toward the tiny figure on the floor, a bearded man the size of a mouse. "Thimble!" Hap blurted.

Dodd popped up from his seat on the other side of the table and leaned over to gape. "By gad, there's the tiny man you've all talked about! So that's the mighty Thimble!"

The little recluse sneered back. In his hand was a spear the length of a dinner knife, and he thumped its end on the floor. "Don't speak my name, any of you, you band of quitters." He turned his head and spat an almost invisible fleck of spit on the floor.

Umber smiled in spite of the dark mood and leaned down with his elbows on his knees. "Thimble, I've become an enemy of the king. Any minute now I'll be tossed into a dungeon. Then I'll be put to death, as soon as Larcombe moves in and discovers that the sorceress has escaped. I don't think a change of scenery is such a cowardly idea under the circumstances. You can come too, you know."

"Bah!" cried Thimble, thumping his spear again. "I say we fight!"

Umber laughed. "Fight the royal army? There are many thousands of them."

"This place is a fortress," snapped Thimble. "And the black door can't be broken. Barricade yourselves and dare them to attack!"

"They'd surround us and starve us out. Besides, a life under siege is a bore, Thimble," Umber said, raising his hands. "No, we'll have to leave. And soon, too."

"What about Smudge?" Balfour asked, prompting a groan from Oates.

"Ah, Smudge," Umber said. "He can join us if he wants."

"You all make me sick," Thimble shouted. He pointed toward the door with his spear. "Go on, get out. The sooner the better. And when those others move in, I'll stick their ankles with poison, one by one!"

"Start with Larcombe," suggested Oates.

Umber rolled his eyes and leaned a little lower. "Come with us, Thimble. It won't be safe for you here."

"Don't worry about me," Thimble said. "I can fend for myself." He stomped off and disappeared into the crack in the wall that he called home. Umber watched him go with a smile at the corner of his mouth.

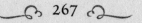

"You'll really leave all this behind, Umber?" Balfour asked. Hap looked around at the countless artifacts on the shelves, the paintings and maps on the walls, and the statues, relics, and other mementos of Umber's remarkable journeys. He thought about the thousands of ancient documents in the archives, the works of art in Sophie's studio, and the books that Umber had written and printed on his press. They could carry away only a tiny fraction of those wonders. The rest would fall into the unworthy grasp of Larcombe and King Loden.

"No choice," Umber said, pushing his chair back and rising. "And Thimble is right. The sooner the better. But if there's any way to steal Fay and Sable away from the palace . . ."

"Lord Umber." Barkin had come up from the gatehouse, and the look in his eye told Hap that something was amiss.

"Barkin?" Umber replied.

"Larcombe is back. With a hundred men," Barkin said. "We dropped the bars to keep them from entering. He's . . . he's demanding your surrender."

Umber ran his hand down his face and tugged his chin. "That was quick. I guess I'll go talk to him."

Hap reached for Umber's arm. "You won't give yourself up, will you?"

Umber patted Hap's hand. "No. I'll tell him I need two days to put my affairs in order. By then we'll be long gone."

Hap followed a few paces behind as Umber walked down the stairs with his head hung low and his hands clasped behind his back. Dodd, Sophie, and Oates followed. The lift clattered into motion, and Balfour rode a platform down to spare his rickety knees.

The small door to the gatehouse was open, but Umber raised his black ring and spoke the enchanted word that caused the wide door of magical black stone to part and swing open. "A little showmanship," he whispered to Hap from behind his hand. He stepped into the gatehouse, and Hap and the others arranged themselves behind him. Only Oates stayed inside, because he feared a question directed his way by Larcombe.

Larcombe stood beside the royal carriage. Behind him was a dense crowd of soldiers on foot, fully armed and armored, filling the breadth of the causeway.

"Larcombe. I thought you weren't coming until after the king's wedding," Umber said.

"Things have changed," Larcombe said. "The king was most unhappy when I reported your insolence. Now you must surrender yourself at once."

Umber shook his head. "Impossible. I need time to make my preparations, and say my good-byes. Come back in two days."

Larcombe's stare was cold and reptilian. "The king is wise,

and predicted your reluctance." He raised his hand over one shoulder and snapped his fingers. Behind him, a man standing beside the carriage opened the door. A short, heavy woman in a plain blue dress stepped out, muscled along by a guardsman who gripped her by the wrist. As she squinted at the sunlight, Hap recognized her scowling face. He had met her several times; most often when he ventured into the headquarters of Umber's shipping company.

Umber shook his head. "Hoyle," he said quietly, and he bent his head forward until it touched the bars of the gate.

Hoyle tugged her arm out of the man's grip. She rubbed her wrist with the other hand and sneered left and right at the men who surrounded her. "Took all of you to bring me here, did it?"

Larcombe stepped close to the gate. He reached for the long knife at his hip and slid it out halfway out of its sheath, making sure that Umber saw it. His voice fell to a thin, grating whisper. "Surrender now, Umber. Or I will spill her blood on your doorstep. And then we will find more of your friends and bring them here."

"That won't be necessary," Umber said. He began to pull the rings off his fingers, starting with the ring that commanded the black door.

"Don't you *dare*," cried Hoyle, stomping her foot. "Let them kill me, Umber! They've seized your shipping company—all our enterprises! Is this the sort of king that rules us now? I'd rather be dead than under the rule of such a thug!"

"Silence her," Larcombe said from the side of his mouth, still giving Umber his predatory stare. The guardsman who had wrestled Hoyle from the carriage clapped his hand across her mouth, and was bitten for his trouble. He yanked his hand away and Hoyle spat on the ground. "Ugh! The sickly taste of vermin!"

"Hoyle, be calm," Umber said. He held his rings out to Balfour, who took them reluctantly with shaking hands.

"Our world is crumbling," Balfour said thickly. Hap felt a lump form at the bottom of his throat, and he saw Sophie with her fist pressed against her mouth. Welkin, Barkin, and Dodd stared grimly, with hands on the hilts of their swords, ready to fight the hundred men if Umber gave the word. Oates stepped from hiding with his muzzle back in place, and he glared at Larcombe with every muscle tensed. Hap was sure that if Larcombe moved within reach of the bars, he would soon be missing an arm or two.

"I need all of you to hold your tongues and tempers," Umber told his friends. He turned his back to Larcombe, pulled a chain up from around his neck, and dropped his magical key into Hap's palm. "Listen, all of you," he whispered.

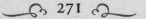

"I've said this before, and it remains the most important thing: Happenstance must be protected at all costs."

Hap bowed his head. "But I still can't do the thing you need me to do."

"*Now*, Umber," Larcombe called out. "I will count to ten, and then she dies. One. Two. Three."

"Balfour," Umber said quickly. "I've told you about a journal in my tower that you must read if anything happens to me. Now is the time to read it." Balfour gulped and nodded.

"Four. Five." Larcombe pulled his knife out again and took a step backward with every count, moving closer to Hoyle. Two guardsmen restrained her, each seizing an arm. "Six. Seven."

"Oates, unbar that door," Umber said, pointing to the small, sturdy door that bypassed the barred gate. "And all of you: Get out of here, to safety, and soon. Go to Captain Sandar and ask him to take you to Nima."

"Eight. Nine." Larcombe was beside Hoyle, who was frothing with rage and kicking the guardsmen in the shins.

"Here I am," Umber shouted. He swung the door open and jogged onto the causeway, hurrying to Hoyle's side. The guardsmen released her, and Umber kissed her on the cheek, whispered in her ear, and directed her toward the gatehouse with a gentle push. She entered and told Oates to bar the door behind her.

Umber waved to them, and with a smile, he stepped into the carriage before the guardsmen could force him inside. Larcombe gave his knife a look of mild disappointment.

Hoyle wrapped her little fists around the bars of the gate and forced her pudgy face between them to shout at Larcombe. "You have no cause to take Lord Umber prisoner!"

Larcombe lowered his brow, casting a shadow over his eyes. "Of course we do. It's not merely his insolence. Umber has to answer for the death of King Tyrian."

Hap's jaw fell slack, and he heard Sophie gasp. "Death of the king?" cried Balfour. "What are you talking about?"

"Tyrian died shortly after Umber's visit," Larcombe said. "Some say that poison ended his life. And it seems that the king was brought his meal while Umber was there."

"That's a lie!" cried Hap.

Larcombe used his knife to point at Hap. "You were in there as well, little green-eyes. An accomplice, perhaps? We'll have to think about that." His glance swept from Hap to the rest of the group gathered behind the gate, and he chuckled. "How charming you all look with those expressions! Someone really ought to paint your portrait." He stepped into the carriage, closing the door behind him. The driver cracked his whip, and the carriage creaked and jostled away with the guardsmen surrounding it on foot.

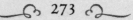

CHAPTER
23

When Hap trudged up to the grand hall, he met Laurel and Lily on their way down. Hap noticed that Laurel carried her medicine bag with her and that Lily had the rest of their things in a satchel. "Are you leaving?" he asked.

Laurel nodded with her eyes downcast. "He is gone."

"We know," Hap said. He heard Oates's heavy footsteps behind him and the soft scuffle of Sophie's feet on the stairs. The clattering lift brought Balfour and Hoyle to the grand hall as well.

Laurel looked up, with one eye squinting at Hap. "You know? How could you know?"

Hap pointed toward the gatehouse. "We just saw Umber taken away. Wait . . . who are you talking about?"

"The patient," Laurel said.

"Willy Nilly? He's gone? You mean . . . he's dead?"

Laurel nodded. Beside her Lily gave a heavy sigh. "He simply gave up at the end," Laurel said. "He told us he was tired. And he said the strangest things. He asked me to tell you something, Happenstance, and so I will, though it makes no sense to me." Hap looked at her, but his vision swam, and her face was blurred. "He said a Meddler must always keep the vow he has made," she said. "And so you must do what you promised to him and to Lord Umber. Or a world of blood will be on your hands."

Hap turned halfway around and threw an arm across his face. His mind felt like it had left his body to go careening off the walls. He wobbled in place, until he felt a pair of hands on his shoulders. When he looked up he saw Balfour staring into his eyes.

"Balfour," he moaned. "I'm lost. I don't know what to do."

Balfour nodded. "I do. Oates, we need to prepare tombs in the caverns, for Lady Truden and Willy Nilly. Have Welkin and Barkin help you. Happenstance, go with Sophie and Hoyle and find Captain Sandar to arrange our passage from Kurahaven. After Dodd drops you off by the harbor, tell him to go find out where Umber is being held. I'll be in Umber's tower, reading the journal as he instructed. We'll meet back here at sunset.

And if by then anybody has a notion of how to help Umber escape, I'm sure we'd all like to hear it."

Hoyle stuck her beefy head out the window as they rode down the causeway. "Ha! They hardly saw that coming."

"Saw what?" asked Hap.

Hoyle leaned back so Hap and Sophie could look past her, at the harbor. "See all those empty berths, where Umber's ships should be?" Hap and Sophie nodded. "They all sailed away," Hoyle crowed. "Captains and crew alike!"

"So Captain Sandar is already gone?" Hap said. He and Sophie shared a worried glance.

"The *Bounder* is gone, so he must be too. But not far, I think," Hoyle said. Her jowls shook as she brushed them with her fingers. "When I was taken, they must have decided to get out of the harbor before the wretched king appointed new captains. I'll say this about Lord Umber: He's not much of a businessman, but he certainly inspires loyalty." She patted Sophie's knee. "Don't worry, dear. We'll get you out of here, safe and sound."

They stepped out of the carriage near the Umber Shipping Company. Twenty of the king's soldiers were standing between the tall marble columns of the great building. Hoyle sneered up at them. "Rodents," she said.

Hap looked at Sophie and saw her mouth drop open and her eyes grow wide, staring at something over his shoulder. He whirled around to find a tall figure dressed in dark clothes coming at him. The stranger had a wide-brimmed hat, and he kept his head tilted so that the brim obscured his face. A rush of prickly panic course through Hap's limbs, and a scream erupted inside his mind: *The Executioner!* But before he could bend his legs to leap, the man raised his head just enough to reveal his face.

"Captain Sandar," Hap whispered, remembering at the last moment not to shout the name. He had never seen the commander of the *Bounder* out of his bright blue captain's coat and snowy white shirt.

Hoyle seized Sandar by the sleeve. "Captain! Where is the *Bounder*? What has become of our ships?"

Sandar grinned down at his stubby but formidable employer. "All moored out of sight, not far from the bay. When the king's guard took you away, we thought the whole fleet might make a good bargaining chip to get you back."

Hoyle snorted. "It's not me we need to retrieve. It's Umber."

"Lord Umber?" Sandar's handsome smile vanished. "What's happened?"

"Taken prisoner by Larcombe, the king's henchman. Loden wanted Umber out of his way. Now he's done it."

"We'll find a way to get him back," Hap said. Sophie linked her arm with his.

Sandar cocked one eyebrow. "Master Happenstance, after what I've seen and heard of you, I believe you will." He looked toward the marketplace, between the harbor and the great palace. A noise like the hum of insects had begun to rise, and Hap could see movement in the crowd—a flow of bodies in the direction of the palace.

"What's going on over there?" Sophie asked.

"Let's find out," Sandar said.

"You go," Hoyle told them. "I'm going to find some of our business partners and see if I can divert our funds from the king's greedy clutches." She stomped off with her dress swishing violently from side to side.

Sandar led them toward the crowd, and when he saw one man heading in the prevailing direction, he tapped him on the shoulder. "Excuse me, friend—do you know where all these people are going?"

"To the palace," said the man. "Haven't you heard? Lord Umber has been imprisoned by the king!"

Hap glanced at Sophie's face and saw the same surprise that he felt. "But what will you do at the palace?" Hap asked.

The man looked baffled by the question. "I . . . I guess I don't know. But it doesn't seem right. After all Lord Umber

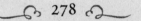

has done, I mean. I suppose we'll ask the king to let him go."

Hap felt tiny bumps sprout down his arms. Near them, dozens more were on the move, and people gathered in small crowds to exchange the news. "Did you hear about Lord Umber?" a woman called as she walked by.

Sandar's mouth tightened and a fierce look came into his eye. Beside him was a stack of barrels lashed together, and he climbed onto them and shouted to the gatherings. "How dare the king take Lord Umber prisoner! People, think what Umber has done for you. His medicines have saved your children. His inventions have improved your lives. Look at the wonders that grace our city! Remember the music he brought you that stirred your souls. Think of the ships he designed that cut like dolphins through the waves, bringing prosperity to us all! And now Loden wants all that to end—and why? Because of petty jealousy. This cannot be! Umber believed in the worth and the power of every one of you. Not only noble folk but commoners like you and me. And now it is up to us to save Umber. To the palace, everyone—if every citizen cries for Umber's freedom, the king will have no choice!"

Heads nodded. The buzz grew. Some who were sitting stood. Some who stood began to walk. And some who walked began to run. Merchants hurried to put away their wares and close up their tents so they could join the crowd.

Sandar hopped off of the barrel and rubbed his hands together. "Let's join them, shall we?"

They paused near the end of the marketplace, where the lane led to an open space with the soaring palace just ahead. "I'm afraid for the people," Sophie said. Hap nodded. He could see a vast crowd gathering outside the walls, grower denser by the minute, converging from the market, the shipyards, and the surrounding streets. They lined the edge of the moat and filled the bridge in front of the mighty oak doors that were clapped shut like an oyster. Guardsmen appeared atop the wall that loomed over the moat, scanning the crowd and whispering to one another. They had bows across one shoulder, but their arrows were still inside their quivers. Voices rose in the crowd, crying, "Free Lord Umber!" and "Let him go!" A scowling officer leaned over the wall and ordered the crowd to disperse at once or suffer the king's displeasure. But nobody moved, and the noise only grew in response.

Hap shivered, but it wasn't from his apprehension over the scene before them. A dull heat warmed his eyes from within. He shut his eyes and knew that when he opened them he would see the filaments again, for the first time in many days. *Hold on to them this time,* he told himself inwardly. *You have to get control.* He blinked his eyes open.

The filaments were there, brighter than ever: thousands of shimmering strands of light. There was one for every person in the crowd, tracing their steps, showing where they'd been and where they were going. *Destiny,* Hap thought. *Every one reveals a person's fate.*

A cluster of filaments hung near his left hand, in the busy part of the lane. He raised his hands and drifted toward them.

He was vaguely aware of Sandar calling after him, "Hap—what's the matter with you? What are you doing?" And Sophie responding, "Captain, let him be—he has to concentrate!"

Yes, concentrate, Hap told himself. *Understand them.* He touched the filaments like the strings of a harp, listening to their strange song, which grew loudest when the light passed through his palms. Some of the threads were discolored. Hap's jaw tensed. He found the darkest of the filaments and searched for its meaning. Words rolled unbidden off his tongue: "Suffering and death ahead."

He heard Sophie whisper, only a step behind him. She had quietly followed him into the lane. "What is it, Hap? What will happen?"

Hap squeezed his lids nearly closed, staring at the filaments. "Not sure. These people . . . in danger. Not just from the castle. There is something else." He looked closer at the bundle of threads that floated by. Even within the brightest were flecks of darkness. And the filaments would dim altogether from time to time, like a candle flickering in the breeze. He felt the urge to repeat the words of the sorceress. *A menace. Something unknown to me.*

"Hap, are we in danger—you and I, and Sandar?" Sophie said. Her voice trembled.

Hap's head snapped up. He could barely believe he was trying to understand the destinies of strangers when the filaments of his friends were right behind him. But as he turned to look, a sound from the crowd distracted his attention so completely that his vision of the filaments shattered into tiny glittering stars that faded from sight.

A man was whistling the tune he'd heard twice before: once here in the market, and once sung by Umber in his elatia-induced mania. The lyrics bubbled up from Hap's memory: *Take me out to the ball game . . .*

He saw a man with puckered lips ambling away from the palace, coming toward them. Hap stared at the whistler. He was a thin man of ordinary height, with a crafty face of pointed features and narrow-set eyes. He wore a tan tunic over a tan shirt and brown leggings—drab and ordinary clothes that wouldn't draw the eye.

The whistler glanced their way. He looked at Sandar without alarm, but his lids snapped open and the tune stopped short when he met Hap's green-eyed stare. *He knows me,* Hap thought. The whistler turned and bolted, heading for the nearest alley between two merchants' tents, a maze in which he'd vanished once before.

"We have to stop that man!" cried Hap, and he sprang forward without waiting for the others, covering a dozen feet with his first stride. Just as his quarry darted down a narrow lane between tents, Hap landed behind him. And when the man's heel rose up in midstride, Hap wrapped his arms around the calf. The whistler stumbled and fell. He struck his shoulder and rolled onto his back with Hap still gripping his leg, dragging behind him. The man looked at Hap with his teeth bared and spittle flying. He kicked Hap across the side of the head with his other boot, and Hap saw orange sparks as pain flared inside his skull. "Let go!" cried the whistler, and he drew the boot back again. The heel was poised in front of Hap's eyes, ready to smash his face. But another boot appeared, stomping down on the ankle and pinning it to the ground. The whistler yelped and threw his arms in front of his face as Sandar's strong hands reached for his neck.

Sandar grabbed the man by the front of his shirt and wrestled him into a seated position. His hand drew back, bunched into a fist. "I ought to knock your teeth out for kicking this boy!"

The whistler winced and turned his face away. "He's the one that attacked me, you know!"

Sandar's face twisted with barely contained rage. "Well, Master Hap?"

Hap stared at the whistler. There was nothing familiar about the man at all. "We just wanted to talk to you, but you ran. And you ran from Lord Umber once before. That song you were whistling: How do you know it?"

The man glanced at Sandar's hand, clutching the material under his chin. He looked at Sophie, who eyed him back nervously, and then at Hap.

"Sandar, you can let him go," Hap said.

Sandar released the man's shirt, and the whistler rubbed his throat and brushed the dirt off his knees. He assumed an unconvincing expression of innocence, with his forehead wrinkled and mouth bowed downward. "Just a song I overheard. That's all."

"Overheard where?" Hap said. Sandar and Sophie looked at him with growing confusion, and he didn't blame them.

"Back home," said the whistler.

"Home? Where is this home? Do you come from . . ." Hap bit his lip. "The same place as Lord Umber?"

The whistler gave Hap a curious stare, and a hint of a grin appeared. "Now this is getting interesting." He chuckled to himself and got gingerly to his feet. "Ah, well. Does it really matter what I tell you now, anyway? Your friend Lord Umber

is in a world of trouble, I think, so it probably doesn't. When I say *home*, little boy, I mean the place I come from. Across the sea."

"The Far Continent?" Hap asked. Sandar stiffened at the mention of that hostile land and looked ready to seize the whistler by the collar again. Sophie took a half-step back.

"That's what *you* call it. We have another name for it. A new name, in fact." The whistler stared at the towering spires of the palace. "This is quite a city you people built. A mighty kingdom, this has been. But things are about to change. Sooner than you know."

Sandar was a head taller than the whistler, and he loomed over the man, glaring down. "I think the boy's first question deserves a better answer."

The whistler tugged his dusty tunic back into place and ran a hand through his hair. "Oh . . . about that song? Why, a man I know likes to whistle that tune. He's a very powerful man. The most powerful in the world, in fact—or soon to be. It was he who sent me here."

"To spy on Lord Umber?" asked Hap.

The whistler lifted his chin and scratched his neck. "Well. I'm not sure I like that word, *spy*. I'm an observer, really. And don't you think Lord Umber is worth observing? It's curious. How can one man be capable of so many accomplishments? The

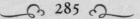

inventions, the medicines, the ship designs, the music, hmm?"

Sandar stared at the whistler with his jaw twitching sideways. He looked at Hap and seemed about to ask a question, but a commotion near the palace drew their attention. The crowd was buzzing anew, but with a different tone this time. Voices rose, and panicky shouts pierced through the din. Then Hap heard the thunderous sound of many feet in sudden motion.

Sophie was closest to the larger path that cut through the market. She stepped back for a clear view of the palace, and her mouth dropped open. "The king's men are shooting at the crowd!" She hurried back into the narrow lane to avoid the first of the people dashing into the market, running from the flying arrows. A group of men turned into the lane, seeking shelter among the tents. The whistler saw his chance and shoved Sandar, catching the bigger man by surprise. He swung his arm and clubbed the side of Hap's head as he passed, and Hap dropped to his knees with his ear burning and his eyes squeezed shut. When he blinked them open again, he saw Sophie holding a reddened cheek and grimacing. The whistler was gone, lost in the stampeding crowd.

Sandar hooked his arm under Hap's and hauled him to his feet. "All right?" he asked, and when Hap nodded, he turned to Sophie. "Did he strike you?" Sophie nodded and dabbed her cheek with her fingers, checking for blood.

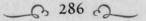

"If I see that spy again, he'll be observing my fists," Sandar muttered, with his breath snorting out of his nose. "Come, you two—let's get you back to the Aerie before the king's army takes to the streets."

They used the narrow passages between the merchant stalls to head for the harbor, avoiding the wider lane that was filled with the rushing crowd. Before long they heard horses thumping nearby, and new cries of fear. From the alleys Hap caught glimpses of mounted soldiers, waving swords and scowling at the people.

At the bottom of the market district, the narrow lane ended near the great harbor wall. In their race to get away from the palace and the deadly arrows, the crowd had run down the sloping roads and gathered there. But instead of heading for the safety of their homes and other buildings, they stood frozen, staring across the water.

"What the devil," Sandar whispered.

Dozens of familiar ships flew into the harbor under heavy sail, racing for the docks. At the prows of the incoming craft, sailors waved shirts and hats and pointed back at the open sea.

Sandar shielded his eyes from the sun with one hand and ground his teeth. "There's the *Bounder*—and the rest of our ships! Why are they coming back?"

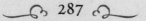

"Something's happening out at sea," Sophie said quietly. "They're running for safety."

Hap stared at the mouth of the harbor. On both sides of the harbor's entrance, the land rose up steeply. Signal towers stood on both of those hills, and plumes of smoke rose from each.

"Something is coming," Hap said, and all the warnings of approaching doom reappeared in his mind. *Something strange in the sea, to the west,* Nima had told them. *Boroon heard it . . . a constant roar of thunder in the water, thumping like a heart.* He remembered Burrell, the terrorized sailor. *Fire monster,* Burrell had called the thing that had destroyed his ship.

As he stood thinking of all those omens, the thing appeared. At first it was only a dark edge, creeping into view from behind one of the tall shoulders of land.

"It's here," Hap said, and his mouth was suddenly dry.

...d the sea g... wander off to ...o a distant land? Or do they hibernate, waiting for the next fool to declare himself... powerful tha...

CHAPTER
24

Even with a mile of water between them, the thing looked immense. It glided through the sea with dark smoke wafting from its innards. Its side faced them, revealing a fierce golden eye at the front of its dark bulk. At first Hap thought it might simply pass by, across the wide mouth of the bay, but then the thing turned slowly, bringing its head to bear on the inner harbor.

"The fire monster," Sandar said, using the name that rumor had given it.

"But it's not a creature at all," Hap said, narrowing his eyes to sharpen his sight. "It's a ship." Its blackened sides were sleek and straight, and it was blunt in shape, except for where its nose narrowed to slice the sea. The glowering eye had been painted

on, to make the craft all the more fearsome. The smoke came from a pair of conical chimneys on its back. Behind the ship Hap could see water frothing, churned from below.

"Listen," Hap said, cupping his hand behind his ear. The strange ship was making a sound: a dull mechanical rumble that rose and fell. It suddenly announced its presence with a shrieking, unnatural whistle, accompanied by a plume of steam that shot up from its stern.

"A ship?" cried Sandar. "But how does it move without sails—there's no leviathan beneath it, is there?"

Hap shook his head. "I don't think so. . . . I think it's a machine."

"But who could make something like that?" Sophie said.

Hap shook his head. He could imagine only one answer: Someone else from Umber's world was here, and it was probably the same man who'd sent the whistler to spy on Lord Umber and the city of Kurahaven.

"I want a closer look," Sandar said, clamping his teeth. He led them through the open gates of the harbor wall and to the docks. The ship was halfway into the bay, and it was obvious that it would dwarf even the greatest ships of Kurahaven. Hap saw men prowling on its broad upper deck, and others coming up through metal hatches from the vast interior of the craft. Many carried objects made of wood and steel, tall as spears, but wider at the bottom. Other structures on the deck of the ship were obvious now: Long, bulky tubular things that angled up, pointing toward the city. The look of them filled Hap with unease.

"There will be a fight," Sandar said, gesturing toward the berths in the center of the harbor, where the royal navy was docked. Sailors and soldiers were on the ships, and two of the vessels cast off their lines and slid out into the harbor. The ships had oars as well as sails, and the oarsmen rowed furiously while archers lined the rails.

Hap felt a shiver run across his skin as he remembered the fate of the ships that had encountered this intruder. "They shouldn't go out there," he said quietly.

"What choice do they have? A hostile ship is in our harbor," Sandar said, but he plucked at his lips and shifted from foot to foot, watching anxiously.

The royal warships glided toward the intruder. Officers stood at the prows, calling out to the strange craft through speaking trumpets. Hap couldn't hear the words, but Sandar explained. "They're telling the fire monster to stop where she is and explain herself, or prepare to be attacked and boarded."

Hap shook his head. The ships looked so small next to the beastly vessel they were approaching. The intruder was twice as tall, three times as wide, four times as long. On the side of the monster ship, panels slammed open, hinged at the bottom, revealing dark rectangles. Hap squinted into the black interiors. His gifted eyes adjusted to the contrast between sunlight and shadow, and he saw long, dark cylinders within.

A man on the deck of the monster ship shouted back at the captains, and more words were passed that Hap couldn't hear. His lungs ached, and he realized that he was holding his breath. From the cylinders within those dark rectangles came an explosion of fire and thunder, so loud it made the bones in Hap's chest hum. Sophie jolted, and Sandar staggered back, stifling a cry with the back of his hand.

Hap caught a glimpse of small shapes flying through the air, out of the smoke. Ragged gaps appeared in the hull of the royal ship that had ventured closest, and it was torn to splinters from within by an unimaginable inferno. Smoke obscured the scene, and then the breeze pushed it away, and when the royal ship could be seen once more it was in shreds. Flaming sections bubbled and sizzled into the depths, and blazing sailcloth fluttered into the waves. Not a single living man could be seen amid the wreckage.

"What . . . *how*?" moaned Sandar. He sank to his knees and clutched his stomach. "All the men on that ship . . . five hundred or more!" In the harbor, the second ship of the navy had been ready to join the attack, but it turned hard, away from the intruder. The monster ship chugged on, closer to the docks.

A horn sounded behind them, and Hap turned to see soldiers atop the harbor wall, calling to the people who had lined the harbor to watch the battle. The harbor wall had numerous tall arches that allowed people and wagons to reach the docks, and the doors that could block those passages were swinging shut to form a solid barrier against invasion. "We'll be trapped," Sophie said.

Sandar rose unsteadily to his feet and took a deep breath to collect his wits. He mumbled his instructions. "Hap, go with Sophie, before all the doors close. Run back to the Aerie. My ship is here; I have to see what happens."

Hap and Sophie exchanged glances, and Hap knew they were of the same mind. "We'd rather stay with you." If necessary they could reach the Aerie in a tiny boat, making the journey at night when Hap's nocturnal sight could guide them.

The intruder was nearly an arrow's flight from the docks when it swung its vast bulk to the right. It was not made of wood at all, Hap realized—or at least, its hull had been plated with dark metal scales. Now that its side faced them, he could see how the thing was propelled: there was an enormous paddle wheel at its stern, like the one that powered the Aerie's lift. As the wheel turned, the ship was thrust forward.

"Vanquisher," Sophie said quietly. Hap realized that she was reading the word painted in silver letters above the golden eye, arching like an angry brow. The demonic ship had a name.

The thumping roar inside the ship fell to a low thrum, and the *Vanquisher* slowed. The wheel stopped churning. Hatches clanged open at the bow and the stern, and a grating, ratcheting sound was heard as anchors dropped and sank under the surface.

From this distance Hap could clearly see the men on the deck of the *Vanquisher,* forty feet or more above the waterline. One seemed to be in charge: a lanky, silver-haired man with thick eyebrows and a prominent nose. He stood on a raised platform, as calm as a statue. The others on the deck would come to him, drop to a knee while receiving orders, and dash off without looking him in the eye.

Hap, Sophie, and Sandar watched as a small boat on the deck of the *Vanquisher* was swung over the side and lowered into the water with two dozen men lining its seats. The silver-haired man stayed on the *Vanquisher*, watching like a falcon perched high. Next to him a pair of men appeared with an enormous conical object, which they aimed toward the shore, not far from where Hap and the others were standing. Hap's heart clenched. He wondered if this was another weapon designed to blast fire and death at them; but then he saw that the cone was hollow, and it served only to project the voice of the man who stood behind it.

The voice carried across the water, and everyone fell still. "People of Kurahaven. You have seen only a hint of what this ship can do. Do not tempt us to show the *Vanquisher*'s true might. Our envoy is on the boat that approaches. Send your highest authority to meet him. Do as he says, or countless more of you will die."

By the time the small craft was rowed to the docks, most of the people had fled. Hap heard the last door of the harbor wall slam shut. It seemed like a waste of time to him; the *Vanquisher*'s weapons could blow those wooden doors into sawdust if they desired.

The men from the *Vanquisher* stepped onto the dock. A small group was there to meet them: Hap saw one fellow who must have been an officer in the king's navy, and another man who looked like a knight.

"Stay here and hide among the crates," Sandar said, and he headed for the dock. Hap and Sophie ignored his orders and followed, earning a stern backward glare.

Someone else was approaching the dock where the meeting would happen. Hap felt a flush of anger when he recognized the whistling spy. He saw Sandar's hands turn to fists. The spy was many paces ahead of them, and he reached the group first. There he was greeted by the thick-chested, black-bearded envoy, who seemed to know him well.

Sandar stopped a short distance away, behind a stack of barrels. They were close enough to hear every word, and Hap could see what was happening through a gap in the cargo.

The naval officer stepped ahead of the others to address the envoy. His throat bobbed up and down, and he dabbed sweat off his forehead with his fingertips. The envoy waited, looking disinterested and picking at the fingernails of one hand with his thumbnail. Behind the envoy, the rest of the men watched with wolfish looks, holding those strange long objects. If they were clubs, Hap thought, they were unwieldy ones, with narrow metal rods at the top fused to thicker wooden handles at the bottom.

"Tell me your name," the envoy finally growled, barely glancing up.

"Admiral Horner," said the officer.

The envoy sniffed. "Admiral? Not exactly the highest authority, are you? Here is what you're going to do, Horner. Tell your king to come to this very spot, within the hour."

"Within the hour?" cried Horner.

The envoy stared without expression. "If he is not standing on this very spot by then, we will do to his palace what we just did to that ship."

Horner looked over his shoulder at the palace, looming at what appeared to be a safe distance. He turned back, and disbelief colored his expression.

"I can see you doubt me," the envoy said. He raised his fingers and snapped them. Behind him one of the men raised a flag and waved it high in the air to signal to the *Vanquisher*. A moment passed, and then another deafening roar and a cloud of smoke shot out from the ship, this time from the great cylinders of metal on its deck. Sophie screamed and clapped her hands across her ears. Something whistled high overhead. After a moment of silence, when even the gulls ceased to cry, there was an eruption of fire and smoke in the building next to the palace. Hap knew the place: It was a theater that Umber had designed and funded. Half of it had been reduced to rubble.

Horner stared with his jaw hanging slack. "I . . . I shall go at once," he said. He cleared his throat. "May . . . may I ask why you require the king's presence?"

"Of course not," the envoy said. "And tell the king to leave his entourage behind; he may bring one servant or advisor only. Also, bring his crown and scepter with him." The spy stepped up beside the envoy, who bent his head to allow the spy to whisper in his ear. The envoy nodded and turned to Horner again. "One more thing. Make sure the king brings

298

Lord Umber with him. Do you know the man I speak of?"

Sophie gasped and clutched Hap's arm. Sandar turned back with goggling eyes, and mouthed the name *Lord Umber*.

"Every man, woman, and child in Kurahaven knows of Lord Umber," Horner said.

The envoy yawned and examined his fingernails. "Then you'll have no trouble bringing the right man." He waved Horner away, and the admiral walked toward the palace as fast as a man could walk without breaking into a run, signaling for the men on the harbor wall to open a door so he could pass through.

Hap saw the spy talk quietly to the envoy again. Hap fumed, touching the tender ear where he'd been struck. The envoy nodded, and to Hap's dismay he glanced in the direction of the cargo they'd hidden behind.

The spy stepped to the front of the group and called out between his hands. "Happenstance! Come out from hiding!" Hap and Sophie stared at each other, and then the spy called out again, guessing their thoughts. "Yes, I know your name. I've been observing you for many weeks. Now get out here, and bring those two with you. That's right—I saw the three of you hiding there."

Sandar stood up first, and the men with those strange metal-and-wood clubs did a strange thing: They leveled the narrow ends directly at Sandar. Hap and Sophie stood on either side of the captain.

The spy put his hands on his hips and looked at them with his head angled to one side. "Come over here, my green-eyed friend. We're curious about you; you always seem to be at Umber's side. But your friends must go; I don't like the way that tall one is looking at me. Hurry, you two, while that gate is open. And don't loiter here, or that will be the end of you."

Hap looked up at Sandar, whose chest swelled with barely contained fury. "Captain Sandar, go on. Take Sophie back to the Aerie. *Please*."

Sandar heaved out a breath. "I don't like leaving you." Sophie whipped her head from side to side. But Sandar knew what had to be done, and he took her firmly by the hand. "Take care, Hap," Sandar whispered. "Get back to the Aerie somehow. I'll get you all safely away."

Hap walked onto the dock. His steps were awkward, and it felt like he was pushing through water. Every man from the *Vanquisher*, and the spy as well, was staring at him. He saw some of them nudge each other and whisper. One of them spoke louder, and Hap heard him say, "Those eyes!"

He stopped when he was a few paces away and stood before them. The envoy gazed at him and talked out of the

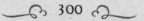

side of his mouth, toward the spy. "There is something special about this boy?"

"It is rumored that he possesses some magical abilities. A seer of some kind," the spy replied. "And it's said that he can leap great distances."

Hap dipped his head and stared at his feet. His face had reddened, he knew; he could feel the warmth in his cheeks. They were speaking about him as if he wasn't even there.

"His eyes are unnatural," the envoy said.

"Yes. At any rate, I thought the Supremacy might be interested," the spy replied.

"He'll be here soon. You men—make sure this area is safe." At the envoy's command, most of the soldiers trotted past Hap and searched the docks.

The Supremacy, Hap said to himself. He supposed it was that silver-haired man. When he looked back at the *Vanquisher* he saw a second small boat being carefully lowered to the water. Like the first it was filled with men armed with those strange clubs. But sitting among them was the silver-haired man himself. He wore a black tunic that fell to his ankles, and carried a tall, silver staff. There was something around his waist that looked, from that distance, like a cluster of large metal rings. They glittered when the sunlight struck them.

The boat lingered beside the great ship for a long while.

Hap wondered why, until he heard hooves and rolling wheels behind him, and turned to see the royal carriage rumbling through the only open gate in the harbor wall. The king was approaching, and these invaders were making certain that it would be the king, and not their Supremacy, who would wait on the dock for the other party to arrive.

As the carriage approached, the driver stared, owl-eyed, at the *Vanquisher*. He stopped the carriage at the foot of the road, right before the wooden planks of the dock. Hap watched, trying to keep his legs from visibly shaking, as the door opened, wondering if Umber was really inside. His stomach soured as Larcombe stepped out, looking frightened and angry. Next, to Hap's great relief, came Umber, who gaped at the beastly ship with his mouth hanging open. Umber normally would have looked at an extraordinary thing with pure delight, but he seemed to regard the *Vanquisher* with dread and even a terrible recognition.

Loden stepped out last, looking ten years older. His face was the color of the oldest parchments in Umber's archives. He gripped the carriage door to steady himself.

"Come here at once," commanded the envoy. Loden and Larcombe hesitated, but Umber gave them a disdainful glance and marched briskly down the dock. Loden was in a daze, but Larcombe tugged his elbow, and they followed.

"Happenstance?" Umber said, with a sudden loopy grin. Hap managed to smile back, and Umber clapped his shoulders with both hands. "My boy. What are you doing here?"

Hap paused while Loden and Larcombe passed by. Loden moved like a sleepwalker, but Larcombe's gaze darted everywhere, and he licked his lips without pause.

"Stop there and remove your weapons," the envoy said. Larcombe sneered at the envoy, but he drew his sword from its scabbard and his knife from his hip and let them clatter to the planks. Loden hadn't moved, and so Larcombe took his sword from him.

Umber shrugged. "I'm not much for weapons myself," he said.

The envoy stared back with narrowed eyes. "Stand here, all of you." He pointed to the space directly before him. Umber put his arm across Hap's shoulder and they walked there together, taking their place beside Loden and Larcombe.

The second boat had reached the dock. Two dozen men climbed out first and stood facing one another in opposing lines, forming a corridor that ended where Umber and the others had assembled.

"Say something," Larcombe said to Loden, nearly hissing the words.

Loden had been gaping at the *Vanquisher*, seeming to barely

comprehend the sight. But his eyes cleared and focused on the envoy. "I . . . I am the king here," he stammered. "You have no—"

"Shut your mouth," the envoy said. The men near him raised those strange clubs, pointing them at Loden, who clamped his mouth audibly. Larcombe's face went purple, and he trembled with rage.

The envoy, the spy, and all of the others swiveled in place, clapped their hands to their sides, and stared straight ahead. Hap saw the tall, silver-haired man step up from the boat. He climbed the rungs of the short ladder and stood at the end of the corridor of men. There was a smile on his face, and then he laughed and clapped his hands together. Hap realized that he was staring directly at Umber, and he turned to see how Umber was reacting to this unexpected attention.

Umber stared back, goggle-eyed. His legs wobbled and buckled, and he clutched Hap's shoulder to keep from falling. "This can't be," Umber said. "It can't be true."

CHAPTER
25

"Who is he?" Hap asked. The silver— haired man strode toward them. Now Hap could see that the circular things that hung at his waist were crowns: at least seven glorious crowns, no two alike, made from precious gold and silver, and studded with jewels.

"It's my friend," Umber said thickly. "Jonathan Doane."

It was Hap's turn to be stunned. Doane was the man from Umber's world who had decided to gather that civilization's vast knowledge of science, engineering, medicine, music, architecture, and more, and store it all on the wondrous machine that Umber had brought with him. And now Doane stood before them, another refugee from a lost world, weeping with joy as he pulled Umber into an embrace.

"Brian! Brian Umber! I wouldn't believe it till I saw you with my own eyes!" Doane took Umber by the shoulders and looked him up and down. "This is the finest day of my second life, seeing you again! Can you believe it?"

Umber shook his head like a dog throwing off water. Hap could see emotions colliding on his face: shock, worry, confusion, and surprise. Umber blinked and choked out a laugh. "I . . . no. I can't believe this at all. To think, you were brought here, just like me."

Doane gave Umber a conspiratorial wink. "Let's not say too much about that, eh?" he whispered. He gazed at the scene around him, from the sleek ships to the handsome buildings. His deep, thunderous voice boomed out again. "Look at what you've accomplished with all your knowledge. Yes, I've heard about everything you've done."

Umber's dazed grin faltered as he looked past Doane to the hulking ship that loomed in the harbor like a thunderhead. "I've tried to be useful. But . . . what have you been up to, Jonathan?"

Doane peered over his shoulder at the *Vanquisher*. His chest puffed, and he flashed his teeth. "Isn't she stunning? But look at your sailing ships—how quaint! Clippers, I think? No, schooners! You'll have to explain why you stopped at such a primitive design, with all the information you possessed at your fingertips." Umber's shoulders twitched at that remark, and Doane's shaggy eyebrows rose and fell twice. "Surely, Umber, you could have constructed something just as formidable as the *Vanquisher*, artillery and all!"

"What?" cried Loden, straightening out of his slouch. He pointed at Umber, stabbing the air. "*You* could have made something like that ship—with those weapons—to safeguard this kingdom from such an invasion? My father begged you to use your ingenuity for our defense! You had that power, and you did *nothing*?"

"I saw no need," Umber said.

Doane turned toward Loden and angled his head. His voice grew cold and stern. "Mind your tone when you speak to my friend."

Loden swallowed, audibly, and struggled to maintain a regal air, but the quiver in his voice betrayed his fear. "Y-your *friend*? That man is my subject, and a traitor at that. I am k-king here, and will speak as I see f-fit." Larcombe was watching the scene with his eyes narrowed and his glance darting from man to man. His tongue slid across his lips again, and he crossed his arms, putting a hand inside the opposite sleeve.

Doane shook his head and smirked at Loden. "Poor little

307

man. You are only king until I take your crown and add it to these." He ran his fingers across the glittering crowns he wore at his waist. Loden gasped and clutched his own throat.

Umber cleared his throat. "Jonathan. You mean to depose this king?"

Doane winked again and pointed at the men assembled with their strange clubs. "Unless he prefers the alternative."

Hap thought that Umber shivered as he glanced at the oddly shaped clubs. Umber blinked and fidgeted, as if some inner struggle was manifesting itself in his hands and feet. But he forced a fragile smile. "May I approach my king for a moment, while he still reigns?"

"Why not?" Doane said, shrugging.

It took Umber five steps before he stood nose to nose with Loden. He stared unflinching into Loden's brown eyes as Loden glared back with sweat on his brow. "I want you to know," Umber told him, "I have never struck a man in my entire life." His hand came up in a flash, and he slapped Loden. Loden's head snapped to one side, and he rocked backward, pressing a hand to his cheek. Umber grimaced and shook his hand. "*That* was for the murder of my friend Galbus. And Argent before him, you unworthy toad."

"Umber!" cried Hap, as Larcombe leaped forward, raising a dagger that he'd concealed in his sleeve. Umber turned to see the blade slashing through the air, and he flung himself backward. The blade missed, whipping through the air, and Larcombe stumbled, expecting resistance when the dagger met Umber's flesh. Umber fell on his back and rolled away as Larcombe caught his balance and came again with the dagger high over one shoulder, spitting with rage.

There was a sound, or many sounds, from nowhere, from everywhere, like cracks of thunder. Larcombe was in the air, leaping toward Umber, and suddenly was pushed aside as if a gust of wind had taken him. He thumped on the dock, as limp as a rag doll, with staring glassy eyes. His mouth moved without making a sound. A leg jerked. And then he was still.

Hap's ears rang from the sound. Umber gaped toward the men with those strange clubs. Some still had their weapons leveled, pointing toward Larcombe. Smoke hung in the air before them, and Hap caught a sharp chemical scent that reminded him of volcanic fumes.

"What . . . what foul magic is this?" Loden moaned. His hands clutched his stomach.

Doane tipped his head back and laughed with a merriment that chilled Hap's blood. "Magic? My boy, those are *rifles* that fire *bullets*, just as your old bows fire arrows. It's not magic at all—it's invention!"

Loden stared at Umber with a child's disbelief. Hap was

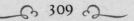

amazed to find himself feeling pity for their enemy. And then Hap saw blood gush from between Loden's fingers. Loden eased down to one knee, and laid himself slowly on the planks, facing the sky.

Doane frowned at the king, and then at the men and their rifles. "Who's the one with the terrible aim? I've told you, make sure of your target before you squeeze the trigger!" He clucked his tongue. "Still, I suppose he brought it on himself." Doane strode to where Loden lay with his mouth open, gasping. He bent down and took the crown from Loden's head. Loden's hand rose weakly up and gripped one side of the crown. Doane tugged back. "Really, Loden, this is pointless." He yanked hard, and Loden's fingers slipped free. There was a crimson smear on the side of the crown.

Doane placed the crown on his head, purposefully askew. "King me!" he said, chuckling. He gave Loden another glance. "As for you, dear Loden, you are gut shot and doomed. Hours of agony and eventual demise lie ahead. So trust me when I say I'm doing you a favor." He crooked a finger and beckoned one of the men with the rifles.

Umber had gotten to his knees, and he raised a hand and screamed. "No—wait!" But another dose of thunder rang out, and Hap was glad that he turned away and saw nothing.

Doane helped Umber rise. Umber trembled from head to

foot and looked like a ghost as he searched his old friend's face. "Jonathan . . . we . . . I . . . have made progress with medicine. We might have saved him."

Doane looked at Loden's still form. His mouth twisted up at the corner. "Save him? Whatever for? Deposed kings only cause trouble. Now, Brian, we need to catch up—how long has it been? So many years! Why don't we have a chat in that tower of yours. I believe you call it the Aerie? And if the reports are correct, you can treat me to coffee!" He turned to the spy. "Spakeman, have that coachman drive you to the gates. Tell those fools that their idiot king has surrendered his crown to the Supremacy. They will lay down their arms and open those gates, or else we will reduce Kurahaven to rubble and burn the flesh from their bones."

The spy, Spakeman, bowed his head and put his hand over his heart. "Yes, Supremacy."

"And bring the carriage back when you're done," Doane said. Spakeman hurried away.

Doane looked at Umber again, shaking his head and smiling widely, and he threw his arms around Umber once more and thumped his back. "My dear, dear Brian. I still can't believe it's really you."

"I feel the same," said Umber, who had found his grip on his emotions once more. He dropped his voice. "Jonathan, how long have you been in this world? How did you get here?" His manner was friendly, but Hap saw how carefully Umber examined his old friend's face.

"About ten years, I believe," Doane said. Hap was the only one standing close enough to hear the conversation, and Doane gave him a suspicious glance.

"Don't worry about Hap," Umber assured him. He tousled Hap's hair. "He knows everything about me, and where I came from."

Doane puckered his mouth. "Ah! A confidante! Good for you, Brian. Well, if you trust him, then I trust him. No secrets between friends like us, eh? Ha! As for your other question—I don't know how I came to be here. The last thing I remember was that mob bursting into our facility. I was trying to get to you, help you save the Reboot computer. There was smoke, and fire, and I was knocked to the ground and trampled, and it all went black. What about you?"

"Same story, more or less," Umber said. He looked over Doane's shoulder and saw Loden's and Larcombe's bodies on the docks. "Can we . . . step away from those two?"

"Of course, of course!" cried Doane. With an arm around Umber's shoulder, he walked twenty strides down the dock. Umber gestured for Hap to follow. When Doane saw Hap tagging along, he laughed. "He's like your little green-eyed puppy, isn't he?"

Hap fought to keep a scowl off his face, and Umber ignored the comment. "Jonathan," he said quietly. "There's something different about you. You are . . . not quite the man I knew."

"Is that so?" Doane said, leaning back. "What do you think is so different, Brian?"

Umber tapped his fingers together. He spoke slowly, choosing his words with care. "When you started Project Reboot, you told me that you did it out of fear. You were afraid that technology—the destructive side of technology, that is—was giving us the capacity to ruin our own civilization, either through malice or mishap. You remember, don't you? We created Reboot to preserve the best of human achievements—in case the worst happened, and survivors needed to rebuild."

Doane lifted his chin and stared at the sky. His eyes lost focus. "Of course I remember that. And I know what you're thinking, Brian. But from the moment I arrived here . . . I suppose I saw things differently. Are you trying to tell me that . . ." A rumble of wheels approached, and Doane glanced at the returning carriage. "Ah, our ride is back. Let us go to your Aerie, Brian—or should I say Lord Umber? I am eager to get a look inside!"

Spakeman stepped out of the carriage and held the door for Umber and Hap. Doane took a moment to bark orders at Spakeman and the small army, giving Umber and Hap the chance for a hurried, whispered conversation.

"Hap, are you making any progress with the filaments?"

"I saw them once. But they went out again."

Umber's jaw slid from side to side. "Remember when I told you that I felt like a changed man, coming to this world? Less cautious, more exuberant?"

Hap nodded.

"I think when we cross worlds, we're altered somehow," Umber said. "It's a crucible that remakes our brains. Jonathan got here the same way as me: A Meddler brought him. And if Willy Nilly brought me, who do you suppose brought Jonathan?"

"Willy's nemesis," Hap said, as the hairs on the back of his neck stood tall.

"Exactly! Pell Mell! I'm sure of it, Hap. And now Jonathan is a changed man, like me. This cruel disregard for life . . . this thirst for conquest . . . that monstrosity he's built! Of all people, Jonathan Doane knew better. He had compassion. He understood where technology run amok might lead us. I have to find a way to reason with him, make him see—" Umber's mouth snapped shut, and he nudged Hap with his elbow. The carriage shifted as Doane boarded and sat on the opposite bench.

"This will be a leisurely ride," Doane said, leaning back and folding his hands over his stomach, as if he'd just enjoyed a great feast. "My men will follow on foot." As the carriage jolted into motion, Doane whistled that familiar song, with horse hooves for percussion. He lifted the crown from his head, and used his sleeve to wipe Loden's blood away. The other crowns around his waist hung from a chain, and he threaded his new prize among the rest. "Look at my trophies, Brian. We cruised in the *Vanquisher* from kingdom to kingdom, and every coastal city fell within hours." Doane shook the chain so that the crowns clanged against one another. "Technology is a beautiful thing, is it not, when the advantage is yours!"

Umber did not react. Doane's eyes crinkled merrily at the corners as he turned to Hap. "So, young man, you know Lord Umber's secrets, do you? Let's see if you can guess this: Do you know how I learned that someone from my world might be here in Kurahaven?"

Hap shook his head.

Doane crossed a leg over the other knee and clasped his hands behind his head. "It was the *music*, of all things." He puckered and whistled a different, unfamiliar tune. "Sound familiar?"

Umber saw the uncertainty in Hap's expression and offered the answer in a weary voice. "Beethoven. It was one of the first pieces I introduced here. The people loved it."

"Exactly!" cried Doane, reaching out to slap Umber's knee. "They loved it, and shared it. That melody came over the wide Rulian Sea, carried from player to player—a virus spreading, a beacon reaching beyond the blue! Finally a wandering musician arrived in my land, and he knew the most glorious music, which of course I recognized at once. It could only have come from my world. *I was not alone!* And so I sent my spies to Kurahaven, to learn the source."

Doane looked at Hap again, with an unblinking stare that felt as intense as the sun. That manic energy reminded Hap, in a strange way, of Umber's exuberance. But there was something frightening behind Doane's fervor. Hap noticed for the first time the tiny twitches in the crags of Doane's face. One eye's pupil was twice the size of the other, with veins of blood spilling into the white. "Can you imagine my reaction when the name came back to me?" Doane said, leaning close. "The music was from Umber, my dearest friend! And in Kurahaven of all places—the grandest city in the richest kingdom of all, the jewel of the world that I coveted most."

"You must have been surprised, sir," Hap said quietly.

"Shocked. Delighted! But, my boy, you must refer to me as Supremacy. Though, Brian, you and only you may use my name." Doane stuck his head out the window and looked back toward the palace. Hap looked at Umber, who took the moment to breathe deeply and rub his temples with his fingers. He glanced back at Hap and raised his eyebrows and hands, as if asking the same question in Hap's mind: *What now?*

With a contented sigh, Doane withdrew his head from the window and leaned back with his arms spread wide. "Brian, tell me something. Are the days a little shorter here?"

"By about nineteen of our minutes," Umber replied.

"I knew it!" Doane crowed, and he nodded to himself, looking pleased with the answer. "Took a little getting used to, didn't it?"

"Hmm" was all Umber said.

Doane's feet tapped on the floor. His fidgeting reminded Hap again of Umber's constant state of motion. "Do you miss anything from our world, Brian?" Doane asked. "Living in this ancient and backward land?"

Umber stared at some distant point, eyes unfocused. "I miss certain friends. Modern plumbing. The lights of the cities. College sports. Pop-Tarts."

Doane rolled his head back and guffawed. "All good, all

good! But, Brian, I have to confess: I don't miss any of it. What I've achieved here . . . what I've created . . . if you told me how to get back, I wouldn't go, not for all the conveniences, all the modern wonders."

Umber's eyes refocused on his old friend. "What have you achieved, Jonathan? How did all this come to be?"

Doane sat forward and rubbed his knees with his hands. His smile jerked at the corner as he gave Hap another inspection, perhaps still wondering if it was safe to speak in his presence. Hap wriggled in his seat.

"I awoke in this world," Doane said, "across the Rulian Sea, in what you call the Far Continent. It had many other names, over there, as many names as it had petty kings and warlords. Brian, you and your neighboring kingdoms rarely venture to those shores. And for good reason. Do you know what people dwell there, young man?"

"No, Supremacy," Hap said.

Umber answered the question. "Outcasts."

"Correct," said Doane. "Men who were banished from these lands. Criminals and pirates populated the coast, while the inlands were full of barbaric clans—and of course the usual roster of goblins and trolls that plague this world. So you see, Umber, I did not appear in such a genteel land as you. I was

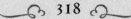

dropped into a lawless, vicious place, where only the fist and the sword mattered.

"But like you, Umber, I found patronage soon enough that helped me rise to power. You found it with a king. I found it with a thug named Thurbor. If what my spies told me is true, your ascent began when you cast down a sorceress. Mine began when I gave Thurbor what he desired most in the world: power. I made weapons for him, things nobody in this world had ever seen before!"

Umber blinked slowly. "It must have been child's play for you."

Doane raised his fists. "Easier than you can imagine. You remember what I studied? My lifelong obsession?"

Umber looked sideways at Hap. "My friend Jonathan was an expert on the history of military technology."

Doane nodded. "With an emphasis on the sixteenth to the nineteenth centuries."

Umber spoke slowly, choosing his words and tone with care. "There was a time when you looked at the progress of military technology and feared that it might end in the destruction of civilization."

Doane laughed and waved the remark away like a bothersome fly. "I don't dwell on the past these days. Or the

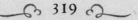

future. Brian, don't you see? I was the perfect man to bring order to that chaos in the Far Continent. But it wasn't just that I *knew* exactly what to do. All the raw materials I required were there in front of me! Gunpowder, that was no trick—a fool can make gunpowder. But, Brian, we had oil, sitting in puddles on the ground, waiting to be ladled up! We had rich veins of ore in the hills. And that was just the beginning. My heart and brain nearly burst as the possibility become clear: the single greatest leap in military might that the world had ever known. Guns, cannons, explosives—I knew how to make them all. I could lead a force and unite the world under a single flag. Something no man has ever been able to achieve, in *any* world." Doane closed his eyes for a moment, savoring the notion.

"What happened to the thug? Your patron?" Umber asked.

Doane's eyes flickered open. He angled his head to one side. "Eventually my people realized who the true leader ought to be. Really, why should power stay *behind* the throne?" Doane scraped his thumb across his throat. "Thurbor was removed by someone who desired my favor. And he earned it—that man is now my envoy. And what you call the Far Continent is now the Land of Doane."

The carriage groaned to a stop, and the face of one of Doane's armed men appeared at the window. He spoke to

Doane with his eyes turned down. "We have arrived at the stone tower, Supremacy."

"Here at last," Doane said. He reached for the handle of the door, pushed it open, and gestured for Hap and Umber to climb out. Hap looked toward the gatehouse of the Aerie and saw Umber's guardsmen on the other side of the bars of the gate, staring at the company that had arrived. Balfour was with them, squinting toward Umber, trying to read his expression and see what they ought to do.

A strange thing happened, and it made Hap's breath stop cold. The light of day dimmed momentarily, and there was a whispery sound like hand passing across silk. Hap had sensed those phenomena before, when Willy Nilly had come and gone. But this could not be Willy. It was someone or something else.

The armed men lifted their heads to peer around. And then Hap saw many of them whirl to stare in the same direction at something behind them. He turned and saw a figure standing on the causeway, fully eight feet tall. It was a creature like Occo, the vicious, relentless, many-eyed being that had once pursued him and nearly killed him.

This was the Executioner.

CHAPTER
26

The Executioner stood on the causeway with his back to them, stretching his arms wide and flexing his spidery fingers. He was either unaware of the small army with their deadly rifles, or he did not care.

Occo, Hap's first enemy, had obscured his shape beneath a flowing robe. But this creature did not care who saw him or his strange, birdlike legs; his only garment was a glittering armored mesh that covered his torso, leaving his head and limbs bare. In the back of his hairless head was a single glittering green eye. A Meddler's eye.

Doane's men murmured to one another, and in the corner of his vision Hap saw the rifles rise up to point.

The creature turned, and the invaders gasped. The mouth

was filled with sharply pointed yellow teeth. The pale face was studded with eyes, in sockets scattered at random across its cheeks, forehead, and chin. Wrinkled lids of gray skin closed over each eye and snapped up again. There were a dozen sockets at least, filled with a menagerie of eyes plucked from unfortunate humans and animals—because this creature was a thief of eyes who could plant any eye into his face and make it serve his brain.

Hap's stomach turned as he saw five more sparkling green eyes in the Executioner's face. *Six altogether,* he thought, wondering which two were Willy's. He looked right and left, trying to choose a way to run if the Executioner sprang upon him.

"What is that thing, Brian?" asked Doane, staring at the Executioner with his lip flared on one side.

"I don't know what it's called, but it's dangerous," Umber replied.

Doane glanced down at Hap. "He has your young friend's eyes."

"Not yet, he doesn't," Umber said, stepping in front of Hap. The Executioner stood still, with only his eyes moving, quivering and peering about as the wrinkled flaps snapped up and down.

Doane put his hands on his hips and sighed. This appearance

seemed more like an annoyance to him than a genuine threat. "Strange and unnatural creatures. I'm told they fascinate you, Brian, in all shapes and forms. For me they are a dangerous nuisance, to be exterminated. And we have the firepower to do so. Shall I?" He raised his hand with a finger extended, and behind him every rifle was leveled toward the Executioner.

Umber bit his lip and frowned. Hap could see him struggling with the question, appreciating the chance to wipe out this threat but reviling the means. "Wait," Umber finally said. He took a deep breath and called out to the creature.

"You there! I will warn you once: You cannot have what you've come for. One of your kind has already died trying. Leave us, and do not return."

The creature's response was a vile slurp that seemed endless. One brown human eye was trained on Umber, while the rest of the assorted eyes focused on Hap. The sight of Hap's eyes seemed to fill the Executioner with an insatiable hunger. A sheet of saliva poured out of his wide, curving mouth, and the needle-sharp teeth glistened with moisture. When he spoke, the voice was so much like Occo's dreadful rasp that Hap covered his mouth to stifle a moan.

"The boy's creation was forbidden," the Executioner said. "And so his eyes must be surrendered. I am the appointed Executioner." He extended the longest finger of one hand.

The fingernail was wide and curved like a scoop, and Hap knew at once what it could be used for. The knowledge made him want to clap his hands across his eyes.

"Appointed by whom?" shouted Umber.

"By fate itself," the Executioner said. He slurped again and began to walk toward them in long strides, on bizarre legs that bent backward at the knee.

Doane tapped Umber's shoulder. "I can help you, Brian."

Umber shut his eyes and replied through teeth clamped tight. "Do it. Please."

Doane thrust his pointed finger toward the Executioner and called to his men: "Kill that thing." The rifles roared, spewing a cloud of smoke. Stones on the causeway sparked and shattered, but the Executioner was no longer there. He had leaped to one side, and he disappeared over the steep embankment, heading toward the water. But there was no splash or thump of a body on the rocky slope. Instead the world dimmed again for a moment, and a silky whoosh could be heard.

Doane stepped to the edge of the causeway and peered down. "I don't see him. Think we got him?"

"Probably not," Umber said. He looked pale and shaken.

"Pity. But that'll teach him to threaten my friends, won't it?" said Doane, clapping his hands and rubbing them together. "Come on, Brian. Invite me in, and we'll talk some more!"

Hap felt like tiny pins were stabbing his nerves from head to toe. At any moment he expected the Executioner to appear again and snatch him away. The size of the creature had shaken him. The Executioner seemed infinitely more dangerous and confident than Occo. *And he's got something Occo always wanted: the eyes of a Meddler,* Hap thought. *No, three Meddlers! Does that make him three times more powerful? He can vanish and reappear—even predict his own fate.* He folded his arms tight against his stomach. It seemed to him that an hourglass had been turned, to show how little time he had left, and the sand was quickly draining.

Doane ambled around the grand hall with his hands clasped behind his back, inspecting the artifacts with a doubtful eye, but admiring the great carved pillars and the machinery of Umber's lift. Hap heard the clatter of utensils and pots in the kitchen, as Balfour brewed a pot of coffee. Half of the armed men had stayed downstairs, while the rest were in the grand hall, spread out and watching in every direction, protecting their leader from any threat. When Oates and Sophie came downstairs, rifles swiveled in their direction. Oates glared back, irritated, and his fists bulged. Umber waved them over to the table. Sophie sat down with her eyes wide and mouth pressed tight.

"Oates, listen carefully," Umber said quietly. "I know you think you could throttle every one of those men, but believe me: Those things they're holding are deadly weapons that would slay you in an instant. And they can kill you from a great distance. So hold your temper and don't do anything rash. Understand?"

Oates stuck his jaw out and nodded. "Should I put on my muzzle?"

Umber sucked on his teeth, and then shook his head. "I can't imagine you saying anything that would make the situation worse. But . . . I'll tell you what. Take Sophie to the archives and wait until you hear from me."

Oates wrinkled his nose. "The archives? With Smudge?"

"Yes, with Smudge. You can stand his company for a short while. Sophie, tell Smudge what's happening. Go on, both of you."

Doane stepped in front of Sophie's latest painting, an enormous canvas depicting the massive sea-giants at rest in their watery cavern. He squinted and snorted. "Brian. You've developed the strangest obsession."

Umber forced a smile. "Yes . . . it seems that coming here had a curious effect on my mind."

Doane gave Umber a sideways glance. Then his expression brightened as Balfour pushed the kitchen door open with his elbow and came out holding a silver tray cluttered with mugs and a steaming pot.

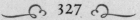

"Is that . . . ?" Doane asked hopefully.

"The world's finest coffee," Umber said. "I know I could use some. Join me." He pulled out the chair at the head of the table, and Doane settled into it. Doane grinned when he saw a bowl with lumps of sugar on the table, and dropped a pair into his mug while Balfour poured. He didn't raise the mug and drink, Hap noticed, until Umber had taken a sip.

Doane raised his chin and closed his eyes as he savored the coffee. "I'd almost forgotten the taste," he said with a sigh.

Umber cupped both hands around his mug. "We need to talk, Jonathan."

"We certainly do," Doane replied over the lip of his mug.

Umber dropped his voice to a whisper. "You must know that you aren't the man you used to be."

Doane smiled back, as if given a compliment. "I won't contradict you."

"It's something that happens to us when we cross between worlds," Umber said. He pushed his mug aside and leaned closer. "It changed me, too. It seems to induce a kind of mania. Look at us, Jonathan. I run around this world like a madman, hardly aware of the danger I'm plunging into. I was never such a thrill-seeker back home. And my emotions—I was always plagued by mood swings, but nothing like the lows that strike me here. And *you* . . ."

Doane's contented smile settled into a horizontal line. "And me?"

Umber took a deep breath and stretched his neck. "Jonathan. My friend. Back home you saw where the wrong kind of technology might lead us. That's why you started Project Reboot. Don't you remember? We did it to preserve the good things, against the possibility that humanity's misguided ingenuity might bring it all crashing down. But now look what you've done. You've leapfrogged five hundred years of military science. And for what?"

Doane sat quietly for a moment. Hap stared at his face, but Doane's emotions were impossible to decipher. Umber's old friend spread his fingers over his heart and spoke theatrically. *"'Is it not worthy of tears that, when the number of worlds is infinite, we have not yet become lords of a single one?'* That's an extraordinary quote, Brian. Do you know who said it?"

Umber's fingers drummed on his mug. "I do not."

"Alexander the Great himself! Can you believe it? More than two thousand years ago they imagined the existence of other worlds. And Alexander wept because even he, the greatest general of them all, could not realize his dream: one world, one conqueror, one ruler." Doane raised his fist and slammed it down. "But I can! Brian, my friend, it cannot be coincidence that I've been given this chance to forge a legacy that will ring through the ages. I had the knowledge, I was given the materials, and this new life has galvanized my brain and granted me the ambition! This is what great men live for: to seize their moment, when it arrives, so that the world still speaks their name with awe two thousand years later!"

Umber stared with his mouth agape. He leaned back in his chair and shook his head. "But you've lost your better self, Jonathan. You've killed innocent people. Sunk defenseless ships. The Jonathan Doane I knew would never have done that."

Doane sat back. A sly smile appeared, and then slowly vanished. Doubt and confusion blossomed on his face, as if he'd exhausted himself with his ravings. He sat in silence for a long while as Umber watched, keeping very still. Finally Doane's fingers came up and tapped against his lips. "The Jonathan you knew. He . . . he wouldn't have, would he?"

Umber clasped his hands and raised them. "Jonathan, you should try it my way—it is deeply satisfying. I've made my impact on this world without hastening its demise. We can do this together—make this the kind of world we both dreamed about. You have so much more to offer than guns and warships!" His chest heaved, and Hap wondered if Umber's heart was thumping as fast and hard as his.

Doane sagged a little in his seat. With his lower lip jutting, he stared at the crowns that hung from his waist. "It doesn't

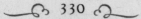

hurt to consider the possibility, I suppose. Let's presume that you are right, Brian. What do you think I should do?"

Umber looked at Doane's armed men on the other side of the room and spoke more quietly still. "We need to undo what you've done, as much as possible. Erase the engineering."

Doane's unruly eyebrows rose. "Erase it? How?"

Umber's knee bounced to a frantic rhythm as his excitement grew. "First, destroy the *Vanquisher*."

A twitch appeared at the corner of Doane's eye. "Destroy it?"

"Yes! Send it to the bottom of the sea. It would be easy. The hold must be full of explosives, correct?"

Doane's forehead wrinkled, and he nodded. "Stuffed like a Christmas turkey. Crate after crate of artillery, rockets, bullets, and bombs. Enough to reduce seven Kurahavens to rubble and dust."

Umber wiped his palms on his thighs. "Order most of the crew to disembark. You and I will take a skeleton crew and steer the ship into deep water, and set a fire. One of my smaller ships will get us all away before the *Vanquisher* explodes."

"And then what?"

Umber rocked in his seat. "Where did you build it? Are there any more like it?"

Doane leaned forward. "I have a shipyard, factories, and

refineries in the Land of Doane. The whole area is walled off and heavily guarded, to protect its secrets. A second ship, identical to the *Vanquisher*, is under construction there, and half complete. It will be called *Destroyer*." Hap saw the fingers in Doane's clasped hands clenching tighter, turning white and red.

"There is hope, then," Umber said, struggling to keep his voice from rising. "The second ship can be dismantled. The factories and refineries too. All the records and evidence destroyed. We can reverse this, Doane, as best we can!"

"You're forgetting something," Doane said. "The men who build the ships. The engineers I've trained. Would you have me send their brains to the bottom of the sea too?"

Umber slumped sideways on one elbow. "That's the trouble with ideas, isn't it? When they are out, they are out. Nobody knows that better than me." He rubbed his temple and squinted, concentrating. Then he straightened again and made a circle with his arms. "Wait. But you keep those men inside the walls of your shipyard, don't you? The same way you keep others outside the walls!"

Doane nodded. "That's exactly what I do. Nobody leaves and nobody enters. I want my secrets to be mine alone."

Umber's eyes shone. "We could isolate those men—take them to an island somewhere, banish them. I'll make sure they're treated well, fed and comfortable. It's mildly cruel, but nothing compared to the suffering we can avert." Umber stood, too excited to stay seated anymore. "Jonathan, it's not too late. We can reverse much of what you've done. It's not a perfect solution—but it can delay the inevitable."

Doane looked up at Umber, and then sideways at his armed men. He sniffed, and as Hap watched, his expression hardened once more. His lip curved into a sneer. "Sit down, Brian," he said in a cold voice.

Umber's color drained from his face, and he sank into the seat, casting a mournful look at Hap. It was suddenly clear that Doane had been playing along, pretending to entertain the idea.

"You think I've gone mad since I came here," Doane said. "Has it occurred to you that this new Doane is the true man, and the other one was the fool?"

"Never," muttered Umber.

Doane laughed. "You want me to help you. But, Brian, my boy, it is you who is going to help me."

"I don't want any part of what you're doing," Umber said.

"I only ask for one small thing."

Umber stared back. "What, Jonathan?"

Doane put his hands behind his head and rocked back in his chair. "Give me the computer."

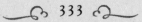

There are r___ of a giant beanstalk __ Londria. Perhaps, when all this is __ I'll wander __ and see if I can __

CHAPTER
27

Umber tried to control his reaction, but Hap saw the way his jaw tensed.

"Computer? I don't know what you mean, Jonathan," Umber said.

Doane leaned his head to one side, propped with two fingers to the temple. "Brian. Give me some credit. Of course you have the computer. You have a first-rate intellect, but you certainly did not produce an entire Beethoven sonata from memory. Or the blueprints for those sailing ships. Or the architecture, or the medicines, or any of your other marvels. It's perfectly obvious that when you came to this world, you brought the Reboot Suitcase with you."

Hap could hear the breath whistling out of Umber's nose.

"It stopped working about a year ago," Umber finally said. "The hard drive crashed."

"Really? Let me see it," Doane said. The last trace of good humor vanished from his expression. He stared like a bird of prey.

"When I knew it was unfixable, I dropped it into the sea."

"Brian, you don't understand. My spy has been observing you for more than a year. Your innovations have never stopped coming. You are lying."

Umber stretched his neck and rolled his shoulders. "Even if it still existed, what good would it do you? Weapons were never the point of Project Reboot. That computer saved the best that our civilization had to offer. Not the worst."

Doane puckered his lips. "Don't be naive, Brian. Technology is technology, and perfectly adaptable from peacetime to wartime." He reached into the fold in the front of his loose-fitting jacket. When he drew his hand out, it was wrapped around the handle of a small object that reminded Hap of the terrible rifles. "But really, at a moment like this, we must be straightforward with each other. History is counting on us."

Umber looked down at the object with undisguised disgust. "Oh, Jonathan. A pistol, too?"

"Brian, I realize you want to be noble. But you're getting in my way. Stop this nonsense and give me the computer. I know it's here. And I know how to make you give it to me." Doane turned the weapon until it was pointing directly at Hap's chest.

Umber's face trembled. "Jonathan, you wouldn't dream of harming this boy if you knew what I know."

"Why don't you tell me what you know," Doane said. "Right after you fetch the computer."

There was a yelp of pain from the other side of the room. One of the armed men reached down and rubbed his ankle. Doane gave him a sideways glance and returned his gaze to Umber and Hap. "What's the matter with that man?" Doane called out.

"Something stung me," the man said. He sucked air through his teeth. "Aagh, it hurts!"

Another man, not far from the first, cried out in pain. He lifted one foot and hopped on the other. Hap realized that both of them were standing close to some bureaus near the side of the grand hall.

"Perhaps we have hornets," Umber said. Doane stood up and backed away from the table, keeping the pistol leveled at Hap.

A third man screamed, even as the first two cried out as their pain grew. "I saw something under there," said another man, pointing. "Get away from the furniture! There's something under there—and it's no hornet!"

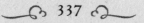

"What is this, Brian?" shouted Doane.

"I haven't the slightest idea," Umber said. When Doane glanced the other way, he looked at Hap and waggled an eyebrow. Hap knew perfectly well what was happening.

Two of the men grabbed the bureau and tipped it over. Hap winced as priceless artifacts crashed to the floor. "There!" cried one of the armed men. Hap saw Thimble at the base of the wall. His tiny feet were a blur as he raced along with a mad grin on his face and his poison-tipped spear at his side. Three of the men raised their rifles. Thimble reached a crack in the wall and darted inside as the rifles fired. Sparks flew and bits of stone were torn from the wall. Another man in the middle of the room dropped his rifle and fell, gripping his knee.

"Stop it, the bullets are bouncing off the walls, you idiots!" shouted Doane, waving the pistol. Umber and Hap stood, and Umber stepped in front of Hap as Doane whirled on them again. The pistol was shaking in his hand.

Hap looked around Umber's side in time to see an arm appear in the opening of the ceiling, where the lift rose up to the third floor. The hand held one of Umber's colored bottles. The bottle was dropped, and it shattered on the floor. Hap was never sure what would come out of one of those bottles—an illusion or a cloud of sleep-inducing smoke— but this one produced a thick purple mist that formed itself into a trio of huge, writhing serpents. Every man who could still stand raised his weapon and fired, but the bullets passed through the phantoms, tearing holes in the paintings and maps on the walls.

Two more bottles fell, smashing on the floor. A red mist billowed out, and as soon as it washed over the armed men, they wobbled and slumped to the ground.

When Doane turned toward his men, bellowing with dismay, Umber spun and grabbed Hap by the sleeve. They ran for the corridor that led to the archives and beyond.

Doane cried out behind them: "Stop!" Another crack rang out, and Hap heard a bullet ping off the wall of the corridor as they crossed the threshold. Umber grabbed the edge of the door and flung it closed. Before it shut, Hap saw Doane charging, leveling his pistol to shoot again. As the door slammed, a bullet struck the other side.

Umber leaned against the heavy door to keep it shut as Doane flung his body against it. Hap joined him, throwing his back against the door. Something hard hammered on the wood, and Doane screamed hoarsely. "I'll kill you, Brian! I'll . . . kill . . . kill . . ." There was a cough, and then the sound of Doane's body against wood, sliding down.

Umber looked with alarm at a thin wisp of smoke trailing under the door. "Don't breathe that!" he said, putting his foot

across the space and pulling his shirt over his mouth. Hap did the same.

"Was that Balfour who saved us?" Hap said through the fabric.

Umber nodded, and Hap could see his eyes crinkling at the corners. "Balfour indeed," Umber said. "Our action hero! And little Thimble, of course."

Oates and Sophie came down the hall from the archives. Sophie looked like a pale ghost, Oates like an angry bear. "What were those noises?" Oates asked.

"Something that doesn't belong here," Umber said. He uncovered his mouth and released the door.

Hap folded his arms tight against his chest. "What now?"

Umber paced in a tight circle, working his mouth from side to side. "I'm open to suggestions. We have a dozen invaders knocked out on the other side of this door, along with the most dangerous man in the world. There are another dozen enemy downstairs, wide awake and unhappy. Welkin, Barkin, and Dodd are in the gatehouse, hopefully out of harm's way. Balfour is upstairs—he kept some of my trick bottles in his room, but I think he's used all he had. Am I forgetting anything?" He came to a stop and scratched the top of his head.

Hap, Oates, and Sophie took turns giving one another

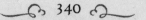

worried, bewildered looks. *We're trapped,* Hap said to himself. He stared down the hall, which led past the archives and plunged deep into the caverns behind the Aerie, where the sorceress had escaped. "Wait," Hap said, even as the idea took shape in his mind. He turned to see Umber staring back with his mouth cinched tight.

"Let's take him," Hap said. "Before anybody wakes up. Just open the door and grab your old friend. You can put him in Turiana's cell."

Oates frowned at Umber. "Your old friend is the most dangerous man in the world?"

Umber ignored the question. "Hap, you're a genius. That is where we keep our dangerous minds, isn't it?" He put his hand on the knob of the door and dropped his voice. "The smoke should be mostly cleared by now. I'll open the door for a peek. If it's safe, I'll throw it open—Oates, I want you to grab the man lying just outside and pull him back in. Ready?"

Oates crept up beside the door and nodded at Umber. Umber grabbed the doorknob. "Hap and Sophie—stand back in case they fire on us." Umber yanked the door open enough to peer out into the grand hall and stuck his face in the gap.

CHAPTER
28

He withdrew his head just as quickly and looked at the others with his jaw hanging loose. Then he swung the door open wide.

"He's gone," Umber said. Through the threshold, Hap could see the bodies of the armed men scattered across the floor with their rifles by their sides. But Doane was not where he should have been, outside the door.

Umber stepped into the grand hall and peered right and left. He coughed and covered his mouth with his hand. The odor of the potion still hung in the air, a sweet and flowery scent that made Hap feel the faintest touch of drowsiness.

"How could he have gotten away?" Hap asked.

"I don't think he could have," Umber said. "Unless

someone . . ." He froze, and then gestured frantically for them to get back to safety in the corridor. There were footfalls on the steps, coming up from below. Before Umber could swing the door shut, they saw Dodd's familiar face appear as he raced upstairs.

"Dodd!" cried Umber, waving to him. "Quick—over here!"

Dodd smiled and raised a hand. "No need to hide, Lord Umber. The Aerie is a stronghold once more." He looked down at the dozen senseless men on the floor. "We'll have to do something about these rascals before they wake up, though."

"Kill 'em!" cried a small voice from ankle-high. Thimble had stepped out from a crack in the wall. The tiny fellow had a knife brandished in one hand, and he whipped it from side to side.

"That's not the kind of folk we are," Umber said, dropping into a squat.

"Not the kind of folk we are," Thimble repeated, mimicking the words as if Umber were a whiny brat. "This will be your undoing, Umber. I heard the whole exchange with this Jonathan of yours. He won't show you mercy. Any of these men will kill you on his orders. Why give them the chance? Don't worry, I'll do it for you. Their necks are down here where I want them. . . . A little nick is all it takes."

"Thimble!" cried Umber, in a voice stern enough to stop

the tiny man in his tracks. "If you slit a single neck I'll bring an army of cats into the Aerie within the hour. Now get back to your hole in the wall and leave this to us."

Thimble grumbled, shook a fist at Umber, and slipped into the shadowy crevice between two stones.

Umber shook his head as he watched Thimble disappear. When he turned to speak to Dodd, his mouth opened into a horrified circle. "Dodd!" he cried.

Dodd had picked up a rifle to inspect it and was holding it straight and staring curiously down its length, as he'd watched the invaders do. He looked up, shocked by the tone of Umber's voice.

"Dodd, put it down," Umber bellowed, pointing at the floor. "Stop looking at it! Stop thinking about it!" Dodd bent to lay the rifle on the floor and stood straight again, stung by Umber's words.

Umber wiped a hand across his eyes and collected his wits. "Sorry, Dodd . . . I didn't mean to be harsh. Listen, tell me what happened just now. Where is the leader of these brutes?"

Dodd cleared his throat and managed a smile. "Welkin, Barkin, and I were downstairs, being watched by a gang of those invaders. Then we heard those banging sounds upstairs— what a commotion! Some of the men rushed up to the grand hall, and they came back, staggering from that sleep potion, dragging that Supremacy or whatever they call him behind them. They carried him outside, and I have to say, they're not the brightest bunch, because all but two of them forget about us. We caught them by surprise and grabbed those death-sticks away, and they ran out after the others. Then we slammed the door after them and barred it."

Umber thumped Dodd on the shoulder. "Wonderful. And where did they all go?"

Dodd pointed with his thumb. "In the gatehouse and on the causeway. Trying to revive their leader."

"He won't be asleep much longer," Umber said. "Let's get busy. Oates, lug these bodies down to the gatehouse. Dodd, tie them up so they won't cause trouble." Umber turned to Hap and Sophie and breathed deep before speaking. "You two. Pick up those rifles. I'll get the ones from downstairs. Don't touch the metal loop near the middle, and do not point the hollow end at yourselves or the others. Stack them in the corner and cover them with a tablecloth from the kitchen. Understood?"

Sophie nodded. "Understood," said Hap.

The lift clattered into motion, engaged from above. Balfour appeared, riding down on one of the platforms. Umber gave him an enormous grin and clapped his hands loudly together, while the old man blushed and waved away the applause.

"This one's dead," Oates announced in a booming voice.

He was standing over the man who'd been struck in the leg by a bullet that bounced off the wall. Hap saw a glistening pool of blood beneath his sprawled form.

Umber's applause ended. He walked over to the body and darted an angry glare at the rifle at his feet. "How easily they kill." He shook his head. "Bring him downstairs with the others, Oates. Quickly. I don't know how much longer they'll sleep."

"I could just snap all the necks," Oates said, twisting an imaginary head with his hands.

"What is it with you people!" Umber cried, shaking his arms. "Just bring them downstairs. *Gently!*" he added, as Oates tossed an unconscious man over his shoulder like a dishrag.

Hap was draping a cloth over the stack of rifles when the voice drifted through the window. "Brian! We need to talk!"

Balfour was closest, and he peered out quickly, pulling his head back an instant later in case bullets flew. "It's your friend, the homicidal madman," he told Umber.

Umber stood beside the window with his back to the wall. He shouted without showing his face. "Jonathan, this has to stop."

"I want the computer. And I mean to have it." The tone of Doane's voice had changed. Before, Hap had the impression

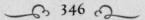

346

that he was wildly entertained by his violent expedition. All that remained was a cold, venomous fury.

"Even if I had it, I wouldn't give it to you," Umber replied. "Look what you've done with the knowledge you have! No, Jonathan. I'd sooner smash it on the rocks. Hurl it into the sea."

A silence followed, oddly peaceful, with only the sound of gulls. Then Doane spoke again. "Listen, Brian. I'm returning to my ship now. My men will guard this causeway, and they'll signal me when you produce the object I'm looking for. If you don't, I will turn every gun on the *Vanquisher* upon this city of yours. And wherever I see your hand at work, I will destroy it. Your sailing ships. Your libraries and schools. Your hospital. Every hint of modern architecture. You would ask me to sink my ship, and undo everything I've accomplished? Then that will be *your* fate, Brian. I suggest you watch from your rooftop. It will be spectacular—like nothing this world has seen before. Do you hear me? You have one hour to give me what I desire. And when you see our flare, you have one minute."

Umber tilted his head back, and it thumped on the stone. He closed his eyes and called out in a voice thick with passion. "Remember who you were, Jonathan. Before you came here. Your mind has been twisted, your ambitions deformed. But I can help you. Send your men away and come inside alone."

There was no answer. Hap heard the carriage door slam.

Reins snapped, hooves clattered, wheels squeaked. The sound faded. Umber risked a quick glance out the window. He blew air out of the corner of his mouth. "He's gone. There are about a dozen men staying behind, on the causeway." Umber clasped his hands atop his head and sighed. "Gather the others, please. I want to talk to all of you."

They stood in a half circle: Oates, Balfour, Sophie, Hap, Welkin, Barkin, and Dodd. Even Smudge had been cajoled from the archives to join the group, but he stood away from the rest, mumbling and twisting his filthy beard. Umber faced them with his hands clasped behind his back. "My friends. Do you trust me?"

"Of course," said Balfour.

"I do," said Hap.

Umber gave Oates a particular stare. "I trust you," Oates said.

Those words made Umber smile. "That means plenty, coming from you. But listen, everyone. You've just heard some things that must have been confusing, and I need to explain. Um . . . how do I say this?" Umber looked down, and shook his head, and chuckled quietly, as if he could not believe that he was about to share his secrets. "Doane and I come from . . . the same place. And I have something that Doane wants, an object that doesn't belong in this land. It's a machine called a computer. A wonderful machine, filled with information on everything you can imagine. Everything I've done here—the architecture, the engineering, the medicines, the music—came from that machine. I've tried to use that power to make this a better world. But Doane would use it to build greater horrors than that warship in the harbor. So I can't give it to him, no matter what. Are you with me so far?"

Hap looked at the others, and they were all looking at Umber with the same mix of surprise and admiration. Dodd broke the silence. "I can't claim to understand all that. But as we said, we trust you."

Umber's mouth twisted and he covered his eyes for a moment with his hand. "Thank you. There is a nightmare before us now. I don't see how we can stop it. But . . . I think we should get ready for what's coming. The final attack will be on the Aerie. They will either destroy it completely or blow it open and storm inside to search for the computer."

"What do you want us to do?" asked Barkin.

"Pack up what you can carry and bring it down to the caverns. We'll be safe from the great guns down there. And if necessary . . ." Umber grimaced and rubbed his jaw. "We might have to escape through the underworld."

"The caverns?" screeched Smudge.

Balfour blanched. "Beyond the gate?"

"But the troll came from back there," Sophie said under her breath.

"The troll is the least of it," Smudge howled. "Those caves are filled with monsters—the horrible things that served the sorceress when she ruled here!"

"But there may also be a way out," Umber said. "It's our last resort."

"Could we sneak out that side door and hide in Petraportus?" Balfour asked. "We might be able to swim to safety."

Umber shook his head. "We'd be seen. The gunmen would pick us off, or the artillery would blow us to pieces. No, the caverns may be the only chance. Everybody, get the stuff you need. Balfour, grab food and water from the kitchen for all of us. Meet back here as soon as you can."

Hap stepped onto the terrace. He inhaled and smelled the blossoms of the tree of many fruits and the other remarkable flora of Umber's garden. The door to Umber's rooftop tower was open, and Hap saw a flickering light through the window. He went inside and climbed the stairs and found Umber in his study, staring at an assortment of books and objects on his desk.

Umber glanced up, biting his lip. "Hap, you shouldn't be

walking around alone. If the Executioner showed up . . ."

Hap shrugged. "We have so many problems, I almost forgot about him."

Umber snorted out a rueful laugh and looked down again at the clutter. "I've been collecting stuff for a decade. How do I to decide what to leave behind?"

That decision hadn't been so difficult for Hap. His existence could be measured in months, not years, and his possessions were few. "I can carry some," he said. The elatia was in its pot on his desk. "We should definitely take *that*," he said, pointing.

Umber didn't seem to hear him. He gestured toward the set of books that he kept on a shelf in his study: *The Books of Umber*, which chronicled his discoveries of all things monstrous and magical. "No room for those of course. And I can't take *these*." He waved his hand over the box of charms and talismans that had once belonged to Turiana. "If we bring them into the caverns and Turiana is still there, I'll be handing them right to her. Better to leave them in the Aerie, where they'll be buried in the rubble."

Hap went to Umber's window and stared down at the enormous ship in the harbor. "Will he really destroy the city? Because you won't give him the computer?"

Umber's head slumped into his hands. There were dark crescents under his eyes, and he looked a decade older, with all his youthful energy gone. He seemed dangerously close to slipping into one of his deadly melancholies. "Happenstance. I . . . I always thought I was doing the right thing. But now . . . everyone would be better off if I'd never come at all. How did it come to this?"

Hap's thoughts whirled in his head. He leaned heavily against the windowsill, looking at the great city, the wonder of its age, about to be devastated. "It wasn't you. Meddlers did this. Willy Nilly brought you here. Willy's nemesis brought your friend to the Far Continent. They set you against each other, like game pieces."

"But now both those Meddlers are dead. And Jonathan is going to win," Umber muttered. "Any minute now, in fact."

At the pier below, Hap saw the royal carriage come to a stop. The Supremacy stepped out and walked to the boat that would ferry him back to the *Vanquisher*. He turned his head and stared up at the Aerie, and Hap felt their gazes meet, even across that great distance.

Hap felt pressure build in his veins. He had the urge to scream out the window and curse at Doane. More than ever he wanted the power to see the filaments, to leap across time and distance. *I could fix this,* he thought. *A Meddler could do it. So why can't I?*

He remembered what Willy had told him, about why his

powers eluded him. *Because you care,* Willy said. Meddlers weren't supposed to care about other people. They were selfish, capricious beings who were concerned only with their fateful games. "How am I supposed to stop caring?" Hap asked aloud.

"What's that?" Umber said, roused from his own dark thoughts.

Hap pushed himself away from the wall and grabbed the hair on both sides of his head. A thought had seized him; a memory from his short but eventful life. "You did something to me once," he said.

Umber's brow wrinkled. "I did?"

Hap rushed across the room and leaned on the desk, staring Umber in the eye. "Yes. When you tried to help me remember my life before this one!"

Umber's head tilted. "That's right. I . . . I hypnotized you. But it didn't go well."

Hap remembered too well how it felt when Umber pried into his mind, taking him back. When Hap had finally approached the memory of his own death, he'd been driven into a blind panic. "You have to do it again. But you won't make me remember this time."

Umber's head wobbled. "I won't?"

Hap thumped the desk with his fist. "When you hypnotized me, you told me to feel things, and I felt them. You told me to feel sleepy. And I did. You told me to see things in my mind, and I did. You told me my arm was weightless, and I *felt* it!"

"But . . . but what do you want me to make you feel now?"

"Nothing," Hap cried. "You have to tell me not to care!"

CHAPTER
29

They sat on the same bench on the terrace, under the tree of many fruits.

"I don't know if there's time," Umber said. His voice quavered, and his gaze drifted toward the harbor, watching for the flare that the ship would send up. *Time is running out,* that flare would say. *Take a seat, Lord Umber, and watch all your dreams laid low.*

"Then you should start now," Hap said, with a harsh note in his voice that he had never produced before. It made Umber's head snap back, but he nodded.

"Right," Umber said. "But wait. Take this." He reached into a pocket and drew out the strange, clear envelope that held the picture of the woman whom Willy wanted Hap to save. "I wrote down some information on her. Who she was, where to find her."

Hap shoved it into a pocket. "Willy said a Meddler has to keep his promises."

"Did he?" Umber said. He shifted in his seat and wiped his palms on his thighs. "So then . . . I guess we'll begin. Close your eyes, Happenstance, and take a deep breath. The deepest you've ever taken. Hold it for a moment, and let it out slowly."

Hap did as he was asked. Umber went on, his voice falling to a soft drone. He told Hap to take another deep breath, and said it over and over again, ten times altogether. The process was ingrained in Hap's mind, and following the commands was as easy as tracing steps in the dust. Umber told him to relax his muscles, one by one. He told him to imagine stairs and to feel more at ease with every step down. He told him to picture a single candle shining like a star in a vast dark room, and imagine that nothing else mattered. When Umber told him his arm was without weight, the limb drifted up with a feathery lightness. Hap felt aloft and detached, and the world faded away.

Even when something in the distance rose high into the air with a screeching whistle and dimly exploded, it did not jar Hap from his trance. Nor did Umber's groan of dismay and muttered words: "The flare."

A voice drifted up from far below. Someone was shouting

on the causeway. Hap recognized the voice of the spy, the whistler, Spakeman. "Last chance, Lord Umber. Give the Supremacy what he wants!"

Hap was not shaken then, or when footsteps approached and Sophie cried out, "Lord Umber—Balfour says those guns are turning this way, not at the city. You have to run!"

With his eyes still shut, Hap reached out and found Umber's wrist. "Keep going," Hap whispered.

Sophie called out again, but Umber hushed her. "Get downstairs, Sophie." Hap sensed Umber leaning close. When he spoke again, the voice was like an echo in Hap's mind.

Happenstance. Your feelings run deep. You care about those whom you've come to know. That was what Willy Nilly did not expect when he turned a boy into a Meddler. And now you must let go of your feelings. Picture them as lengths of cord, binding each of us to your heart. Sever those cords, Happenstance. One by one. Cut the cord that ties you to Sophie. In his mind Hap saw himself surrounded by the people he cared for. The string that linked him to Sophie snapped, slashed by his will, and Sophie drifted from sight. *As the cords are severed, your feelings go with them. Now Balfour. And Oates. Nima. Thimble. Fay and Sable.* One by one Hap's circle of friends diminished.

And me, Happenstance, Umber's voice finally said. *Most of all, cut me loose. Be the Meddler you are meant to be. Free your heart. Embrace your powers. When you open your eyes—*

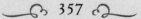

There was a crack of thunder, and an eagle's screech, and it sounded as if the air above was torn in half. Umber rushed out the words: "You will be a—" But his cry was drowned out by an all-consuming roar. Hap opened his eyes in time to see a great red and black firestorm fill his vision. Umber stood and was blown off his feet, into Hap, and they tumbled across the terrace and sprawled on the stone. Hap rose up on his hands and knees and then stood, with a deafening ring inside his brain. A second explosion rocked the Aerie, striking the side of the tower somewhere below. Dust and ash stung his nose and made him cough. Smoke hung in the air until the sea breeze pushed the cloud aside. He felt a hand on his ankle. Umber was reaching out for him. Umber's head bobbed unsteadily, his chin an inch off the ground. Blood trickled down his forehead from beneath his hair. He let go of Hap's ankle and pointed.

Hap looked. Umber's tower atop the Aerie was torn open, half of it lying in rubble. Flaming paper rained down; torn fragments from Umber's books. They were everywhere, like the leaves of autumn.

"Jonathan lied," Umber said. "Tried to kill me."

Hap felt only a vague curiosity for Umber's shock and fear. He was more interested in the luminous filament that emerged from Umber's chest. Even before he touched it, he heard its song, filled with wonderfully obvious meaning.

More threads emerged from the stairs that led to the terrace. *Oates,* Hap could tell, just by looking at one. *Sophie,* he knew, stepping forward to let his hand pass through the other.

The guns of the ship fired again, and the Aerie shook as the artillery slammed into its side. Oates and Sophie dashed onto the terrace. Sophie screamed at the sight of the ruined tower, and Oates rushed forward and scooped Umber up like an infant. "Get downstairs," he roared at Hap.

"Right behind you," Hap said, but when Oates and Sophie ran, he did not follow. He stared down at his own filament, narrowing his eyes. It suddenly seemed to him that it was hollow. And if he stared at it a certain way, it might turn before his eyes and reveal a different angle, an unexpected dimension, and he might even be able to step inside, and who knew what he might see then?

The thread told him there wasn't much time. A heartbeat or two. "Better hurry," he said, almost singing the words. He felt calm and bemused despite the jeopardy. There was another roar of the guns, and a rising screech even louder than the first, flying straight for his ears. The terrace was enveloped by flame, and the tree of many fruits was blasted away, limbs on fire. Hap was there, but yet not there, because he had slipped inside the filament.

He was in the Neither.

CHAPTER
30

Neither here nor there, Hap thought.

The Neither was a void, bitterly cold. The land and sky were gone and only filaments remained, glittering gossamer against endless, starless black. There was a strand for every living being on the wide, round world. He saw the footprint of civilization, cities and villages where filaments clustered, seas and wastelands devoid of humanity, and roads where people traversed.

Time itself had ceased to be when he entered the Neither. He knew this, because every thread was poised, unmoving. *No, not every thread,* he told himself. His was filled with life and energy. It darted in every direction, flying across the globe, wherever he directed his thoughts, and it carried him with it.

When it crossed another thread, he felt a glimpse of the life of the person it touched, as if a breeze were blowing across open books, flipping pages for him to read. He sensed what was happening, and how it might be altered if he were to drop back into the world and intervene.

"This is how a Meddler meddles," he said. His voice was barely audible, the sound conducted only through his own flesh. He raised his hands in front of his eyes and was mildly surprised that he'd maintained a physical form in this ethereal realm.

The cold began to penetrate. His ears stung. His feet tingled and lost their feeling. He wrapped his arms against his chest, but it gave him no comfort.

A jolt went through him, but not from the cold. He'd been so transfixed by the Neither and preoccupied by the cold that he'd almost forgotten: the Aerie was being destroyed by the guns of the *Vanquisher*. He looked below where he floated, and counted the threads that represented his friends. None had been extinguished yet, he saw. His filament turned and flew down among them, and he slid along the thread like a spider to better perceive their fates.

His friends were going to die. The guns would go on battering the Aerie high and low. When a hole was opened near the gatehouse, the guns would pause and the armed men

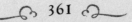

on the causeway, who had withdrawn from harm's way, would rush in. Oates would charge at them, and five or six of the invaders would die before Oates fell, his body riddled with lead. Umber would tell the rest to surrender, but the guns would still blaze. There would be no mercy. And then, as the guns of the *Vanquisher* turned upon the rest of the city, the search for the computer would begin.

That must not be, Hap thought. The iciness of the void was beginning to muddle his thoughts, and he knew he could not stay inside for much longer. He saw where the *Vanquisher* floated in the water; its shape was defined by another cluster of filaments. As soon as he considered it, his own thread shot across the space between, and he soared with it.

Hap stepped out of the Neither, onto the deck of the ship. After the icy serenity of the void, his senses were assaulted by the sight of the *Vanquisher* and the battered Aerie, the stinging scent of the great guns, and the thumping roar of the engines. He rubbed his hands together and blew on his palms, and hopped from foot to foot to drive away the dead, numb sensation.

The Supremacy was there, smiling with his jaw clamped tight, his eyes filled with a savage glee. There were a dozen men near him, but all eyes were upon the Aerie, which was obscured by smoke. They were waiting for the smoke to clear, before the guns would aim and fire once more.

Doane leaned out, holding the railing at his waist. *A little push would change things,* Hap thought. But his mind recoiled at the notion. That was not how Meddlers operated, he knew. There could be nothing so blunt, so direct.

"Hey!" cried a voice. "You there!" Hap looked over. He'd been seen. A man was pointing at him. Then everyone was looking. Doane's face transformed itself—the malicious smile opened into a gaping circle. The eyes popped. Hap wanted to laugh out loud.

"Time to go," he said, as men rushed toward him. He tried to slip back into his filament, but nothing happened. "Oh yes," he said, not caring who heard. "Can't vanish when someone's watching." He sprang up and away from clutching hands. The leap carried him over their heads. He landed, crouched, and soared again. One or two of the men were armed, and he saw rifles swing his way. But he was gone, over the railing, plummeting past the steep side of the great ship, out of sight.

Hap slipped into the Neither, but only for a moment, before he reappeared inside the *Vanquisher*. He stood in a corner, hiding from the men who moved about inspecting the gears and works that filled the room. The heat was oppressive, and the air stank of oil and sweat. The noise was clanking and unpleasant, unlike anything he'd heard. Near the back of the ship was a massive, plated mechanical thing with steam whistling through pipes, and thick metal arms that moved in circles when engaged. Hap supposed that those arms turned the paddle wheel that propelled the ship, but the idea did not hold his interest for long. He looked about, tapping his lips with a finger, and then decided to move on.

The next place where he appeared felt more promising. He was on a balcony that overlooked a vast hold. Beneath him were hundreds of long boxes, and barrels lashed together with great care. It was all carefully secured with ropes to keep the cargo from shifting.

Hap's mind went back to a conversation between Umber and Doane. Umber had asked: "The hold must be full of explosives, correct?" And Doane had replied: "Crate after crate of artillery, rockets, bullets, and bombs. Enough to reduce seven Kurahavens to rubble and dust."

Hap rubbed his fingertips together. "Perhaps. But now what?" He heard men shouting and feet pounding the planks above. "Find him," someone cried. "Searching for me," Hap said, chuckling quietly.

Filaments hovered in the air before him: the paths of men who'd come this way, and who were yet to pass. He reached among them and perceived that two men were soon to arrive, hunting for the intruder. Violent, greedy souls, one with a lantern to light the way. In Hap's mind, he pictured a sequence of events unfolding. "But what makes the sequence begin?" he wondered. And then he saw a strange aura surrounding the chain he wore around his neck: a silver locket, seashell-shaped, that held an enormous pearl of extraordinary value. "The cause," Hap said, almost singing the words.

He saw a glow appear in a threshold not far away, and heard voices murmur. Quickly he took the chain off his neck, opened the locket to reveal the pearl, and set it on the planks, close to the balcony. And then he vanished, reappearing below, where he could peer up from between two crates.

The men prowled along the balcony, searching. Both had cudgels in their hands, ready to batter the intruder. The first man, who held the lantern, stopped suddenly and dropped to his knees. He put the lantern on the ground to free his hand so he could scoop up a small, glittering object. A conversation began that soon turned angry.

"What was that?"

"Nothin'."

"Don't tell me it was nothin'—it was somethin'. Looked like a pearl as big as my eye!"

"Forget it, I tell you."

The words became shouts, and then a wrist was seized, and the two men slammed into the balcony. As they scuffled, a

foot struck the lantern, pushing it perilously close to the edge. Cudgels swung, and the first man was struck in the face. Blood flowed, and the first man struck back, cracking his crewmate on the temple. The second man staggered and groaned, leaning heavily against the railing, and a shove in the chest sent him tumbling over the rail. He crashed headfirst into the cargo below, not far from where Hap was hiding, and was still.

The man above staggered into the shadows, half-blinded by the sheet of blood pouring into his eyes. The lantern remained, perched on the edge above.

Hap smiled. The sequence was in motion. And it was beautifully indirect, as Meddlers like it.

He felt an uncomfortable tug at his conscience. The ship had to be destroyed, but could he let so many perish? Entering the Neither, he drifted among the filaments, judging the invaders and their destinies. They were grim men, accustomed to killing, intent on pillage. In another hold were the riches they'd stolen from the kingdoms they'd conquered. They had done unspeakable things to people who'd begged for mercy.

"That answers that," Hap said, and he searched for the thing he needed next. It was there, as his instincts had promised, on the horizon. When he saw what it was, he shivered with delight. He was there in an instant, standing on the back of the great leviathan. A slender, black-haired woman, clad in sealskin, stood with her back to him, staring at smoke and fire in the distance. She sensed the dimming of light and whispery sound that foretold a Meddler's arrival, and then she turned around and gasped.

"Happenstance!" she cried. "How did you…" She stepped closer, and her eyes grew wider. She reached out and touched his hair.

"It's all white now, isn't it?" Hap asked her.

She nodded. "White . . . but it dazzles. Like the sun in the water. What has become of you? Are you all right?" She raised her arms, but Hap backed away from her embrace.

"Nima, listen carefully," Hap said. "You were thinking of doing something to help. Even though you and Boroon are afraid. Weren't you?"

She nodded again and looked toward Kurahaven. "We have seen what that ship has done. How it destroys the Aerie with fire. Is . . . is Lord Umber safe?"

"Would you like him to be safe? You should do something, then."

Nima detected the change in Hap. She gave him a wary look.

"A wave is all Umber needs," Hap said. "An enormous wave, beside that ship. But don't go too close, understand? Or the guns will kill Boroon, and the gulls will feast on his flesh."

Nima's hand rose up and covered her mouth. She stared at Hap. "Don't mind me," he said, shaking his head. He felt giddy and impulsive, liable to say anything, despite the danger his friends were in. "I'm not quite myself at the moment. Say, what's that over there?"

Hap vanished again as soon as Nima turned to look. A moment later he was at the top of the royal palace. In its highest tower, under the magnificent clock, was a porch, big enough for two to stand side by side and look across the bay. Behind him was a pair of glass doors that opened to a room reserved for visiting royalty. This was where Fay and Sable were staying, but neither of them was inside.

"Such a view," he said, turning back to the open air.

Far below he saw a pair of tiny figures running from the palace. One was short and one tall, both in dresses. "There you are!" he said. His curiosity was teased, and so he slipped into the Neither to read their filaments.

He listened to the song, and smiled. The news of Loden's death had caused chaos in the palace, and Sable and Fay had slipped past the guards who kept them there against their will. Now they were racing toward the Aerie. Hap felt his heart warm, knowing how Umber would feel if he saw Fay again, but he warded those feelings away so they would not loosen his grip on his emergent powers.

He reappeared in the tower. The guns of the *Vanquisher* roared again, gashing the walls of the Aerie. Hap saw the carved face at the corner, the place that had once been his room, break away and fall into the water below. "That wasn't nice," he said to the distant ship. Doane was on the deck, applauding the destruction. Men ran about, still searching for the strange boy who'd vanished.

Beyond the *Vanquisher*, deep in the bay, Hap saw water rise up into a mound that surged straight at the ship. Boroon was charging, swimming just under the surface.

A man on the deck pointed to the disturbance, drawing the attention of the others. Doane rushed over for a closer look, and his arms waved. Men cranked wheels, and one of the great guns on the deck turned toward Boroon.

The gun roared. A plume of water shot up in the center of the mound. Boroon's progress slowed for a moment, and dark debris floated up. *Was he hit?* Hap wondered. The leviathan had no filament to tell the story, and he could not read Nima's from where he stood. A wide swirl appeared, and Boroon's broad tail breached the surface for a moment as he dove.

There was a breathless silence. Doane and his men rushed to the stern of the *Vanquisher*, straining to see where the threat might have gone. And then the leviathan roared out of the sea a hundred feet from the starboard side.

Hap saw Nima, tiny from this distance, clinging to the leviathan's back in her usual perch. The barge that was strapped to Boroon was damaged, with a gouge blown into its center by the swiveling gun, and water poured from its usually airtight space. Boroon himself was unharmed. The guns on the side of the *Vanquisher* were unprepared for the appearance of the sea-beast, and they failed to fire. Boroon hung in the air for a moment, his enormous crescent flippers flung wide like wings. Then he fell, and his bulk crashed deep into the sea, hurling up a pair of towering waves. One sped toward the *Vanquisher*.

A smaller boat might have been upended by the wave, but the *Vanquisher* was enormous. When the wave struck it broadside, it rocked but did not capsize. Doane held the railing to stay on his feet, and Hap could almost hear him screaming orders to fire the guns and kill the creature that dared to confront them.

Hap closed his eyes. He pictured the lantern on the edge of that plank, almost falling back into place, but finally tipping and tumbling onto the crates below. They were crates made of wood and packed with straw; crates filled with the deadly materials that threatened Hap's friends and the city that he called home.

The starboard guns finally responded, punching the sea and tossing foam into the sky. The swiveling guns atop the

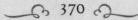

Vanquisher spun and roared. But the invaders could only guess where Nima and Boroon had gone. Hap supposed that Boroon had swum to the depths of the bay and was already moving stealthily out to sea.

The guns went silent. Doane pointed to the Aerie again. The swiveling gun began to rotate back. Hap tapped his foot and drummed his fingers. There was something thrilling about the anticipation. Then, at last, he heard the sound he was waiting for.

It was a low thudding sound, like a boulder dropping to earth: *whoomp!* It caught the attention of every man on the deck of the *Vanquisher*. They froze in their tracks and stared at the planks that shuddered under their feet.

The sound came again, louder still, and men fell to the deck. A hole appeared in the side of the *Vanquisher*, and flames and black smoke poured out like dragon fire. Doane sprawled flat and struggled to his hands and knees, crawling toward the side of the ship where other men were already leaping into the sea.

The ship burst apart with a violence the world had never known. Pieces flew in every direction, radiating from the heart of the explosions that came rapid-fire, as blinding as the sun. Planks twirled through the air. The deck was lifted straight up, and a swiveling gun flipped like a coin. A billowing black-red chaos consumed every man on deck and in the sea. The roar was so great that Hap felt the palace tremble.

It was too loud for him to hear that faint whispery, silky sound. But he noticed the way everything dimmed, only for a moment. He turned and saw the Executioner standing on the other side of the glass doors, staring at him with five green, glittering eyes among the many that studded his face. A tapering tongue slid over the points of his yellow teeth.

Hap jumped back, startled, and the railing pressed against his waist. He froze there, looking back at the Executioner, who made no move to open the door. Instead the multieyed creature raised his hand and said, "Wait."

important to distinguish natural w...

...from their more dangerous magical

...unterparts, some of which are kno...

...peak and walk on two legs...

CHAPTER
31

Hap stood petrified except for the quaking of his knees. The Executioner put his mouth to the narrow gap between the pair of doors. "I have been watching you. I saw what you intended and thought it best to let you finish. That thing did not belong in this world." The words ended with a horrid wet slurp.

Hap glanced at the Executioner's hands, making sure they were not reaching for the handles of the doors. A shiver shook his spine when he saw the sharp, curved nail that the Executioner would use to carve out his eyes.

"I have your gratitude for that?" the Executioner asked.

Hap nodded and gulped. Every muscle twitched. His legs

were ready to spring and send him flying into the atmosphere. "And now?"

"Now you will thank me by facing your punishment. You know what must be done. It is the law."

"Wh–whose law?" Hap stammered.

The green eyes blinked at random. "I do not know. The crimes of Meddlers are made known to me. The task is assigned. I must reclaim the essence that made you a Meddler, because the laws were broken: No Meddler may harm another Meddler, and your maker did. No Meddler may create another Meddler, and your maker did. No child shall be made a Meddler, and here you are."

"I don't care about your laws," Hap said. "I wasn't the one who broke them."

Three of the green eyes rolled upward, two of them narrowed. "You break them by existing. Now stay where you are. There is no sense in running. Your maker tried to run, but I still took his eyes." The Executioner pointed with that terrible curved nail to one green eye on his right cheek and another on his forehead. "Accept your fate, outlaw."

The Executioner plunged his long-fingered hand straight through a pane of glass. Hap arched his body back as the nails raked his cheek. He spun over the railing and fell off the balcony, accompanied by glittering shards. The ground rushed up, but before his body smashed onto the castle wall below, he slipped into the Neither.

He stared around the blackness. The ravenous cold gnawed at the fresh wound on his cheek, and he felt the trickling blood turn to ice. He looked right, left, up, and down, wondering if the Executioner would appear. *Move,* he told himself. He soared into an empty black space and looked behind him.

A filament was approaching. In the distance it slithered right and left, probing the Neither like a tentacle. *It's him,* Hap thought. He couldn't see the physical form, but he knew it was his enemy. *Tracking me.*

How can I lose him? His teeth chattered, from fright as well as cold. He didn't know what would happen if the Executioner's filament crossed his, here in the strange void, but he was certain it would be the end of him if it did.

As the thread approached, he wondered where to go, what to do, and how to escape his pursuer. He seized the first notion that came to mind.

His filament had two parts. The brighter portion showed where he might go, and would bend according to his wishes. The dimmer part revealed where he had been, and was fixed. If he followed the fainter thread, he would not go back in

time—that was impossible, even for a Meddler. But he could retrace his journeys across lands and oceans. He raced along that path, hoping to find an advantage on familiar ground. The Executioner's filament gave chase, like a comet with an endless tail in its wake.

His filament sang of dueling fates: *He catches you. You get away.* It warned of danger and torment. But the meaning began to blur. It made him think of what Willy Nilly had said, words that Hap thought were just feverish ramblings. *It's cold in the Neither, and if you stay long enough, move fast enough, it confuses the signs, makes the filaments hard to read. . . . But I grew tired, let my guard down, and he caught up with me . . .*

Hap focused his will and soared faster across the inky expanse. There was no wind to add bluster to the cold, but still he knew he could not stay in the Neither for long. Already his thoughts were growing hazy.

"Fendofel," he said through chattering teeth.

The old wizard looked up from the table where he was sorting through a pile of odd-looking seeds. "What? Who are you? Wait, I know! You're Umber's ward, that green-eyed boy . . ."

"Happenstance," Hap said, hopping up and down and shaking his arms. He glanced over his shoulder.

"Now, Dendra," Fendofel said, wagging a finger. "None of

that. This is a friend!" Hap looked up and saw one of the muscular vines of Fendofel's carnivorous plant poised like a viper about to strike.

"Happenstance, how did you get here?" The wizard's gap-toothed mouth curled up in an open smile. "Is Lord Umber back? Has he come to visit me again?"

Hap shook his head. He spun in a circle, looking anxiously through the open archways in the white dome. "No, sir, it's just me. I need a favor—from Dendra, actually."

Fendofel's shaggy eyebrows rose. "Eh? From Dendra? What sort of favor?"

"I'm being pursued by a horrible thing—a tall creature with many eyes—and I thought Dendra might—" Hap gasped and looked behind him again. The world had dimmed, and the familiar sound whispered.

"How odd! The same thing happened a moment ago," Fendofel said, squinting up at the rounded ceiling.

"He's here," Hap said, crouching low.

"Would you like something to eat?" Fendofel said. He picked up his cane and got to his feet.

"No, thank you," was Hap's distracted reply. He spun in place again, looking every way. His hope was that the Executioner would appear, and Dendra would seize him. But his enemy was wary—perhaps the filaments had warned him.

"Where are you?" Hap muttered. He moved to the center of the room, away from the openings. His own thread darkened, warning him that danger was approaching. "Never mind what I said," Hap told the wizard.

"Eh?" said Fendofel.

"Good to see you," Hap said. He ducked under the table, out of Fendofel's sight, and slipped back into the Neither. For a moment he was amused by the thought of the old wizard wondering where he'd gone. Then panic consumed him again, the blinding fear of the mouse as it flees from the cat.

Move faster, he urged himself. *More space between us.* The iciness of the void was affecting him sooner than before; he wondered if it had been unwise to return to the Neither so quickly. He looked behind and saw the filament chasing him, closing in fast. Like a blade, he sliced his way into the physical world. He appeared where he once stood on the deck of the *Bounder.* But of course, with no ship there, he plunged straight toward the sea. No matter; he was getting better at this, and after another brief passage through the Neither, he landed where he wanted to be.

He flattened himself on the rocky floor of a deep crevice in the sea-cliffs, thankful for a clutter of jagged stone in front of him. His muscles were so stiff from cold that it was hard to draw breath.

Something heavy slithered on the other side of the rock. He peered through a crack and saw glittering, golden scales. The creature inhaled deeply, and then a fiery glow erupted, illuminating the crevice in waves of orange and red.

Hap watched as the dragon poured fire from its jaws, bathing a cache of crystal eggs. He wondered if some of those eggs were the ones they'd retrieved from Sarnica. It occurred to him that the flickering light and roaring flame might disguise the signs of the Executioner's arrival. When he looked behind him he saw his pursuer appear, nearly on top of him. The multitude of eyes swiveled down to stare at Hap, mad with hunger. The long arm shot out and seized him by the shoulder, before Hap's frozen muscles could muster a reaction.

A roar came from the other side of the jagged rocks. The Executioner shrieked and threw his arms in front of his face as a fountain of flame obscured him from sight. The heat forced Hap to turn away, and when he looked up again, the Executioner was gone. A whiff of charred flesh hung in the air. *How badly was he hurt?* Hap wondered, but he had only a moment to ponder the question, because he saw the dragon's frightful head appear over the clutter of stone, searching for the intruder.

Hap flew across the Neither, feeling a thrill of hope. *He didn't see the danger coming—he made a mistake,* he thought. His

optimism faded a moment later when he spotted the filament slithering behind. Its color had shifted; Hap could sense pain and fury, so powerful that it radiated across the distance.

He stood on a lost, uncharted islet with the bones of shipwrecks scattered across the shore. There was a barrel on the sand. He'd clung to it once, when he was washed overboard and lost at sea.

The cold had penetrated his brain, sinking deep. He rubbed his palms against his temples, trying to warm his mind. It was hard to think, and harder still to read his filament. He hoped the Executioner had the same affliction.

The day was calm and the skies were clear. When the dimness came, and the now familiar sound that was not so different from the gentle waves rolling onto the shore, he was ready. He leaped onto an outcropping that was surrounded by deep pools of briny water. His frozen muscles shrieked in protest.

The Executioner stood on the sand with his chest heaving, shivering from his cold passage. The skin on his arms was charred, with fluid oozing between the cracks. Some of his eyelids were burned away by the dragon fire, and the green orbs stared, full of malice.

"Y-y-you're hurt," Hap said, with his teeth clacking together.

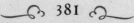

"I w-will not underestimate y-you again," the Executioner said.

"Willy told me I w-would b-be a powerful M-meddler," Hap replied. "Maybe he was r-right. Maybe I'm t-too much for you."

The Executioner sneered, and his muscles and tendons crackled as he rolled his head on his long neck. "I was only g-going to take y-your eyes," the Executioner said. He stepped toward Hap on his long, birdlike legs. As he flexed his fingers, he hissed with pain. "B-but now I think you should suffer more."

Hap gulped. "If I d-don't run, will you have mercy?"

"Perhaps," the Executioner said. "Stay where you are." He stepped closer, covering an uncanny distance with one stride. His bare foot came down beside a deep crevice filled with water. A claw rose out and clamped on his foot.

The rest of the soul crab bubbled to the surface. "Castaways," it cried in the brittle voice of an old woman. Hap heard claws scrabbling all around, as dozens more of the massive crabs sprang to life. The Executioner screamed and drove his fist into the crusty shell of the claw. The shell cracked, and the fist plunged inside, but the claw only squeezed harder.

Hap didn't wait to see more. He slipped into the Neither.

CHAPTER
32

Hap sprawled on the sand of Desolas, the island of the bidmis, and let the volcanic heat that poured from the surrounding fissures warm his body. It was another unpleasant spot with terrible memories, but again it was a place that he knew and his pursuer might not.

The last trip through the Neither had nearly finished him. His mind had been befogged almost instantly, and he'd barely mustered the will to reemerge into the world. His bones felt like icicles, and there was a pain in his heart, as if it had nearly frozen solid. "Think," he muttered aloud, and his cold lips barely articulated the word.

The Executioner was badly burned and had at least one gruesome wound on his foot. Hap wondered if the creature would break off the pursuit, to rest. "Probably not," he decided. The look in the Executioner's eyes spoke of an all-consuming hunger. Like Occo before him, this thing was relentless.

The world dimmed, and the Executioner appeared, up to his waist in the water. He saw Hap and tried to take a step toward him, but he stumbled and fell into the shallows.

His aim is getting worse, Hap thought. *Like mine.* He'd learned that it was impossible to appear precisely where you intended. There was guesswork involved, and you might pop up a few strides away from the mind's target. And with the senses impaired by the icy void, the aim suffered even more.

The Executioner rose up again, dripping. He spat seawater and stared with his eyes swiveling in all directions at the bizarre sights of Desolas: the mile-high wall of boiling steam that encircled the island; the lofty obsidian palace; a half-finished staircase to nowhere, spiraling high; and the titanic statue in the likeness of Caspar, the last fellow who'd fallen victim to the island's curse.

Those strange sights didn't hold the Executioner's attention for long. He turned every eye toward Hap again, and limped onto the sand. Hap noticed that one of the long, birdlike toes was missing.

"G-give up yet?" Hap asked. The Executioner hissed back, baring tooth and gum.

Hap turned and ran as fast as his frozen legs could take him, into the tunnel that plunged under the island's surface. He ran until a wall blocked the passage. There was a short, wide door in the middle of the wall. It was made of dark metal and looked as old as the world itself. A brass ring in the center of the door could be used to knock, and words were etched in an ancient language: *Knock thrice and master you shall be.* Another message was scrawled in chalk, in Umber's hand: *Beware the curse. Do not touch this door.*

Hap heard the Executioner advancing down the tunnel with one foot dragging. "Hope I know what I'm doing," Hap whispered, as a vivid memory of Caspar's tormented face arose. He grabbed the ring and slammed it once, twice, three times against the metal door.

When Hap turned around, the Executioner was almost upon him, crouched inside the low tunnel, with his hands spread wide, sharp nails screeching against the opposing walls. The eyes that still had lids narrowed with pleasure when he saw the wall behind Hap, preventing escape. "You run b-because you are too cold to fly." He chuckled darkly and slurped his own drool.

With a dreadful screech of ancient metal, the ancient door swung open. Thousands of small feet pattered toward them. The Executioner's eyes goggled as he looked past Hap into the dark space behind.

As the footfalls swelled like an approaching storm, a single pale, naked creature stepped across the threshold, as tall as Hap's knee. "Who has knocked?" it asked.

"I am your master now," Hap said. "But look: Do you see the intruder?"

The Executioner's cruel crescent mouth opened in a scream. Somehow he found the energy to bound away in long, awkward strides as thousands of bidmis rushed out of the doorway. They flowed around Hap like water with their white teeth gnashing, filling the tunnel.

Hap knew he had to depart before the bidmis came back and asked him for tasks to perform—he might never escape their sight otherwise, and manage to slip away. But he couldn't bring himself to enter the icy void yet. A warm gust of air flowed out from the threshold, and he trotted through, hoping to drive away his chill.

The passage sloped into an enormous round room with a ceiling so low his head nearly scraped it. A pool of molten rock roiled at the center. The walls were pocked with thousands of niches where the bidmis must have lain dormant when there was no master to drive insane. "You would have enjoyed this, Lord Umber," Hap whispered. It wasn't wise to linger, he knew. The warmth had helped him recover enough, and so he slipped back into the Neither.

As he flew through the frozen nothing, tethered to the dim filament that traced his past, he was startled to see the thread in pursuit once more. *So you got away from the bidmis after all,* he thought. *I wonder how much more you can take. Where shall we go next, then? Someplace not so warm, I think. No comfort for you.*

Hap reappeared with his heels teetering over the ledge of the sea-cave. His arms pinwheeled, and he bent at the waist and lunged forward. When he caught his balance and looked up, he thought for a moment he'd come to the wrong place.

"No," he said aloud. "This was it—I was here."

It was the den of the sea-giants. Many weeks before, Umber had brought Hap and the others here, and they had seen the terrible giants dozing on the rock, in a century-long hibernation. But now the ledge was barren, with only a trace of enormous footsteps in the sand and dust. Hap scratched the back of his neck, staring at the empty cave. "Where have you gone?" He was sure they weren't heading back to Kurahaven; he would have sensed the impending doom. The giants, like most creatures, had left no filaments behind for him to read, so he was left to wonder.

The thought of the threads made him think of the Executioner, just as the warning signs came. The darkness fell over him like a shadow, and the whispery sound was as close as someone blowing in his ear. The Executioner blinked into the world, and he could have reached out and seized Hap, except that he was grappling with a pair of bidmis that had latched their jaws onto his shoulder and leg. He had covered their eyes with his hands, to allow his escape. Water poured off of him, and he coughed and sputtered as he pulled one bidmi off his shoulder and hurled it away. The bidmi took a mouthful of flesh with it, and dark blood oozed from the wound. The little creature struck the cavern wall, fell to the ground, and sprang back to its feet, unharmed.

The other bidmi leaped off the Executioner before he could pry it away, and both stared at their surroundings. They raced to the brink of the ledge, leaped into the water, and swam out of the sea-cave.

"Going home, I suppose," Hap said, backing away. "It'll b-be a long swim."

The Executioner snarled at him and staggered. He stared at his wounds with his chest heaving. His body was racked by wild, convulsive shivers.

Are you done yet? Hap wondered. *Maybe not. One more trip might do it.* "You're soooo close," he said, drawing out the words to taunt his foe. The myriad eyes swiveled and stared, boiling with pain, hunger, and hate.

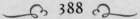

"Come on," Hap said. "Don't you see how powerful these eyes make me? They're grander than yours. You *need* these eyes."

The Executioner's lips pulled back farther still. His breath hissed in and out.

Hap pointed and laughed. "Look at your face. What is that eye on your forehead, a simple hawk's eye? And that one—a dog? Wouldn't you rather have mine?"

The Executioner blundered toward Hap with his arms out, grasping. Hap stepped off the ledge, dropping from sight, and slipped away once more into the icy netherworld.

Hap fell onto his stomach. He'd drawn out the chase as long as he could, with his enemy's thread in pursuit, screaming with agony and malice.

How fitting if the chase ends here, he thought, as he stared up at the simmering peak of the volcano, Mount Ignis. *The place where Happenstance was born.*

He was on a wide flow of volcanic rock. Underneath the looming mountain was Alzumar: a city that was lost once, buried under ash, and was now lost again, its entrance sealed by a fresh river of lava.

The signs told him the Executioner was coming. Hap braced himself, in case he had to spring away, but his pursuer

appeared farther up the flow, where the slope was not so gentle. The Executioner toppled, and rolled senselessly down. His elbows, knees, and skull thumped against the stone, leaving splotches of blood. He finally stopped halfway down the slope, staring at the sky. His ugly, sharklike mouth opened, and an animal screech of agony rang in the air.

Hap stood and steadied himself. Only one of the Executioner's eyes rolled toward him. The others wandered in their sockets.

"I want you to leave me alone," Hap said.

"N-n-never," said the Executioner.

Hap shook his head and laughed bitterly. "Can't you see what folly this is? You won't catch me."

"You were c-c-clever," the Executioner said. "L-lured me into a chase. . . . W-won't make that mistake again." With a great effort he raised a quivering arm off the ground. He tried to point at Hap, but half the finger was gone. His shoulder was torn like a garment, with tattered skin hanging. Hap wrinkled his nose; he could smell the flesh that was seared by dragon fire. "These wounds will heal," the Executioner said. "My k-k-kind always heals. And then . . . you will forget to be wary . . . like the others . . . I will have your eyes . . ." The arm fell limp. A leg jerked. And then the Executioner was still.

Hap watched him for a while and saw the creature's chest

rise and fall. He crept closer—careful to stay out of reach of those long, clutching arms—and passed his hand through the Executioner's filament. With the cold of the Neither still gripping his brain like a frozen fist, he found the song of the thread foggy and hard to interpret. He concentrated, searching for meaning. He hoped to learn that the Executioner had seen enough of his prey and would give up the chase. Or at least that the wounds would take a long time to heal. But the only things he sensed were a terrible, unquenchable hunger, a pure unbridled hate, and a lust for revenge.

The restless volcano rumbled, deep and low. Hap looked up its headless summit. There was a scuffling noise behind him, and he turned to see the Executioner lunging. He leaped, but the clawed fingers curled tight around his ankle and he slammed to the ground.

Drool poured from the creature's mouth, even as the charred face contorted with pain. "Now," the Executioner said, crawling up and over Hap's legs. Hap grunted through clenched teeth and kicked at the hand around his ankle, driving his foot into the stump of the missing finger. The creature howled and swatted the foot away with his free hand. He crawled up and gripped the front of Hap's shirt. Hap kicked again, with all the desperate strength his frozen muscles could muster, and planted his foot in the Executioner's chest. The Executioner twisted sideways, lost his balance, and started to roll farther down the slope, pulling Hap along by the shirt.

The world spun as the rock battered Hap over and over again, hammering his limbs and spine. The back of his head struck the stone, and sparks filled his vision. He heard the Executioner grunting with the same pain as they tumbled together, arms and legs flailing, until they reached the bottom of the flow and sprawled on the beach.

The Executioner's elbow fell across Hap's chest, pinning him down. The awful face loomed overhead, grinning madly with every eye, animal and Meddler, bulging and quivering with anticipation. "You can't leave now. I'm watching you," the Executioner said, as a line of drool dangled from the corner of his mouth. He plucked a pair of dripping animal eyes out of their sockets and let them fall to the sand. And then the hand came for Hap's face, with the long scoop of a claw extended, aiming for his right eye. Hap seized the wrist with both of his hands, trying to ward it off.

The Executioner's strength was failing, but still the claw came closer. Hap turned his face to the side, pressing into the sand, but still the claw drew near, until it touched the corner of his left eye. Hap's cheek pressed into the sand, trying to escape another inch. *Sand,* he thought, and with one hand he clutched at the beach and flung a handful into the Executioner's face.

392

The wrinkled lids flapped shut as the grit struck it, but the sand stuck to the wounded, lidless eyes, and the Executioner turned his face away, spitting grains.

With no eyes to watch him, Hap slipped into the Neither. And to his shock, the Executioner was with him, his physical form intact. *Because I carried him here,* Hap realized. He was still gripping the hand that meant to pluck his eye.

They floated in the emptiness. Hap kicked away, holding the Executioner at arm's length. His enemy's filament passed through him, and he felt a change in the song. This time there was fear. The Executioner tried to shake him off, but the effort was weak.

"Now I'm watching *you*," Hap said, hearing the words dimly. He flew across the Neither, pulling the Executioner with him.

The creature's crescent mouth moved, shaping words that might have been *let me go*. Spasms shook his arms and legs.

"You'll j-just come after me again," Hap said. He knew what the Executioner was feeling. The cold was harsher than ever. His skin felt like leather, his teeth like slabs of ice. The numbness was in his brain, slowing his thoughts.

The Executioner's limbs jerked violently. Hap nearly lost his grip, but doubled it with the other hand. "I'm . . . s-stronger than you . . . ," he told the creature.

The spasms slowed and stopped. And then all the stolen eyes stared lifelessly. Hap released the arm, and the Executioner drifted in the void, stiff and motionless, gently spinning. His filament faded from sight, like the smoke of a snuffed candle.

Spasms jolted Hap's body from head to toe. His enemy was finished. But he wondered, thickly, if he had left himself with strength enough to return from the Neither.

CHAPTER
33

Umber wandered over the ruined terrace,
picking through the blackened, blasted remains of his tower. A
stack of charred books rested on a fallen block of stone. The
Molton wriggled out from a pile of rocks, limping on his iron
peg, with an armful of tattered and half-burnt parchments in
his stony arms.

"Put 'em with the others, Shale," Umber said quietly. He
glanced at the sky, which had suddenly dimmed. Then his
body snapped up straight, and he whirled around. When he
saw Hap, he barked out a curious sound, part laugh, part cry
of surprise. He rushed forward, stumbling over the wreckage,
and wrapped his arms around Hap's head.

"You're still alive, my little Hap, you're still here, and just look at you!" Umber held Hap at arm's length. He was a man who smiled frequently, and broadly, but this was the most elated grin of them all. "Hap—your hair. It's all . . . it's completely . . ."

"I know," Hap said. "It's part of what I've become."

Umber wobbled and sat abruptly on a fallen stone. He covered his face with his hands, and his shoulders trembled. "It's a shock seeing you. No—a miracle. We thought you died. I was holding on to the tiniest hope that you'd suddenly gotten a grip on your abilities and vanished in time. I mean . . . that *is* what happened, isn't it?"

"It is," Hap said.

Umber brushed his hair back from his eyes with quaking hands. "We made it, Hap. Just barely. Sophie, Balfour, Oates, Smudge, the guardsmen . . . we all got to safety in time, before the explosions."

"I know," Hap said brightly. "Even little Thimble survived."

Umber chuckled and wiped away a tear. "I guess you know a lot of things now."

True, Hap thought. He knew, for example, that Fay and Sable were downstairs as well, and that Fay held Sable cradled in her arms, consoling her over the loss of young Happenstance. And he knew that Fay kept looking toward the stairs, waiting for this strange and unpredictable Lord Umber to come down again so she might speak to him, and take his hand, and ask him if everything would be all right.

"The computer was crushed, by the way," Umber said. "It'll never share its secrets again. Shale found it in the ruins."

"But the elatia lives," Hap said, pointing at the plant, charred but still half-green, in a cracked pot.

"Small victory," Umber said. His chest swelled, and he exhaled long and slow. "We were lucky, Hap. Half the Aerie was destroyed. We might've been killed if the *Vanquisher* hadn't exploded. We're still wondering how . . ." Umber's eyes narrowed. The side of the terrace closest to the harbor had been blown away, offering a clear view of where a few blackened ribs of the *Vanquisher* stuck out of the water. He gestured with his thumb. "Er, I don't suppose you had something to do with that."

Hap glanced at the wreckage, and his eyes gleamed. "The possibility exists."

Umber lowered his head. "It was a terrible thing, but it was for the best. I hope it's not haunting you."

"Not at all," Hap said. There was something in the tone of his own voice that surprised him: a hint of mirth and mischief.

Umber heard it too, and his face paled. "You really have changed, Happenstance."

Hap sat on his own block of stone and folded his hands atop one knee. "But I had to, didn't I? It couldn't be avoided."

Umber rested his chin on his hands. "And now a lot of things can't be avoided. The *Vanquisher* is gone, but people have seen it. They know such a thing is possible."

"And that makes it inevitable?" Hap asked, echoing words Umber once had spoken.

"Right. I even convinced those men on the causeway to surrender and give up their rifles. The guns are at the bottom of the sea, and the men will be banished to an island. But you can't kill an idea. Not even a bad idea."

"Still, we've bought time," Hap said. "Delayed the inevitable."

"I doubt it. You're forgetting the Far Continent. Doane had factories there. . . . They were building another warship."

Hap stood up. "Yes. About that. I was curious and did a little exploring before I came back here." He extended a hand. "There's something you need to see. I will take you."

Umber's eyebrows flew up. "Take me? Meddler-style, you mean?"

Hap smiled.

"Wait," Umber said. "It won't make me any crazier than I am now, will it?"

"No," Hap said. "Only the trip between worlds does that, I think. To regular folk like you."

Umber took a deep breath, and then took Hap's hand and closed his eyes. "All right. Then, show me!"

When they winked back into the world, Umber gave an exhilarated shout, even as he shivered. "Ha! Is that what it's like to fly with a Meddler? That was the most—" The elated look vanished instantly when he saw what lay before them.

They stood on a rock that jutted from a narrow inlet of the sea. "It's the Far Continent," Umber said. "Doane's shipyard."

The blue sky was corrupted by filthy black smoke. The shipyard and the industry that surrounded it were in ruins. And there, prowling among the broken structures and demolishing the few that still stood, were the sea-giants.

"They've awoken," Umber said.

"Yes," Hap replied. "A hundred years ago, when the old king of Kurahaven declared himself master of the world, they destroyed his kingdom. Now they have been roused again from their slumber, to prove that there are limits to man's dominion."

The sister ship of the *Vanquisher* was lying on its side in shallow water, and the greatest of the sea-giants, the one named Bulrock, clawed the boards off its sides and hurled them into the sea.

There were long, low buildings that might have been used to manufacture Doane's guns and artillery, and other giants were stomping them into dust. Hap could feel the crushing strides even this far away. Other buildings were afire, and a refinery had been reduced to smoldering coals. As they watched, a she-giant lifted a broken chunk of a building, and three men scurried out like mice. The she-giant roared and crushed them under a single foot.

Umber made a choking, strangled sound, and he covered his mouth with his hand. "All this death," he mumbled.

"They're destroying it all," Hap said. "But do you see the wall that Doane spoke of, the wall that kept his secrets from escaping? It still stands."

Umber rubbed his eyes, as if he could wipe away what he'd seen. "It's just . . . terrible, that's all. And who knows how much time we've really bought?"

When the voice spoke up beside them, Umber nearly stumbled off the rock into the sea.

It was the voice of the sorceress. "More time than you know, Umber."

CHAPTER
34

The rock where they stood was not the only one that rose from the water. Turiana stood on another, with only a short band of water between them. The wind made her long dark hair and the sleeves of her dress flow behind her like pennants. It would have been the portrait of perfect beauty, except for the last of the thorn imps huddled at her feet, shriveled and parched, near the end of its short life.

"I summoned the sea-giants, Umber," the sorceress said, touching a pendant around her neck. It was one of the talismans retrieved by the thorn imps. "Those weapons, those ships of war, they were abominations. They would have been the end of creatures such as them. And such as me. This danger must be extinguished, before it spreads."

Umber stared at her with his lips pressed tight and his arms rigid at his sides.

"I told you to release me, Umber," she said. "I warned you about this threat. I might have put an end to it sooner. But you kept me in that cell, out of fear."

Umber didn't reply for a while. Other sounds filled the air: splintering wood, screeching metal. In a burning building something exploded. Men screamed, and their cries were snuffed out. "And will you rule here now, Turiana?" Umber asked bitterly. "The way you ruled Kurahaven after the sea-giants ruined that city?"

Turiana's red lips curled up at the corners. "Perhaps. I know what you are thinking, Umber. You presume the worst of me. But don't you see that I could have sent these giants to the Aerie first? Don't you understand that I could bewitch you and force you to love me? Isn't that proof enough that my works of evil are behind me?"

Umber's mouth twisted, and his voice was hoarse with sorrow. "Someone I cared about died in your escape. Thanks to your helpers." He jabbed a finger toward the miserable, shriveled creature at Turiana's feet.

The sorceress lifted her chin. "You mean my keeper, Lady Truden? Blame yourself for her fate. You should have set me free."

Umber closed his eyes and whispered, "Take me home, Hap. Get me out of here."

Hap waited until the sorceress turned to watch the destruction. And then he and Umber slipped back into the Neither.

"This isn't home. Where are we?" Umber said, shivering from the cold passage. "Wait—I know! It's where I started—where I first came to this world!"

"That's right," Hap said.

They were on the road that led down the long slope of farmland toward the great coastal city of Kurahaven, sprawled below. Umber paced around the spot and pointed. "I woke up right here. And then—over there! Balfour rode up with his horse and cart!" Umber's expression was still haunted by the encounter with the sorceress and the rampage of the sea-giants, but he mustered a nostalgic grin. "But why are we here, Hap?"

"This is where I depart," Hap said.

The words rocked Umber like a physical blow. "Depart? Now?" He sank down to sit on the grass by the side of the road, with his knees tucked against his chest. "I suppose there's a reason it has to be now."

"There are a billion lives at stake in another world. I promised to save them for you."

"A billion and one," Umber reminded him.

"I will keep both my promises. It is the way of Meddlers."

"That's one good quality at least," Umber said. "Will you add one more promise? To stay another day and say good-bye to your other friends?"

Hap shook his head. "I can't."

"What—is it that Executioner? Is he after you?"

"He's not the reason," Hap said. "It's you, Lord Umber. And Sophie. And Balfour. And the rest."

Umber gaped back at him, shaking his head.

"Don't you see?" Hap asked. "It was friendship that tied me to this world and kept me from becoming what I had to be. I can still feel the tug of those bonds on my heart. I sense them, reaching for me again."

"Ah. I understand." Umber sniffed and rubbed the corners of his eyes with his thumb. His voice was raw. "Happenstance. I meant to do so much more to prepare you. I don't know what to say."

"You could say nothing, and still I would understand."

"Why here, though? Why is this where you leave us?"

Hap looked at something that Umber could not see. "When my powers came to me I still didn't know how to travel to the other world. There was nothing in the Neither that I could see. I learned the answer the first time I went to the Far Continent. I saw it there, in the physical world: a passageway."

"Invisible to the rest of us, I assume. What does the passage look like?"

"A handful of filaments, funneling into nothing, where only a few have passed. When I saw it there I knew it was how your friend Doane was brought to this world. And that meant there would be another passageway here, where you appeared."

Umber sighed, deep and long. Then he stood and gave Hap a sad, crooked smile, and spread his arms. "Well. Is there anything I should know about my destiny?"

Hap laughed and passed his hand through the brilliant filament that emanated from Umber. "Your adventures aren't over," he said.

"Thank the fates for that," Umber said. He tousled Hap's hair. "You grew up so suddenly. I never had a son, but it must be just like this. One day you realize he's not a child anymore. And it happened when you weren't looking."

Hap's green eyes glittered. "Tell the others I will miss them."

"You'll come back?"

The mirth drained from Hap's expression. "Despite all my newfound abilities . . . I honestly don't know."

"Well. I can hope." Umber closed his eyes and embraced his young friend.

And suddenly he was holding nothing at all.

EPILOGUE

Umber blinked at the darkness. He yawned and rolled to his side, swinging his legs out of the bed and onto the cool stone floor. It was nowhere near daylight, but nevertheless he shrugged his way into a wooly robe and fumbled for the spectacles he kept at the side of his bed. When he pulled the cloth off his jar of glimmer-worms, soft light oozed out, and he caught a glimpse of his thin gray hair in the mirror, and the wrinkles that creased his skin.

He walked down the stairs of his rebuilt tower, moving gingerly as the blood started to flow through his veins and his aging muscles warmed. He opened the door and stepped onto the terrace. With his head tipped back he caught a whiff of the terrace flowers, and then he breathed deep, drawing in a great lungful of sea-scented air.

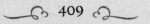

There was a moment of darkness as if a great wing had passed across the moon, and a thin, whispery sound. Something shifted at the corner of Umber's eye. When he turned, the sight caused his knees to quake.

An ancient man stood there, shivering. Wrinkled skin hung loose on his face. He was dressed in clothes that Umber hadn't seen since his days in his former world: pants made of heavy blue fabric. A zippered coat with a hood hanging down the back. Glasses with black lenses. The names for those things fluttered out of the dustbin of Umber's mind: *Jeans. Hoodie. Sunglasses.*

Then he noticed the old fellow's long, white hair with colors flickering within. As the visitor's trembling hand came up to remove the sunglasses, Umber knew that a pair of glittering green eyes would be revealed. And they were.

Umber's mouth trembled and his lips curled inward. He stared at the face—a countenance worn by time, and a portrait of utter exhaustion. Finally he recognized the faint reminders of the boy he'd known. He forced out a whisper. *"Happenstance?"*

The sunglasses slipped from the green-eyed man's hand and struck the stone with a plastic clatter. The long-forgotten sound stirred Umber's memory.

"Hap, is that really you?"

The ancient man's eyelids fluttered and his knees buckled.

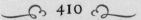

He looked around him for a place to put his hand and brace himself as he lost his balance. Umber rushed over and wrapped his arms around the visitor. For a long time they stood there, with the man's head resting on Umber's shoulder.

"My friend," Umber said, patting the ancient man on the back. "You've come back at last. It really is you, isn't it?" He felt the pressure against his shoulder as Happenstance nodded. The strength in Hap's legs failed, and Umber eased him down. They sat on the terrace floor with Hap leaning heavily against Umber's side.

There were so many questions to ask. Umber fumbled for words. "Hap, you were gone so long. It was thirty years in this world . . . but many more for you, wasn't it?"

Happenstance swallowed, and his throat bobbed. A faint smile appeared, and he finally spoke in a dry whisper. "Well. About that. Couldn't come . . . any sooner. You can't imagine the responsibility. That world—so much more populous, so much more complex. Never found a moment when I could leave. If I did, I would lose track of all those threads, all those possibilities."

"Of course," Umber said, squeezing Hap's shoulder.

Hap clutched Umber's hand. "May I call you Father? Because that is how I thought of you all those years, when I wandered through your world. As my father."

"I would like that very much," Umber said with a sniffle. It was so strange speaking to a Happenstance who was older than him. "Hap. It must have been so hard, and you were just a boy. How could I have asked so much of you? I'm so sorry."

Hap wagged his head from side to side. "Sorry? Never. I don't regret a thing. Of course, it was difficult. For each crisis I turned aside, a new challenge grew in its place. There were momentous decisions to make. Should a million die so ten million will not meet a worse fate? Should a generation suffer so a better nation can be born? Should a wicked man live so a greater villain does not take his place? Those were my choices. That was my existence. But it was filled with the kind of meaning that others only dream about. I had the chance to make a better world—just as you did here. I could have walked away long before I did. But I grew to love what I was doing. And so I stayed, until I felt I could leave."

Umber leaned closer and spoke quietly. "So you did it after all."

Hap nodded. "Father, how would you describe the world you knew as a young man?"

Umber scratched his temple. "Messy. Far from perfect. Full of marvels. But marred by intolerance and misunderstanding."

The nod grew stronger. "It's still messy," Hap said. "Still marred. But it's still there, Father. Still there."

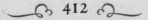

Umber leaned back and allowed himself a sad smile. "You really did it. Rescued an entire civilization." His eyebrows rose. "And the woman that Willy Nilly wanted to save?"

Hap's eyes were half closed. "She lived for a long time, an ordinary person with an ordinary life. Nobody ever heard of her. And she found something like happiness."

"Willy would have been glad to hear of it."

Hap shrugged. "I saved her only to keep my promise. It was your mission that mattered." His eyes rolled up, and his head bobbed. "What's the matter with me now? Father, I think I could use some of that coffee you loved so much. I became fond of it in my later years."

Umber chuckled and shook his head. "Would you believe I don't have any? I can't touch the stuff anymore. It does unspeakable things to my digestive tract."

"Shame," Hap said, and the strength left his body, and he sagged against Umber's shoulder.

"Hap?" Umber said.

Happenstance did not answer, and did not move.

"Hap?" Umber said again, giving him a little shake. His voice rose and cracked. "Hap!"

Hap's eyes fluttered open. With his head sunk deep in his pillow, his gaze turned right and left, taking in his surroundings, and finally settled on Umber, who watched him from a chair next to the bed.

"Your new tower?" Hap asked.

"Took a while, but we rebuilt things pretty well," Umber replied.

Hap frowned and rubbed the inner corners of his eyes. "What just happened to me, Father?"

Umber leaned toward the bed with his elbows on his knees. "Don't you know? You fell asleep, Happenstance. For quite a while."

Hap laughed and closed his dazzling green eyes. "So that was sleep. It was a pleasant thing after all. Floating in a warm oblivion. The mind finally at rest."

"Nobody ever deserved it more. Did you dream, Hap?"

Hap opened his eyes again and clasped his hands behind his head. "Ah. Those visions while I slept. Yes, I finally know what it is to dream. I saw my old friends, the ones who lived here. They were always in my thoughts while I meddled in your world. Tell me about them."

Umber smiled. "Of course. But . . . don't you already know their fates?"

"I could find their filaments and read them. But . . . I've spent a lifetime doing that, in the other world. It would make me happy now if you just told me."

"Then I will, of course. Who would you like to hear about first?"

"Your artist and archer. Sophie."

"Ah, Sophie," Umber said. "She is still the artist for my books. And do you remember the young man who turned out to be your brother? Eldon Penny?"

Happenstance nodded.

"If you recall, I found a position for Eldon in one of my shipping offices in another port. He turned out to be a very talented fellow—made an excellent reputation for himself. Eldon came back to Kurahaven a few years later, a changed man with a healed heart. Clever, confident, and kind. When he and Sophie met, it wasn't a week before they were deeply in love. And they remain so to this day."

A smile took root on Happenstance's face. "And there was the strong man who was compelled to speak the truth. Tell me about him. Did he ever escape from that curse?"

"Oates," Umber said, chuckling. "No, the cure for him was never found. But a few years after you left I went to a tavern with Welkin, Barkin, and Dodd—perhaps you remember them, my personal guard. While we were there a barmaid tossed a mug of ale into a sailor's face and sent him out the door with a kick in the hindquarters. She called him a liar and shouted that all men were liars, and that if she ever met a truly honest one, she'd marry him on the spot. I told Dodd to get to the Aerie as fast as his horse would take him and fetch Oates. And that is how Oates met his wife."

"And is Oates still with you?"

"Sleeping downstairs, I imagine. His wife cares for the Aerie now. Would you like to see him?"

Happenstance shook his head. "No. I have their faces now in my mind, now that we've talked of them. I want to remember them that way. As I knew them." He sat up in bed and stretched his arms. "The sleep did me wonders. I haven't felt so good in years. Now . . . the woman who rode the leviathan barge. Tell me about Nima."

"Still my dear friend, and willing to take me wherever I ask to go."

Happenstance narrowed his eyes, concentrating. "Balfour," he finally said, more a statement than a question.

Umber stared out the window. "Dead and gone for many years, I'm afraid. As is little Thimble."

Happenstance bowed his head, and after a long silence he lifted it again. "And you, Umber. Have you been well?"

"I have. You know, Fay came to me the night you disappeared, and she never left. We were as happy as two can be for many years. And her niece Sable became a physician, and a great one at that." Umber's mouth twisted. "I lost Fay two years ago."

"Ah," Happenstance said, wincing. "And were there more adventures for you after I moved on?"

Umber chuckled softly. "I've had the time of my life. And you know, after Loden died, Celador did what all kingdoms do: It replaced him with the nearest living relative. The new king isn't a bad fellow, and he's allowed me a reasonable amount of progress."

Hap swung his legs over the side of the bed and got to his feet, bouncing with a newfound strength. "I really do feel refreshed!" He reached out and waved his hand in front of Umber's chest. His green eyes shimmered and twinkled.

"I'm not sure I want to know what you're seeing," Umber said.

Hap reached out for Umber's wrist. "Come with me, Father."

"Go with you?" Umber said. "To where?"

Hap stared back into Umber's eyes.

"To my old world?" Umber asked. His voice was quiet and hoarse.

"To the new world that I've made of your old world. You don't have to be afraid for your mind; the trip won't drive you mad. In fact it will undo the troubles that have plagued you since you arrived. And aren't you curious?"

Umber kneaded his chin with his fingers. "You know me, Happenstance. I am forever curious."

"Then come with me. We are old men now, you and I. But there is still time to share one great adventure."

Umber gulped. He took a deep breath and lowered his head. "I knew you'd come back someday, Happenstance. I didn't think it would take this long. But I was sure I'd see you again." He lifted his face, and his cheeks were damp. "And I have to tell you . . . I've had the feeling lately that my days here might be coming to an end. Yes, I'll go with you. But there is something I'd like to do first, with your help."

"Of course," Hap said.

"Wait here," Umber said. He stepped out of the room. When he returned he was fully dressed and had a wooden crate under his arm. He pulled a note from his pocket and placed it on the table beside the bed. Hap looked down at the first words: *Dear friends. This may come as a surprise. Or maybe nothing I do surprises you anymore . . .*

"Now, then. Let's go," Umber said.

The wind made Umber's long coat flutter as they stood atop a great palace in a distant land. Umber pried the lid off the crate.

Inside was a stack of papers. He slid his hands down the sides and pulled out as many of the sheets as he could hold between his thumb and fingers. "I had these printed up years ago, to be distributed upon my death," Umber said. "But this is so much better, doing it myself!" He flung the papers over his head. The wind lofted them high and scattered them far across the rooftops below. Umber whooped with delight.

"What do they say?" Hap asked as the pages floated and soared.

"They speak of freedom for all people. The rights that every man, woman, and child ought to enjoy. I must admit, I stole the words shamelessly from several famous documents in my world's history. Now, Hap, there are a few more kingdoms I'd like to litter with these. Can we move on to Fenn now?"

Hap put a hand on Umber's shoulder. An instant later they stood atop the wall that surrounded Fenn's greatest city, and Umber flung his parchments to the wind. Umber named more places in more lands across the known world, and Hap took him there, until finally the box was empty. Hap gripped Umber by the forearm again, and at last they stood on the hill above Kurahaven, shaking off the chill.

"Are you ready now?" Hap said.

"You're really taking me back to the world I knew?"

"Yes. But you may not know it so well anymore."

Umber scrunched his features and tapped the side of his head with his palm. "It's all so baffling, Happenstance. If you changed the course of history, why do I remember it as it was? And if my civilization was never destroyed, and I never escaped to this world, why am I here at all?"

Hap raised his hands and smiled. "That is a question not even a Meddler can answer. But now it's time to see this new world you made possible."

Umber cleared his throat and shifted his feet. He looked down at the great arches and columns of the city, and the Rulian Sea twinkling under the stars, and the Aerie, tiny from this distance.

"And then," Hap said, "when you have seen it, we will journey forward. That is how you and I will spend the time we have left. Alighting across the centuries like birds on branches."

Umber's eyes grew wide, and a smile spread on his face. "How far into the future?"

"As far as can be." Hap stared into the heavens, beholding the passage that Umber couldn't see. "All Meddlers are drawn to it, Umber. It grows stronger with the years until we can no longer resist. I ache to see it. The end of time."

"The end of time," Umber repeated. His voice was mellow with awe. "But what is the end of time, Hap? Is it our sun devouring the earth as it swells? Is it the galaxies colliding? Is

it the cosmos cooling until everything is frozen and dead? Is it the universe collapsing on itself, only to reignite and expand again? Or is it something we can't even imagine, something out of myth?"

"There is," Happenstance replied, "only one way to be certain." He locked elbows with Umber.

"Wait!" Umber said. "One last look." He gazed at the vista below. "You know," he said after a while, "when I scattered those papers? I was a bit of a Meddler myself, wasn't I?"

Happenstance shrugged. "Aren't we all? Now close your eyes."

There was a sound like the breath of an infant, and a blush of darkness, and they were gone.